The Healing of

Howard Brown

A Novel

Jeb Stewart Harrison

THE HEALING OF HOWARD BROWN

Copyright © 2016 by Jeb Stewart Harrison

For information contact :

Babybingusbooks@gmail.com

http://www.babybingusbooks.com

Book and Cover design by Katherine M. Harrison

ISBN: 153090028X

ISBN-13: 978-1530900282

First Edition

10 9 8 7 6 5 4 3 2 1

FOR MY FAMILY

Fathers, Mothers, Wives, Husbands, Sons, Daughters, Sisters, Brothers, Nieces, Nephews, Cousins, Uncles, Aunts, Ancestors, In-laws and all those we did not choose but still must learn to live with, even if just a memory.

SPECIAL THANKS

To David Cates, Greg Glazner, Jim Heynen, David Huddle, Rick Barot, Stan Rubin, Judith Kitchen, the MFA faculty at the Rainier Writing Workshop of Pacific Lutheran University, and my colleagues Sarah Blaser Murray, Warren Read, and Jenee Stanfield. And to my wonderful wife Holly, my sister Katie Cassou, my children Jack and Katherine and the ever faithful and understanding Mister Boo.

BOOK I
KENTFIELD

To become aware of the possibility of a search
is to be onto something.
Not to be onto something is to be in despair.
– Walker Percy, *The Moviegoer*

1 Trying To Die

I could tell he was trying to die – really trying, as if by the sheer force of his iron will he could command his heart to stop, like he had so often commanded me, my sister, my mother and a great many others to stop, to halt, to shut up, to do this or that. He was in that familiar state of stern, steely concentration, laid out on the rented hospital bed at the foot of great grandmother's regal plantation four-poster, his knuckly fingers rolled into fists, his jaw clenched, his brow furrowed, and the afternoon sun illuminating his gnarled and knobby toes. What, I wondered, was responsible for their profound disfigurement? Was it the miles of fairways, tees and greens he had trudged across in his 85 years? Or was it the endless hours pacing to and fro in San Francisco courtrooms, trying to command the thoughts of judge and jury?

Whatever it was, I decided then and there it should be avoided. I bent over my massive midriff and studied my own toes in the crusty white shag. Aside from the yellowing, curled nails, they didn't look unusually bent or knobby, at least not yet, but I feared that like many of the failing factory parts of my six/six, 240-pound frame, they would eventually join in the cacophony of inflamed and screaming joints that had accompanied me into my 60th year.

My father's exit had become unreasonably complicated. I could understand why, on a purely emotional level, he felt like dying. So did I, even on that exquisitely lit late summer afternoon. We had, both of us, a rough go of late.

It started with my mother succumbing to the "awful awful" (my father's term for Alzheimer's) in a quiet but possibly premature fashion, after which he promptly broke his hip, got pneumonia, and forgot how to swallow. Subsequently, his life quickly became a revolving door of hospitals, rehab centers, surgeries, more hospitals and rehab centers, skilled nursing facilities, and finally home to a house full of caregivers, hospice nurses, pills, purees, and us: me, my ever-patient and long-suffering wife Sandy, my winsome son Tripp, his equally winsome girlfriend Elke and the world's most prescient, possibly telepathic chocolate lab Mr. Booper. On occasion my mercurial shape-shifting sister, Sisi, might show up, but those visits had become increasingly infrequent.

What made my father's last days so devilishly complicated was this: my sister had decided she was burned out on care-giving and needed a break, so she informed everybody she was going on a three day backpack trip with her new post-divorce boyfriend, a rotund biker who smelled of Cool Ranch Doritos, with a doo-rag atop his shaved dome – the polar opposite of her hail-fellow-well-met husband of 22 years. Our father was horrified, convinced that this creepy recovering alcoholic was going to rape and murder his daughter, chop her up into bite-sized chunks, pack her up in double-strength trash bag and unload her in a Quincy dumpster. So when she didn't answer our phone calls at the appointed time on Monday, Hal Brown got a little nervous. Then more than a little nervous. When she wasn't back by Tuesday morning he was beside himself. Spiked a fever. We all started calling around to see if anyone knew of her whereabouts. By the time I learned from her employer that she had walked off the job in a huff it was too late. The old man's vision of his daughter as a raccoon midnight snack had sent him into delirium, so he laid down on the rent-a-bed, closed his eyes, and told his broken heart to stop.

There I was, stuck between a father who was so bereaved by his daughter's apparent abandonment that, like a grief-stricken Dickens character, he could just lay down and die, and a sister that obviously didn't give a shit. Where would this leave me, once my father was dead and my sister gone? Would I be a 21st century version of young Rasnolikov, abandoned by humanity, my body in tatters, my mind tortured, twisted and inflamed, and my heart throbbing with a cold, nameless ache; nothing more than a branch broken off the family tree, left to rot on the ground? After thirty years of teaching high school English and coaching basketball, with my remaining years stretched out before me like the last flight of the proverbial stairway to heaven, I felt like I couldn't take another step.

A strong breeze, the kind that usually heralds the arrival of ocean fog, had begun to whip the branches of the oaks, bays and redwoods outside my father's bedroom. I stepped away from my post at the foot of his rent-a-bed, Mr. Booper following me with his ochre eyes, and opened the sliding glass door, thinking a blast of chill wind might revive the old man, or at least dry the nervous sweat at the nape of my neck.

It was then, if my memory serves, that I felt something break through the dull, frozen undefined ache in my heart, like a poisonous baby viper cracking its egg: anger. Big, red, hot burning anger. I felt like taking my father in my arms and hurling him across the room. *Fuck this goddamn dying charade*, I thought. Then I was angry with my sister for being angry with our father. I was angry with death, angry with God. And above all I was angry with myself, for always being so angry with everybody and everything else.

"Dad," I barked after slamming the sliding glass door, "you can't die now. We've got some things we need to talk about."

He didn't move one single cell, but I could hear his voice in my head: *Yes, of course. About money, I suppose. And the land you and your sister will inherit in Louisiana. What else could there be?*

I gripped my big, square head in my massive paws and gave it a violent shake. "No, no that's not it at all!" I whispered, even though it was, or at least part of it was. He must have heard me because I heard his voice, though his thin lizard lips didn't quiver a micron.

What else is there besides the money and the land?

"What a smartass!" I hissed quietly, not wanting to alarm Sandy and the caregivers. *What is he seeing in his fading mind's eye?* I thought. *A six-foot, six-inch tall slimy green leech, with countless little sucker pods trying to latch onto him?* Though there were many unresolved issues regarding his estate, I honestly didn't want to talk about it. Not to the exclusion of everything else, at least. That's what he wanted to talk about, but not me. I sincerely and angrily wanted him to know how much I loved him without having to tell him so, but I didn't know how. Still, he appeared to be unconscious, so why not? He might hear me, but wouldn't be able to react.

"I love you, Dad." *Is it love?* I immediately wondered. *Or is it gratitude for the material comforts he had heaped upon our family? Can a child love a parent that once hurled his little body around the room like a football? Can a boy love a father for whom none of his efforts were ever acknowledged as good enough?* Maybe I should have asked him straight up: "Was I ever good enough?" But I didn't, at least not that afternoon in his bedroom. Besides, I already knew the answer, or thought I did.

Then I heard my father's voice in my head again.

Oh...no you don't love me. You can't. How could you after all the psycho-terror I heaped upon you and your sister? I may have been a good bank, but not exactly a good dad. But thanks anyway.

A good bank? I thought. It was the same sarcastic, self-deprecatory bile that we had grown up with. *Is the proximity of death causing him to actually mean what I imagine him to be saying?* I wondered.

Distracted by the peculiar clarity of his voice in my head, my anger began to dissipate. Quite suddenly, I went from hopping mad to complete exhaustion. Numb, frozen, bound, gagged, sad, hollow – I felt victim to an emotional gang rape. So I abandoned my post at the foot of the bed and collapsed into the low-slung rocking chair I had spent so many hours in as an adolescent, practicing my guitar and reading science fiction novels. Soon Mr. Booper laid his long, soft and silky head across my own tortured toes. After a few minutes I took up the old nylon-stringed guitar that was propped against the bed and absent-mindedly plucked at it, watching my father's chest rise and fall and listening to the purple finches singing "chit chit chit" while they flitted about the swaying feeder outside.

Eventually I dozed, dreaming of the two of us, father and son, locked in a friendly golf match, emerald fairways crossed with the dark shadow bands of the redwoods and Monterey pines, golden Northern California hills glowing in the soft twilight. We knew that we were basking in the natural grace of the Golf God, seventy four degrees, not a breath of wind, the late summer scent of sweet vanilla rising, greens soft and forgiving, fairways trimmed to perfection, two tall dixie cups full of cold draft beer in the golf cart. My father put a seven-iron swing on the ball like George Archer, tall and loose, an easy backswing that started down slow, then caught the ball with a crisp whoosh-click, pulling a six inch divot skyward. The ball soared in a soft fade over the flag, kicked up a tiny tuft of green, then rocketed backward into the cup as if on a string.

At the very moment the ball rattled into the cup, I was jarred awake by Sandy, my wife of 32 years. "Well, how's he doing?" My eyes popped open.

"He's faking it. The whole thing. It's just a ruse to get Sisi to show up."

"Howard! What a thing to say!"

"Look at all that snot. His body is supposed to be shutting down, but his shnozz is a regular booger factory." It was true. Yellow crust had built up around his cavernous nostrils while a steady stream of sinus butter spilled across his upper lip and down his whiskered cheek. Sandy took a clean rag and wiped.

"Howard, just because his nose is running…"

"Look at his toes, Sandy, those aren't the toes of a dying man." I knew that there was no validity to my claim, just as I knew that my attempts to brighten the gloom of impending death with my banal levity were insensitive and inappropriate. But it didn't stop me. "He's obviously possessed by aliens," I said. Sandy paused and looked me over with mild contempt.

"Here your father is dying and all you can do is joke about it. Boy, Howard. You sure can be a jerk sometimes."

Sandy was right, of course. My father was dying, and as his only son I felt I had the right to be as flippant and selfish as I pleased.

"Death will do that to a guy," I said. Sandy shook her head, gave the old man a kiss on the forehead, sighed, and left the room.

I remained, slouched in the antique armless rocker with my size-15 feet under Mr. Booper's warm chocolaty muzzle, and considered what had become of the master bedroom. It was now a virtual hospital: the fully automatic, adjustable hospital bed was just a few feet from the foot of his real bed, the antique four-poster, and an oxygen tank hissed at the base of the pole that held the fluids and liquid food that got pumped directly into his gut through a peg tube. Atop his chest sat his little transistor radio, a single wire snaking up to the plastic earphone jammed halfway down his ear canal, and on the table next to the bed sat a plastic bag full of tiny triple A batteries. A few feet from the foot of the hospital bed stood a brand new 24 inch flat-panel TV on an antique end-table, its remote control aside the radio on his chest.

At one point after my mother's death, my father asked if dying was painful. I told him that, quite obviously, I had no idea, but in case it was we would be prepared. So, my father being a great believer in better living through chemicals, I had his caregivers arrange a robust pharmacopeia atop his giant mahogany antique dresser. This I sampled generously, not only as my father's acolyte, but also in the interest of ensuring efficacy of the various pain meds. By the time of my sister's disappearance I was pretty certain that even death by sledgehammer would be pain-free.

That afternoon, after Sandy had pronounced me "jerk of the day," I thought a little morphine sulfate under the tongue might perhaps make me feel less of a jerk, and I knew it would relieve the throbbing knot in my lower back. But I also knew it would make me numb, light, dreamy, drowsy – I might fall asleep and miss my father's big event all together. There was also a healthy supply of Ativan in case one of us got nervous, and the Haldol, should we get psycho, but neither of those were called for at the time. So I decided to take a healthy swig of his liquid hydrocodone, the Vicodin cocktail. Within minutes the knot at the base of my spine had unraveled, and I was wondering how it was possible that my wife could consider me, big Howard Brown, the world's greatest high school basketball coach, a jerk.

I felt alert, imperturbable, as strong and solid as the redwood tree in the front yard. My brain parted like the Red Sea, with me on one side observing me on the other side – self abstracted from self, the watcher and the watched.

I closed my eyes as my Vicodin-laced brain pulled sparkling clean memories out of the mental soup with pristine clarity, and eventually recalled a scene of Mom and Dad and a pact they made three years ago.

That day, the old man sat us down at the kitchen table next to his overstuffed club chair. Then he cleared his throat as if he was in the courtroom about to address the ladies and gentlemen of the jury. "Mom and I have agreed that we don't believe in any sort of life after death," he announced, leaning forward on the edge of his chair and running his twisted fingers through his long, silver-blue hair. "We've decided that this is the end."

He looked like the end had already happened, his giant hawk nose a roadmap of booze-busted capillaries, snot perennially coalescing in the nostril fuzz, his grey eyes broken down into pools of uninvited tears hiding in the shade of his overhanging silver brows, his terse upper lip shielding what was left of his teeth.

My mother had no comment. Alzheimer's had made such concepts as "death" and "the end" as meaningful as "spoon" and "poop." She might have been wondering what happened to her usual daytime rerun companions: Lucy, Ricky, Matt Dillon, the Brothers Cartwright, Bob Barker. She might have even wondered why we kept her friends holed up in that box in the corner of the kitchen.

But Hal Brown was serious, so I did what I could to paint a brighter picture: "That's the great thing about death, Dad. Nobody knows for sure what happens so you can make up whatever you want." This was probably the most metaphysical thing I had ever said to him in my entire life, and though both of my parents converted to Catholicism upon their arrival in San Francisco, Dad from the South and Mom from Chicago, their religious affiliations had more to do with blending into the City than with any faith in the Holy Trinity. But as it turned out on that particular day, he wasn't interested a theological debate, nor was he interested in my theory of eternal party after death, or even to make lively discussion over Pascal's wager (which to me was, and still is, the only logical way of looking at it). Instead, as always, there was an immediate practical purpose, a command, a fatherly directive that he meant to impart:

"Well, we don't want any last rites or anything like that. And if you put on a little memorial get together we don't want any priests or religion involved."

Bullshit! I wanted to shout. *If that's how you've decided it's going to be then why did we waste all that time at St. Sebastian's getting baptized and going to catechism and*

8

getting confirmed and playing CYO basketball? Was that all so you could play God in the Christmas Pageant with your big ass God-like voice booming through the church? What about all the stuff we learned about venial sin and mortal sin and how to decide which was which and how big a mark a sin might leave on your soul and how much penance you had to say to wash it off? Weren't these the rules we were taught to live by, so when we got to where you are now we could relax, knowing we were going to Heaven to hang with Jesus and The Holy Ghost in super clean super white robes and golden halos? Now you're shitcanning the whole business, right when it matters most? Now that you've spent your whole life paying the premiums you're saying you don't want the insurance after all?

But I didn't say any of that. I glanced over at Mom who was now looking right at us. If the old man had his way, both he and Mom would be holding hands and, on cue, the lights would go out.

Here, and then...*flick!* Nowhere. No pearly gates. No exit interviews. No purgatory. No limbo.

But despite my father's commanding presence, few of his efforts ever went according to plan. As my consciousness drifted back to the rocker by his rent-a-bed I wondered what had become of my sister, and if her cruel disappearance had been planned to purposefully force the old man over the edge. *What the fuck were you thinking? Can you imagine what it must be like to be at death's door with no idea if your child is dead or alive?* Abandoning our father in his increasingly tenuous and precarious state appeared vicious beyond comprehension, and I soon realized there was no making sense of it. Regardless of how hard I wished, hoped, visualized or otherwise cogitated, I couldn't make Dad's final days a loving family sendoff any more than I could climb Mt. Everest.

As the afternoon faded into evening, so the did the strength of my chemically induced clarity. Sitting there in that old rocking chair, Mr. Booper stretched across my feet, I became hypnotized by the rhythmic rising and falling of my father's chest, all the while making wagers with God: *which breath will be his last? This one? The next? How many more? Five? Eight? 50? 100? Come on, Higher Power, when are you going to flip the switch?*

2 Choosing To Live

At first I thought that I must have dozed off again, and was dreaming. There was old Hal Brown throwing his covers off, swinging his mottled, bony legs over the edge of the hospital bed and fixing me in an angry stare, shouting "Goddamnit, where is she?" – which might have been a normal occurrence in a dream, but impossible, I thought, in the current circumstances. But then he tried to push himself up off the edge of the bed, and I had to jump up from the rocking chair and grab him before he fell on his face. Suddenly Sandy was next to me, helping me lower him back down on the bed, and I knew from the acrid stench of his almost-dead flesh – an odor that, with a little olfactory concentration, I can conjure to this day – that it was no dream.

"Oh my God," my wife blubbered, tears forming at the base of her tired, bloodshot eyes. "We thought you were a goner!" But the old man wasn't interested in reunion hugs. Instead, he looked at the gold stretch-band watch that hung loosely around his veiny matchstick wrist. He smiled.

"Hey pal, go get me a beer, will ya?"

I didn't pause. I didn't wonder. I didn't ask questions. I only knew it must have been past five PM. I took one look at Sandy who was standing in front of the almost-dead man in amazement. I loped down to the kitchen, cracked open the fridge and grabbed a couple of Sierra Nevada Pale Ales, then turned around to see Angela and Shirley, the caregivers, slack-jawed and bug-eyed.

"Mister Hal?" Shirley, the duo's more practiced English-speaking spokesperson, asked in a half-whisper. I nodded toward the bedroom, looked down at the beers in my hand, and shrugged. I could no more have thought of something to say at that moment than I could have sung an aria. They fell in behind me as I headed back to the room at the end of the hall, all of us speechless.

He was still sitting on the edge of the hospital bed and Sandy had her arms around his scarecrow shoulders, still blubbering, "Oh Hal, this must be some kind of miracle!"

"Mister Hal!" the girls cried, tentatively touching his hands and arms as if he might crumble into dust. Sandy stepped back as I twisted the cap off a Sierra Nevada and handed it to him. He cradled it lovingly, at a slight tilt, studying the label, then held it up in toast: "To me! The man that couldn't die!"

My father and I drank while the girls studied him, comically twitching their noses at the fetid odor of his jilted deathbed. Soon Sandy went to the bathroom and returned with a wet washrag, and the old man, now intimately familiar with sponge baths, instinctively lifted his arms above his head. The three girls pulled off his lousy white T and proceeded to wipe him down like a muddy pup, gently working the zipper-like scar from his throat down to his gut – a souvenir from aortic surgery – as he smiled at me, almost as if to say "now *this* is *the life*." Then, after a couple more sips of Sierra Nevada the old man cleared his throat, as if ready to deliver a closing argument to a packed courtroom.

"I feel like a new man!" he pronounced, his booming voice – THE VOICE – clear, deep and strong, turned up to about seven. Sandy and I had grown so used to his dramatic, sartorial authority and commanding presence around the house that I could only smile, at the same time burying all the memories of the times when that same voice reduced me to a cowering cur.

"How long have I been napping?" he wondered. So I brought him up to date on the events of the past week: the disappearance of my sister, his excellent attempt at dying complete with two days of death rattle, and finally the fine weather we had been having. He nodded. "The last thing I remember is the Giants were beating the Phillies seven to three. Did they win that game?"

I wondered why he cared; the San Francisco Giants were having a miserable season. But before I could answer he changed the subject.

"Why isn't your sister here? Did you forget to tell her that I'm waiting for her?" It was his signature tone of disappointment. Was I supposed to be out looking for her? Hadn't I been doing the right thing by being there with him, gently shuffling him into his personal void? Of course I was leaving messages every fifteen minutes wondering where she was because her father was now dying and she was supposed to be here. But it wasn't surprising that she wasn't returning my calls. It didn't matter if she was backed up against a boulder with her ankles over Mr. Doo Rag's shoulders in some national forest campsite or, as Hal Brown suspected, chopped up into bite-sized chunks and tossed in a Quincy dumpster; she wasn't where she was supposed to be and it was my fault.

"Where's my fine dog?" he suddenly asked, perhaps even sensing my disgust with his stupid recriminations. Mr. Booper came over and stretched his soft, warm tummy over my father's gnarled toes. Then he lifted the bottle of beer to his cracked lips, opened wide and poured the amber liquid down his gullet with a dangerously big swig. The "guvner" in his throat had lost the ability to distinguish liquids and solids from air – a condition known in medicine as dysphagia – which often resulted in foreign shit, like Sierra Nevada Pale Ale, ending up in his lungs and causing pneumonia. But instead of launching into one of his historic coughing fits, he wiped his lizard lips and bared his yellow teeth at me, because he knew that I knew how much he loved to drink his Sierra Nevada Pale Ale. I could tell that, contrary to what I presumed to be his sentiment just a half hour before, he was glad to be alive – his eyes were as bright and snappy as sapphires. He was most certainly happier to be alive at that moment than I was – a whopping wicked headache was coming on and I had a bad case of the withdrawal sweats. I felt like I had several times that day already: like I was going to jump out of my own skin. I looked at my watch and sure enough my body was telling me it was time for another Vicodin cocktail.

"Well, pal, believe me I hate to make you go do this. I suppose I could hire a private dick but knowing your sister she would probably screw the guy so silly that he would forget why he was looking for her in the first place."

Angela, a Seventh Day Adventist, stood up, shocked. I was a little shocked myself, having rarely heard my old man be quite so blunt. Sandy giggled quietly. I headed to the drug bar.

"Oh, I'm sorry, girls," he said, waving his Sierra Nevada bottle around. "You're such good girls I don't know why I am being so crude. But you don't know my daughter like I do. She is a complete slut. She sleeps around. That's why she's divorced, you know. She's been two-timing her husband from day one, shacking up with her second cousin in Louisiana, shacking up with that alkie biker, shacking up with the cable guy, the mailman, the golf pro. You name it. "

My ears perked up when I heard about our second cousins in Louisiana. Sisi always said her long weekends were golf outings with members of the golf club ladies' auxiliary. I guessed that Hal Brown had innocently inquired about the outcome of the golf matches with a couple of male members, and somehow arrived at the conclusion that his daughter had been sneaking off to Baton Rouge or to the old family plantation north of St. Francisville, Briarwood.

"Now she's pissed off because I didn't die according to her plan. I didn't want to sit down and discuss fucking end-of-life issues with her and those butt-ugly hospice nurses. I mean, end-of-life issues? What issues could there be?"

I wasn't sure if "closure" and "end-of-life issues" were interchangeable, and I didn't ask. Nonetheless, it was clear that my father had decided to give up on dying, which had simply proven too difficult for such an old man without any end-of-life issues, and had decided to try and live instead, if only for as long as it took to find my sister and bring her back. I wondered if I could get him to explain why he couldn't die without her, and whatever this thing was that he wanted to give us, or say to us. Maybe he just wanted to say goodbye to her, but I also had a hunch that there was more to it. Maybe he wanted to give her promiscuous ass a good spanking. Whatever it was he seemed to be pretty certain that death would wait. In the meantime if there was going to be any watering of our distressed and dehydrated family tree, the watering can, or maybe the hose, clearly belonged to me. Once again, my old man had thrown down the gauntlet: find Sisi and bring her back. And though he didn't say it, I knew what he was thinking: This is your last chance to do something right, son. Don't fuck it up.

3 Odes to Mr. Booper

My name is Howard Brown and that is what I am called. Not Howie, not Hal (that's my father, not me), not Harry, especially not Harry. Not Ward. Not Brownie or HB. Not even Junior, or at least not anymore, except by my sister who used it just because nobody else did. For thirty years I answered to "Coach," and still do when one of my ex-hoopsters or students spy me buying smokes at the Seven Eleven. I don't mind still being "Coach;" it conjures a vision of youthful vitality that, like clean living, has all but faded from my view. In truth, I remember getting out of the shower, just a few days after my father's miraculous change of plan, and almost fainting at the sight of my supersized old man-boobs in the mirror. Had there been a scalpel handy, I might have performed a spontaneous double self-mastectomy. It was a moment of truth that I'll never forget: standing before myself in the mirror, praying for the miracle of booblessness and wondering *how the fuck did you get so old?*

Outside observers might have accused my Mom, Marjorie Brown nee Evans, of negligence in the matter of my potential existence long before I was born. The seeds of her negligence were not just seeds; they were chocolate covered peanuts, specifically. And candy bars, cookies, glazed jelly donuts, pistachio ice cream, pineapple upside down cake, potato chips, corn dogs, cheeseburgers, and every sort of crap a girl could stuff into her pudgy cheeks on a Lake Michigan beach in Evanston, Illinois, 1934. My mother, Marjorie Brown, told me with pride that she was once referred to as "Large Marge," "Marge the Barge," "Heavy Evans" and just plain "fatso" in the schoolyard, the Indian Hills swimming pool and the Johnson Street Beach.

But when her hormones, kicked in and she began take an interest in boys the eating abruptly stopped. All manner of eating. Two years later, at sixteen, she became a model for the J. Walter Thompson advertising agency and started to show up on local billboard and magazine ads, always bearing plenty of leg and a tight sweater. "Large Marge" was now "Take Charge Marge:" the miracle weight loss model of Chicago.

Unfortunately, when it came time to make babies my mother's famous figure was not be tampered with. Fueled by a steady diet of scotch, cigarettes and Librium, she gained just 11 pounds, five of which were me, a grossly underdeveloped wet rat with a disturbing hole the size of a dime in my sternum. Much later I was told that this mysterious hole brought about an endless battery of medical tests for the first year of my life and that my parents fretted over it to distraction. Later, when I started to get a handle on language, I learned that my mother referred to my hole as my "chown hoon dong," though it would be many years before I knew what that meant. Had I known how that little hole would wreak havoc upon my life, I might have asked for it to be plugged up with something. Chewing gum. Concrete. A dog turd. Anything!

Then I started to grow, and grow, and grow some more at an unusually rapid clip. At 10 years old I was five feet, nine inches. At 12 I was six-two. At 15 I was six-six, 160 pounds; one of those skinny guys that disappears when they turn sideways. And I was so hopelessly uncoordinated I couldn't even walk down the street without falling all over myself. Now, I see it as the beginning of what was to be a long, acrimonious, dysfunctional relationship with my body; a body that seemed to have a mind of it's own, completely independent of the supposed control panel in my cranium.

It started with the hole in my sternum. Then, when I was around 11, an orthopedic surgeon noticed my unusually upright stance on the putting green and announced to my father that I had a serious back problem. Later, tests revealed that a crucial factory part – the "Scotty's Collar" – had failed to fully develop in my lumbar vertebrae. Or it became deformed as a result of playing too much golf during my remarkable growth spurt. Regardless of the cause, the doctor ruled out contact sports (much to the chagrin of the football coach, who figured all I had to do was stand in front of the opposing quarterback with my arms raised) lest my spine crack and confine me to a wheelchair for the rest of my life. Basketball was okay – hoops being a different game in those days – even though I had a hard time running from one end of the court to the other without falling on my face. Golf was never in question, regardless of my broken back. It was what Howard Browns did, period. I imagine that even if I had been born with my head screwed on backwards, golf would still have been okay.

Golf exacerbated my back problems, of course. So did everything else. By the time I retired from teaching at 55 everything I did, from taking out the trash to sweeping the patio, caused excruciating pain, accompanied by lightning bolts shooting down my thighs. I felt supremely gypped. I had been looking forward to retirement, albeit in a rather vague and hazy way: I would get back to my landscape paintings, practice my guitar, walk Mr. Booper in the watershed, hone my cooking skills, tinker in the tool shed, putter in the garden, and join a men's group. Instead, I was afraid to move.

I recall one summer's day a couple of months after retiring, before my mother's death and my father's subsequent demise. I was in the storage room off the garage of our little ranch-style house in San Anselmo, assessing the potential risk of trying to fetch something from an upper shelf, when I heard Sandy talking to someone on the phone. As she often did when she wanted to speak with someone in private, she was holed up in our son's bedroom.

Since the wall between the bedroom and storage closet wasn't insulated, Sandy sounded like she was sitting in my lap. Once I learned the conversation was more or less about me, I moved a box of nails and a Coleman stove off of the Igloo cooler and carefully sat down, hoping I wouldn't smash it in.

As I remember it, the conversation went something like this: "It's kinda scary to tell you the truth," Sandy said. "He's become a patio potato, I don't think he's been anywhere but the backyard and his parents' house in the past two months!"

At first I couldn't tell who was on the other end of the line. It might've been one of her two remaining brothers in Appleton, both of who were suffering through the last years of amyloidosis, the incurable disease that had killed her father and oldest brother. Or one of her old basketball chums from Colorado, who she called every few months. She and my sister were still on speaking terms at that time, but avoided one-on-ones, and her only local chum had succumbed to ovarian cancer two years prior.

"Yes, the situation with his Mom is only getting worse," Sandy said, referring to my Mom, who was on her last legs. "She puts on a good front, but I'm pretty sure she doesn't know who we are anymore. Just the other day I heard her ask Hal, Howard's father, who the tall girl with the long brown hair was. Ha! Ha!"

There was a short pause. I could tell it was a woman's voice on the other end of the line – that's how clear the sound from Tripp's room was in the garage storage closet.

"Oh, I know it's not funny at all, but sometimes you have to laugh to keep from crying," Sandy said, then listened.

"Yes, I think it bums him out," she said, meaning me. "It bums me out, and Howard's mom hasn't exactly been Miss Lovey Dovey with me over the years."

There was a short pause. It's true. Since Sandy is a few years older than my sister, my mother had expected her to tutor Sisi in the social graces, a job doomed to fail.

"Yes, it has gotten better, now that she's so out of it most of the time."

A long pause. No doubt it was her old basketball chum, Diane from Indianapolis, who played guard with the CU Buffaloes and had since become a wide load. I expected Diane was postulating her theory about what was happening to me.

"Well maybe. But you should see him, Diane. He gets up around nine-thirty, sometimes not 'til ten, puts on his sweats, eats his gluten-free muffin, takes his pain meds, drinks his coffee, reads a little of the paper, checks his emails and by eleven he's in the backyard smoking and chucking the ball for Mr. Booper. I'm surprised Mr. Booper hasn't dropped dead! Plus he makes up these silly little songs and sings them to the fucking dog, Diane! Oh Mister Loopy this and Mr. Loopy that and Mister Loopy wants to play with his daddy all day and on and on. It's driving me nuts!"

I briefly pondered my random and purposeless singing habit in the ensuing pause. The singing was really just a way to liberate and relieve my brain of it's incessant yammering, but, in retrospect, I can understand why Sandy was concerned.

"Yeah, his real name is Mr. Booper but Howard calls him Loopy, then he goes around singing "little Latin loopy Lou."

Diane must have said something funny at this point.

"Ha ha! You got that right. Howard's the loopy one! Oh, yes, no question. His dad has struggled with depression for years. Howard said if it wasn't for the invention of Prozac the old man would have probably exploded. And his sister is certifiably insane, so, yeah, he's definitely been depressed."

Diane was buzzing away again, just like a big fat mosquito on the other end of the line.

"Yes, he takes something that is supposed to help with depression and pain. But on top of that he takes pain meds. So now that he doesn't have to get up and go to school five days a week he's…I don't know…kinda lost, I guess."

Diane buzzed for a little bit, then Sandy said:

"Well, he actually talked about coaching summer basketball maybe next summer, if his back gets better. But CYO…that's a good idea. He hasn't mentioned it. You know he's a Catholic? Yep. Baptized, confirmed, the works. No, he doesn't go to mass, or if he does he doesn't share it with me. But CYO basketball would be perfect for him. I think he likes being around all the priests and the nuns. Maybe he thinks a little holiness will rub off on him for coaching the Pope's hoop squad."

I couldn't recall even thinking about coaching CYO basketball, but given my strict regimen of self-medication in those days, I might've said anything. The truth is, I was done coaching basketball, just as much as I thought I was done being a Catholic. My back hurt, my legs hurt, my feet hurt, all the yelling gave me a headache, and I was too busy shuffling my parents into the afterlife. I had been with my mother for four hours three days a week, along with the caregiver, so old Hal could go play dominoes with his cronies. After she passed, my father took on the death march duties, and he was a full time job.

A little later that same day, as I sat on the patio contemplating Sandy's conversation with Diane, I realized that I had put my personal interests on hold so I could help – or maybe just watch – my parents die. It wasn't so much a morbid fascination with death as it was a commitment I felt compelled to fulfill. If I wasn't helping over at 156 Woodland I was thinking about it, even if it looked like all I was doing was singing and playing chuck-it. I also realized that putting life on hold to attend to our dying father was exactly what my sister was refusing to do. Several years after I initially had that realization, she proved that my assessment had been correct: she decided to go backpacking with Mr. Doo Rag, leaving me to watch our father die. Or not.

It would be inaccurate and unfair to say that Sisi's disappearance, along with several incidents leading up to it, did not have a profound impact on my wife. Not only were we – Sandy and me – expected to pick up the slack. When Sisi made her occasional appearances, it had become an increasingly tense exchange between sister and sister-in-law. So, on the day of the old man's resurrection – when Sandy heard that he wanted me to go on a recon mission, find my sister, and bring her back kicking and screaming to his bedside, her reaction was predictable. "When is it going to stop? She's gone! Finally! And now you want to go find her and bring her back?" I had no logical, argument, no comeback, no sensible retort – I wasn't about to tell Sandy that I really *wanted* to bring my sister back, especially since she would soon be my only remaining connection to the first 20 years of my life, the sole witness to the sometimes farcical and sometimes terrible dysfunctionality of the Howard Brown family. On top of that, several Sierra Nevadas, a shot of scotch, and a couple of oxycodone, had made an intelligent conversation impossible. "Think about it, Howard." Sandy continued as we motored back from Kentfield to San Anselmo, "Your dad's gonna die, and your sister is giving you a 'get out of jail' free card for who knows how long by not showing up and making a Hallmark horror moment out of the whole thing, and you're gonna bring her back?"

"It's what the old man wants, Sandy! He wants to die and he wants Sisi to be there. He wants to die knowing that she didn't get thrown in the chipper." I should have explained that I actually *wanted* to help my crazy sister avoid the chipper, but I didn't want my wife to drive us off the road in a fit of righteous anger.

"You've spent your whole life doing what your dad wants, Howard." Even if this had been true I would've never admitted it. Coaching basketball and teaching English was the last thing Hal Brown wanted his son to be doing. "The question is: what do *you* want, Howard? You've spent the better part of the past year singing to your dog and shuffling your father from hospital to rehab back to hospital and on and on, all along taking shit from your sister. Soon he's going to be gone, hon, and hopefully your sister, too. Right? Then what?"

"No," I responded immediately and without a second thought. "I don't want my sister to be gone. I want her to get better. I think the combination of her divorce and putting our parents down has been too much for her. Hell, it's been too much for *me*! But I want to give her a chance. She's the last family I've got."

Sandy mulled this over for a minute. "So that's what you want? That's what this is really all about? Then have you spent the last year playing chuck-it on the patio with Mr. Booper trying to figure out how to fix your sister? How many times have you written her off for some insane Facebook post, or for insulting me, you, Tripp – anyone within screaming distance? I'm sorry, Howard, but I think you're still just doing what your dad wants you to do, and that you don't have a clue what you really want. I'm not criticizing you, honey. You spent thirty years trying to help high-school kids think, trying to help them win, trying to help them feel okay about their lives. And now, it seems like the shock of waking up every morning and having nowhere to go, nothing important or exciting to do, nobody to talk to…I mean, what have you been talking to your therapist about all this time? Rescuing your sister from her own bullshit?"

When we were young, Sisi and I had the world on a string. A yo-yo string. One minute Sisi and I would be co-conspirators, partners in crime, boyfriend/girlfriend scouts, authors of the wiseass encyclopedia. The next minute we would be archenemies, at each other's throats. But the bad times of late had all but erased my memories of the good times, and I was finding it difficult to conjure those increasingly rare moments of peaceful coexistence and kinship.

Sandy was right about Sisi, and doing my father's bidding, of course. I hadn't given a thought to what *I* wanted. Only to what I didn't want: for my old man to die and my sister to disappear into a home for the criminally insane, which at the time seemed like where she was headed. I had seen the inevitable train wreck coming, yet still I thought I could throw the switch and save the day.

I also knew, on that day of my father's resurrection, that my post-retirement routine was coming to a rapid close, starting with the search for my sister. It didn't occur to me that perhaps I should be searching for a sense of direction or some sort of marker in my doped-up wilderness that might help put me on track for what remained of my life. I also found the popularly-espoused idea that "everything happens for a reason" to be completely irrelevant. I was 60 years old, and had, as the saying goes "been around the block a few times." I guess I felt like Frank Bascombe, the Richard Ford character that branded the final third of his life as "the permanent period," where a man knows what he likes and likes what he knows.

And so, doped up to the point that I thought I knew what I was doing, I set out on the search for my wayward and wandering sister and her new best friend, Mr. Doo Rag.

4 The Search, Phase One

Sandy knew that fulfilling my father's wishes was rarely an easy task, and that this search for Sisi would likely be no different. So when she cooled off the next day, she even decided to help me pack. We stared at the duffel on the bed we've shared for the last 30 years – the last seven in San Anselmo, California, which boasted the only town square in the world with statues of Indiana Jones and Yoda – wondering what I might possibly need for a sister hunt: Camping gear? Fishing gear? Golf clubs? Stun gun? Guitar? I wasn't sure about the guitar.

"Don't you wanna take a break from playing the guitar? You've been serenading your dying parents for the last five years. Your fingers must be exhausted," Sandy asked while folding my J. Crew double-x pocket-tees, which had slowly replaced my entire collection of undersized vintage Hawaiians. Sandy was famous for having exquisite yet understated, uncluttered taste in just about everything, and a J. Crew pocket tee stretched out like a tent on a 60 year-old 240 pound-moose was the epitome of high fashion in her view. I looked over the rims of my chi-chi Barton Perrier's, her choice for my glasses, and thought of eagle-eyed, agile, statuesque Diana, the bow and arrow goddess, a wild doe in her sights. My heart leapt into my throat. *What a specimen! What a catch!*

I fell in love with Sandra Eriksson, "six-foot Sandy" as she was known then, while watching her shoot free throws on a Sunday morning at the CU Fieldhouse in 1974. She had a move to the basket that was more ballet than basketball, and after watching her sink forty seven free throws in a row with the same identical motion – her long dark chocolate ponytail bouncing up and down on her back the same way time after time, her knees flexing precisely four inches, the muscles of her thighs tightening and releasing, right elbow bending as her forearm, perfectly perpendicular to the floor, drawing the ball back to her forehead, left hand guiding as she arched the ball to the basket with a quick flick of the right wrist – over and over and over, swish, swish, swish. I was so hypnotized, so incapacitated and breathless with longing, that when she finally missed a shot and my turn came up I couldn't move.

To say it was love at first sight might be a stretch. I had seen her before around campus and on the basketball court and had made specific note of her, only because she was within the realm of physical and sexual possibility, meaning that I didn't have to get on my knees to hug her like I did with most of my previous girlfriends. She was also the best looking amazon of the bunch, with the proportions of Wonder Woman – impossibly long and shapely legs, a solid, generous derriere below a thin, flat tummy with breasts that made a sports bra look sexy. There was something about her ballet dancer's graceful swan neck and arms emerging from her number 58 CU Buffalos basketball jersey that, once I had studied her foul shot for a half hour, hooked me deep inside.

After she missed free throw number 48, she walked the basketball over to where I sat in the third row of the stands and said, "If you make more than 48 you can take me to dinner tonight," and plopped the ball into my lap. Tiny beads of perspiration clung to the soft down by her ears, across her upper lip and in her light sienna eyebrows that she left naturally bushy and unkempt. Her flashing umber eyes highlighted with flecks of yellow and gold and surrounded by irises as white and pure as fresh milk were so unabashedly playful that I had to accept her challenge or excuse myself. When I missed the first free throw she laughed and said, "Okay, I'll settle for a drink. Dinner can wait. Geez, I don't even know your name." Later she admitted that she did in fact know my name and actually knew more about me than I knew myself.

As we did the romance dance her old soul wrapped itself around me, thick and comforting, and calmed me down. There was something about the soft, comforting chestnut brownness of her presence, along with her down home Appleton, Wisconsin goodness and the almost imperceptible scent of freshly washed gym socks that cloaked and hypnotized me with warmth. I could still feel it three decades later as we packed for the search in San Anselmo.

"Yes, my fingers are tired," I admitted, pulling a handful of boxer shorts out of the white Elfe System wire basket – white is by far Sandy's favorite color – and throwing the little pile on the bed. I stopped and looked at my big hands, then at the tips of the fingers on my left hand where guitar callouses usually form. "For some reason I'm not getting calloused up like I used to. After an hour or so of playing the tips of my fingers are killin' me," I mused while Sandy took my left hand in hers, which was large by female standards, examined the tips of my fingers, then placed it solidly on her firm left breast.

"How does it feel now?" she asked.

"Ooooh! Much better!" I covered her right breast with my other hand

and twisted both of them left to right. "Dialing in, Will Robinson!" I announced in my mock "Lost in Space" robot voice. Mr. Booper, dismayed by my pending departure and his Mom and Dad's apparent disregard for propriety, whimpered and departed, toenails clicking on the hardwood floor of the hallway. Before we knew it my jeans were around my knees and Sandy's lovely bare bottom was on top of my neatly folded J. Crew tees and the little pile of boxers. That was the other best thing about going on a solo journey: she almost always made sure that I knew exactly what I would be missing while I was gone.

When our brief spontaneous bouncy-bounce was over, we went back to packing for my sister hunt, Sandy neatly refolding the J. Crew tees while I pulled a couple of pairs of jeans off their hangers and laid them across the bottom of the duffle. The rest Sandy packed for me as if I were a traveling salesman, though without the back seat hanger for sport coats, ties and button down shirts - Sandy was pretty sure my sister wouldn't be someplace that required coat and tie.

"But you can never tell, can you, hon? I think she's reinvented herself as many times as Madonna!" she said from the bathroom where she was loading up little daily packets of pills – opiates, anti-spasmodics, anti-cholesterol, anti-high-blood-pressure, healthy liver milk thistle capsules, sleeping pills, laxatives…it was a ridiculous cornucopia that, with a couple of cyanide capsules added to the blend would have been perfectly suited for a Baby Boomer – or more specifically, *this* Baby Boomer – "going out in the world."

I thought as I have many times in the last 35 years that my wife was unequivocally right. My sister had reinvented herself as least as many times as Madonna, starting before high school as a cheerleader and Miss School Spirit, to private girls' school androgynous hippie, to wild partying sorority girl, to earnest student to strident corporate ballbuster, glowing mommy, perfect parent, community organizer, church scandal-maker, landed gentry, writer, golfer and noble equestrian, recovering alcoholic, bitter divorcee, and then, simply missing. Now, when I look back on her chameleonic personality, I can understand what it must have been like to try so many things on, and have none of them fit. But then, short-sighted and somewhat cold-hearted as I had been in the years leading up to the search, I was expecting yet another capricious costume change, if only to throw her family off her trail.

My father set my itinerary. I was to drive to Downieville on the North Fork of the Yuba River and the north end of Highway 49, which snakes north/south through the Sierra foothills and the California Gold Country.

There were several portals into the west side of the Lakes Basin Wilderness near Downieville where I could look for her car, or more likely Bob's camper. Bob Rosenberg, my father was certain, was the fellow she was taking on her backcountry fuck fest. If I came across a suspect vehicle I was to wait there. Literally pitch a tent and hunker down. If I struck out in Downieville, I was to head to Graeagle and check out the various eastern portals into the Lakes Basin and Buck's Lake Wilderness areas. If I couldn't find the car or the camper, and the locals couldn't provide any clues, I was to play a round of golf at the Graeagle GC and head back. Why my old man included a round of golf in my itinerary is a mystery to me to this day. He knew that I could no more play golf than hike across Antartica.

Having finished packing and saying goodbye to Sandy, I drove over to 156 Woodland Road. The old man was sitting on his family room club chair, which was situated on special risers to make it easier to navigate in and out of the walker, and watching The Golf Channel. "Got your clubs?" he said when I walked into the kitchen. The caregivers had been cooking Asian food: a sweet/sour odor hung in the stuffy, sundrenched room. I opened the slider to the deck.

He had on his widest grin and his grey eyes sparkled like marbles. It was the first time I'd seen him in anything but boxers and t-shirts in several weeks and he looked like he was going to a luau. He wore a yellow short-sleeved Murakami shirt, the feeding peg in his stomach pulling it up to one side, and a pair of unbuttoned khaki slacks so his scarred gut could hang out unencumbered. If he didn't have the oxygen tubes in his nose he might have been wearing one of his big Sam Snead straw hats.

It was early for him: 11:30 AM. He was always a light sleeper, and had taken to propping himself up in the old four poster with his crosswords, novels, magazines, newspapers and ever-present transistor radio with the single earplug and dozing off and on, day and night. The whole concept of early and late had dissolved in the face of his impending death, and it looked like he was now content to mark time by the daily Sierra Nevada Pale Ale.

I can picture him there on his throne with the TV remote in his prehistoric-looking claw, one of the girls standing close by, a zipper-like line of stitches up the middle of his chest where his ribs were lashed together with super glue and bailing wire, and a tube of disgusting brown liquid dripping into a hole in his gut. It was hard to believe that the rest of him was still working relatively normally. He could breathe, pee, shit, drink beer, laugh, smile, and operate the remote. His mind was still sharp, and all he wanted was a goodbye kiss from his only daughter, close his eyes and drift away. I gave him one last look as I backed out the kitchen door, his eyes glued to the female golf channel and a stunning array of ass jammed into so-called golf shorts. I chuckled quietly to myself and shut the front door behind me, just as certain as I could be that my father would be right where I left him when I returned, and that Sisi in all her maniacal glory would be at my side.

5 Born Disappointments

My sister's name is Elizabeth Brown, but the only person who ever called her that was our mother, and only when she was angry with her, which was often. Otherwise my sister was called whatever her name du jour might have been at any given time. This wasn't a problem until later, when her contacts with old friends became more infrequent. She could be Crystal in January and Kris by July, much to the dismay of everybody who hadn't spoken with her since January. If it was someone that hadn't been keeping track of my sister's frequent name changes, they defaulted to the one name that stuck: Sisi, which we first pronounced "Sissy," or just "Sis." Later, after I learned about the volatile and disturbed Empress Sisi of the Hapsburgs – the one who never cut her hair – I started pronouncing it "See-see." By the time of her disappearance and my father's resurrection, Sandy had started referring to her as "Cruella," for she often had that same demonic laugh, the impatience with the "idiots" around her and, around that time, the streaky black and white hairdo.

I had no idea what her name du jour was when she quit her job and took off for the mountains with Mr. Doo Rag, and I had forgotten to ask my father. For all I knew she might have gone by Oprah. Fortunately it didn't matter much what she called herself: she couldn't escape her chiseled Audrey Hepburn profile and willowy body, her thick, sculpted brows or her deep-set umber eyes. That's not to say she didn't try. She often made valiant attempts to attach an aggressive, controversial Day-Glo hairdo to her name du jour, but for my detective purposes it made no difference. Anybody who saw the photo I carried on my phone would have recognized her in an instant. "Oh, how could I forget her?" I imagined folks saying.

After bidding the dying man adieu, as I was driving down College Avenue in my black Saab – custom fitted to allow the driver's seat to push all the way to the back so I could stretch out my tree-trunk legs while hanging my left arm out the left-side backseat window – I thought as I often did of Kentfield's slow small town death over the course of my 60 years. I pictured my famously slender mother – tan, buxom and blonde as if she had just stepped out of a Coppertone ad – driving around town with us: the tow-headed boy and the chestnut-headed girl, in her powder blue convertible Buick Skylark, going from the drugstore to the grocery store to the hardware store to the stationery store and finally to the Eat and Run drive-in for corn

26

dogs and chocolate milkshakes, all of it on College Avenue. When a couple of lanes were added to the main Ross Valley artery, Sir Francis Drake Boulevard, and the Rexall pharmacy got replaced with a turning lane, the town just went belly up. Before long the drive-up window at the Eat and Run was a drive-up ATM and the College of Marin football field was a parking lot.

College Avenue frequently bombarded me with memories of the early sixties, and that day – the first day of my search for Sisi – the memories were especially vivid. I pictured a pack of fifth grade boys sneaking into College of Marin football games under the misty Friday night lights, followed by that same pack racing around town in baseball uniforms on Stingrays with Topps baseball cards flapping in the spokes. I recalled how Sisi and I felt, liberated from the boy and girl at home who could seem to do nothing but disappoint their parents, regardless of straight As, .650 batting averages, top drill team honors, the lead part in the Ballet Aquacade, and the ability to play "Classical Gas" at age ten. Whatever our accomplishments were, they either weren't right or weren't good enough, at least not for our father. We could never quite figure out what we had to do to please him, besides suddenly growing up and being the top money winners on the P.G.A. and L.P.G.A tours.

Our mother was not nearly so enigmatic. "Howard," she said one evening shortly after my betrothal to Sandy, "I wish you would quit this teaching business and get a decent job. I didn't raise you to be a teacher."

"Oh?" I replied. "What exactly did you raise me to be?"

"Successful," she cried, getting flustered. "With your looks and your golf game, Howard, my God! You can write your own ticket!"

"What ticket is that, Mom?" I was baiting her as I often did. I knew that if I drilled her for specifics, regardless of the topic, she would buckle. It was an instinctual tactic, vindictive and cruel, and had I known that her mind would soon vacate her anorexic, emaciated body, perhaps I would've shown a little charity and cut her some slack. But I didn't, or at least I didn't until after it was too late.

"Oh come on, don't act like such a dullard, Howard. You know what I'm talking about," she insisted. But I didn't know, not exactly. Was she saying that there was a way to make a good living –not just a good living, but a way to get filthy rich – simply by looking good, being tall, and hitting a driver 280 yards? Was she saying that people would pay great sums just to have an overly tall, somewhat handsome, well-read, articulate man with a good golf swing hanging around?

"But what would I actually do, Mom?"

"Play golf! Do deals! Drink Scotch! Play dominoes and sign contracts!" she cried.

Such memories often clouded my consciousness in the years following her death, and on that first day of the Sisi search the recollections were unusually intense. Suddenly nauseous with regret, I turned east onto Sir Francis Drake Boulevard, named for the British privateer that claimed Marin County and quite possibly the entire western hemisphere for the Crown. Ahead lay the bay, blanketed in summer fog that stretched from the Golden Gate to Berkeley like a long, grey, fuzzy gym sock.

I was debating easing my nausea with a cigarette when my mobile buzzed. It was my son, Howard Brown, III, sometimes referred to as "the turd" but generally called Tripp. Being his dad, I had a million nicknames for him, but I generally defaulted to the universal "Buddy," "Bud" and "Pal." I reserved "the turd" for special occasions.

"You need to come get me," he said in a straight deadpan. "Mom said you were taking a road trip…"

"Hey, Buddy. Yeah I was just about to call you to see if you wanted to get out of town for a couple of days." I lied. I had completely forgotten to call my son and tell him what had happened; how G-Hal, as he was known (short for Grandpa Hal) didn't die and was actually doing better than he had in months, and that I was to go find Aunt Sisi.

"You need help with the driving, right?" he said, knowing it would coax a chuckle. My son was at that time legally blind. Even so, he wasn't so blind that he wouldn't get behind the wheel, which I was pretty sure he'd done with some of his friends. He also was the most talented (which is to say luckiest) legally blind fly fisherman on the planet. Once Sandy had told him that I was going on a "harebrained boondoggle" to Downieville on the North Fork of the Yuba River and then Graeagle on the Middle Fork of the Feather River, with the Truckee River close by, he was checking the fishing reports. Hearing his earnest voice on the phone, I couldn't believe that I hadn't planned to take him along, the distraction of my father's self-willed resurrection notwithstanding.

I can picture what happened next as if it happened yesterday. I was just about to head north off Sir Francis Drake onto highway 101, but to fetch Tripp I had to go south. I looked in the rear view: there was just enough space to cut over a couple of lanes and get to the southbound exit, so I put on my blinker, shoved my gorilla arm out the window and hit the gas. Still, there was no way to avoid cutting off a couple of drivers, who started honking, naturally. Then I saw this one driver – a red-faced Fu-Manchu dude with mirrored sunglasses and an Oakland Raiders cap in a junior-sized blue Ford Ranger – getting really pissed, shouting and flipping me off violently. So, like I always did when I upset a fellow driver back then, I blew him a kiss. This was a bad idea: Mr. Fu-Manchu got so close behind me on the freeway onramp that I thought he was going to bump me. Then he pulled up alongside, shouting unintelligibly through the open passenger window. He was so close I could see the throbbing blue vein in his red forehead, but I just kept blowing him kisses like I was Marilyn Monroe on the stairs of an airliner, bidding adieu to her adoring fans. What the world needs now is love sweet love, right? Well, I was giving it to Mr. Road Rage, who I could now see had a shaved head under his mesh-top Raiders cap and was just getting more and more infuriated. Then he made his move: he cut in front of me diagonally so I had to swerve to avoid him in the heavy Saturday afternoon traffic: brake lights flashed, horns blared, tires squealed and I could see several vehicles fishtailing behind me to avoid a pileup.

"Holy motherfucking shit that fucking cocksucker almost killed us all!" I hollered, dropping back in traffic until the blue pickup was out of sight. Feeling like I was having a heart attack, and realizing that I had been out in the big, bad world very little in the five years since my retirement – driving around Marin appeared more dangerous than ever – I took the next exit and pulled into a parking space beside a Chevron Extra-Mile mini-mart, thinking a beer or five on top of a little oxy would calm me down.

"Dad!" I heard Trip's tiny voice. He sounded like the little boy that couldn't seem to scream "DAD!" loud enough. "Dad are you there?"

"Buddy! I can't find the phone!" I shouted in the general direction of where his voice had come from under the driver's seat. All the swerving around on the freeway had dislodged the phone from its harness. So I opened the door and, knees on the pavement, fished around under the seat, then did the same under the passenger's seat. No phone.

"Dad, I'm over here!" I could hear him chuckling as I peered between the passenger seat and the center console. There it was, wedged in snug and cozy. I lay my plus-sized gut across the driver's seat with my gargantuan ass sticking out the door and tried to liberate the phone while Tripp reported on fishing conditions at the Yuba. "The water is pretty low, and it's been a pretty dry summer up there, so we're gonna wanna look for pools with deep channels where we can just swing a fly right across the bottom." With the mention of "bottom" somebody gave my ass a powerful, violent shove that pinned me against the seat.

"Hey! What the fuck?" I shouted, trying to get up, but whoever it was had squashed my crotch against the electric seatback control. Suddenly, my wiener was in charge; a little shift against the button I could recline or incline the seat.

"You're some hot shit race car driver, ain'tcha?"

Oh for fuck's sake, I was thinking. *It's the shaved-headed Oakland Raiders fan, Mr. Road Rage. He has tracked down my custom-designed Saab and is going to chop my balls off, then jam 'em down my throat.*

"Dad?"

"Hey, Buddy," I said, bemused. "There's a fella here trying to buttfuck me in the Chevron parking lot."

"Shut the fuck up, fag!" growled Mr. Road Rage, shoving me even harder. He stunk of beer, gin and vomit so powerfully that I felt a sympathy barf welling up. I also recall worrying that the asshole had a gun trained on my bald spot, which I was told existed but had never seen.

"That's him, the buttfucker," I reported.

"Hey, you shut up, asshole!" Tripp shouted, picking a fight from the cell phone stuck between the seats.

"Turn that fuckin' phone off, dickface."

"I can't! It's stuck between the seats!"

"Yeah, can't you tell, shit-for-brains?" Tripp yelled. I could imagine the sneer on Tripp's face.

Then I felt this giant upwelling of superhuman power as I shoved my angry wiener against the seat control, inclining the seatback as forward as it would go, which enabled me to get a grip on the sides of the seat. With a bloodcurdling war whoop, I pushed myself back against my attacker who, with one foot on my ass and the other on the ground, lost his balance and fell backward, his acrylic Raiders cap bouncing on the pavement. I spun around, ready to blanket him with my immensity, when two uniformed mini-mart attendants blasted out of the double glass doors side-by-side like Butch and Sundance, arms waving and yelling "Stop! No fighting here! No fighting! You must stop!"

Instead they stopped, about 10 feet away from where I stood over the vanquished butt stomper. The station managers were looking at us as if we were combustible materials.

"Why for you like fight?" one of them shouted, almost melodiously. My rage was draining and my crotch was throbbing.

"Dad? What the hell is going on there? Dad?" Tripp yelled. The station managers were now studying my Saab, marveling at the odd configuration of the driver's seat.

"Sir," one of them said, "your phone. Somebody is talking."

Mr. Road Rage was snickering and hissing like a Disney anaconda.

"I'm sorry about this," I said to both of them, avoiding the gaze of Mr. Road Rage, who was probably fifteen years younger than me and pretty good sized, a kangaroo to my grizzly bear.

Mr. Road Rage hopped up from the ground and brushed himself off, glaring at me while he hissed, "You are such a fucking fag. You wanna kiss me now, asshole?" His sleeves were rolled up over the elbow with a dragon's tail stretching across his freckled arm. His face was still fire engine red. I paused to retrieve the phone, telling my son that I couldn't explain it all at the moment but would call back later.

This was not how I had planned to re-enter the world. After five years in relative hibernation – on the patio with Mr. Booper, at 156 Woodland with parents, caregivers and my frequently ill-mannered sister, and in bed with Sandy – I had forgotten that even marvelous Marin County streets and highways were tinderboxes of pent-up frustration and rage just waiting to explode, like my new acquaintance had just demonstrated. I briefly contemplated going home and calling off the search – I was grossly unprepared for the dangers of American highway culture – but then an alarm went off inside the mini-mart: a half dozen kids were making off with bags stuffed with as much mini-mart crap as they could carry, mostly twelve-packs of Bud Light. The station managers were after them in an instant. I jumped in my car and ducked behind the dashboard. But these kids were hardly dangerous. Instead they looked like the backfield for the Redwood high school football team: ripped dudes with crew cuts, tattoos peeking out from under tank tops, shorts falling off their asses. I got the feeling that the theft was more of a prank than a serious robbery – they probably didn't even open the cash register – so I got out and hobbled behind the running security team, when along came Mr. Road Rage from behind, streaking across the blacktop to where the guys were jumping into the back of their truck, one kid ripping the gas hose out of the tank. The station managers and I froze as the all-star wrestling Fu Manchu maniac hooked an arm around the football player with the gas hose and slammed him into the side of their big boy pickup truck, beer cans erupting out of the twelve pack in a glorious explosion of golden suds. One of the other kids jumped out of the pickup bed onto Fu-Manchu's back, wrapping his legs around his waist and whomping on his shaved head with a free hand while Fu got the other football player by the nape and was banging his forehead into the passenger side window. Just as the glass shattered into a million tiny shards sparkling against the blacktop, my phone rang.

"Dad!"

I went running back to my car, which waited with the keys still in the famous between-the-seat Saab ignition. "Hey Buddy you won't believe what is happening here." I described the scene, which, as I pulled out of the Extra Mile, had developed into a sort of scrum with Mr. Road Rage Fu Manchu getting the shit kicked out of him by a half-dozen beefy teenagers. By the time I turned into the freeway entrance, the kids were peeling out of the Extra Mile and the station managers were attending to Mr. Road Rage on the ground who, I supposed, got more fight than was originally planned when he followed me into the parking lot, as had I. And the real search for Sisi hadn't even started yet.

I drove back into the flow of freeway traffic, headed to Tam Junction and the Shoreline Highway that would take me out to Bolinas. Soon I would lose cell service. I scanned my rear view for the blue Ranger, paranoid as always that some random nut case out there would pull up alongside me and blow my brains out with an assault rifle, or toss a grenade into my lap. "I'm gonna lose you in a little bit," I said as I crested a hill past Muir Beach and met the broad aquamarine expanse of the Pacific, but Tripp was already gone.

That particular stretch of Highway One, after the road climbs out of Muir Beach to the ridge, revealing the craggy cliffs that fall into the seething foam of the ocean, has, in its arresting panorama, always forced a moment of reverence and reflection. Instead, on that particular afternoon, I found myself imagining how I would have loved to pop Mr. Road Rage's bald, red head like a big pimple. Terrified by my own violent visions, I started to wonder: *what am I getting into here, and why? Was leaving my patio, my chucker, Mr. Booper and my wife's broad, creamy bottom worth a harebrained boondoggle for the sake of fostering some final family harmony?*

Then, as if Baba Ram Dass had started dancing on the hood of the Saab chanting "be here now," I finally came back to where I was, gazing across breathtaking blue-on-blue stretching across the Pacific Ocean into infinity. I wished my father could see it. I wished my son could see it. I wished my wife could see it. Most of all, I wished my sister could see it. At least then I would know exactly where she was.

6 Pit Bulls and Coyotes

My mother had always espoused platitudes like "you attract more bees with honey" and "kill them with kindness" when dealing with rude people, including murderous motorists. The only problem was that, for some reason, whenever I applied Mom's conflict management theories – like blowing kisses – the approach almost always backfired. After my run-in with Mr. Road Rage, I vowed to stop blowing kisses and instead, now that I was back in the so-called real world, employ the expected three-fingered salute.

"Fuck off!"

"Okay, no problem, have a nice day!"

When I got out to Bolinas, a famously secluded burg on the tip of Punta de Baulines, with the lights of San Francisco visible thirty miles to the southeast and the wilds of the Point Reyes National Seashore to the northwest, I called Tripp to let him know that I had arrived. "You're sitting in your car outside my house?" he asked. And then there he was, a dwarf compared to me, in his ever-present backwards cap and wrap-around Vuarnet sunglasses, his prominent and perennially sunburned beak poking out like the Brown family crescent, like that of six Howard Browns before him. The classic "Why don't you shave that shit off" ratty blond pubic whiskers were still there over his lip and sprouting out from his dimpled chin, between a golden thicket of tangles falling to his broad shoulders.

"Yes, but now I am getting out," I said, and just as I popped open the door a mature, healthy female coyote trotted into the yard. "Uh…wait a sec. Don't move," I whispered, slowly pulling my legs back into the car. It was rather early in the day – late afternoon – for a coyote to be making an appearance. Such appearances can indicate that something is amiss with the beast, like rabies, though this gal was beautifully turned out with a thick muffler of silvery fur around her neck and down to her upper foreleg.

"Tripp," I whispered, "There's a coyote in the yard." Immediately I realized that telling Tripp there was a coyote in the yard was like telling the late great "Croc Hunter" Steve Irwin that there was a poisonous, deadly creature nearby. Like the Croc Hunter, Tripp would want to see how friendly he could get with the wild animal, even if all he could make out of it was a blurry, monochromatic outline. Sure enough he tiptoed across the porch with his cell phone still up to his ear and his ever-present white stick in his hand. It seemed weird to be talking to someone on a cell phone when they were only fifty feet away, but between the two of us was a sizeable coyote sniffing around the base of a Gravenstein apple tree.

"Is she over by the apple tree?" Tripp whispered, looking in my general direction.

"Yes, she's eating an apple." This surprised me – I didn't think coyotes ate fruit, though Mr. Booper loves apples.

"Yeah. That's Carrie. She'll eat anything," Tripp whispered as he came down the front steps in ultra slow-mo, his tanned toes curling over the edge of the lip of each stair. The coyote, to my amazement, was completely oblivious of Tripp's approach though it wouldn't have surprised me, since they were on a first name basis, if Tripp invited the canine in for a beer and a milk bone. Then Tripp jerked his head up as if he had just heard something. I looked over to see three coyote pups run out of the willows, blackberries and brambles that lined the little creek behind Tripp's house, yipping and rolling through the grass up to mom under the apple tree.

"Three pups?" he asked.

I had never been so close to something like this in my life, but for Tripp it sounded like an everyday thing. I wouldn't have been surprised if he had names for the pups too. They made for mom's belly but she nudged them away. Eventually they found some of the bits of apple mom had chewed up and left on the grass. Tripp slowly sat on the stoop and stared sightlessly across the yard, listening to the almost imperceptible sounds of the coyote and her pups.

Then, like somebody had hurled a hand grenade into the yard, mom and pups scattered for the ferns. From around the corner of the house ran a snarling, ferocious grey and white pit bull mutt, a real spiked dog collar around his neck. He was lightning fast and had one of the pups by the scruff of the neck in an instant, but mom was far faster than the domestic breed and, twisting around in one quick motion she latched onto the pit bull's neck, dog blood squirting out in all directions. She bit in harder and gave the dog a rip, tossing him like a rag doll ten feet back into the yard. The pit bull lay there motionless as Carrie and her family raced back to the creek and the safety of the overgrowth.

I sat in the driver's seat stunned, not sure if I should get out and tend to the dog or what the hell I should do. "Tripp," I finally exhaled into the phone.

Tripp didn't answer because he was bounding down the stairs two at a time, one hand sliding down the rail while his white stick bounced alongside. When he got to the grass he rushed directly over to the dog and got down on his haunches, and, even though I had seen him do far more remarkable things in his blindness, I still asked myself *How did he do that? Did he have the dog's scent? Was he sniffing the air as he ran, or was he hearing his way?*

Now he reached instinctively for the dog's jugular, then wiped his bloody hand on the grass. Then I was with him, my heart pounding in my throat and my big hand on his shoulder. "Shit," he muttered. "Elke!" he shouted, but his lithesome girlfriend was already out the door, phone in hand.

"Yeah, Danny. A coyote got him on the neck," she explained on the phone as she knelt next to Tripp, one hand on his where they were trying to staunch the flow of blood. "Right. Doug Dennikan's dog," she added with an odd hint of wariness.

Only then did I observe that the evening fog had arrived and was swirling around the dim nautical sconce by Tripp's front door, the only outdoor lighting on the property. More dogs were barking down the gravel road in the direction Carrie the Coyote had gone with her pups. Then from around the corner a red Fire Chief's pickup came flying, sending up plumes of dust as it slid to a halt. Two volunteer firemen rushed to where the dog lay, one with a veterinary medicine kit. They worked fast: stuffed the wound with gauze, taped her up and carried her back to the truck and hopped in. Elke shouted out, "Is he going to make it, Danny?"

The fireman shook his head. "I wouldn't bet on it," and before the dust from their arrival had even settled they sent up another plume, fishtailing down the loose gravel road with a portable red light flashing atop the cab.

"Jesus. Buddy better live, that's all I can say," Tripp said to no one in particular, standing up and brushing himself off. "His owner is a first class asshole."

"Ha!" I couldn't help but chuckle at the idea that some dog owner would try and pin the blame on a coyote that happened to be eating apples with her pups in my son's front yard, especially when Buddy the pit bull was clearly the aggressor.

"Dad," Tripp interrupted. "Logic isn't a factor with this guy. He's a dangerous, violent drunk, and he would like nothing better than an excuse to fuck with me."

"So, the guy lives nearby?"

"Yeah." Tripp nodded down the street. "Third house down."

The place looked like a halfway house for car parts and other indeterminate metal objects; a rusted vintage Wedgewood stove from the thirties, several piles of old tires, odd-shaped objects hiding under bungeed tarps and...wait. My breath caught. That blue Ford Ranger. I knew there must be a million of 'em prowling around the 101 corridor, but this one was almost calling out to me, saying, "Hey haven't we met someplace before?"

"So Tripp," I said, not taking my eyes off the pickup. "What does..." but I caught myself. I almost asked my blind son what his asshole neighbor looked like. Instead I clapped him on the back.

"Don't worry, Pal. Those pit bulls are unkillable. He'll be fine."

7 The Accident

Tripp was packed and ready to begin the search for his aunt Sisi, so after bidding Elke adieu, we hit the road. About halfway to Vallejo, (named for General Mariano Vallejo, the Mexican that was briefly in charge of Alta California in 1836 when the USA moved in) we got a call from Elke telling us that the dog was alive and out of the woods.

"Well, baby," Tripp sighed over the phone, "Mister MacDickfuck is going to blame Carrie either way." It didn't surprise me that Tripp referred to his neighbors with such understated reverence. It was Bolinas after all, so it was a wonder that Tripp had managed to live three doors down from someone whose name he actually knew. Mr. MacDickfuck. *What a great name,* I thought. Then I remembered Mr. Road Rage. I started to interrogate Elke over the phone: did Mr. MacDickfuck drive a blue junior-sized pickup? Yes, according to Elke. Did he have a shaved head and a Fu-Manchu? Elke said it was pretty lame, yes. And if that wasn't enough, did he wear a cheap nylon trucker's cap backwards and move like a fat rhesus monkey? Yes and yes and yes and oh my God did I feel good then? YES! Tripp's coyote had just seriously fucked with that motherfucker's worthless, violent, aggressive dog!

Random coincidence? Divine justice? Here a bad human had attacked another smartass but not altogether bad human in a mini-mart parking lot – unjustifiable behavior by anyone's, especially God's, measure – and was now paying with his almost-killed dog. I knew it wasn't the dog's fault that he ended up with drunken maniac for a master, but I could help wondering if such an event belonged in the "everything happens for a reason" category, or did such events just happen? An impossible question, but I had inkling that I hadn't heard or seen the end of Mr. MacDickfuck and his bloodthirsty pit bull sidekick, Buddy.

Once we were out of the Bay Area and beyond the happy lights of the fast food colony at the junction of interstate 80 and 680, which I've always viewed as sort of a welcome mat and indoctrination to the deep-fried Frappuccino experience of the Sacramento Valley, I cross-examined my son about every wave he had ridden, fish he'd caught, seminar he'd taught, and interview he'd given since we last had the opportunity to speak of such things. By the time we got to I-5, the big central valley north/south artery running right up the belly of the state, we were riding in silence. Tripp had his ear buds buried deeply and was listening to something that didn't sound any more like music to me than the Beatles must have sounded to my parents, his chin on his chest rocking forward and back like Ray Charles at the piano.

Our son was not born blind, nor did he become blind as a result of disease, like Ray Charles. Up until July fourth 1998, when he was nine and a half, he had eagle-eye vision so sharp he could see the subtle ripples of a trout eyeing a fly on the surface before it struck. He could identify bugs in the air from their flight patterns, as well as dozens of species of songbirds and waterfowl. He could tell you the species, size, age and likely whereabouts of almost any animal from tracks in the mud. He was so visually and preternaturally attuned to the natural world that local naturalists at Point Reyes and Mt. Tamalpais State Park would invite him to help guide local nature walks, particularly for kids his own age. When people asked us why our son was so familiar with nature, we told them that once he read *My Side of The Mountain* there was no stopping him. By the time he was nine he had read every single Tom Brown "tracker" book in the library and was already making fire with a hand drill. Until July fourth, 1998, Tripp Brown was not only a bona-fide naturalist; he was a fly-fishing prodigy to be reckoned with. Like many parents of gifted children, we would often look at each other, shake our heads and say, "Where did this kid come from?"

My unforgettable recollection of that July fourth evening plays like a horrific highlights reel in my personal hall of shame. There were three boys in the driveway of our neighbor's little San Anselmo hillside home: the stocky thirteen-year-old Ballard twins, Steve and Ben, were in their daily white crew neck T-shirts and buzz cuts, crowded around my skinny little burr-headed blond boy, who was unusually small for his age, particularly given his supersized parents. The neighborhood was alive with popping firecrackers, whistling Piccolo Petes and pinwheels, and the multi-colored spray of sparks from fountains of every size and color: the "Liberty Tower," the "Big Blast," the "Krakatoa." The air was thick with the smell of gunpowder and the local dogs were howling louder than any of it except our Mr. Jones, Mr. Booper's hound dog predecessor, who had burrowed into a corner of Sandy's closet and made a fort of plus-size designer sportswear to protect him from what must have surely sounded like the canine apocalypse.

The night was warm and unusually clear for the Fourth, when the summer marine layer of fog and drizzle usually crept far inland, shrouding the various fireworks celebrations around the Bay under a dense gray cloud that could only hint at the colorful explosions underneath. Sandy and I, Vivian

Ballard and her husband Jim, along with several other couples were drinking margaritas and talking about what was known locally as the China Camp murders: a local teenager and her boyfriend had murdered her parents and then fried their bodies in an ancient cistern years ago and somebody had written a song about it. For a while we had been paying close attention to the boys, and had instructed them to lay the firecrackers on the ground, light the fuse, then run away. The older boys seemed to know what they were doing, and Tripp followed their lead. After a few more of Jim Ballard's very stiff fruit jar margaritas, we began to gossip about who was cheating on whom, and those of our so-called friends we wouldn't touch with a ten-foot pole, and so forth, and forgot about the boys and their explosives.

It was well past Tripp's bedtime when I heard him cry out from the street in unison with an explosion – a loud pop, then screaming, like a giant balloon full of crows had exploded. All the adults jumped up. I saw Tripp's hands go to his face. Sandy ran to him as I stumbled on the cracked pavement of the driveway and fell headlong into the privet hedge. Scratched and bleeding I got up as Tripp, hands still over his face, started to half stagger, half run down the empty neighborhood street, Sandy trying to get a grip on him, both of them yelling incoherently. Then Tripp rammed into the rear of a parked car and fell hard to the pavement. Sandy and I knelt over where he lay fetal with his hands still to his face, neither of us exactly sure what had happened. He was screaming, crying, moaning, sobbing all at once. Then the slack-jawed twins were standing behind us. Their father, who had a reputation for being a hothead with the neighborhood kids, started shouting. "What happened? What the hell happened? Goddamnit Ben, Steve what just happened?" He grabbed the boys and spun them around while I gently covered Tripp's hands with my own and tried to calm him down, but the howling just got louder. When Sandy sat on the pavement and cradled his head the howling slowly fell to a loud, steady groan.

It was now pretty obvious that a firecracker, or something bigger, had somehow exploded in our son's face. Tripp knew he was not under any circumstances to light a firecracker, so we suspected one of the other boys lit one and perhaps threw it at him. Or it had been lit on the pavement and, when it didn't go off, the older boys convinced Tripp to go get it so they could relight it. None of the adults saw what happened, and were probably too drunk to register any impending danger. Getting the straight story out of the Ballard brothers was hopeless.

Soon the continuing cacophony of exploding fireworks was complimented by screaming sirens and whirling, flashing red lights as the firemen arrived and cleared us all away. We still didn't know for sure what had happened. Then a fireman saw Tripp and knew immediately.

"What was it?" he asked the Ballard boys, knowing that Tripp was still in no shape to take questions. "A cherry bomb? An M-80? Roman candle?"

"No, just a firecracker. A fat one," one of them said. Just a firecracker?

"Also known as an M-80," the fireman said. The paramedics had arrived along with two cop cars, one from San Anselmo and the other a county sheriff. The paramedics had the stretcher out and slowly slid it under Tripp, whom they had finally coaxed into a supine pose. His hands still covered his face but his howling had been quieted to a steady groan punctuated with a whimper. Then the paramedics slowly pulled his hands away.

There, in the swirling, flashing red and yellow lights of the emergency vehicles rhythmically illuminating the little hillside houses, faces staring out of the darkness from front lawns, inside the din of popping firecrackers, whistling Piccolo Petes and pinwheels, the voices over the walkie-talkies, smell of smoke and gunpowder; there, in that moment before the paramedic applied the cold compresses to our son's blackened face, when we saw his eyes staring skyward and sightless into the darkness, the devil took a bite out of our souls.

Later, the ophthalmologist gave Tripp's eyes a 10% chance of someday being usable. The surgery he proposed would either improve what was left of his eyesight – now reduced to a world of indistinct, fuzzy shapes, grey or brown against a background of darkness – or turn out the lights completely. We decided not to take the chance in hopes his eyesight would improve on its own.

Call it an error of omission, a momentary lapse of parental diligence, a security breach. Call it responsibility, shirked. Call it shit, happening. Every parent knows it, and every parent knows that the heartbreak can't be fixed. Even though the wound may heal, the scar that remains just gets thicker and tougher, to the point where it feels like the heart itself is nothing more than a purposeless pump, sheathed in an impenetrable shell.

That was 17 years ago. Like the rest of the failing factory parts of my jumbo body, I sensed the shell around my heart was weakening, as well. It must've been. Otherwise, why didn't I just let my old man die and let my sister go live her truth in whatever crazy fashion she pleased? Had the harebrained boondoggle – the search for a woman who clearly did not want to be found – been proposed ten, or maybe just five, years ago, I would have said "no way." Instead, with my blind son asleep in the passenger seat of the old black Saab and my heart thumping its inexorable rhythms, I drove onward.

8 A Man's Truth

It didn't take long to get a line on my sister. Her former boyfriend, Mr. Doo Rag, was practically waiting for us at the St. Charles Hotel Bar in Downieville.

When we arrived the sidewalks of the town had been rolled up for the night, all except the St. Charles, which had been a red hot bordello back in the gold rush days. But the place had fallen into dusty disrepair, with a 20 year-old life size cardboard Elvira hawking Coors Light on Halloween and real spider webs on the jumbo double hung windows.

Tripp and I walked up to the bar and were just about to hunker down on the red naugahyde brass-pinned stools when I did a double-take. There at the end of the bar sat a backpacker with a sweat-stained David Foster Wallace bandana wrapped around his head. Alone. I hesitated. After my friend-making experience with Mr. Road Rage earlier that very same, very long day I was really not in a reach-out-and-touch-someone mood and this guy did not look happy. Then just as he got up, shouldered his backpack and stumbled toward the swinging Wild West barroom gate the bartender – a buxom, tattooed, peroxide blonde – shouted: "Hey asshole! Where do you think you're going?"

The backpacker, his bloodshot eyes painfully red like the skin on his face, swayed under his heavy pack, then lurched with a spastic top heavy step to his left, followed by another lurch, and another, picking up speed as he went crashing into the pool table.

"Yeah!" shouted the blonde, "you think you can sit in here and drink all day then just walk out without paying?" Considering the backpacker was now on the planks, arms and legs splayed out from underneath his pack like a squashed four-legged bug under a big red shell, we couldn't help but laugh. But the poor bastard on the floor was out cold. Then the bartender handed me a pitcher of ice water and said, "here big boy – give our friend a bath. It's almost closing time and I'm not taking any boarders tonight."

Feeling empowered, I gave the backpacker a thorough facial douche. He lurched up, lost his balance and fell over on his back. Now he really looked like a helpless bug and I told Tripp so, because he could remember how many things looked and even though he couldn't see them they were alive in his mind's eye. Conjuring the image of a black beetle on his back, six legs flailing in the air, Tripp shouted out, "Dude, you look like a fuckin' stinkbug!"

I stood over the backpacker, who even in the peaceful slumber of borderline alcohol poisoning looked troubled and overwrought, four days of spotty growth on his jowls, eyes puffy with several days of crust around the edges, and possibly second degree sunburn on his heroically hooked beak. I couldn't picture him as my sister's type but as she had said herself her latest primary criteria for partnership was the capacity for real love, which I supposed had been lacking in her marriage. This fella didn't look like the real love type either, with his hairy belly bulging out from under his tank top and tufts of wiry hair on the back of his upper arms.

The bartender supplied me with another pitcher of ice water and I was just about to give the backpacker another douching when his eyes opened up to see me staring down at him. It was when I finally got a good look at his hopelessly bloodshot and burning eyeballs eyes that a flash of recognition ran through me like a 40-volt cattle prod, but I was struggling to put a name to the face. Then he said in a hoarse whisper: "Howard? Howard Brown? What the fuck?"

We ended up taking Mr. Doo Rag, aka Bob Rosenberg, back to his camper near our motel at the confluence of the Downie and Yuba rivers. He made coffee and pulled a couple of folding chairs out onto a levee overlooking the water, where he commenced to tell me his Betty Jo (name du jour) Brown story. Within minutes I was nodding off to the voices in the gurgling water. All I was really interested in was her destination, but he was determined to make me suffer through the whole wretched blow-by-blow.

The moon had ascended over the canyon, illuminating the white trunks of the spruce on the steep hillsides, the granite boulders in the river and the sparkling riffles. A chilly breeze blew upriver, rattling the leaves and making me wish even harder to be under the covers, where I imagined Tripp was snoring like a baby gorilla.

"Man, I'm beat," I told him. "You wanna have breakfast tomorrow?" It seemed like he didn't even hear me. But then his story began to get more and more bizarre, and before I knew it I was all ears, wide awake as the hoot owl across the river.

I think I said about three words in the hour or so that I spent listening to Rosenberg drone and watching the moonlight dance across the riffles. I was too busy trying to figure out which parts of his story might be believable and which parts he was making up to save face. In a nutshell, my sister decided that Rosenberg was gay and ditched him on the trail.

"But the truth is she got the hots for this other guy we met and wanted me out of the picture," Rosenberg whined while I was trying to keep from falling out of my chair. Turns out on the second night out they met a couple of other guys who were camped on the other side of a small lake. Rosenberg told me that Sisi, who he knew as Betty Jo, had been watching the guys fish off a couple of granite boulders that were part way out into the lake, and when he took a look through the binoculars himself he realized that they were probably twins, both with real backcountry Patagonia bright white teeth sparkling in the sun. He also noticed they were butt naked. Normally my bullshit meter would have been tripped by this little tidbit if I hadn't spent quite a bit of time gallivanting around the mountains in nothing but hiking boots, socks and a day pack in during my college years.

After watching them catch almost a dozen good-sized trout through the glasses, while Rosenberg caught none, my sister decided she would invite herself over to their campsite for dinner. "It was almost as if she was going to make me stay at our campsite and eat Rice-a-Roni because I couldn't catch a fucking fish!" Rosenberg wailed. "Of course I wasn't going to stay at our campsite while she ate trout with the naked fishermen." So they joined the two thirty-something backpackers at their campfire. "They were Czechs, from Prague, which surprised the hell out of me," Rosenberg admitted. "I've never heard of a backpacking Czech, especially in California."

Several crispy breaded trout and sierra cups of Beam later, once the moon was casting shadows of the lodge pole pines across the granite, Betty Jo and one of the twins disappeared into the woods "to collect firewood." When they returned Rosenberg was passed-out by the campfire, as was the other Czech fisherman, their arms around each other. "Nothing happened, I swear," Rosenberg whined, but as far as my sister was concerned the die had been cast. Her female allure had not been powerful enough to keep her new boyfriend from living his truth as a gay man, and for this she was wonderfully happy. "She said she was so glad that she had helped me discover my sexuality. Jesus. I passed out and the Czech dude decided to spoon me, which I've heard is not particularly easy to do in Prague. Still, I can't be responsible for what I do when I'm asleep!"

"So where did she go?" I finally asked, having not let on what Tripp and I were doing in Downieville other than fly-fishing.

"She took off with one of the twins! When I woke up early the next morning, freezing my ass off lying in the dirt by the dead fire with a Beam headache that you wouldn't believe, she was gone. But she left me this ridiculous note about helping me live my truth and how wonderful I must feel. What a crock of shit. I burned it." Obviously Rosenberg did not know where my sister and the other Czech were going, or even if they were together, though I suspected she would have preferred company to hiking around in the Sierras by herself.

It was past 3AM and I had heard enough, though I was wondering what, if anything, my sister had said about our father's condition, and the very good chance that he might die while she was gone. "Oh, that was the main reason for going. At least that's what she told me. She didn't wanna do the death watch like she did with your Mom."

"Why?" I cried. "Did she say why she didn't want to help her old man in his final days?"

"Oh yeah. She said she just couldn't stand the old man ordering her around any more. You know. She said every five minutes it was another emergency. She couldn't wait for it all to be over."

This I could imagine to be partially true. Ever since Mom had died he rode Sisi, and I pretty hard. *Well,* I thought, *damn right it'll be over soon! She couldn't stick it out for another week?* Of course she had no idea that our father had put the whole dying thing on hold until he could say whatever it was he had to say to her – to us together – before checking out. She wouldn't know until I found her, and I just couldn't imagine the old man just going on day after day. How could he?

There was one other thing I needed to know before I could say good riddance to Mr. Doo Rag. Something that was important to me then that I wouldn't even think of asking now. "So what about the other twin? What happened to him?" Rosenberg paused, poured out the last couple of drips of coffee, then got up and stretched.

"Oh..." he said at last. "He's asleep." He gestured toward his old jalopy of an RV. "I told him I would give him a ride back to the City. Turns out he's staying right around the block." Then he reached out and gave me a quick man-to-man shoulder hug. "You take care, Howard. And tell Betty Jo it's okay, I forgive her." He backed away with an almost romantic look, as if he were inviting me into the camper for a frisky three-way with his new boyfriend. I remember feeling like I wanted to bust him in the esophagus, not unlike the feeling I had when I thought of popping Mr. Road Rage's head like a juicy zit, as if both of them were responsible for my father's impending death. There I was, back in the real world and feeling murderous, twice in the same day. As I watched Rosenberg scamper back to his camper, where, as my sister would have put it, "his truth awaited," I thought that if I didn't get back to Sandy, Mr. Booper and my patio soon, I would likely end up in jail. It had only taken a day, but right then I was convinced that the real world was no place for Howard Brown.

9 A Blue-Winged Olive

Toward the end of our conversation, before I had my sudden, unwelcome homophobic urge to beat the shit out of him, Mr. Doo Rag asked how my blind son had become a celebrity fly-fisherman. Either Sisi had told him about Tripp, or he had seen an article in *Outside* magazine, or one of several stories about him on the fishing channel online. I didn't ask how Rosenberg knew about our son; I just answered, as briefly as possible. I explained that Tripp was a sort of child prodigy with the fly rod before the accident, and, with the help of a companion, he could navigate the waters with amazing efficiency. But all I wanted to do at that point was go to bed, so I didn't give him the whole story.

Immediately after the accident we all thought our nine-year-old son's fishing career had met a premature death, along with every other sport and pastime that depends on clear vision. Then one spring evening our son discovered that he had supernatural powers – or at least they seemed supernatural at the time.

Sandy and I were sitting in the family room listening to a Giants game on the radio – we avoided TV in those early days of Tripp's blindness – when we heard odd noises coming from Tripp's bedroom – clicks, taps, whistles, pops, and shrill, high-pitched barks that almost sounded like yapping, yipping coyotes. I had heard him making such noises before, but never thought anything of it.

"Now, what do you suppose *that's* all about?" Sandy wondered aloud. It was about a year and a half since the accident, and Tripp had adjusted surprisingly well to his new, more or less sightless world, far better than Sandy and I had adjusted to having one blind son instead of two healthy, happy little hell raisers.

"Sounds like he's trying to commune with the animal kingdom," I said, curious but not overly concerned. "Either that, or he thinks he's Dr. Doolittle."

Suddenly Tripp burst through his bedroom door, held his white cane triumphantly over his head and shouted, "I did it! I did it!"

Sandy ran towards him as she always did, expecting to take him by the arm and guide him through the furniture in the family room.

"Mom!" he shouted before she could grab his arm, "Stop right there." She froze just two steps short of him.

"What did you do, buddy?" I asked from my chair. Sandy shot me a wild look, clearly distressed by our son's sudden strange behavior.

"I…" he said, giving his cane a couple of quick taps, then tossing it onto the couch with amazing accuracy and raising his arms in the air like wings, "am Batman. Junior."

Then he slowly walked around the coffee table to the couch, retrieved his stick, and tapped it a few times on the hardwood floor. Then he barked – one quick, short, high-pitched yip, the kind of sound we might have made for echoes – and slowly walked around the coffee table to the chair Sandy had been sitting in, reached out for the overstuffed arms, turned around and plopped into it. We were dumbfounded, but he just sat there, a Cheshire cat grin under his wrap-around shades. *Batman Junior?* I thought.

Sandy looked at me, then back at Tripp, and said, "how did you do that, Tripp?"

"I don't know how, exactly. I only know that I when I bark like a coyote, or sing like a whale, I hear echoes. Just like that time we found that place in the mountains when I was little, where we could shout and hear our own voices echoing back. Except now the echoes turn into pictures into my mind. I can see how big things are, and where they're located. It's weird."

It was very weird, especially listening to our little 11-year-old in his faded Ninja Turtles t-shirt, cargo shorts, and mirrored Vuarnet's tell us about seeing things "in his mind," and barking like a coyote. We wondered then if our son was somehow touched by an angel or otherwise blessed. I wondered, in secret, if God had decided to even the scales by giving our one remaining son supernatural gifts in his blindness.

After learning that our son had this unusual ability, we started doing some research. The next day we located a doctor, Dan Kish, who ran a program for blind kids that specialized in the development of "perceptual mobility." After a couple of years of training, Tripp's ability to walk into a river and catch fish like he was shooting ducks in a barrel became a sensation in fly-fishing circles. When the experts saw that he could cast dries or nymphs upstream or swing them cross-current downstream, or bounce a Copper John along the bottom of a seam like an indicator fisherman without the indicator, every single one of them finally said, "Okay, this I gotta see!" Which is why Tripp's annual income as a "pro" fisherman eventually doubled what mine had been as an English teacher and coach.

The next day, after Bob Rosenberg and his Czech boyfriend steered west down Highway 49 and I finally got out of bed, Tripp and I headed for the river. Rather than fish the stretch that Tripp had been fishing all morning upstream from the confluence of the Yuba and the Downey, we decided to drive downstream to a spot that supposedly held some of the biggest brown trout in the Sierras. It was also the opposite direction from the popular pocket water upstream in Ladies' Canyon, and further away from the thunderstorms brewing in the high country near the headwaters. I could see towering black thunderheads with their white parfait tops in the rearview mirror to the east, and while post thunderstorm evening fishing can be some of the best, we were happy to be headed west where it was less likely to rain.

I parked at the bridge where Highway 49 wound up and out of the river canyon at the head of a dirt forest service road. We packed for the 20-minute hike down to where the dirt road met the river again. When we arrived it looked like the fishing could be promising indeed, since at some point in the not-too-distant past somebody made camp there, complete with a boarded up, rusted out, RV camper and several iron grated fire pits. I was figuring it was a makeshift forest service station that doubled as a camp for family gatherings, or it was a hermit's hideaway, or perhaps a mini-meth lab. God knows the Sierra foothills were crawling with meth heads and denture salesmen following them around with rent-to-own rot-proof teeth. Regardless, nobody had been at that camp for a long time from the looks of things, and I thought it might be a good spot to nap a little later.

I led Tripp down to the water's edge and described the river: pocket water upriver, mostly; small pools between big VW Bug-sized boulders surrounded by smaller stepping-stones. The pools spilled into each other between the rocks; mini-waterfalls creating bubbly froth where fish wait on the bottom for something yummy to tumble out from under the bubbles. Further down river the pocket water gave way to a broad riffle divided by a small willow island that broke the water into two long, deep runs that eventually washed into another riffle and then more pocket water.

Tripp was sitting at water's edge, his face tilted skyward, arms raised and palms open as if he was praying to the fish gods for the king of these pools and riffles to come forth and meet his human master. What he was really doing was catching the spinners – mayflies that had completed their short lifecycle from the bottom of the river to the surface to the trees and back again, spent, to the river to be gobbled up – to check their shapes and sizes, along with any other bugs that alight on his open palms, so he could tell me what to tie on.

"Let's try a blue-winged olive on three-x," Tripp said as he turned his head to where I was standing in the water looking at the rocks on the bottom. It was usually better to get Tripp situated in the river rather than on a boulder, considering the consequences of falling off a boulder, and particularly when we were lashed together around the waist.

I led my son across a fairly deep channel to a gravel bar about three feet below the surface, close to the center of the river and just below a medium sized pool when I saw a trout feeding on the far side just below a large boulder. Once I got Tripp oriented to the center of the river he blew his high-pitched echo-locator whistle and listened with his blind man's ears for the imperceptible echoes. But he didn't need his whistle this time, because I had spotted a feeding trout. "Rising at two o'clock, about 30 feet," I whispered. Tripp stripped out some line and started false casting – I didn't have to tell him when he had 30 feet, he could sense it by the flex of the rod – then after three false casts he dropped the blue-winged olive dead center in the circle of ripples and the trout took it in an instant. Tripp set the hook with a quick upwards jerk of the rod and a yank of the line in his left hand and the fish – a fat, 10-inch rainbow – shot straight out of the water trying to wriggle free, but to no avail. He plopped sideways back in with a splash, and Tripp with his rod tip high let out a hoot.

"Ha ha!" he laughed. "Feels like a three-pounder, at least!" The line squealed as the trout dove for the bottom of the pool, then up to the head, down to the tail and to either side, looking to get a big rock in between him and his captor. Tripp let him run for a bit until the manic darting around the pool began to subside, then he began to haul him in with slow pulls interspersed with reeling, until the trout was at his feet. He reached around behind him for his net and, holding his rod high with his right hand, scooped up the fish with his left. I reached down with my mini-calipers and delicately removed the tiny fly from the trout's lip, then Tripp, his rod under his arm, reached down under the water and gently caressed the fish head to tail.

"Nice 10-inch female rainbow," he remarked. "Pretty good sized for the Yuba!" I admired the sparkling multicolored freckles over the phosphorescent pink stripe of the rainbow, marveling at the mystery of nature's creation, which hardly seemed designed to fade into the underwater background with its brilliant colors. Then Tripp dropped the net and, holding the trout's head into the current with both hands under the water, slowly released his gentle grip. The fish lay still for a moment as if to acknowledge its kinship with a fellow creature, then slowly wiggled away.

Tripp caught another half dozen trout – bookies, rainbows and a couple of big browns – over the course of the next hour. I even hooked one myself, though I lost it, fly and all as I typically do. We moved downriver some, fishing the deep seams around the island and the pocket water below, with much more success in the pocket water since most of the action was on the surface. Much of my time was spent untangling my line from the bushes and tree limbs, but I was quietly ecstatic to be with my son; all my thoughts of Sisi on the run and our father on his deathbed had floated off downstream and it was just the two of us, about 15 feet apart from each other, lashed together at our waists, casting upstream to where I could see fish rising for the spinners that drifted like snowflakes from the cottonwoods. If I could turn that last hour of golden light flashing across the riffles and seams and the sight of my son with a fish on the line into an eternal loop that just kept playing over and over in my mind, undisturbed by the cares of the universe, I would.

10 I Lose My Legs

The next day when I remembered why we had made the journey to Downieville in the first place, it occurred to me that the one clue I had to my sister's whereabouts – Mr. Doo Rag and his camper – had returned with his newfound truth to San Francisco. Knowing there wouldn't be any cars with Czech plates parked in the various backcountry access parking lots, we called off the search and headed home. Sisi couldn't disappear into the Plumas National Forest forever, and someday she would have to check in with me, if only to find out if the old man was still kicking.

When we arrived back at Tripp's place, Elke was sitting on the front steps with the injured pit bull, a radar cone around his neck to prevent him from licking out his stitches. For some inexplicable reason she had renamed him "Odo," after the interior designer from the movie *Beetlejuice*. I had just sat down with her and Tripp on the steps to ask her what had prompted the odd name when a man's shout ripped through the thick evening air: "Hey Brown, you little fag! Where's my dog?" There, across the anemic fescue lawn, one arm hanging out the driver's window with a smoldering cigarette between stubby fingers sat my mini-mart marauder, Mr. Road Rage himself. I had been trying to avoid thinking about him on the drive out of the Sierras and through the central valley to the Bay Area, but it was impossible. My blind son lived three doors down from what appeared to be a violent, drunken methhead, and his comely blond girlfriend had absconded his dog.

I had the feeling that he wasn't referring to me as the "little fag," since I doubted that he recognized me from the mini-mart, he couldn't have known my name was Brown, and I am anything but "little." It would have been better if I really was the "little fag;" perhaps my reaction wouldn't have been so extreme. But he was referring to my boy, and it triggered my paternal killer instinct, my inner homicidal maniac, my blossoming rage against the real world. I was ready to rip the fucker's lungs out with my bare hands.

"I know this guy…" I began.

"Suck any hot cock lately, super stud?" MacDickFuck shouted as if he was trying to make sure the sea lions could hear. "I know your girlfriend has!"

I don't know if I tried to get up too fast, or if spending all day in the car had somehow reconfigured the vertebrae in my lower back, or if God in his

52

infinite wisdom had decided that ripping Mr. Road Rage's lungs out with my bare hands was a bad idea, but when I tried to stand up a searing pain shot down the back of my thighs and my legs folded underneath me like a collapsible card table.

"Howard!" Elke shouted, reaching for me as I toppled over. "Tripp, your dad's collapsed!" I crashed down the long stairway as if I had been shot, somersaulting head over heels until I reached the bottom.

"Ha!" yelled MacDickFuck. "Whassamatta? Can't hold your liquor?"

I tried to push myself up but my legs were completely numb, as if the circuit breaker to that part of my body had just blown and the power had gone out. Then, as I tried to roll over onto my side, another lightning bolt of pain rocketed through my left shoulder. Tears came to my eyes as I rolled over, and through the stinging, watery haze I could see MacDickFuck stumble out of the pickup, a beer in one hand and a leash in the other.

"Gimme my dog, you little bitch," he growled as he stumbled across the lawn.

"Jesus, Doug!" Elke cried. "Are you fucking blind? Tripp's dad needs help!"

"So? Call 911 if it's a big fuckin' emergency. I just want my dog."

I closed my eyes and pressed my face into the grass, thinking I could hear Tripp on the phone with the 911 dispatcher in the background while Odo whimpered on the front porch. Quickly, Elke picked up the dog and went inside – I could hear the "click" of the front door locking.

"Goddamnit!" MacDickFuck hollered, practically tripping over my supine frame as he made for the stairs.

I remember thinking I should say *Hey, haven't we met someplace before?* Maybe I did say it, but a growing roar in my ears drowned it out. Or perhaps it was the crazed neighbor pounding his fists on the front door and yelling "give me my fucking dog or I will burn this fucking shithole down and everybody in it!"

Then, as the outside world faded into unconsciousness, I imagined myself erupting into the Incredible Hulk, ready and able to flick the toy pickup over the cliff and into the waves of the Pacific a block away with my superhuman green pinky. I had to protect my son. I had to pulverize his attacker into dust. I couldn't, wouldn't, look away like I had that Fourth of July 17 years ago.

Images of flashing fireworks invaded my consciousness, explosions of Day-Glo chartreuse, cerulean, crimson and yellow burst across the backs of my eyelids, while thundering blasts of bombs and rockets ricocheted through my ears. The smoky stench of gunpowder and charred flesh filled my nostrils while the ground burned below me. Flames leapt and curled around my legs, around my arms, around my body, pulling me deeper into the boiling inferno. And through the din of what I thought must surely be my final battle, I heard my own voice like a mantra, repeating *God, save my son! God, save my son!* until I slipped beyond thought and into the darkness.

11 One-Handed Family Hygiene

In a way, my precipitous collapse on Tripp's front steps had helped defuse, or at least defer, an ugly confrontation. The paramedics, firemen and sheriff's officers were intimately familiar with Doug Dennikan's drunken circus, and were able to shoo him away like an annoying housefly when they arrived on the scene.

"You can't do this," he had shouted back to Elke on the porch, Odo in her arms, when he departed. "You can't just steal my fucking dog. He's mine, goddamnit! This ain't over!"

By the time I heard what happened after I lost consciousness, I was in the surgery recovery room at Marin General Hospital, where several of my lumbar vertebrae had been fused together with titanium pins, my rotator cuff had been sewn up, and my left ankle, which I had broken in the fall but didn't even notice through the numbness, had been set.

I couldn't help but think that, if I hadn't heeded my father's order to find my sister, none of this would have happened. But, as the surgeon explained, I was a spinal fusion surgery just waiting to happen. "Besides, you still have a few good years left in you. Hell, you might even want to coach a little basketball." *What a card,* I thought.

Still, it was obvious that the search for my sister had precipitated the whole ugly mess, and had I any sense at all I would have sworn her off for eternity right then and there. And I did swear her off. Just not for eternity.

Several weeks later, with autumn in full swing, I finally got up the gumption to go visit old Hal Brown, who had heard about the debacle and, I suspected, was none too happy with the results. I was held together by black Velcro: my left arm was lashed across my chest in a super sling with a half dozen adjustable straps to keep my left shoulder immobile; my left ankle was in a black plastic boot up to my knee with another dozen Velcro attachments along with an inflatable bladder to ensure I didn't cut off the circulation in my attempts to keep the boot snug. I also wore a bone growth stimulator around my lower back to help solidify the disk replacements in my spine.

While I had been recuperating, Sandy had been a regular Florence Nightingale, going to see old Grandpa Hal almost every day, mostly to give the caregivers a break but also because she honestly loved the old guy, especially since he didn't have my Mom to torment anymore and my sister had left him high and dry.

My father and I had been sitting in the kitchen, purposefully avoiding any further conversation about Sisi and where she might be, and watching The Golf Channel. After a half hour or so – a long time for him to be sitting up – he decided he wanted to get back in the hospital bed. But first he had to go to the bathroom. I looked around, and when I didn't see one of the girls I called for them. "Angela! Shirley! Hello?" No answer. I limped out to the driveway. No car. I remembered they said they were making a quick trip to The Woodlands Market down at the base of the hill, but I hadn't noted how long ago they had left, nor could I remember how long they would be gone. Sandy had dropped me off, but was now out shopping as well. It was just Mr. Booper and the two of us, and I wondered how I could have possibly imagined that the dying geriatric and his crippled son could manage without help.

"Come on," Howard Brown senior commanded. "I gotta go." He smiled. "And I guess I'm gonna need your help." I situated the royal blue walker in front of him with my one good arm and he took hold of the handlebars with his arthritic knob-knuckled claws, blotched with sickly yellow and purple bruises and open sores, and leaned his upper body as far over the front of the contraption as he could. Then I heaved him up by one armpit, my other arm watching from its sling. He slowly straightened until he was upright, unlocked the brake and started shuffling across the hardwood kitchen floor, then continued down the long hall to his bedroom. I couldn't help but marvel that his matchstick legs, equally covered in nebula-patterned blotches with a bloodstained gauze pad hanging from a bit of surgical tape, could still transport his considerable beer belly and formerly six-foot, 4-inch frame the twenty or so steps it took to get from the kitchen to his bedroom. I walked immediately behind with one hand under his armpit should he waver and start falling backwards.

His days of using the regular flush toilet were over: he might have been able to sit down on the real crapper but it would have taken a crane to get him back up. The geriatric toilet sat near the bedroom window looking out across the canyon through the shimmering heat to the thick forest. A portable swamp cooler had been left on so the bedroom was relatively bearable. I steered him over to his shit throne, pulled down his boxers and sat him down. A few minutes later my one good hand was navigating between his soft white flabby butt cheeks, cleaning him up the best I could while he just chuckled. "God knows I've wiped your ass more than a few times." I felt like I was cleaning a raw breast of chicken in preparation for the broiler. A very stinky chicken.

He stood there hanging onto the bars of the geriatric shit throne, still grinning, while I hobbled in my Velcro boot into the bathroom to flush his creamy turd, which looked like a perfectly youthful and healthy turd to me vs. a turd produced by a failing internal organ, down the real can. While there I took a healthy swig off the bottle of liquid Vicodin, then kicked myself for not hitting the sublingual morphine instead. It wasn't as if I needed any additional pain meds – I was well equipped so I could deal with my various injuries – but I just couldn't help it, and the liquid stuff soaked into my brain like a cushion of cool whip.

When I came out of the bathroom with the clean pot he had this look of triumph on his face like he had just repaid me for a lifetime of ignominy and embarrassment. It was almost as if in making me wipe his ass he had settled the score and we could now move forward into the final phase with a balanced budget. I, of course, didn't share his odd sense of equanimity, but I wasn't holding an express ticket to the afterlife either. Not that I cared. The soft, Cheshire grin of the synthetic opium-eater had crept across my face and the sense of complete disassociation with the task at hand was settling in.

I gave his smooth Charmin-like ass a final wipe down with a cool jumbo-sized sanitary Handi-wipe, concentrating mostly on the interior of the cheeks where some residual skid marks needed attention lest he soil his relatively clean boxers and add to the general odor of dirty diapers that already hung thick in the room.

I helped him over to the hospital bed, then lowered it down to where he could sit on the edge. Then I lifted his legs onto the mattress, cradling them lightly, worried that I would rip his translucent skin and pieces of leg would tear off the bone like the shanks of a Hawaiian pig at a luau. Then I pulled the sheet over his legs just enough to leave his driftwood feet sticking out in front of the flat screen TV.

"See if the golf is on, pal," he said, his sweet, loving "please take care of me" smile on his face. I turned to the Golf Channel, where the golf is always on, with the sound on low, and he lay his head back on his pillow and closed his eyes. I stepped over to pull the curtains across the sliding glass door to the deck and noticed that the old bird feeder was nearly empty. Still, the branches of the bay tree were full of purple finches, jumping down to the deck railing and the feeder perch to alternately grab a seed in their beak or knock the few remaining seeds out of the feeder onto the deck where the other finches dropped off the tree branch, had a seed, then flitted back up to safety. When my father could still lie in the big four-poster bed he liked to watch the birds, the little transistor radio on his shoulder and a single earplug in his ear tuned to NPR or a ball game or sports talk. But getting in and out of that bed, which was probably five feet from the floor, was too much for him now.

I thought of setting him up with his transistor, but he looked peaceful and, after hearing the girls return, I was ready to leave. Just as I was about to walk out the old man reached out and grabbed my arm with a surprisingly iron grip. "Pal?" he asked. "Why are you so good to me?" It wasn't the first time he had asked me that question.

"You're my dad. It comes with the territory."

"Oh I don't think so," he intoned rather gravely. "I've been pretty tough on you." He looked up at me with that same helpless smile.

"Are you serious?" I asked, my voice reverberating inside my skull as if it were hollow. "Geez dad, I don't think so. You've been the greatest dad a guy could ever ask for." I honestly didn't know what else to say. At the same time I felt like sticking to the script was a typical dope addict cop out. I had been presented with an opportunity to share the truth – an extremely rare and possibly once in a lifetime occurrence – but I skipped right over it. Too real, too raw, and I was ready to go home. It didn't matter anyway, I told myself, because soon enough he would be gone.

"Aww. That's nice, Buddy. You've got a great wife; you know that, don't you? Be good to her."

I promised that I would, and his head sank back into his pillow. Still, he held onto my arm like I was helium balloon about to float away. A few moments passed, and then without opening his eyes, he said, "Do you think she's alive?"

Suddenly he opened his eyes very, very wide and tried pulling his head off the pillow in a state of great anxiety, as if he had a vision of his daughter in the display case of the meat department, neatly laid out on trays: flank, breast, thigh, leg, wing...

"Dad!" I cried in serious earnest, thinking the old man wasn't going to go quietly after all, and that his ramshackle ticker, lashed together with spit and bailing wire, had finally exploded. "Of course she's alive. I know for a fact she's alive!"

"No way!" he repeated, and I was still thinking that if this wasn't a heart attack it was one about to happen. "If she were alive she would come and see me. I've been calling her every day for six weeks! I swear that ponytailed-alkie-biker son-of-a-bitch took her out into the woods and chopped her up. I swear on a stack of Bibles. She wouldn't just leave me here to die! She can't! How can I die? What did I do?"

The effort triggered his signature wall-rattling cough, shallow at first but soon working itself into what sounded and looked like an effort to expel a large, mangy, waterlogged rat. I handed him a crusty handkerchief and he hocked something into it, his face a deep crimson, tears streaming down his cheeks, a runaway glob of thick pale yellow lung butter hanging off his white whiskers and the veins on his neck threatening to explode. I propped the pillow up under his head and, finally, the fit passed. Several minutes ticked by as he caught his breath, the thumb and forefinger of his right hand pinching the bridge of his nose where his red and watery eyes met, his left hand still gripping my arm and showing no signs of letting go, perhaps for fear of coughing himself right through the ceiling and getting sucked into the ether.

"You okay?" I asked after a bit, feeling a bit pissed at God for heaping such a supersized helping of indignity on my old man, as plain old nasty as he was, from the ass-wiping to the lung butter to the snot caked into his nose-hairs.

The last rays of the sun streamed across the faded bedspread of the grand four-poster and reflected off the mirror on the giant mahogany chest where he once hid *Playboys* under stacks of wool and cashmere cardigans in the second drawer. The coughing fit had cracked open my drug cocoon, though I suspected the chemicals were at least partially responsible for the memory of the stack of *Playboys* under the cashmere, which struck me as an odd memory to have at the time. The bedroom had begun to cool off and the thought crossed my mind that I should turn off the swamp cooler. I moved slightly and felt my father's grip on my arm tighten. He dabbed at his eyes with the pale yellow, bloodstained handkerchief and ruminated:

"I may have been tough on you guys, but I wasn't so tough that she should desert me like this, was I?"

"Of course not!" I cried, grabbing the hand that squeezed my arm like a tourniquet. "Don't worry, Dad! Please, don't get all worked up. She'll be back, I swear. I'll bet she'll be here tomorrow for sure! She's just trying to get her head together after the divorce. She probably thinks you're just fine and that she's not needed here. That's probably it. You've got the girls, you've got

Sandy. She probably feels like she's the fifth wheel." It hadn't occurred to me to put it that way before, and it suddenly struck me that Sisi might in fact feel that way, as feeling threatened had always been one of her greatest points of leverage.

"Oh, I don't know, Pal," he moaned. "I don't know."

"Well, I know," I announced, and I did know, but what I knew – that Sisi might have been sitting in the driveway at the very moment but would never, not in a million years, come back to say goodbye – was far, far worse than the most egregious lie I could tell at that moment. Now I felt more confident than ever that my father and I could both lie our way around every real and perceived heartache that had ever been visited upon this family, and end up topping our monumental pile of horseshit with the juiciest maraschino cherry the world had ever seen.

"Okay," he said quietly, gazing up at me with that same patented "pity me" smile, his grip on my arm lightening. "If you say so, then that's what I'm going with." Then, for the first time in my life I felt like my old man, for no concrete reason and certainly based on no solid evidence, truly trusted me.

He laid his head back on the pillow and closed his eyes while I leaned over and kissed him on the forehead. Then he let go of my arm and weaved his dried up and knob-knuckled fingers across his chest. "Thanks, Pal," he whispered, still smiling, eyes still closed. I pulled up his cover, turned off the TV and the swamp cooler, limped down the hall with Mr.Booper at my side to say goodbye to the girls, and stepped out into the driveway where Sandy was, to my surprise, sitting in the car reading the paper.

"Had enough?" she chirped. I assumed this to be a rhetorical question, slid into the passenger seat and pointed up the driveway.

12 Wind in the Redwoods

The next night the wind came up. It started like the usual late summer winds that herald the approaching fog on the coast and promise cooler air to neighborhoods like ours out in Leave It To Beaver-land where it was not uncommon to bemoan the lack of A/C when the fog didn't do its duty. But it was late in the season for fog, and a little early for serious rain – approaching the end of the Indian Summer and hinting at Halloween – though as all the climate change pundits around here knew, it wouldn't be long before mile high spouts of boiling sulphuric acid, gaping maws of molten lava and tsunamis big enough to douche the entire state would be common occurrences thanks to our relentless destruction of the ozone layer. A powerful wind in autumn could only foretell bad juju, or at least that's what the cold pit in my stomach seemed to be saying.

To say I was in bad shape on that Autumn-pretending-to-be-Winter evening would be to state the obvious, but there was more to it than the painful souvenirs of surgery; my brain felt like it hadn't fully returned from the those few moments of semi-conscious terror at the base of Tripp's front steps. My brain. Pfft. My entire consciousness felt powerless against the flow of memories – bad memories, recollections of things that shouldn't have turned out the way they did because I wasn't paying attention. Tripp's blindness: If I was even remotely present… Or losing my Mom. Or Sandy's Mom. Did they really have to die or did I take my eye off the ball just long enough to set the process in motion?

What was worst about all the pointless recrimination was that it prevented any kind of direct experience of the present. It was a self-sustaining cycle that felt like it wouldn't end until I ended, which fired up a whole library of ugly, irresponsible thoughts that I was embarrassed to admit even existed and that were likely to do me in for that very reason. A clean slate was needed, but where I once had acres of mental acuity – for a high school English teacher, that is – stretching as far as the mind can wander, I had fireworks, artillery shells, mortar and shrapnel.

It was around 9:00 p.m. when I first noticed the ghostly howl in the tops of the tall Monterey pines and redwoods on the steep hillside in the neighbor's backyard. Redwoods have the power to transform what otherwise would simply be air moving through air into the lonely moans of hell, and even though it scared the piss out of me and stirred the ice around in my gut, I could imagine Sandy smiling on her side of the bed, for she knew the scary wind would eventually get me spooning her in desperation, holding onto her hard as I could, free of the black plastic Velcro contraptions that held my various injuries inert and wary of sudden movements or pressure that might zap me with pain. Still, I would be spooning her, even if only to melt my frozen core. But even at our advanced age and in our physically and psychologically injured states, spooning was more than a simple thawing procedure. Even after 30 years, spooning was still a surefire precursor to lovemaking. And even though this ostensibly simple, natural act now required profound effort and commitment, I would do anything to drown out the howling wind.

That night I felt a need to crawl way up inside her, all of me as far in as I could possibly go where it was dark and warm and quiet and not even the loudest of the lonely wailing redwoods could reach me, far away from dying fathers and crazy sisters and all the goddamn drugs and iceberg intestines and even Mr. Booper. Yet even with some temporary distance I could still see the vague shape of trouble on the horizon. *Give me deeper, give me darker,* I thought, *let me hide out inside my lovely warm-hearted girl, my tiny baby* (as I often refer to her still, though she has never been particularly tiny). She, and perhaps even this long marriage, was perhaps the best port this coming storm had to offer.

She was thinking something similar and with a pill and a little concentrated manual effort I was ready for her to "hop on up" as we so romantically and practically referred to it, especially since it had been years since my back could handle thrusting and parrying like the old days. We got going and it was very, very good, her breathing quickening with the gusts through the trees that were no longer lonely or wailing but just the sound of the wind in the trees. I wanted her to open up all around me like bubbles rising in a warm bath to swallow me whole...and it worked, all this together. (Except for Mr. Booper who with a whimper excused himself from the bedroom).

Within seconds of Sandy's controlled and focused climax when she held her breath momentarily and we froze together through her gentle shudder, right after that point of exhalation and release, the fucking phone rang.

Mr. Booper jumped up and rushed into the room with a single bark as if to say, "I'll get it. You guys are busy!"

"Oh for fuck's sake..." I grumbled. It was Angela, one of old Hal Brown's caregivers, calling from his house.

"Howard you must come now! Mister Hal is very afraid for you. He is very afraid of the big trees and that they will be falling on your house." I flicked on the light.

"Mister Hal, he is very scared, Howard," she continued with a little hint of hysteria in her voice. I put the phone on mute.

"Angela obviously isn't familiar with Dad's acting capabilities," I told Sandy, who responded with an unexpected "pfft", followed by:

"Howard, I really don't think your Dad knows whether he's being manipulative or not at this point. I imagine he's scared to death, literally!" She rolled out of the sack on my side, pulled her little white lacy nightie over her head and made for the closet to get dressed. I guessed we were going to the old man's house to fend off falling trees.

"The weatherman says this storm is very big and has earthquakes too!" Angela pronounced, though I suspected that the weatherman was simply making the observation that odd fall weather had accompanied earthquakes in the past, most noticeably the 1989 Loma Prieta quake thirty-five years ago. She probably overheard folks at the market talking about earthquake weather too, and had obviously taken it quite literally.

"Well, don't worry about earthquakes, Angela. Heart attacks are probably more likely," I said.

The drive over to 156 Woodland had become an obstacle course. Tree branches full of autumn foliage were flying through the air, bouncing off the windshield and crashing onto the street in apocalyptic chaos. As we dodged our way down Kent Avenue into Kentfield the lights in the houses suddenly went out, then flashed on again, then went out and stayed out all the way to the old family home.

As we pulled into the downhill driveway, our headlights flashed across the dark entry and landed on a strange-looking vehicle I had never seen before, a cross between a van and a truck, tall and boxy like an electrician's travelling shop. And I thought *well maybe one of the girls called someone with an emergency generator.* As we inched down the drive I could see that this was no electrician, or if it was he was travelling in style. The vehicle was a new Mercedes Sprinter, the $100,000 RV for two.

"Who's car...or truck...or van?" Sandy half-whispered.

"I have no idea. At first I thought it might be an electrician here to fix the lights. Would be just like the old man to figure his was the only house in the neighborhood to have the lights go out."

"Ha! One luxury electrician, I would say!" she observed, trying to smile. Neither of us had made a move to get out of the car when a tall guy with an athlete's V-shaped upper body and a small beanie atop his chiseled visage stepped out of the shadows of the carport, a cigarette glowing between his fingers.

"Are you...the brother?" he asked loudly through Sandy's driver's side window, his central European accent as thick as his chocolate brown unibrow. Sandy lowered it just enough to hear, even though it was obvious Sandy was nobody's brother.

"You mean Howard?" she answered.

I eased out of the passenger side door, crutch in my armpit, thrust my hand forward and introduced myself. For a moment the man just stood there dumbfounded by my imposing size. At around six foot two himself, he was probably not accustomed to being looked down upon. Slowly, he took my hand. Then Sandy came to my side and looked the man up and down as if he was the male version of Mary Poppins blown in with the storm.

"What kind of accent is that?" she asked, uncharacteristically abrupt.

"I am Arno, from Praja in the Ceská republika. It is most pleasure meeting you. Your sister is your big fan, yes?"

"My fan?" Sandy chuckled. "Ha! She hates my guts!"

"I think he means me, hon."

"Yes. But I am sorry she is not liking you. She can be...what is the word?"

"A judgmental conniving lying bitch?" Sandy said. I couldn't believe what had come over her.

"Yes, judgmental. That is the word," Arno said, smiling politely, pale blue eyes flashing like mancala pieces under his dark brows.

Then, in a delayed reaction, it hit me: my sister was obviously in the house. I tried to speak but my tongue felt like a wet carpet sample and I was kicking myself as best I could with my Velcro boot for not listening to my goddamn intuition and staying at home with my tiny baby and Mr. Booper in our nice warm bed. But Sisi, or Sisi and our father, wanted me to come over, using the storm as an excuse. Surprise! The last time I saw Sisi she was having a meltdown in the Cal Pacific hospital elevator, on our way to the waiting room while the old man was having his aorta sewn together. Sisi was pissed that we were going to the trouble and expense of saving his life by having his aorta repaired. "It's our money," she had said, "or at least it will be if we don't spend it all." I didn't take her sentiment seriously at the time, but I should have.

My leg was throbbing in concert with my shoulder and my feet were being attacked by thousands of microscopic archers firing flaming poison arrows. I limped over to the big flagstone front step, out of the wind, and dropped my head into the position it knew so well, lolling just above my lap in a sordid sway. Sandy joined me with a sigh.

Arno, so lava-soap clean we could smell it in the hurricane, joined us. The brown fuzz that sprouted under the beanie was too short to be disheveled by the wind, and his prominent Adam's apple leapt like Ping-Pong ball when he talked or swallowed. He was also sporting a very cool soul patch under his full lower lip, which made him look youthful and hip. I guessed he was around 45, only 10 years younger than Sisi or thereabouts.

Sandy let Mr. Booper out of the car, all waggy-tailed as he greeted Arno on the step, just as a swirling dust devil full of brown, dried needles from the redwood blew into our faces. After the mini-tornado passed I looked up at the 120 foot-tall tree, a dark spire swaying to and fro over the roof of the house and thought, as I had many times before, about what would happen if it came crashing down. It was perched at the top of the steep hillside so I didn't think it could fall on the house.

"Jesus," I said, covering my eyes from the airborne assault of unswept driveway flotsam. "Let's go inside!"

"Oh," Arno said. "Your sister told me to wait here because she has private business with your father."

I checked my watch. *Private business with the old man at this hour? By candlelight?* I thought.

Arno rolled his eyes, stubbed out his smoke, got up, said good night and climbed into the Sprinter. I studied the vehicle for a moment, wondering how my sister could have possibly afforded such a purchase.

"So, where do you think Sisi got the dough for a ride like that?" I asked Sandy. At that same instant the answer dawned on me. "Don't answer that," I quickly added, shaking my head and realizing that I had just become the involuntary half-owner of a luxury RV.

13 Blind Spots

Just as Sandy, Mr. Booper and I walked into the entry of the old family home – an entry that looked like Roman Catholic Offertory, with votive candles arranged like choir singers on the top of the huge antique chest – I heard a few fat drops of rain on the tar and gravel roof. I had always loved the hypnotic, steady thrum of rain on the roof of our family home, but when it lashed against the floor-to-ceiling plate glass windows, accompanied by the screaming trees, I could barely stand it. I clenched my teeth when, as if on cue, the living room windows shuddered and wept in the gale.

We moved down the dark hallway past the kitchen where a few candles flickered in the side bedrooms, past two giant oil pastels of my sister and I at around three and five respectively. Music was coming from somewhere, which I thought was impossible without electricity, but it was Sandy's ring tone. She pulled the phone from her purse.

"Ah! Saved by the bell! It's Tripp!" I guess she was relieved to at least temporarily avoid the inevitable cold sisterly greetings because she rushed back to the kitchen to talk to our son. Then the front door, the one we just came through, blew open with a blast and the braying storm came rushing through with Arno, who had to put his back into the door to shut it against the wind.

"Change of plan?" I asked. He rolled his eyes.

"Lisbet called me! In the van. Says I'm to bring her medicine." He held up a prescription jar. My guess was Arno, who had by now been with my sister several months, thought to bring the pills in himself, as he probably had been told that things could go sideways when my sister and Sandy were in the room together. My presence usually didn't help either.

I expected to see her when we got to the end of the hall and slowly pushed open the door to the master bedroom, but instead Angela sat on the chair next to the hospital bed, fiddling with a jar of something in the candlelight. She looked up at us, a quiet, knowing smile on her face, and I gathered there had been some emotional carnage, which I realized was why she called me in the first place. She knew if she had called and told me that my sister was berating my old man for being a capitalist pig while she plundered his bank account, I would have unplugged the phone, turned out the lights and buried my head underneath the pillow until the storm was over, one way or the other.

I peered into the darkness: a lone candle burned atop the darkened TV at the foot of the bed, the flame straight and true, and another on the night table next to my father's silvery head. His eyes were closed, but he was alive, perhaps just barely. I took his lizard-claw hand and his eyes opened suddenly like I'd interrupted him from a great dream, but he just smiled one of his classic born-to-lose smiles.

"You're being robbed, Pal," he said with a feeble waver in his voice. Sisi stepped out of the shadows in the corner, as if the whole scene had been carefully staged. The old man's sarcasm was apparently lost on her.

"Oh, is that what you think is going on here, Dad? Being fair to me is robbing Howard? Is that how you feel about it now? Just a minute ago you thought it was the right thing to do!" Sisi declared in an edgy, dry tenor.

"Hey!" I exclaimed with as much enthusiasm as I could muster. "Sisi! How ya doin' sweetie? I haven't seen you since..." I wanted to say since your last breakdown, but restrained myself. The candlelight lent a sinister glow to her gaunt features, accentuating her high cheekbones and her long, slender nose, but turning her deep-set eyes into empty black sockets under her strong brow. Had I not been so familiar with her long neck, willowy figure and sculpted visage I might have mistaken her for a ghost, or a death-eater, perhaps. Still, her appearance in the candlelight was shocking enough. I broke out in a full body sweat, so I quickly made for the drug emporium in the bathroom, adding as I went, "Well, it's been awhile, hasn't it?"

I heard Sandy's footsteps padding down the hall and was relieved when she said, "Tripp and Elke are okay! The power is out in Bolinas, Stinson, and pretty much all through West Marin." She went to G-Hal's bedside and gave him a kiss on the forehead. "No need to worry about your grandson, Mister Hal. Tripp is safe and sound." I could tell by his tired smile that Tripp and Elke were far from his thoughts.

In the bathroom, the jars, boxes, bottles, tubes, wipes, tanks, vials and so forth were all arranged on a towel folded neatly in the corner between two large pillar candles like a sort of shrine. I was inclined to drop to my knees and give thanks; instead I reached for the morphine dropper. *No!* squeaked a little voice in my head. *You don't want to pass out, then wake up to find us all picked to the bone.* Instead I opted to wash down 50 milligrams of oxy with a swig off the hydrocodone bottle. Almost immediately the warm opiate paraffin spread a protective shell across my cerebral cortex, a shield against the poisoned arrows that were most certainly to come.

Outside the wind continued to scream through the trees, rising and falling, each gust getting progressively stronger and longer than the last. Then, like somebody on the roof decided to dump a bucket of water on the bathroom skylight, the rain arrived in force. It washed in great horizontal sprays over the roof of the old sixties post and beam, crashing against the floor-to-ceiling windows as if we were a ship at sea, pitching and yawing in mountainous waves.

"This is it!" I heard my father's booming voice through the bathroom wall as if the storm had challenged him to a duel. I hurried out of the head. "The grim reaper is coming to get me!" His eyes were bugged out, glazed-over like silver Christmas ornaments, staring at his daughter as if she had donned hooded cloak and taken up the scythe herself. She was, in fact, wearing a familiar navy blue cashmere cloak, scarf or blanket around her shoulders. Sandy had given it to my mother for Christmas several years prior.

"Ha! Dad, you are really too much!" Sisi said with a sarcastic chuckle. "If you had been following your truth The Lord would be taking you unto his fold in peace and harmony, but no, you've got to make some kind of battle out of it! It wouldn't be worthwhile if it weren't a competition. Right, Dad?" She sneered and took a long, slow, cruel golf swing. Competitive sports, in her view, had been the epitome of parental psychological torture.

Arno deposited Sisi's meds on the nightstand and hastened his retreat. My sister moved around the bed in three giant ballerina steps, snatched up the bottle and shook four pills into her hand. "This," she announced, "looks like it's going to be a long night." The old man was watching her every move now, eyes still slightly buggy, propped up on a hospital pillow.

"What are you going to do with those?" he asked, wondering what kind of fresh pill had been introduced to his daughter's pharmacopeia. Sisi walked over to the bed and put her birdlike claw onto our father's shoulder.

"Well, Dad. You're the one who introduced me n' Howard to better living through chemicals. Now I need 'em just to get up in the morning." It was then that I noticed that Sisi was wearing an unusually eclectic collection of jewelry: turquoise rings, silver diamond-studded, bracelets and necklaces, elaborate hoop-style earrings – all of it from Mom's collection, all of it just to make Sandy jealous.

"Oh that's not true! You make it sound like I was giving you uppers with your corn flakes! Seems to me you just helped yourself," our father said, though I didn't think Sisi or anyone who was not standing right next to him could hear because the rain slashing across the roof was even louder than the wind.

Before Sisi could retaliate a loud crack cut through everything, followed by the sound of crashing branches free-falling down the steep, densely forested hillside across the canyon.

"Well maybe we won't have to worry about dividing up inheritance, since it looks like we'll all be buying the farm right here tonight!" the old man cried, pleased with the prospect of a synchronized, clean ending for the three of us. Maybe Sandy and the caregivers, too.

"You would like that, wouldn't you, Dad?" Sisi shouted over the din. Across the canyon the neighbors down below were shining flashlights through the rain up to the slope where the trees would have fallen, but the rain threw the light back onto their hooded slickers and in less than a minute they were back inside. Did a tree really fall in the forest? We heard something, but what was louder in my mind was the idea of unseen forces on the move, just waiting to bump into something.

"God, he's just joking, Sisi! What's wrong with you?" I asked, instantly regretting the direct question, which was bound to open a floodgate of vitriol.

"What's wrong with me? What's wrong with me? Aren't you asking the wrong person, Howard? How about what the fuck is wrong with you? How about what the fuck is wrong with him?" She screamed, pointing at the dying man. "And her!" she added, pointing and glaring at Sandy with all the squinty-eyed spite she could muster. "What about her?"

I realized then, in that instant when the director should have called for lightning to catch her expression in a flash and save it for eternity, that her irrational anger wasn't about any real or imagined mistreatment from her dying father, though there was plenty of it and plenty to be angry about. Nor was her acidic spitfire reserved for me, though there was plenty of that left on reserve for a subsequent showdown. No, that night there was only one person that she truly and honestly wanted to hurt, and not just hurt but cast out like Eve from the Garden, the one person that had stolen and ruined her once funny, blond curly headed brother, and then went and commandeered what was left of the heart of her wobbly dad...my wife of 30 years, my six-foot Sandy Brown.

I limped over to where Sandy sat at the foot of the hospital bed staring at my sister like a deer frozen in the headlights and put my arm around her. It painfully obvious to everybody that Sisi had gone too far. She had shown her proverbial hand; most if not all of her recent neuroses and suicidal, possibly murderous breakdown antics appeared to be the result of stupid in-law jealousy. Or perhaps Sandy was just the target du jour? This was entirely possible because I had seen it happen before, but never with such dramatic energy. It could have been the cacophony of the storm, the dark shadows and the candlelight flickering off the polished mahogany, and the dying man hocking yellow sputum into a rag on the rent-a-bed. Perhaps all of it in concert had triggered the actor in my sister.

Now she appeared to be waiting for us to go around the room and explain precisely what was wrong with each of our individual selves, in our own words, then changed her mind and started her mobile.

"Arno, sweetie, are you there?" she cooed. Instantly, she had transformed into an entirely different person just by the sound of her voice. We couldn't make her out over the storm, but then she turned and blurted: "Goddamnit! Looks like we're gonna have to stay here tonight, lovies. I know you're thrilled. Maybe we could make s'mores and hot choco?"

"Why do we have to stay here?" I asked.

"Well of course you're going to have to stay here," our father chimed in with a bit of his old strength and authority. I was surprised. I thought he had fallen asleep, or maybe even died, he had been so impervious to his daughter's rants. "No way you're gonna be able to get anywhere tonight. There must be trees all over the roads."

"Yep, Dad, you're right," Sisi said. "Arno looked up the road info and it is blocked about 3 houses down from here, and further down on the flats too. Hope you don't mind sleeping to the sound of chainsaws, Sandy," Sisi jibed, but Sandy didn't even look up. I looked closer and could see the hint of a smile as if she was saying *oh yeah the road workers will be out here all night in this storm sawing up the trees on the road while praying more don't fall on them.*

"Wait!" Sisi shouted. "You have a chain saw, don'tcha Dad? Howard, you and Arno could probably cut a swath wide enough for the Sprinter to skinny through." At this, Sandy could take no more.

"You know what, Sisi? You really are nuts! Even if there was a chainsaw here, which there isn't, your brother has a torn shoulder, a broken ankle, and just had spinal fusion surgery!" She got up from the corner of the hospital bed and put her hands on her hips. Then, like pulling a gun, she pointed at my sister. "And you think he's gonna go out there with what's his name in a fucking hurricane and clear the road so you can take off in your hundred grand luxury SUV, purchased by this man laying right here…"

Sisi started to object, but Sandy shouted her down, jabbing her index finger at her, "…no, don't lie, Sisi. You thought you could get us to believe Arno bought it, but he just told us on the way in that it was a gift from dear old Dad!" Arno, of course, did not say this, but Sandy had a feel for who was holding and who wasn't and Arno wasn't. Then Sandy walked over to the old man and picked up his limp claw, "Did you know that, G-Hal?" she asked in a quieter tone. "Did you know that you just bought the most expensive camper on the market for your loving daughter?"

Sandy paused and caught her tirade-blown breath, when suddenly dad threw both his matchstick arms up in the air over his head, nearly knocking over a candelabrum on one of his adjustable side-tables. "Of course I knew it!" he shouted in a voice just as loud and strong as it was when called me a loser for missing a short putt. "I had to! How do you think I got her to come over here and say goodbye?"

The wind momentarily subsided as the rain fell in a steady, hypnotic wash, quiet enough to hear the old man start a low hum. The hum built into a blast of geriatric laughter – laughter at the thought of having to bribe his daughter with a $100,000 camper to get her to bid adieu to her dying father. I couldn't help but to laugh along with him until, of course, his laugh turned into a vicious, hacking cough that sounded like he was trying to expel a buried bullfrog. His face turned crimson and the veins in his forehead were visible even in the candlelight, and this went on and on while Sandy rubbed his shoulders and Angela prepared a morphine dropper, until at last he hocked what might have been several small mammals into his phlegm rag. "Ooooh," he groaned. "Listen, I'm bushed," he pleaded, holding Angela's hand and giving her his best "please take care of me" look. Then he smiled, addressing the rest of us in the room like we were the ladies and gentlemen of the jury. "It's been such a pleasure having you here and I'm really so glad that you've all decided to stay the night. I'm making French toast and mimosas in the morning and we can all watch the golf together. Won't that be grand?"

I hadn't heard my old man say so much at once in a week, and even though the local authorities predicted that the electricity might be out for some time, eliminating the possibility of watching the golf or anything else on TV, I had to commend his spunk. He had just seen some profoundly dysfunctional but not unusual behavior, and if he said it was a pleasure I believed him. His children were with him and he was pleased. Fuck the storm, fuck dying, fuck a hundred grand for his selfish greedy daughter's new wheels. Fuck his son's surgeries. It appeared he honestly didn't give a shit anymore, for as long as his kids were around, regardless of how messed up they might be, he was going to be happy in spite of it all.

14 From The Bottom, Up

Few people believe what happened next was physically possible. Now that a few years have passed since that fateful night, I have a hard time believing it myself. Had I known how the forthcoming events of that evening – whether or not they were physically possible, or, as the insurance company put it, "acts of God," – would put in motion the host of calamities to come, I would have opened all the doors and windows to the house and let the wind blow the Brown family into deep space. But even if I'd had a premonition that everything was about to go from bad to much, much worse, I would've been too stoned to notice it.

Our little master bedroom summit meeting was over. Nothing had been resolved, and nothing had changed except the configuration of the forest across the canyon, and the unwelcome fact that we were all trapped in the family home high up on the slopes of the mountain known as The Sleeping Lady, and she was having nightmares. I had also learned that somehow Hal Brown had agreed to buy his daughter a car, which I imagined he expected to be a practical Japanese sedan: a Honda, or perhaps an Infiniti or Lexus. If the knowledge that he had just bought a two-person Mercedes camper that could run well into the six figures was a surprise, it didn't appear to register as such.

It registered with me, though, even in my opiated condition. Despite the ugly exchange in the master bedroom, I wanted to see what the tall blue box on wheels was all about, especially since half of it would be mine once the old man finally checked out. Sisi was shocked when I asked her if I could have a look at the Sprinter: her eyes bugged out, her nostrils flared and the blood ran out of her already pale face. But then, as had happened so many times in her past, her sudden brain cramp did a complete 180; her color returned, she smiled, and her hazel eyes sparkled like she had just tasted a transcendental French chocolate truffle.

"Of course!" she squeaked after several strained moments. "Didn't I tell you? The van is for both of us!" She grabbed my injured shoulder and gave it a squeeze, but I was so doped up and bewildered I hardly noticed the shooting pain. Here was my sister acting as if it was perfectly normal for our dad to try and bridge the gap between us by sending us out to tour the world together in a box that wasn't even large enough to accommodate my burgeoning paunch.

.

While Sandy and Angela ministered to the old man, Sisi took me by the arm and steered me, hobbling in my Velcro boot, down the dark hallway. The rain and wind assaulting the house outside aroused my distracted consciousness and it occurred to me that, actually, the last place I wanted to be was sitting in a camper van – even a six-figure camper van – on the driveway underneath that giant redwood. My tour could certainly wait until morning. But Sisi was now dragging me along like a nun dragging a recalcitrant child to the principal's office, her energy growing more manic by the moment.

In the entryway I noticed that about half the candles in the votary had gone out, and wax was dripping across the top of the antique cabinet. "Oh shit!" I cried, trying to postpone our inexorable march into the storm. "Sisi, look!" I was yanking her back and pointing to the wax dripping down the front drawer. She paused as a bemused expression crept across her wild-eyed visage.

"Ah…I've never liked that piece," she said, looking it up and down. "You can have it." It was the first time I had thought about what was going to happen to the furniture, and all the other junk, when the old man checked out. I swooned but Sisi grabbed me. "Come on," she commanded as she slammed the heavy double-sized front door.

Outside, cold muddy rainwater had pooled over the clogged driveway drain about eight inches up the tires of the Sprinter, but it didn't faze Sisi. She pushed me through the giant puddle and barked "Arno!" as she pounded on the Sprinter door. It was at that moment that I felt something move under my submerged bootless foot, something pushing up on the asphalt, then receding, followed by several large bubbles popping on the surface. *I'm imagining things*, I thought. *Gophers, trying to escape their flooded tunnels through the asphalt.*

Arno, clad in nothing more than a g-string, opened the door. "Arno, honey, we're going to sleep in the house tonight. It's too dangerous out here in the van," Sisi said as she took his arm and yanked him down the step.

"Okay, dear," he mumbled, as if just awakened from a peaceful slumber. I thought the Sprinter must be pretty soundproof to allow somebody to sleep through the shrieking storm. When Arno saw the huge puddle he hesitated, obviously confounded, then shook his head stepped in. A second later he gasped and looked down at his submerged feet, bubbles popping midway up his calf. I guessed that the strange imaginary gopher had given him a little nudge, but Arno wasn't interested in sticking around to find out what it was.

He jumped out of the puddle and scrambled to the front step, his near naked body glistening with rain.

Sisi was just as eager to get into the van and yanked me up the step. I scrunched myself up and tried to squeeze through the little door, scraping my noggin as I passed through. "Goddamnit!" I howled, grabbing my pate. Inside, I couldn't even stand up straight. And this box was something we were supposed to share.

"Jesus," I said in amazement. Sisi must have been able to see how constricted I was in the little space, but she didn't say anything. "I could really use a glass of red right now, just one," I said, thinking she might pity my bent condition.

"Howard, you know I don't have any red! I don't drink and neither does Arno. We met at a meeting, didn't I tell you?" She was sitting on a small bench in the mini kitchen and unless I wanted to sit in the cab I would have to squeeze in next to her, leaving one butt cheek hanging such that I had to grab the other side of the table to keep from sliding off the bench. I was nonplussed to hear the lie about meeting at an AA event, though I knew she had been to a few. Still, I decided to let this little conflict in her story slide because I knew if I started cross-examining her at that moment she would either shut tighter than a cold clam or go ballistic.

She reached up and pulled a small towel out of a wicker basket in one of the cabinets across from another bench, which folded out into a double bed. The taupe leather swivel captain's chairs in the cab were turned back toward the living/dining/sleeping area, which was too luxurious to even comprehend. But the most amazing thing about this 5-star hotel on wheels was the unsettling silence. I hadn't heard a drop of rain or a gust of wind since I walked in.

"Sandy's gotta see this," I blurted, immediately regretting it. Sisi got a little pink in the neck but continued to towel dry her hair.

"It's not for Sandy, Howard." She pulled the towel away and her high cheeks were flushed. The vigorous toweling had smudged her mascara and her processed black locks were now pushed every which way, reminding me of the Disney version of T.H. White's "Mad Madam Mim." All Sisi was missing was about 200 pounds and eyes that rolled around like marbles in their sockets.

I sensed that a heart-to-heart talk was about to erupt, even though I prayed that there was still hope for a simple, quick tour of the Sprinter interior and a hasty exit. I wanted to see the various nooks and folding tuck-away crannies that I'd heard were all through it.

"So did Dad tell you what's happening with Tripp's tuition to the Watson Wilderness School?" She rested a bony hand my knee. I shook my head, but I knew what was coming. The Watson Wilderness School is a private institution for the blind in Duvall, Washington, and didn't even enter our thoughts when deciding where to send Tripp after he had completed grammar school-level education because one semester cost about half my annual salary. But my parents insisted, especially my Mom who felt that nature was the world's greatest healer. Not only had my parents insisted – they also agreed to pay for the full four-year program, plus room and board.

"Dad's decided that in order to be fair, half of the total cost of the tuition has to be reimbursed to me out of your half of the estate." She took her hand off of my knee and rubbed it in the damp towel, smiling. "I've got the contract right here." She patted the little canvas haversack hanging from her shoulder. "You need to sign in the presence of a notary and…"

"STOP!" I yelled, surprised at the volume I could muster in my narcotic numbness. "Let me see this supposed contract. This agreement that I won't agree to."

Sisi stood up and moved over to the little table in the back, perched on its edge. "Oh you don't have any choice, Howard. Dad signed it in front of the neighbor down below. Bill something. He's a notary."

"Let me see it!"

"I don't know why you have to see it now when you're obviously so upset. You're in a reactive mode right now, Howard. And we're all very, very tired. I shouldn't have brought it up. I just thought that since we've got this wonderful RV to share that you would understand." Something had shifted inside her mercurial brain and her psychotherapist persona was starting to take over.

"Do you want a glass of wine? It might help you calm down." She opened a storage bin under a bench seat that had a cat-print cushion, something that I never would have selected for my half of the van, and extracted a bottle of Merlot. I have a vivid visual memory of that moment, along with the palpable sensation that I was in an Altman film and my sister was one of Lily Tomlin's characters – completely insane. Just minutes ago she was a recovering alcoholic.

"NO!" I yelled again. "I want to see this contract! This addendum! This whatever!"

I reached out to where she was standing and tried to snatch the canvas haversack off her shoulder, but she had put the bottle down and was holding on with both hands, pulling away from me with all her strength, which was mightier than her emaciated body suggested. I thought *this is bullshit there's no contract*. And then the obvious thing happened – that thing that anybody watching would have been eagerly anticipating: the haversack's strap snapped with an audible "pop" and, since I was already sitting, my head and shoulders whiplashed backward into one of the industrial strength tinted side windows with a loud thump. Through the little cartoon birds that tweet, tweet, tweeted around my head I saw my sister fall as if in slow motion, the haversack flying from her hands as her body hurtled backward, her damp silver and black Morticia locks a mass of spaghetti as the side of her head cracked into the corner of the little bolted-down brushed chrome table. She collapsed to the floor like a marionette cut loose of its strings.

For what seemed like a very long moment I was frozen; glued to the blackout window with one end of the broken strap in my hand, letting the sudden quiet fill the space. Then, without warning, the sound of the roaring rain and wind burst through the tense silence, like someone had opened a window. It was all I could hear; the god-awful gale ripping through the 120-foot-high redwood tree above us. I wondered if I had imagined the soundproofed silence.

Sisi's face on the floor was oddly riveting, damp locks of hair loose across her ivory forehead, the smudged mascara under her eyes and her mouth open just slightly, her arms arranged in an almost purposeful gesture of peaceful sleep, palms open, welcoming. It wasn't until I saw the first rivulets of blood trickle out from underneath the crown of her skull that I realized what had just happened and the urgent need to act, but I remained transfixed by my sister's face.

Could this be the same woman that had just attempted to bilk her own brother out of tens of thousands of dollars based on some twisted sense of equanimity I thought? This pretty little dark-headed waif with such elegant and royal features; the high Audrey Hepburn cheekbones and dimpled chin, the full painted lips and broad smile, the dark, sometimes brooding and sometimes flashing umber eyes under such an uncommonly strong brow. Even her bushy eyebrows, purposefully unmaintained, it seemed, hinted at a royal lineage – an elegant Southern Belle cryogenically preserved by the ghosts of *Gone With The Wind*.

The driveway burped again: a roiling gas bubble just under the asphalt surface. Perhaps Angela was right and earthquakes really were in the forecast.

.

But this was no earthquake. I would've dialed 911 but it hadn't been long since the report of downed trees on our road and it was unlikely they'd been removed, though emergency crews might have been able to land a copter on the almost flat roof of my parent's house. Sisi had not moved, so I started looking for a first-aid kit. Then it occurred to me that I should go get Arno, who would have known where everything was in the luxury contraption.

I had just opened the back door when the van lurched from side to side, and this time I could see the rippling pavement just beyond the massive puddle that encircled us. It looked like giant anacondas slithering just underneath the surface of the asphalt. When I saw one start to crack the pavement my brain jerked into one of its rare, focused moments: I had to get my sister out of our chared luxury love mobile immediately or we were both going to be fucked.

I closed the RV door against the ripping storm, went to the little sink, filled a plastic cup with water and splashed it across my sister's peaceful expression, but to no avail. I yelled, barked and shouted her name, stomped my feet – also to no avail. So I was left with the prospect of schlepping her through the pond, or taking the chance to run into the house and enlisting the help of Arno. And it was impossible to know how much time we had before the anacondas did whatever it was they had in mind.

Suddenly it dawned on me that trees don't fall from the top down, they fall from the bottom up, and that the anacondas under the driveway were the famously shallow roots of the giant redwood beginning to tear loose from the deeper, longer, skinnier roots below. It was propitious timing for the Sprinter to take another disturbing lurch, this time perhaps indicating which way the tree would fall, which if we were lucky would be down the steep hill east of the house and into the neighbor's pool.

The second I grabbed my sister under the armpits her eyes fluttered open. "Howard?" she whispered, her voice squeaky, broken.

"Yes honey, it's me."

"What happened? My head hurts."

"You fell."

"Ooooh," she swooned backward, seeing the pool of blood on the floor, "I don't feel so good." The driveway bulged up, further this time, and then crashed back down.

"What was that?" my sister cried, bug-eyed and now quite awake.

"Come on, hurry," I said, hooking my good arm around her so she couldn't fall. I dragged her down the steep steps into deepening puddle, now bubbling like a boiling cauldron. Just as we cleared the van we heard a deafening slurping, cracking growl as the surrounding driveway erupted like emerging alien beast, water pouring into the opening fissures, and sending Sisi and me headlong into the mud, roots, sticks and slime. Sisi screamed and I shouted, partially from the pain shooting through my ankle and my shoulder simultaneously, and then there was Arno in his g-string at the door screaming and shouting too, bounding into the muddy puddle and dragging us out just as the immense, monstrous root system ripped the asphalt into chunks and the gnarled arteries, veins and capillaries of the alien redwood tree emerged from the earth, dislodging boulders the size of garbage cans and chunks of asphalt eight to ten feet in diameter, pushing them further up. The luxury RV, now on its rear wheels, looked to be praying to the god of Mercedes from where I lay on the front step. I strained to see up into the darkness where the top of the tree was now falling over, heading towards the neighbor's house. Amidst the terrible roar of the driveway being ripped asunder and the pride of German engineering rolling onto its back like a doomed Junebug I could hear the shouts of the neighbors below. Then the tree ripped through the woods down the slope, slower than I thought was possible, while the van crunched and galumphed end over end down the hillside until after what seemed like a very long time it landed with a massive splash amidst the branches of the treetop in the neighbor's pool. Within minutes we saw a flashlight and a shout went up, then another flashlight, but we were too far up the slope for the beams to reach where we sat on the front step aside the giant hole in the driveway.

It wasn't long before the lingering sounds of the freakish disaster had all but died away. The neighbors were probably hitting the vodka bottle and going back to bed, each of them probably hoping to awaken in a few hours to talk about the bizarre dream they had the night before. In a few moments I noticed the sound of Sisi's muffled sobs had departed as well, and I was left standing on the doorstep, my arm draped over Sandy's shoulders and hers around my waist, listening in the dark to the hole the giant redwood had left in the sound of the wind.

15 Imaginary Imposters

Later that night I laid in bed listening to Sandy's gentle snore, trying to convince myself that what had just happened was physically possible and not some supernatural cosmic interference. I grew up with Sequoia Sempervirens, the Coast Redwood. I had hiked trails from the Oregon border to Santa Cruz where the giant root balls of the downed trees could be up to 20 feet in diameter. But I had never seen a root ball wide or thick enough to toss a one-ton vehicle down a hillside.

Like the unlikely coincidence of Mr. Road Rage being one and the same as Mr. MacDickFuck, the coyote and the pit bull, the disappearance of my legs at the top of Tripp's front steps, this event seemed to fit right in with the recent string of bizarre happenings. Ever since my father's remarkable resurrection, life had started to take the shape of a fever dream: portentous meetings, uncanny coincidences, random scatology and inexplicable natural events. I suppose if Mr. Booper had jumped up on the bed at that moment and started singing to me instead of the other way around it wouldn't have surprised me in the least.

When I finally fully awakened it was 11AM and the forest was filled with the whines of chainsaws. I'd dozed off in my Velcro and straps, sling across my back and shoulder immobilized, the wet wonder boot fully secured around my throbbing ankle. Out the window the cloud cover was still dark and heavy, still dropping steady curtains of cold rain. I'd never seen so many trees down or so many mudslides, gaping like open wounds between the million-dollar homes dotting the hillsides.

Not long after my eyes fluttered open there was a loud banging on the front door. Sisi got there just a minute before I did, dressed in a skimpy nightie that did little to cover her good-sized synthetic breasts, along with a bloodstained ace bandage wrapped around her head and her hair, discolored with blood, sprouting up like julienned beets out of a sushi hand-roll. I imagined she had a gargantuan headache but she also seemed eager to talk to our neighbors. I didn't know if she had dosed up on Vicodin when she woke up or if the pain was waiting in the wings, ready to pounce at any moment.

"Why hello nayuhberrs," she twittered like she had just stepped out of a Flannery O' Connor story. "How y'all doin'? Hold on and I'll get the help to take your coats." I was so zonked that this opening salvo of insanity flew right over my head. The neighbors, in matching yellow raincoats, pulled their hoods back. The male neighbor then tried to take Sisi's outstretched hand for a little shake, but she took it away. Perhaps she was expecting a kiss on the hand or a couple on the cheeks, I couldn't tell. But if she was peeved she didn't let it show.

"You can call me Sissy Mae. I'm up visitin' from down home in Laurel Hill, Louisiana," my sister said, a look on her face like I had never seen before. It was as if her head was vacant, like the person that usually lived in there wasn't home and the caretaker didn't quite have the lay of the land yet.

I was immediately reminded of an article I had recently read in the local paper. It was the cover story that caught my eye; a photo of a very pretty, blue-eyed faux strawberry blonde with high cheekbones and perfect white teeth framed in a lovely smile. The headline announced something to the effect that this handsome woman was stricken with frontal/temporal dementia, a version of Alzheimer's that attacked the front of the brain and had a different impact than the memory loss usually associated with Alzheimer's. In the moment that my sister suddenly became Sissy Mae from Laurel Hill, a large tract of land that had been in our father's side of the family since the days of the Declaration of Independence, the image of this sick young woman suddenly jumped into my consciousness like subliminal advertising.

I remembered the history of dementia on my mother's side of the family: Mom, Grandmother, Aunts and Cousins aplenty, all stricken. Shortly after Mom died I warned my sister of the very likely possibility that the dementia gene was floating around in her, but it only pissed her off. Sisi was far too sharp to be outsmarted by dementia and scoffed at my suggestions for testing. I hoped then, as I continued to for far too long after, that her Beverly Hillbillies routine was just an act.

The neighbors exchanged puzzled looks, and I must have looked equally puzzled. We all stared at my sister like she was having a high school flashback and was once again in the cast of *Oklahoma!* on the stage of the little theater.

"You mean you didn't grow up here, in this house?" Mrs. Neighbor asked.

"Oh no, honey. You're thinking of my cousin Sisi. It's always rankled me that they call her that, since I'm the real Sissy. Or Sissy Mae, but what difference does it make, you know?"

I touched Sisi's arm and whispered in her ear. "Hey I think the water's boiling, Cousin. Do you want to go see about that coffee?" My sister, now Sissy Mae, retreated to the kitchen. "I better get her to a doctor," I told the neighbors. "She took a nasty rap on the noggin' last night and it seems to have disoriented her just a little bit."

"Seems the mini-van is a little mixed up as well," chuckled Mr. Neighbor. I laughed but not nearly as much as he thought his little comment warranted, though I appreciated that he wasn't crazy pissed either.

"Yes, yes, I'll get that taken care of." Thankfully Mr. and Mrs. Neighbor didn't ask me *how* I planned on taking care of it, because I didn't have a clue.

When I got back to the kitchen Sisi was drinking coffee from a huge bowl-shaped mug with both hands, her elbows on the kitchen table. She wore a thick pink terrycloth bathrobe that had belonged to Mom, and if it wasn't for her unique Eraserhead hair-do I might have thought Mom had been resurrected. Sisi was an inch or two taller and maybe 20 pounds heavier but gaining on Mom's target weight of 95 alarmingly fast.

Arno was still asleep, and Sisi didn't want to wake him, so, despite my surgeries I was elected to take Sissy Mae to the emergency room. Sandy didn't seem at all surprised that my sister was having identity issues, especially with a Southern persona. But she was also certain that Sisi's behavior was scripted, all part of a grand act that played into whatever plans she had to milk our father's estate as dry as a bone.

"Don't sign anything, don't agree to anything. Best-case scenario: don't say anything," Sandy warned half-jokingly. I suspected the various mistakes I had made justified my wife's circumspection, but I would've felt more confident if she had displayed just a little trust in my ability to manage my younger sister. She had little reason to, but she could've faked it.

The rain was falling straight down, a beaded curtain of grey drowning the sorrows of the injured forest and the homes of its inhabitants, and I wondered if there would be flooding. Since the rainy season had yet to arrive, the ground was a thirsty sponge soaking up every drop, so I concluded that flooding would be unlikely. Later in the season when the ground was saturated a storm like this would have been ten times worse, trees popping out of the mud and flying through the air. But like most freaks this thing would exit just as surreptitiously as it arrived and aside from the damage and the temporary observations about climate change, all would go back to a slightly modified, slightly denuded state of normalcy.

The sight of my sister in one of her standard circus outfits calmed me tremendously. She had changed into her usual potpourri: fluorescent pink Nike's with yellow laces, black leggings under a denim skirt, an "I Love NY" red text over black t-shirt, a Day-Glo green Patagonia fleece vest and the ace bandage roll o' fries hair arrangement. She was atrocious, but better than Sissy-Mae in the pink terrycloth bathrobe.

A little later we hit the road, which had been cleared of debris for the most part. The rain was still steady but getting lighter by the hour and the wind had left town altogether. My prediction was that we would now have about two weeks of a full-fledged Indian Summer, with warm, slightly hazy days and chilly nights, until the real seasonal rains returned for Halloween, just in time for the little trick or treaters.

There was no way I could let my sister drive. Obviously. But I wasn't exactly in prime driving condition either. Still, I took the sling off and took hold of the steering wheel. The boot on my left foot didn't get in the way much, and fortunately there was little traffic, so we managed. Sisi brought her bowl of coffee along, freshly recharged, which she held with both hands as if receiving the to-go sacrament of Christ's blood. Steam fogged her glasses but it didn't appear to bother her, and we drove in silence until we passed our old school.

"You went to grammar school there, didn't you?" she asked with some antipathy. I got the distinct sense that this was a continuation of her amnesia act.

"Of course I did, Sisi! So did you!" I shouted, making her jump.

"Jesus, Howard, I know. I was just asking. It was a long time ago," she whimpered.

"Oh. I thought you were asking…" I started.

"I know what I said. Just forget it, Howard," she said, warming up her waterworks. I pulled up to the stoplight in front of the school and she looked across the open area where the kids gathered into little groups after school to walk home or wait for their rides. A couple of small trees had been uprooted in their planters and now lay on their sides in the rain.

"I don't know what's wrong with me," she said, still looking across the sad trees to the playground beyond. I didn't know if I should agree that something seemed wrong, which might send her into a complete breakdown, or simply reassure her that nothing was wrong. I took the middle ground.

"You took a pretty hard whack to the head last night. It's not unusual for your brain to be a little shaken up," I observed. It was a fact that really couldn't be argued. She rubbed the area around the gash where her hair was still matted with dried blood.

"Ow!" she cried. "Shit, that really hurts. Jesus," she added, tears rolling down her cheeks. She looked at me and put her hand on my knee. "You think that…I don't know…these things. All these strange things that have been happening, you know…with Dad. I mean, with Dad and me, do you think that…" she trailed off, sniffling.

"All I know is that you need help, Sis."

"No, it's more than that, Howard," she said, her voice lowering, smoothing out. "I've got some…issues. Family issues. Stuff I can't talk about with anybody. It's driving me crazy." *Family issues?* I thought. *No kidding!* But I didn't want to let her get going on all the things she might have thought were wrong with her and what had transpired with her family after the divorce. Not then. Our dying father was the one with something wrong, and he was stealing Sisi's thunder.

We crossed the short two-lane bridge over the Corte Madera Creek and Marin General Hospital, with its attached urgent care clinic, came into view. Sisi cried out: "Oh no. Do we have to go there? Howard? I can't!"

"What? We've been talking about coming down here all morning!" I complained.

"We have not!" Sisi insisted. "I don't care," she added. "I'm not going. Take me home!" she screamed, pounding her fist on the dashboard. I sighed and pulled over to the curb in front of the hospital.

"See what I mean, Sisi. This is why I'm worried about you. You're acting like an eight year old."

"Well you might too if your dad was dying," she said. I reached over and took her by the chin, turned her face towards mine and looked into her bloodshot eyes.

"Sisi, I'm your brother and I love you. Now, you've got to try and pull yourself together. Dad is going to die, very soon. It's a wonder he's still alive. His heart is filled with fluid and pretty soon it's going to stop, and I need you to help me because there's going to be a lot to do."

I had been planning on trying to appeal to whatever sense of kinship she might have still had with me, which until our respective marriages was pretty strong. Had Sisi and Sandy hit it off, we might still have a strong, albeit different, bond. But Sisi didn't have many female friendships, and those that she had tended not to last. Still, appealing to our shared childhoods seemed as good a place as any to start. "We need to work together on this, Sisi, like a brother and sister. As good a team as there ever was, right?" I chucked her shoulder and her lips finally formed a meek smile. The rain ran down the windshield in fast rivulets, and she put her finger up against one of them and traced its path.

"Howard, I love you too. Don't you know everything I do is out of love for you? Dad is Dad. He obviously loves you a lot more than he ever loved me, and I just can't bring myself to forgive him. The things he's done, Howard. You can't imagine." She turned her face away and looked across the crowded hospital parking lot at the modernized edifice. "Maybe someday I'll be able to talk about them. I can't even talk to my therapist about some of the shit he pulled on Mom. He's an evil man, Howard. And he's suckered you."

The transition from weepy grammar schoolgirl to angry middle-aged woman was as clean as punching a button on the remote between stations – there was no semblance between little Sisi #1 and big Sisi #2, not to mention Sissy Mae from Laurel Hill.

"It all comes from love, Howard. I'll tear up the contract for Tripp's school. That was Dad's idea. You know how he and Mom wanted to make everything equal between us, and when Kenny refused the money Dad insisted that I take it in secret, in some other fashion. So, the contract. But it's gone now, right? Down in the pool."

I looked across the little patch of wetlands that had been saved from landfill to the subdivision where my parents first settled: Kentfield Gardens. I had fond memories of the little Leave-it-To-Beaver neighborhood. It was really a moveable play date for the kids, who simply walked out their front doors in the morning, hooked up with the homies for some adventures, came home for lunch and then went out for afternoon hijinks. My baby sister, with her dark pixie and oddly sallow complexion, was a popular plaything for our little posse. We liked to see how high we could push her on the swing; how fast we could bowl her down the slip n' slide; how long we could haul her around in her little red wagon towed behind our Stingrays before she fell out. I wondered how many times we dropped her on her head.

"But I'm gonna need that money, mister," I heard my sister say, yanking me out of my reverie. I thought for some reason she was talking to somebody on the phone and that I had somehow missed the prologue, but now I realized she had done a remarkable, instantaneous, schizophrenic about-face on "the contract."

"What?"

"I'm gonna need that money. The ninety thou. I'm divorced, you know. My job doesn't pay shit and Kenny's alimony payments are a pittance compared to what I'm used to. I don't know how I'll afford the next roll of toilet paper." It still sounded like she was talking to someone else.

"So, is this what 'coming from love' is all about? You love me and my family so much you decide to retroactively collect on a gift from grandfather to grandson? Help me understand what piece of that is yours?" I was starting to get really angry now, and was thinking I better get her to the clinic before I gave her another reason to have her head examined.

But she'd burst out in tears. Major bawling, as if my ribald honesty was so unabashedly mean that she had no choice but to break down. I raced up to the clinic entrance and tried to haul her out of her seat and through the automatic doors but I was too crippled to get a grip. The pain broke through the opiate wall and left me squeezing her arm as hard as my arthritic fingers allowed when an orderly showed up with a wheelchair, plunked her into it, and wheeled her up to the admissions desk. She ripped the makeshift bandage off her head with spastic flailing that looked more like a seizure than a crying jag, exposing the wound, which she had managed to scratch open so that her blood was creating purple dreadlocks. When the triage nurse saw her condition she took her back immediately, allowing me in to pretend to be the compassionate caregiver, designated to fill out the forms. We had managed to butt in front of a dozen other storm-injured folks that had probably been waiting patiently for hours, but it didn't matter and I didn't care. I was through with her bullshit. Finished. I thought I would call my father and propose that we put her up for adoption.

They wheeled her to a curtained-off bed, the triage nurse asked me a few questions and then plugged her into an Ativan drip. Within 15 minutes she was staring at the lights, snot still dribbling and enhanced by a stream of drool at the corner of her open mouth. I hoped I could remember her that way because it was the only way I would be able to walk out of her life for good.

The nurse said she would call me and took my number. She said they would repair the gash and run a few tests – three or four hours – to determine if she needed to stay overnight for further observations.

"That's fine," I told the triage nurse. "Keep her as long as you want. At least we'll know that we're safe, for awhile."

The nurse, who under normal circumstances would activate my rather lame but cute old guy charm, gave me an odd look and a quizzical smile. I nodded and shrugged with open palms.

"Thanks," was all I could say.

16 A Tee Time in Heaven

By the time I got back to 156 Woodland my sister had escaped the hospital. They told me that she yanked the Ativan drip out of her hand, walked right out the ambulance bay and hit the road without a single stitch in her wounded head. If the hospital personnel put up a chase it was either pathetically half-hearted or she out-foxed them. She certainly knew the territory around the hospital. When we were kids we called it Tractor Hill because of all the apartments being built in the area. She could have hooved it cross-country all the way to Sir Francis Drake and hopped on a bus, for all I knew. She'd abandoned Arno as well, without a goodbye kiss or even a goodbye phone call. As for her dying father, her disappearance was practically expected.

When I heard that she had escaped, I went weak in the knees, short of breath, and broke out in a full body sweat. "Fuck!" I shouted, slamming down the ancient Princess phone in Sisi's old bedroom so hard it cracked into three pieces. Then I went into the bathroom, drew a glass of water, downed what remained of my daily dose of pain meds, went back to the bedroom and sulked.

"Howard!" Sandy shouted from the kitchen. She found me head in hands sitting on the edge of Sisi's former bed.

"Man, I've fucked it up this time. I never should have left her there. I should have stayed until they were finished with her. Now she's gone. I'd be really surprised if she comes back after a spazz attack like that. She must think I hate her guts." Sandy took my hand. "Dad's gonna kill me," I added. Then I told Sandy what had transpired in the car; how I lost my temper and Sisi had one of her famous breakdowns, how I stormed out of the clinic hoping they would send her straight to the lockup. Her disappearance had triggered the little recorded loop in my brain: "It's all your fault, it's all your fault, it's all your fault," even if it wasn't.

"Howard, you sound like a guilty teenager. Your sister is a grown woman. She's old enough to make her own decisions," said Sandy, her arm across my slumped shoulders, hand kneading the knots in my neck under the strap of my sling. The dope was coming on so strong she probably could have smacked me with a hammer and I wouldn't have noticed.

"No, honey. She's not. That's just the thing. Something is happening. She's losin' it." I briefly thought about crashing through the plate glass window and running screaming into the forest.

"Well, you know as far as I'm concerned it's for the better. I know you don't want to hear that, but you need to face up to it, hon. She's poison, she hates me, she hates Tripp and she hates her father most of all."

"What about me? Do you think she hates me too?" Despite how Sandy felt about her, I really didn't want my sister to hate me.

Sandy paused, wrapped her arms around me and gently pushed me back on my sister's former bed. Then she he climbed onto my trampoline tummy and pinned me to the mattress. She bent forward and kissed me, just a grazing of lips, really. Then she kissed me again until I started kissing her back.

"Does it really matter now?" she said, her face inches from mine. "You just said yourself that she's nuts. She could feel one way about you one day, one hour, one minute, then feel exactly the opposite the next. She loves you, she loves you not."

She shrugged, straightened and tousled my hair. "Here's what I think you need to do, Howard. Think back on the best times, when you guys were young and played together, or later when you all partied together. Whatever it is, you have to build a little photo album of the happy times in your mind; a little video loop; a slide show; all of the above, whatever is has to be, and you have to hold on to that."

I closed my eyes and dug through my memory banks for images of the happy moments. Sandy went back to the kitchen and left me there thinking, but all I could find was drama, suspense, danger, mystery…a regular library of knock-down-drag-out fights, shouting matches, crying jags, slamming doors…it wasn't long before I gave up. I didn't feel like getting up so I called my son on the cracked Princess phone, which worked fine as long as I held the mouthpiece and the earpiece together.

"Buddy, you should make it over here as soon as you can and say goodbye to G-Hal."

"Oh. Really? I thought I just said goodbye about a month ago?" Tripp replied calmly, and there was no denying it. We had all said our goodbyes, except Sisi. Then the old man decided that dying was too much work and that he would wait until he had a chance to have a few words with his daughter.

"I think this is it," I told my son. When my father realized that his daughter was probably gone for good, he gave up. Death had been waiting long enough.

"Is Aunt Sisi there?"

"No. She escaped from the hospital. Disappeared completely. We have no idea where she is."

"Oh! Jesus, that's intense. Sorry."

"Well, what do you think? Can you and Elke make it over the mountain for one last final-final goodbye?"

"I would, but Elke's not here. She's been helping out at the vet clinic a few hours a week, working off Odo's bill." There was no rancor or even irony in Tripp's voice, and I could only assume that he thought that appropriating Mr. MacDickFuck's dog for humane reasons was perfectly normal. Maybe it is in Bolinas, but I still had the feeling that the crazy drunk wanted his dog back, if only to roast it on a spit.

"Well, how about I put you on the phone with old man?" I told Tripp. "I'll hold the phone up to his ear, but I can't guarantee that he'll say anything or even acknowledge your presence, but at least you can say you tried, right?" I had been told by the Hospice people and had read that hearing was the last sense a dying person loses.

"Sure," Tripp said without hesitation, "put me on with GHal."

I slowly heaved my broken body off the bed, laid the cracked phone on the side table and limped down the hall to the dying man's bedroom door at the end of the plush carpeted hall. He was still there, pose unchanged, mouth open, head listing leftward on two pillows, breath ragged and regular. Angela was lying on the big four poster, barefooted in a tank top and pedal pushers, watching TV in Tagalog. For some reason it struck me as the cutest goddamn thing, as if she and the old man had just finished a surreptitious session and were now back in their designated stations. She clicked off the tube and jumped up when I walked in.

"Mister Hal is good, very quiet. I give him a drop under the tongue, and he is happy now," meaning she gave him a dropper-load of morphine sulfate under the tongue, and I thought great he'll be in no mood to talk to his grandson. But I was completely, utterly wrong. As soon as I held the phone up to the old man's ear and I heard Tripp say "G-Hal, what's happenin'?" his grandfather's face lit up, his eyes like pinball bumpers, all bells and whistles and ringing and dinging. He shouted:

.

"Hey old buddy old pal! It's my favorite person, the big number three! Awwwww..." and instantly he started to fade. "I want...you know...hey you're so sweet... my buddy... I'm so happy..." and his head started to sink back into the pillow, "just so happy..." he said and I could hear Tripp saying:

"I love you, G-Hal!" but the old man was gone again, back to wherever dying people spend their final days, hours and minutes. I lifted the phone to my ear.

"Man, buddy," I whispered, now that the old man was back to sleep, "you should have seen his face."

Several days later the hospice nurse came by on her rounds and officially unplugged Hal Brown from the fluids that might perpetuate his vegetivity indefinitely, so unless he invoked the "no dying without daughter present" clause it was just a matter of interminable time.

It wasn't long before it became clear that he'd given up for good. I had been sitting by his rent-a-bed all day and he hadn't even twitched. As I watched him from the rocker, guitar in hand, my long legs stretched out in front of me, Velcro boot removed and Mr. Booper's warm tummy stretched across my aching feet, I got this inexplicable feeling that he was waiting for something else. Something he needed to take with him on his journey to the country club in the sky.

I pushed myself up with a grunt, my ankle warning me against any sudden moves, and limped around the room he shared for so long with the unsinkable Marjorie Brown, and then unwillingly made his own as his unsinkable one sank steadily into the depths to a place where it didn't matter where she slept; a place where the once tall, gallant, silver-haired trial lawyer with his ever-present pipe between his teeth became just another vaguely familiar figure around the house; a place where her own skinny little daughter and big sack o' potatoes son became just another pair of caregivers changing her diaper and forcing evil food between her puckered lips. When it came time for her to go, she too checked out in a rented hospital bed, but not in the master bedroom. She died in Sisi's old bedroom, where the chain that once locked Sisi in still hung on the molding by the handle. To Mom the room might have been anywhere.

My father's breathing was getting shallower, and I wondered if he wanted something of Mom's. Maybe something from her dressing room; a pile of cashmere sweaters or a smart senior outfit in the peppy fire engine red that Mom, ever the attention-getter, liked to think made her look vivacious and bold. Perhaps a memento from her writing desk, which still stood under the double floor-to-ceiling windows overlooking the highest branches of the ancient live oaks. I glanced through a couple of drawers but it was mostly empty, cleaned out after her exit.

I went back to the old man's bedside and looked him over: his long shining silver hair was taking on the soft, light tone of yellowed parchment in places, fading like the pages of an old book. His fingernails were getting gross and twisted and his toenails were far worse, but I didn't dare take a clipper to them. I might have slipped and lopped one off like a knob of ginger. The purple, blotchy skin of his legs was as translucent as a sheet of phyllo dough, and it hung off his toothpick arms like a braised ham shank. And to think those arms could once blister a tee shot 280...oh! Then it hit me. *That's it! If he's headed to the links in the sky, he's going to need his clubs!*

I gave him a little peck on the forehead, strapped on my Velcro boot and galumphed out the back door to dad's little six-hole Astroturf putting green. Immediately Mr. Booper charged across the Astroturf, snarfed up a golf ball, then ran back to drop it at my feet. "Okay," I told my slobbering pup. "That's the one." It was a red Titleist three, appropriate for seniors. *What a smart pup*, I thought. I then picked a goofy putter with a rusted shaft and a head that looked like a Schlitz bottle, feeling the extra bonus of finding objects that represented two of my father's favorite things: golf and beer.

I headed back to his bedroom, Mr. Booper on my heels, wondering what the hell I was doing with the golf ball that I was supposed to throw. Sandy and the girls were sitting on the deck in the sun but didn't look up as we passed. Back at his bedside, I put the red Titleist three in his open upturned palm and gently closed his fingers around it. Then I laid the grip of the putter across the palm of his right hand, so that the beer bottle-shaped head was atop his gnarly bare feet.

It was five o'clock, perfect time for nine holes in the warm Indian summer twilight, with the dark shadows of the Monterey pines, willows, and redwoods stretching across the bright chartreuse of the sunlit fairways. There is no better time on the golf course. Even when old Hal Brown could no longer play a normal round of golf he loved to take a cart out at twilight, drop a few balls around a green, chip and putt, and watch the small herds of deer graze on the luscious grass.

After a few minutes nothing had changed: his swollen-knuckled fingers did not fold around the ball or the grip of the putter, his eyelids did not flutter nor did his breathing quicken. I stepped back, picked up my guitar from where it sat on the grand four poster bed, slowly lowered my aching frame into the rocker, and began to play a Jimi Hendrix ballad: *Angel.*

Midway through the second chorus I heard Sandy. "Howard," she whispered.

I opened my eyes and there was her soft smile in the doorway. I stopped playing. She came over, put her hand on my shoulder, turned to face her father-in-law, then whispered as if afraid to wake him: "I think he's gone." I stood up and she hugged me, then quietly retreated down the hall.

A few minutes later, after I'd held my fingers to his jugular, put my ear to his mouth, and laid my head on his chest, I realized that old man's body had shut down. Most people would say that he was dead, but unlike Mom who didn't have much of a body left when her spirit abandoned it, my father was too substantial to be completely dead. How could anybody who shouted "hey old buddy old pal" two days ago be completely dead?

Then, with a reflex I couldn't control, I reached down and popped open one of his eyelids. There he was, staring back at me, his eye of blue steel just as shiny and sparkling as if a tear might well up and roll down his wrinkled cheek. I held it open for a split second but when I took my hand away the goddamn lid wouldn't shut, naturally, and there he was, the one-eyed jack staring back at me. *Shit,* I muttered under my breath, frozen by the old man's eye. I don't know how long he held me in his supposedly dead man's gaze but I reached down and slid that eyelid closed as soon as I was conscious of what was happening.

I felt suddenly like a puppet on a string, following my father's unspoken orders. "Son, go get that old putter and a ball – a red Titleist three, I'm sure there's one out there." Given his uncanny control over the time and fashion of his ultimate exit, I felt like a force had been unleashed – his spirit, perhaps – that had been lying in wait just to fuck with my head.

Then came the sweats, the shortness of breath, the heart palpitations, my surgically repaired shoulder and ankle throbbing in unison; the back throbbing; lightning bolts shooting down my thighs and calves into my feet. I steadied myself on one of the old bedposts and looked at him lying there on the rent-a-bed with the golf ball and the putter, feeling like I had just witnessed a paranormal event. Was I having a heart attack? Was there an angel in the room? An angel disguised as a caddy that heard my ministrations and saw that the old man was ready to go play nine on the celestial links? *Who's here?* I heard myself shout, *Show yourself! Who is it?*

Then, for a moment, all went black.

I came to just seconds later, thinking Sandy or the girls must have heard me yelling, but there was only silence. I pulled myself up on the hospital bed, and noticed the peeps and whistles of the purple finches at the old feeder in the bay tree overhanging the deck. Then there was Sandy and the girls talking quietly in the kitchen, waiting for me to be done with my private bon voyage so they could similarly bid adieu. Some bon voyage. I staggered over to his medicine table and took half a dropper of the liquid morphine. In a moment or two I was feeling the warmth of the sun against my face.

After I'd caught my breath and the morphine has encased my blazing cerebral cortex in a soft, cool glow, I called Sisi's cell phone, knowing she wouldn't pick up but also figuring that she would know why I was calling. "He's gone," I said. And then out of sheer spite I added, "He was asking for you up 'til the very end." I hung up with the distinct feeling that regardless of whatever ugliness had transpired between her and me in the past, the real work was just beginning.

It occurred to me then that we should have tried to move the old man into the grand antique four-poster so he could die with a little more dignity, in the same bed that had heard the dreams of generations of Southern kinfolk in West Feliciana parish. But, just as he insisted that his remains be cremated instead of buried in the ancient family cemetery where his mother and father lay in Laurel Hill, Louisiana, he probably would not have wanted to die in that old Southern bed, just as he didn't want to live anywhere near his Southern relations.

Though it wasn't the proper time for such musings then, I can now see that the bed, and my momentary glimpse into lives of the people that once slept there, was a harbinger of things to come. Instead of my father's death signifying the end of something, it turned out to signify what was to ultimately become a beginning. Standing there next to his dead body in the master bedroom, I got this anxious, uncomfortable feeling that there was a part of the old man that was now loose in the spirit world and looking for a live body to move in with, and that my future had become, as they say, a whole new ballgame.

I called the mortuary, and in 45 minutes he was bagged up with his putter and golf ball and headed for the incinerator. A half hour later the caregivers had packed up and returned to their cousins to await the call from another American family that didn't know what to do with their old folks.

Despite a strong feeling that I wanted to see the house and everything in it vaporize into thin air, I knew that after an attempt at sleep Sandy and I would be back, packing up 40 years' worth of whatever my parents felt was worth keeping and whatever was worth recording about their lives and the lives of their ancestors, which I felt must have been hidden somewhere in the ungodly mess, and pitching the rest.

And then, before I closed the forest green double-sized front door, I heard a faint but distinct call for help. It was as if the house itself, home to the Browns for over fifty years, was pleading for me to stay, if only long enough to mend the remains of our fractured family. At the same time, just as I stepped off the front landing, I felt like I had been completely cut loose of my moorings, left to drift alone in uncharted waters, abandoned by the only other remaining survivor of the Howard Browns: my sister. Had I decided then to let her go, had I decided to turn my back on her and walk away, just as she had done to me and our father, had I just listened to my wife…oh! Had I just listened to anybody, anything besides my own foolish heart, this tale of woe would end right here, right now.

Instead, it's just beginning.

BOOK II
BRIARWOOD

Hope springs eternal in the human breast;
Man never is, but always to be blessed:
The soul, uneasy and confined from home,
Rests and expatiates in a life to come.

— Alexander Pope, *An Essay on Man*

17 My Soul Hole

The buzzing in my birthmark – the strange hole in the center of my sternum that, by the time I turned 60, was a discolored depression about the size of a thumbtack – started that night. I was lying on my back in bed, still bundled up in my Velcro rig and all abuzz with narcotics, when I got the feeling that someone had attached an electrical stim node to the hole in my chest and turned the juice up to ten. The label that had been unofficially assigned to my deformity – Chown Hoon Dong – surged into my addled consciousness, and I was presented with the kind of vivid memory that is usually reserved for dreams.

I was just a baby, probably no more than a year old, and I was being studied intently by the man whom I would recognize later as the proprietor of the local Chinese laundry in Larkspur. He looked like a Chinaman from a children's storybook: *The Five Chinese Brothers* or perhaps *Ping, the Duck*. A silvery mustache like gossamer threads fell from the corners of his leathery lips, tickling my bare chest as he peered through thick spectacles at the hole there. He oohed and ahhed, while he circled my birthmark with a long yellowed fingernail. "Your son," he finally said, "He is very special."

My mother, who I somehow knew was tempted to snatch me up from the laundry counter and run, said in a shaky voice: "How so? Does he have some kind of curse?"

The laundry man laughed and bared his tobacco-stained teeth. "In China, the Chown Hoon Dong is great honor."

"Chow what?" my mother cried.

"Chown Hoon Dong. It is the soul hole. A conduit to the afterlife."

Lying there in bed, I remembered the feeling of having unique, super-secret powers that were mine and mine alone. It was a feeling that had manifested periodically in dreams throughout my life, and had without fail boosted me out of whatever blue funk I might have been in. But this time it was accompanied with a powerful sense of foreboding, along with the palpable buzzing/tickling/burning sensation on my skin.

Soon enough I learned that the buzzing was, quite literally, a signal, a warning of sorts that either my father had a message for me, or that I was in the presence of ancestral ghosts. At first it was just a voice in my head; the visions didn't come until later. When I told Sandy about it, not long after the old man's final exit, she called her "intuitive," a woman most folks would refer to as a "psychic" (and that I referred to as a "psycho"). After Sandy put me on the phone with her for a few minutes – I was not to speak – she informed me that my dead father had taken up residence in my third chakra, and my third chakra had been wired to my soul hole. Hence the buzzing. *Hello? This is Howard. Please leave a message at the beep.*

I had heard of chakras and energy healing – hard to avoid in Marin County – but wasn't aware that the spirits of the recently deceased, unwilling to depart their earthly domain, could hole up in the third chakra, which I pictured to be somewhere near my large colon. The psycho intuitive told me that I had to command my father to leave; cast him out like a demon, without sympathy or compassion for his bodiless state. But what was I supposed to say?

I considered going to a Western doctor about the buzzing in my soul hole, thinking perhaps there was some sort of electrical imbalance that might throw my heart out of whack. But there was something about the psychic's interpretation that appealed to me, if only because I figured that two could play at this "telephone" game, and here was my chance to set a few things in the family record straight without fear of retribution, before my father left the physical world altogether and I lost contact. It was also an excellent, even if totally lame, rationale for the aberrant behavior that came later.

The problem with this arrangement was that the dead man, as I imagined, could now monitor our execution of his last will and testament. Such documents often abound with various challenges and tests of mettle that must be successfully completed before the treasure is released: precarious rope bridges over rocky chasms and rivers boiling with ferocious piranha and razor-toothed crocodiles; perilous climbs up sheer granite cliffs crawling with rattlers, tarantulas, and scorpions; treacherous expeditions into the burning molten bowels of the earth to battle beasts unknown to man or God – who knows what parents might require in a will to ensure their progeny is worthy of their hard-earned inheritance?

It also meant that I was still on the hook to locate Sisi, since dividing up his estate according to his wishes meant that we, brother and sister, had to actually work together and come to an agreement on a wide variety of gifts, most notably a 100-acre tract in the woods of Laurel Hill, Louisiana, on what was once the Briarwood plantation. Dividing it up, selling it, keeping it – all this could be worked out in due time once my sister had decided to make herself available for such discussions. Trouble was nobody had a clue where she'd gone. And I wasn't entirely sure I had the will or the energy to go looking for her. She would have to turn up, eventually. Or leave her inheritance to me.

It was an apocryphal phone call, just a week or so after my father's death, that set our future in motion. Sandy and I had just returned home after collecting our son in Bolinas for an extended visit. Meanwhile Elke, tired of Mr. Road Rage's daily harassment, took Odo to visit some friends in Nevada City. When we arrived back in Sleepy Hollow, there was a message on the voice mail that, to put it bluntly, took everything I thought was true about my sister and our family, threw it all onto the roulette wheel and with one sweep of a mighty cosmic hand let it spin.

18 The Return of Elizabeth Stewart

At first I thought the message must be from somebody that read Hal Brown's obit in the SF or Marin news and wanted to know when and where the memorial service would be, which we hadn't figured out yet. Then I thought it might be the Bolinas Sherriff's department wondering why the town drunk – Mr. MacDickfuck – was camped in Tripp's front yard. As it turned out, it was neither.

"Hello this is a message for Howard Brown. I hope I have the right numbuh. Our cousin Anne wasn't sure if y'all's family information was up to date or not. I called your daddy Hal's numbuh and have heard that he is deceased. We are all very sorry to heayuh that."

On hearing the caller's unmistakable Louisiana twang Tripp's ultra-sensitive ears perked up. "Who the hell is that?" he shouted with incredulity.

"I have no idea," I said. Then, as if he had been listening to our conversation, the caller on the voicemail identified himself.

"My name is Eddie Sublette, your second cousin by way of your father's first cousin, Claude Jr. You may remember me from a time back when our families met at a reunion in North Carolina."

"What's he want?" Sandy cried from down the hall.

"Don't know! Hold on!" I cried in return, wishing I hadn't put the message on speaker. I remembered Eddie as a skinny 18-year-old with a concave chest, cutoff jeans and a pack of Kools that he kept hidden in his tackle box. I figured he was probably in his early seventies now.

"I'm calling to inform y'all that a woman we believe to be your sistuh is makin' a bit of a fuss down heayah in Saint Francisville and has gotten into a little trouble with the locals on a couple of occasions. If you could please call me back at your earliest convenience I will be happy to provide the detail…"

I collapsed, painfully, onto the family room sofa in complete catatonic shock. For a fleeting moment I had a vision of leading a somewhat normal life again, once my limbs had healed and my father's estate was subsumed or liquidated and I had engaged in some sort of gainful employment. Instead, the shit kept coming. And coming. And coming.

My first inclination was to erase Eddie Sublette's message and pretend it never happened; just file it under "hallucinations" and be done with it. But I knew Tripp, who has always felt that having a sibling is a divine gift, having lost his own, would not let me simply blow her off. Had Elke not flown the coop Tripp would have never known about Eddie Sublette because he wouldn't have been sitting on the living room sofa with Mr. Booper atop his bare feet.

Both my son and my wife would have been perfectly comfortable making the decision whether or not to respond to cousin Eddie on my behalf; I was so whupped that I was inclined to let them figure it out. But when I picked up the phone to call Eddie back, Sandy was already on the line. My soul hole started buzzing the instant I heard Eddie's voice.

"Hello Eddie, this is Sandy Brown, Howard's wife," Sandy said with a familiar, unmistakable air of team captain authority.

"Hello, Sandy. I am pleased to make your acquaintance," twanged Cousin Ed.

"Yes, I just wanted to let you know that Howard and his sister are estranged, and we really don't have anything to do with her."

I gulped hard, suppressing the temptation to blurt out something rude to my overly assumptive wife, though I knew Eddie was familiar with estrangement. Several of my Southern cousins were not on speaking terms from what I had heard.

"I am so very sorry to heayuh that," Eddie said softly. "Though I must say it's not uncommon in families as mixed-up as ours."

"Uh…excuse me," I said, bursting in, "uh…hello Eddie, this is Howard Brown."

"Well hello, Howard!" Eddie cried, "You know since I left that message I've been thinking – didn't we meet years ago at some family outing in North Carolina? I seem to recall a certain bottle of Kentucky bourbon and maybe a little locoweed down by the lake, and you were playin' your gee-tar and singin' up a storm and…oh, well. It was a time!"

I was probably a little young for Kentucky bourbon and locoweed to be involved, but Eddie was older. I didn't know. It was all a blur. "Why sure, Eddie. I have a dim recollection…"

"Well, of course, of course," said Eddie. "Funny how our brains forget the best times and hang onto the worst."

I could hear Sandy breathing impatiently, still on the line in the bedroom.

"Now let me say somethin' 'bout your sistuh," Eddie continued. "Y'all may be estranged and like I say that's standard operatin' procedure 'round these parts, but y'all gotta unnerstand that there's certain family obligations that must be fulfilled, and if one your kin is causin' trouble in the family – spreadin' lies and rumors and that sorta' thing – it is up to the kin to straighten that sort of thing out, y'all unnerstand what I'm sayin?"

"NO!" shouted Sandy without hesitation.

"Sandy!" I shouted back, shocked by her rudeness. "Just a minute, Eddie." I put the phone down and stormed into the bedroom, but before I could say anything she started in:

"Howard! Under no circumstances are we going to Louisiana to rescue your goddamn sister!" she screamed, hand over the mouthpiece.

"Nobody said we were!" I yelled back. "What the hell is wrong with you? We don't even know what the hell she's doing to cause trouble. Hell we don't even know if it's her!"

After what my sister has said about the devils in our Southern tribe I was amazed that she would go anywhere near West Feliciana Parish. "Now, please hang up and let me find out what's going on. That's all I ask. We're not going to Louisiana to rescue her. I promise, if we ever go there it will have nothing to do with her."

Sandy just sat on the bed glaring at me. Then she lifted the phone to her ear. "Eddie?" she cooed softly, "my apologies for the little outburst. As you can imagine Howard's sister has done a little damage in these parts as well, which is why we've sworn her off." Sandy fixed her hairy eyeball on me and waggled her index finger like a grade-school teacher. "Anyway thanks for getting in touch," she continued without missing a beat, ensuring cousin Ed couldn't get a word in. "Goodbye," she said, and hung up.

"WHAT?" I hollered. I went limping back to the living room where I hoped Eddie was still on the line to find Tripp with the phone.

"Just a minute, Mr. Sublette, my dad is on his way," he said, smiling. I gave Tripp a pat on the shoulder and he offered up the phone.

"Eddie, I'm so sorry. As you can see my sister is a loaded topic around here, and if I told you some of the stories you would understand why we're avoiding her, I'm sure. But at any rate I would like to understand the trouble she's allegedly causing. I might have a suggestion or two."

"Well first let me say, Howard, that we're not lookin' fer suggestions. We're lookin' for somebody to come'n git her and take her north where she belongs. A white person simply can't behave like her in these parts, not if they don't wanna get knifed."

Knifed? I thought. What could my sister, the 97-pound waif with matchstick arms and a neck so thin it looked like her head might droop over like a dead tulip at any moment; a woman of translucent, almost lavender skin and bones that pressed out at sharp angles as if she were more of an exercise in graphic design than she was a real person – how could such an odd, shrill little reptile like my sister deserve a switchblade in her ribs?

I noticed that Sandy had returned to the family room and was sitting on the sofa nuzzled up to her son and Mr. Booper, watching me like a cat at a mouse hole. She had the other phone in her lap.

"May I put this on speaker phone with the mute button on?" she asked politely, and I figured why not. There was no point in keeping the conversation secret.

"Knifed?" I asked Eddie in amazement.

"Well that might be exaggeratin' the situation a bit, but your sister…this woman that claims to be Elizabeth Stewart and kin to Mr. Alexander Stewart who as you probably know first settled this area in 1783 – this woman has takin' to bein' her ghost at the Myrtles."

I gasped, thinking back to the day after the giant redwood tree fell in the storm several weeks ago, when Sisi greeted the neighbors as "Sissy Mae Brown from Laurel Hill." Now it sounded like she was taking the charade a few steps further, or a few steps back, into the complex genealogical swamps of planters, Southern Belles and ghosts.

"What makes you think that this woman is my sister? I mean, she was here just a couple of weeks ago before dad passed away. The whole thing made her a little upset, as you might imagine, but I expect once she calms down a bit she'll be back to help liquidate the estate. Not only that but as you might know our father owned 100 acres of Briarwood that's now split between us, so…I don't know. It's just another thing we need to work out. She's never behaved in the way you describe, so I really doubt that it's her."

I admit I was acting far calmer and level-headed than I felt, for I knew full well that Sisi was bi-polar and maybe even schizophrenic, even if my parents never spoke of it.

"Okay," Eddie said, hesitantly, "I will text you a photograph. What is your cell number?"

I gave Eddie the number and Sandy jumped up to grab the cell phone before I could get to it.

"Oh my God!" she shouted, almost gleefully, "Oh Howard you're not going to believe this!" Sandy handed me the phone and there she was, a full frontal head shot, well-disguised in a black period wig parted in the middle with nautilus curls on either side and festooned with black ribbons, her face powdered and rouged so she looked more like a 19th century doll than a real person. It occurred to me instantly that anybody could have Photoshopped this portrait if they had a picture of Sisi's face, but if it was a fake it was a damn good one. And there was no way to prove that this wasn't actually her unless I met this Elizabeth Stewart character in person.

"Sure looks a lot like my sister," I said to Eddie, not wanting to admit to anything. This was looking to be a bad business all around, given Sandy's strong desire that I let my sister stew in her own bad brain chemicals, and my sense of duty to my family, a big brotherly responsibility that had been ingrained in me by both father and mother when I was very young. If there was one thing above all else that was expected of me, it was that I look out for my little sister. Sandy, with three older brothers, had no such sense of familial duty. Her brothers could take care of themselves.

"I know she looks harmless, Howard, but when she goes out on the town all gussied up in her hoop skirt, fancy hat and parasol, or even worse, starts hanging around the old plantations, the tourists are put off. She'll barge right into the exhibits like it's back in the day, sitting in the antique furniture with some ancient porcelain teacup, talking to the tourists like they're houseguests and she's throwing a party."

"Is she drinking?" I had to ask, grasping for some explanation. Sandy had retired to the other room again and was having a good laugh, but I could sense a much darker, dangerous development afoot here, one that might lock my sister up in a mental institution for good, for this was far beyond mere bipolar disease or even clinical depression; this was out n' out schizophrenia, though it could have also be a bizarre reaction to alcohol, which had never set well with Sisi.

"I don't think so. I personally have not seen her take a drink, nor have I seen her drunk, at least not normal drunk," Eddie explained, serious as a judge. "No, the real problem is this, Howard: when she is in her role, so to speak, as a planter's wife from the 1830s, she treats the local citizens of our community like servants."

"Oh my God! She's completely off her rocker!" Sandy yelled exuberantly, almost victoriously, as if my sister's serious problem was the best thing that had ever happened to her. Even Tripp was outraged.

"Mom, shut up!" he barked, his annoyance boiling over. He could imagine the anger that was building up inside me because he felt it himself. It just didn't feel right to wish ill upon a family member, but both Tripp and I knew that Sisi had been blatantly heaping ill will upon Sandy from the day they met. Still, laughing about my sister's obvious departure from reality seemed to be going too far. Way too far. Mr. Booper agreed and went outside to lie on the warm bricks of the patio.

Eddie, perhaps suspecting the deep enmity between his cousin Sissy Mae and my wife, continued: "Howard, ah need you to understand just how serious this situation is. A white person can't expect to live long in these parts callin' folks 'boy' and 'sonny' and 'girl' and especially the 'N' word, which I can't even bring myself to say. The community is up in arms, but you know you can't arrest somebody for play-acting, though the police, the mayor, and the reverend have given her a stern talking-to." Eddie finally paused to catch his breath.

I asked Eddie if Sissy Mae was even aware of her play-acting as Elizabeth Stewart.

"Not that I am aware of, but it's difficult to know if Sissy Mae is telling the truth. She claims to have seen the crazy woman, as Sissy Mae refers to her, around town."

"Bullshit!" Sandy shouted from the living room.

"Mom!" Tripp shouted back.

"She's lying, Tripp! This whole play-acting business is a charade! She just wants to be the center of attention like she always does."

"Mom, please!"

I covered my other ear. As far as I was concerned it made no difference whether she was aware of her 180 year-old evil twin or not. Was Dr. Jekyll aware of Mr. Hyde's anti-social antics? What's more, if Elizabeth Stewart gets knifed, so does Sissy Mae, Sisi and all the other people my sister has tried to be over the course of her life. They all die, and under the circumstances I wasn't willing to let that happen. Especially with my father riding shotgun in my third chakra.

"Okay, Eddie," I sighed, exhaling deeply, massaging the hole in my chest while trying to relax the muscles in my neck and upper back, noticing that the pain in my shoulder had returned with a vengeance. "What she needs is a doctor, a psychiatrist. She has probably run out of her medication and when that happens she forgets that she's even *on* medication."

"I can set you up with a psychiatrist the minute your plane lands in Baton Rouge, Howard," Eddie said, indicating with curt finality that her safety was my responsibility and nobody else's. Several days later the thought occurred to me that local social services deal with crazy people on the streets all the time, so why not my sister? But by then I had booked my flight.

"Let me make some arrangements," I told him, "I'll get down there as soon as I can."

"Good, I am sure the family will be tickled to see y'all. We can put you up in the old plantation house in Laurel Hill: Briarwood. You've been there, have you not?"

I told Eddie that indeed, I had been to Briarwood, though not since college, now almost forty years ago. The place had not been restored since some time in the forties; the mattresses were stuffed with hay, the kitchen was in an outbuilding and the house was stuffed with so many dusty antiques, many covered in sheets, that it was difficult to find a place to sit. But I had heard that it had been beautifully restored and even added to the National Register of Historic Places.

Finally, I warned Eddie not to let my sister know of our impending visit because she would disappear in an instant, to which Eddie said: "Hey now there's an idea. We tell her you're coming and she disappears! Problem solved!"

"Maybe for you, Eddie, but not for me," I said, half-chuckling.

"Of course," Eddie said. "Well I do indeed look forward to meeting your wife and son, and you too, Howard. It's been far, far too long."

I hung up and went to the living room, where I suspected I was going to have to do some expert coaxing to get Sandy to accompany me on this rescue mission, but when I turned the corner into the living room the front door was standing wide open. I rushed outside and looked down the street, thinking perhaps she needed a quiet walk to think things over. But all I saw was her car, rolling away in the silent, still, uncommonly warm afternoon, until she turned and was gone.

19 An Impossible Choice

Had I known Sandy was going to pack her bags and move out, I might have taken a different approach. Instead, I was lost in a 3-D twilight zone of "what ifs?" swirling about my head like moths to a flame. What if I had said this? Or done that? Or crossed my legs and put my cap on backwards?

Just before she left, she said: "Howard, if someone said the things your sister has said about me…if someone ever told such horrid, hurtful, hateful lies about you, don't you think you would want to avoid them?" She was leaning forward in the brick red wingback chair in the family room, next to the forlorn, empty fireplace that had been mothballed as a result of the shitty autumn thermal inversion air quality.

I told her that she didn't need to have anything to do with my sister ever again, and that she could do as she pleased in Louisiana: go fishing with Tripp, stay in New Orleans, take the train to Memphis, just so long as we were more or less together.

"Howard," Sandy interrupted, her voice growing more intense, strident, insisting, "you're not hearing what I've been trying to tell you since the argument in your father's bedroom."

I recalled that night, the night of the storm, the night Sisi and I almost got catapulted into the neighbor's pool in the Mercedes RV. But whatever Sandy was trying to tell me that night had been erased.

"Your sister is not good for you, Howard. She cheats you, lies to you, steals from you, puts you down…" Sandy went on to enumerate the many times Sisi has fucked me over out of pure malice, as well as the many times the fucking over had a negative impact on our little family. "And if you continue to insist on having her in your life, well…I don't know if I can take it anymore."

Big tears welled up in Sandy's deep brown eyes so I handed her my handkerchief, my thoughts like bubbles, rising to the surface, popping, rising, popping, never pausing long enough to see. Even after all these years of enmity between them I never thought it would come to this. But there it was. A clear choice. My choice. The more I thought about having to make such a choice the angrier I got. Didn't Sandy hear Eddie Sublette's description of Sisi's condition?

I tried to make a deal with her. I told her I would never speak Sisi's name in her presence, and we would make arrangements so that she would never have to see, hear, think or otherwise consider her existence, but it wasn't good enough. I knew as soon as the words came out of my mouth that I completely missed Sandy's point.

"Goddamnit!" Sandy screamed. "I'm not talking about me, Howard, I'm talking about YOU! I'm saying that I can't handle seeing you get your face rubbed in shit every single time you talk to that fucking bitch!" Sandy leapt to her feet and began to pace back and forth, her reflection in the dark windows aping her every move. "Don't you see that every time you come skulking back here with your tail between your legs because of the latest insult du jour, I'm the one that gets the brunt of it? I'm the one that has to play the shrink and get you back on your feet! For what? Don't you see that, Howard? It's unnecessary! There's no reason you or I or Tripp or Elke or anybody else should have to put up with it. It doesn't matter if she's your sister, Howard. She might as well be Genghis Khan for all I care. Just because she happens to be the child of your mom and dad, like you are, doesn't mean that you are required by law or anything else to have anything to do with her!"

"Wait a sec, honey. And please try to calm down," I said, finally grasping a thought bubble before it popped. "In order to sell the land Sisi is going to have either sign the deed or be declared insane and have a proxy signer. But I'm not sure that we should sell our piece, since it belongs to you and me, and I don't think we should do anything until we see it, walk around on it, maybe camp out and roast weenies." But Sandy didn't even grin. Instead, being far outside the sphere of reason, Sandy charged off down the hall and into our bedroom, slamming the door behind her with such force that the entire house shuddered. I dropped my face in my hands and massaged my temples. I simply didn't understand why I couldn't go down to Laurel Hill, get Sisi squared away in a mental institution, execute whatever real-estate transaction needed to be executed, kiss my cousins goodbye and come home.

Well, actually I did understand, though I am hard pressed to admit it: these two women had it in for each other from the beginning: the day I brought Sandy to 156 Woodland for Easter dinner thirty years ago. My parents still loved dying eggs and having a hunt, so we had arrived early afternoon for the traditional ceremony. Sandy, having recently completed a graduate degree at the Rudolph Schaeffer School of Design, managed to dye some very fashion-forward eggs that made Sisi's eggs look like monkey turds. And so the jealousy, which I guarantee every sister has for their brother's wife, kicked in immediately and without pretense. Sisi was lobbing snark-bombs at Sandy before dinner had even started, especially since Sandy consistently found more eggs. Childish, I know, and it may not be politically correct to say it, but when some women square off there is no diplomat or peacemaker in the world that is going to keep them from gouging each other's eyes out.

I realized then that Sandy was far beyond even wanting to understand the most business-like, practical reasons for making the trip. But she also refused to agree that my sister was mentally ill and that you have to separate the aberrant behavior from the patient, who may or may not know that what they're doing or saying is wrong. Sandy said that while Sisi was starting to look like she'd gone bonkers, it hadn't always been that way. As far as Sandy was concerned Sisi has been a conniving, double-crossing, backstabbing witch from that fateful Easter, borderline personality disorder and all other disorders notwithstanding. As far as Sandy was concerned, I was walking into a trap that my sister had carefully laid, a trap that would trick me out of every last dime of my inheritance, land and all. And there I was, on the opposite end of the spectrum, thinking that Sisi was no more capable of laying a trap for me than she was capable of swimming the English Channel.

When I heard the wheels of one of our travel duffels roll across the hardwood floor and emerge from the bedroom my heart sank so fast and so hard that I feared I was going to have a stroke. All of my injuries started howling like the hounds of hell, the pressure behind my eyes was pounding as if trying to push the tired orbs out of their sockets, so before I went to confront Sandy for what might be the last time I grabbed a few oxys – maybe more than a few – and washed them down with a big chug of cold sake right out of the bottle.

"Howard, I'm sorry," Sandy said when I saw her standing by the front door all packed up and ready to go. Tripp joined me, his arm hooked around my neck, treating his mother's departure as if were a fait accompli, an inevitable bridge that must be crossed if we're to carry on as a family unit. He also wanted to fish the bayous and the gulf and no doubt wrote off his parents' little disagreement as spasms old people have. It wasn't the first time he had heard us speaking different languages. I suspected he had come to see our rare brain cramps as a periodic release of pressure that might have been easily avoided with a fishing trip or a week shooting tubes in Costa Rica.

"Why do you have to leave, honey?" I pleaded. "Can't you see that I've got a responsibility here? Besides, what about the land? Don't you want our fair share? Who's going to take care of Loopy?" Looking around for our brown pup I saw that she had already leashed him: he was on the front stoop sniffing at the bag that held his traveling kibble. "Honey! I can't do this without you!" I howled.

"Sure you can. You've got Tripp."

I looked at my son in his Cat Eye Vuarnet's, cap on backwards and golden ringlets of straw-colored hair popping out every which way. Assisting his dad in the hunt for his aunt didn't appear to be on his mind.

I should have said something about the intermittent buzzing in my chest that had arrived with Eddie's call and wasn't going away, and the silver blue bullet my father shot into my heart with his final breath. Sandy knew the old man had taken up residence in my third chakra, and I could have said that it was him forcing me down here, because he wanted to at least visit the old place before departing for good.

After she was gone I lit a cigarette, sat down on a patio chaise and stared into the autumn night, bare tree branches silhouetted against clouds illuminated by an invisible moon. Tripp was in his bedroom tying flies for his bayou fishing adventure, which was being sponsored by *Outside* magazine, Sage and Patagonia and was going to result in a half-hour video for ESPN. Tripp wouldn't be able to see the final result, but he was buoyant just the same.

While Tripped tied flies and rapped along with Fifty Cent, or NWA, or Dr. Dre – it all sounded the same to me, which was exactly what my parents said about the music of the British Invasion – I had a premonition. Suddenly I felt that Eddie's story was just a ruse to get me to come down south. And how did I know that it was even my cousin on the phone? Something about Sandy's extreme over-reaction to what appeared to be nothing more than practical family business made me suspicious. I couldn't put my finger on anything in particular, outside of the sheer outrageousness of Eddie's story, but I was wary just the same.

I looked skyward through the thin layer of light clouds, imagining the stars beyond and thinking back on the many times I'd searched the heavens hoping for a sign, a message from God that everything was going to be all right. Sometimes I stared until my eyes watered and my neck cramped into spasms, whispering *come on, you can do it, just one little twinkle, one little shooting star, hell even a satellite will do*, but it was all one blank curtain of grey. *It's okay*, I thought. *Perhaps I should save God's sign for a time when I am really, totally screwed.* So I pushed my aching frame off the chaise, my shoulder reminding me to go gingerly, and went to bed.

.

20 Welcome to West Feliciana

When Tripp and I arrived at the Baton Rouge airport I was expecting to be met by Cousin Eddie, who said he would be happy to shuttle me from Baton Rouge to Briarwood, where there would be an extra car. Tripp was met by the *Outside* writer and videographer in baggage claim while a few other fishing enthusiasts gawked and pointed. I wanted to shout out, "Yeah, that handsome kid in the big shades that everybody is making such a fuss over? That's my boy!" But I didn't, and within 10 minutes he was whisked away in a celebrity hubbub. I was turning to look for my bag when I heard him shout from the door to the loading zone, "Love you, Dad! Wow, it's humid as fuck down here!"

Instead of meeting Eddie, I was met in baggage claim by the Briarwood caretaker, Johnny Stubbs, a stooped, grizzled, gray-headed and impossibly old, faded man in threadbare denim overalls. He wore a beautiful hand-knitted zipper front cardigan of soft brown wool with vertical dark rose-colored stripes, about four inches wide down either side, which reminded me of some of my father's cardigans from the fifties and sixties, all of them now irreparably moth-eaten. Johnny Stubbs's cardigan looked like an exact replica of one I'd seen in pictures of Hal Brown, most taken on the golf course. I suspected the sweater was a perfect fit for Stubbs about 20 years ago, but now he looked like he must be pushing ninety and shrinking into oblivion. The sweater fit him like a bathrobe. Eventually his kin would be able to mummify him in it and send him on his heavenly way.

"Welcome to the South, Mr. Howard," Stubbs said as we shook hands, his droopy eyes popping out of his head. "We've been missin' you a very long time. It's good to have you back, though I must say you've grown a little since I last saw you." He laughed and chucked my elbow, which was about as far up as he could reach. I must've looked like Frankenstein, with my left ankle still in the black Velcro boot and my arm in a sling. Johnny took note: "How did you get so banged up?"

"Oh, I'll tell ya later," I said, not wanting to try and explain how I had collapsed like a ragdoll in the face of Mr. MacDickFuck's wrath. "It's a long story."

"Yes, they're all long stories round here," Johnny said, nodding.

My chest started buzzing lightly, and I had the first sense of having stepped into an ancestral dream, as if a long dead branch of the family tree

110

was suddenly wick again and I was a bud on the branch, waiting to pop. Or as if I had finally shown up to claim a fully furnished, luxuriously warm and inviting room in a vast ancestral hotel that had been reserved for me since birth and had been anxiously awaiting my arrival for sixty years.

It was all so familiar, yet so completely and utterly foreign that I might as well have stepped off a plane in Botswana. Even the air that greeted me as we exited baggage claim was like nothing I could remember: a dense, heavy vapor, thick with the odor of rotting vegetation and gasoline. Instantly I was blanketed by an enervating dampness; my jeans and T-shirt clung to my skin, my glasses fogged up, even moving my lips was challenging.

When we arrived at Johnny's pristine 1966 Ford Pickup, he introduced me to his daughter, Toya, a curvaceous, well-proportioned, solid woman in her mid-forties, wearing jeans and an LSU hoodie. "How'd you get so banged up?" she immediately asked, helping me get situated with the sling, careful not to jar anything. She had put the seat all the way back so that she had to sit on the front edge and lean forward to hold onto the wheel while I slouched down as far as I could so my head wasn't bumping against the headliner. I gave her the same response I gave Johnny, knowing that the story would have to be told, but at the same time praying they would forget about it. I decided then that I would lose the boot and the sling and take my chances.

"So we've heard y'all's been havin' some family difficulties," Toya started, in a voice so silky smooth and melodic I couldn't help but think of Ella Fitzgerald. We pulled onto Highway 61 north, the "Blues Highway" made famous by Sunnyland Slim, Johnny Young and Bob Dylan, that runs from New Orleans along the Mississippi all the way to Wyoming, Minnesota. Dylan's lyrics popped into my head:

Well Georgia Sam he had a bloody nose
Welfare Department they wouldn't give him no clothes
He asked poor Howard where can I go
Howard said there's only one place I know
Sam said tell me quick man I got to run
Ol' Howard just pointed with his gun
And said that way down on Highway 61.

I explained the family situation to Toya who said she had heard about it from Eddie's younger brother Binx. I asked her about the local mental health services, and if my sister had actually been arrested or detained in any way, or if anybody knew where she was living.

"Binx would know," Toya said. "Me and daddy ain't never seen her. Thank God." Toya and Johnny laughed the way people do when they absolutely don't give a shit about what you think of them, which hit me like a fresh, cool breeze, being as I was then so totally consumed by my own angst-ridden existence I could barely move my bowels. It was then that I first heard a little voice; maybe it was Sandy's voice, saying *focus*. That's all. Just *focus*, as if the task of chaperoning my parents to the afterlife the past three years had cut me loose of my moorings so completely that all I could do was drift.

"Damn, I should have rented a car," I said, out of the blue. What was I thinking? How could I chase Bixi down without my own ride?

"Oh no," Johnny said. "Mister Eddie has that all worked out for you. He's got an extra car and if it breaks down, which it could seein' as it's 'bout as old as Eddie is, you can use Toya's car. She just needs to get to the school and back and she can use my Bessie's car."

"Bessie?" I asked.

"My wife," Johnny said, "goin' on sixty five years."

I felt my interest in these people, their lives – Eddie, Binx, Johnny, Toya, Bessie – spark in a tinder ball and flame up. But the voice, Sandy's voice, was on me: *focus, focus*.

"That's great," I said appreciatively. "I was thinking on the plane that one way to figure out where she is, if nobody has actually seen where she goes after one of her little performances, is to call her cell phone. If she's got location services on it will at least indicate what town she's in."

"Location services?" Toya asked. "Well, who ever heard of such a thing? Heck, I sure could've used that back when my ex-husband was out sowin' his wild oats around the parish!"

Again, laughter as sweet and happy as a child skipping down the sidewalk. I wanted some of whatever it was that made people laugh that way.

We traveled in silence for a short while, and out the window there wasn't a single light on for as far as I could see in any direction. I saw the tips of the bigger trees jutting above the top line of the forest silhouetted against the backlit clouds, their branches beginning to lose their leaves in the waning days of autumn. Then I decided to dial my sister's number. Again. Disconnected.

"I know your sister," Toya finally said, bringing me back to the task at hand. "I've known her for a long time. She's been down here before you know, pokin' around y'all's family history. I think she might have come down here for a medical procedure a long, long time ago, when I was just a little girl. You know what I'm talkin' about?"

I had no idea what she was talking about and at that moment I didn't want to know. I wanted to know how to find her and what kind of social services I could enlist for help. Then, as I asked Toya if she or Johnny had any idea what the going rate was for an acre of woods, every pore in my body opened up and starting leaking beads of sweat; ants started crawling over the back of my neck – I had missed my evening dose and my body wanted the drugs. So I squirreled around on the seat, fished out my pillbox and swallowed them dry, the bitter chemical taste sweet on my drug-loving tongue. Toya was curious.

"You all right?" she asked. "You look like you're having a heart attack."

"No," I explained. "I forgot to take my meds, that's all. I was overdue. But thanks."

At this Johnny chuckled and nodded his big head, looking out the passenger window. "Yeah, I know all about *that!*" he said in a raspy, Louis Armstrong grumble. I imagined that Johnny Stubbs might know a few other things about my family that hadn't made it north of Natchez.

We drove for a little while just listening to the tires on the pavement and the faint strains of the blues on the radio, Albert King, *Crosscut Saw.* I pondered Eddie's description of my sister's supposedly dangerous, "knifeable" behavior, which so far bore no eyewitnesses. The whole idea was crazy. After she had these episodes when she felt like she was living in the 1820s, how then did she gather her skirts into a Chevy Cruze and drive off? Did she see the car as a horse and buggy? Did she shout "git up" when she turned the key in the ignition? And then what? How did she snap out of it? Did she simply go home to sleep it off?

"Eddie's story makes no sense at all," I declared with a long sigh. "She wakes up in the morning, looks in the mirror and lo and behold it's Elizabeth Stewart! So she dresses up in her black taffeta and drives up, or down, or across to St. Francisville to harass locals and play living history on the plantation tours? I've heard of schizophrenic but never anything like this."

Toya slowly turned to look at me, the whites of her eyes as big and round as any eyes I've ever seen, and slowly grinned as if to say "you got that right" while Johnny gave me a playful slap on the thigh.

"Heh heh heh," he sniggered. "You sure got your work cut out for you, Mister Howard."

We stopped at the Piggly Wiggly in St. Francisville to pick up a few supplies, Johnnie's half-gallon of Beam and a few bottles of red, then continued to roll up Highway 61, headlights slicing through the heavy, cool mist, only now and then passing a solo roadside business, curio shop or Baptist church. The Bible thumpers, it seemed, had monopolized the billboards:

"The LORD is close to the brokenhearted." Psalm 34:18

"I have loved you with an everlasting love." Jeremiah 31:3

"Come to me, all you who are weary and burdened, and I will give you rest." Matthew 11:28

"Cast your cares on the Lord and he will sustain you." Psalm 55:22 NIV

These were all swell ideas: who could argue with everlasting love, rest, and sustenance? Still it had never been clear to me how to go about getting these things, other than perhaps promising to give the ten commandments my best shot, which shouldn't have been too difficult considering I grew up Catholic, went to Catechism, got confirmed, went to confession, ate Jesus and drank his blood. I knew venial sin, mortal sin, the seven deadly sins – for a long time "sin" was practically my middle name. I felt like I didn't have the energy to sin anymore, though I certainly thought about it a lot.

But right then, sitting between folks whose ancestors I assumed had been owned by my ancestors – owned, like cattle or goats or horses – I felt an overwhelming guilt, remorse and embarrassment. Why should these two have any concern whatsoever about my complications with my sister, other than a desire to get a troublemaker off the streets of St. Francisville? Especially considering Sisi's claim that our old man had fathered hordes of illegitimate children right along this stretch of highway. It seemed to me that I probably didn't qualify for everlasting love, rest, and sustenance, especially considering the "sins of the fathers" clause.

"We're almost home," Toya sang as she made a right turn off of Highway 61 onto a narrow two-lane blacktop. The almost invisible burg of Laurel Hill, once a thriving town bigger than St. Francisville, was just 2 miles ahead and the turnoff to Briarwood just short of it, but there was not a single streetlight, house light, firefly light, star light or anything besides the Ford's headlights shooting their beams into the impenetrably dark, dense broad-leafed shrubs and the trunks of a dozen different hardwoods.

"Where do you folks live?" I asked as Toya pulled the Ford around the circular drive up to the broad brick steps of the old house.

"Oh, we're not far from here. Daddy's little house is just right over there next to the abandoned stables," she said, pointing into the black nothingness where a single light shone above a plain wooden doorway.

"Yep," Johnny said, slowly sliding off the bench seat to the gravel driveway. "Lived there near 75 years." I guessed that this would have made him about 90 years old, just five years older than my father.

"And how about you? Where do you live?" I asked, immediately regretting the question, thinking it might be too forward.

"Oh, we're not far from here. Just the other side of 61 on Sligo Road. Just a little country place. I teach math down at the high school in St. Francisville."

"Really? I taught English and coached basketball for thirty years," I said, leaving out the golf because...because...I don't know why, I just left it out.

"I know," she said, laughing. Somebody, it appeared, had established contact with the northern clan of Browns and was keeping the southern posse up to date. Odd, I thought.

When Johnny flipped the lights on in the central hall I was immediately awestruck by the vast expanse of space between the polished oak floors and the high ceiling, and the huge portraits and landscapes that bedecked the walls. Though I knew from my pervious visit that Briarwood was not a classic baroque mansion in the columned tradition of Rosedown, Wakefield, The Myrtles and all the others on the Plantation tour – Briarwood was more of a bungalow, by comparison – still, I felt as if I had walked into a museum. Then the smell hit me: fingernail dirt, cut with Lemon Pledge and seasoned with old hay. I swooned.

Johnny told me he would be around in the morning to show me the lay of the land and so forth, and offered to take me over to my inherited property, but I politely declined his invitation. I had to get down to St. Francisville and file a missing persons report that I hoped would get an official manhunt under way. Then I wanted to poke my head into Stephen Hart's office, our Louisiana family attorney, and either set up a subsequent meeting or sit down right then and sort through the various options I had to liquidate my portion of the property and probably Sisi's piece as well, considering she might need to be declared incompetent to deal with legal issues.

As I finally hit the hay – the last time I had been to Briarwood the mattresses were literally stuffed with hay – I had the feeling that the forthcoming proceedings would all be handled with reason and good will, and that once Sisi was stabilized and back on her meds I could go in peace within a day or two.

Nothing could have been further from the truth.

21 Sibling Forgery

The pictures that I had of my sister, all of them on my phone from better times before she took off on her backpacking expedition with Mr. Doo Rag, were nothing like the way she looked when she escaped the hospital. Based on the description I'd given the state police in St. Francisville the following morning, they decided to have their courtroom artist draw a composite sketch, one in the beanie and another in a wig and bonnet circa early 19th century. Then it went out on the missing persons wire statewide and I just had to sit and wait, unless she showed up for one of her infamous performances at a local plantation tour.

After the 3-hour morning marathon at the state police office, which was conveniently situated right next to the high school and had a horrifically wrecked automobile displayed like a sculpture on the front lawn – as a reminder, I'm told, for kids that drink and drive – I motored Toya's Chevy over to the St. Francisville Courthouse where the attorney's offices seem to have had the old building under siege – all four blocks surrounding the building were quaint Victorian law offices, and one of them was Stephen Hart's.

When I made contact with Hart's office the receptionist was so happy to learn that I was in town I thought she might put on a state reception. I had never met the woman, of course, but I got the idea that having a Howard Brown in town was cause to celebrate, which was far better than the lynch mob I had expected based on my father's escapades.

Around noon the sky started to drop and the air grew thicker: a storm buildup was underway, though it wasn't expected to explode until the next day. Before I crossed over to Hart's, I took a short walk around the courthouse – literally around the outside walls of the old pre-civil war building – to see the Union cannonball that was supposed to be lodged in the bricks on the northwest side. According to the history books, St. Francisville fell without a fight shortly after the Union took New Orleans and went upriver, but I guess there was a skirmish of some sort and a cannonball made it all the way from the Mississippi to the courthouse wall. But I couldn't find the goddamn thing, though there was a marble block in one corner of the building, about 5 feet up. That's all. No commemorative plaque. I wondered if a move was afoot to rewrite the history of the South.

The thought stuck in my craw as I crossed the street to Hart's office: *was it now politically correct to wipe out history's big fuck-ups? Are Southerners embarrassed to admit that certain mistakes happened? Where is that goddamn cannonball? Did somebody decide that it was uncool to show that this country was once at war with itself, and that St. Francisville was on the wrong side of the fight?*

"Howard! Look at you! Hell and I thought I was a big fella! You're a spittin' image of...well, gee, come here and let me get a closer look. Hell, it ain't your daddy. Maybe your grandpa, yes that's it. He wasn't a giant like you, but you have some of his features: the curly hair – was it blond at some point? – that big schnozz and the fuzzy eyebrows, the eyes – hazel, aren't they? The natural frown. Damn. I'm sorry, Howard. He was one fearsome fuck up."

Stephen Hart was a very large man, pink as a carnation with a shock of silver gossamer thread atop his eat-a-peach head and jowls that would make a bulldog jealous. I took one of his thick freckled paws and had a seat in a chair that was relatively puny compared to the grandiose throne behind his desk. Had he been in any sort of good physical condition he might have been considered imposing, as I am imposing, but there was an old-man softness about him, as if he were made of watermelon jelly, that made his presence almost porcine, like a giant pink cartoon pig. I figured he must be 80, at least. And still practicing law.

"First, let me express my condolences for y'all's daddy. I must say he was one of the most genteel and professional men I've ever met. And that laugh of his; I'll never forget that laugh!"

Anybody who has had the good fortune of hearing my father laugh says the same thing: it was truly unforgettable. My friends would often imitate Hal Brown's laugh, especially after several joints and a six-pack, because it was just that kind of laugh that would make everybody else in the room laugh even if they didn't find the joke or whatever might have been said the least bit funny. When I really think about it, though, it wasn't the laugh itself that was so oddly unique, but the revving up, like a motor that takes a long time to catch: hrmmm, hrrrrmmm, mmmrrrmmm...down in the deepest recesses of his larynx, like a very long grunt, slowly rising up in pitch as it moved up his throat and then HA HA HA: big guttural blasts that might knock a person over. Sometimes the laugh would never make it up and out, but instead would die back down into the depths from whence it came, which had a very unsettling effect on people. Is he going to laugh? Is he going to say something? Is he going to throw up? Yes, anybody that heard that laugh wasn't bound to forget it any time soon.

We spent a few minutes talking about my family; how my mom's Alzheimer's had basically killed her twice, such that the woman that died was not really the person I thought of as my mother. I described my father's subsequent demise, which seemed like it lasted for years but all told was only 18 months, starting with the broken hip, the rehab, the dysphasia, the pneumonia, the aortic dissection, and finally the congestive heart failure that put him under. I even described the episode with the golf balls and the putter, which Hart took very seriously, nodding his jowly head slowly and pulling on his fuzzy earlobes. I intermittently looked around his small office, noticing that the original panes were still in the windows, as they were in the parlor of the plantation; the glass was so wavy and bubbly in some places that the outdoors looked twisted and distorted. Aside from that, and a portrait of Daniel Webster on the wall, the room was solid bookshelves, overflowing with volumes and volumes of law texts, some of them very old. I have been in a few law offices and had seen pretty much the same thing, even in the high-rise fancy firms; all just for appearance, I'm sure of that. I don't think I've ever seen an attorney actually open one of those books, or even take one down from the shelf.

When I told Hart about the effect my sister's disappearance had on the old man I could see him getting nervous; even in the icebox air conditioning sweat began to bead across his forehead and in the silver threads above. Finally, after hearing the whole story without a single word, he clapped his big mitts down on his desk and said: "Son, we have a problem."

He turned around in his swivel throne and grabbed a couple of thick manila folders labeled in fine cursive "Brown," and slapped them down on the desk before him.

"Howard, I would like to describe the events of the last several weeks to you, and if you wouldn't mind holding onto your questions until I'm finished, I think you'll find everything to be quite clear." Then he buzzed his assistant, who was so close in the tiny office adjacent to Hart's that she couldn't help hear our conversation, and said, "Hey darlin' could y'all get us a couple Cokes? Whaddya like Howard? Diet? Regular? I like this new Uno – no calories, which as you can see I hardly need."

After "darlin'" had brought in the drinks – I thought I might try a regular Coke, which I honestly couldn't remember drinking in the last thirty years – Hart began:

"Howard, I know part of y'all's intention comin' down here was to sell off that little piece o' property your daddy willed to you and your sister. Well, son, I hate to tell you this, but your sister already sold it."

Upon hearing this I actually surprised myself: I didn't jump up and pound my chest or curse her and the world and everybody upon it, nor did that familiar feeling of being trapped in firefight overtake me. Instead, I raised my eyebrows and looked over the rims of my glasses, nodding, wondering how somebody who sometimes believes she is an antebellum princess could possibly devise such fraud. She would have had to forge signatures, convince the buyers that I was on board, provide the old man's death certificate...I didn't think she was in any condition to manage such a task on her own.

"Okay, Mr. Hart, but..." I started, but he stopped me, wagging his Jimmy Dean pork sausage index finger.

"Ah, ah, ah, Howard. Just hold on."

"Okay, okay, but I don't see how..."

"You'll see. I promise."

He paused, shuffled a few papers, then looked up and fixed me in a benevolent, almost father-like gaze with his soft baby blue eyes, as if he could tell just by the way I carried myself around that this latest bit of news might unravel my fragile brain. "Okay, before I go on, I want you to know that there are ways to remedy this situation, hopefully without a lawsuit. So please don't despair. Unnerstand?"

I told him I would try to keep my chin up and he smiled, again in that fatherly way as if he knew I felt like a naked child lost in the woods.

"Now, here's what's transpired in the last several weeks. On Oct. 25th I received an email from your sister informing me that your daddy had passed and she had been instructed to sell the property, and that you were in agreement."

I was tempted to open the manila folder that sat before me, for I was sure the email was printed out and sitting in that pile, but he put his meaty paw on the stack and continued.

"We'll go through all of this later. I want you to get the lay of the land, unnerstand?"

I took a sip of Coke, which was over rocks in a crystal cocktail glass, and my cheeks felt like they might explode. The stuff was pure sugar, as far as I could tell, and my mouth was so unaccustomed to such sweetness that my tongue just about fell out of my mouth.

"You okay? Good. Okay. Now. I told your sister that in order to execute anything related to your daddy's estate, she would have to provide a death certificate. Which she did, first as an attachment dated Oct. 26, and Fed-exed the following day."

"Okay, hold on," I cried, getting up out of my chair and nearly knocking over the Coke. "That death certificate is a forgery. My father died on Oct. 31. I have the official death certificate right here."

I zipped open my backpack, pulled out my old leatherette, extracted the death certificate and laid it on his desk. "Cost me 200 bucks for five copies."

Then it was the lawyer's turn to be shocked, and I almost felt good about it despite the big man's overall genteel likeableness, for he was a lawyer after all, just like my father. And just like Eddie Sublette.

He scanned the real death certificate, patting his forehead down with a white handkerchief, his face as pink as an overripe watermelon. Then he opened one of the manila folders, extracted the forged death certificate, compared them, then looked up at me and said "Why? I mean why would your sister want to predate the death certificate? And why didn't she just sell her half of the property and leave your half alone? It makes no sense whatsoever."

"What my sister is doing, Mr. Hart, is trying to make sure that my wife, Sandy, who she's hated from the moment they first met, gets as little benefit from my father's estate as possible. I'm just an innocent bystander who happens to get reamed in the process."

The big man leaned back in his cherry wood wingback swivel chair with a dramatic exhalation as the furniture squeaked in protest. "Ahhhh. In-laws. I would probably be out of business if it weren't for good old in-law feuds."

He laid the death certificates on his desk so I could compare them, and besides the date they were identical. Even the excellent forgery of my signature.

"I mean…really, Mr. Hart, think about it. You've heard about her latest antics around St. Francisville, right?"

"You mean the little antebellum act she's supposedly putting on? Yes. And it's entirely inconsistent with what we're seeing here. Don't you agree?"

I sighed and looked up at the crystal chandelier hanging from the ceiling, the light refracting and reflecting so that the actual source could have been coming from any one of the crystals. "My sister is like this, Steve," I said, gesturing to the chandelier. "She lives in her own house of mirrors. Not only is she bi-polar, be she's showing signs of paranoid schizophrenia as well, at least if her Elizabeth Stewart charades are genuine. But in this case she feels that she's been emotionally and financially short-changed by the old man in favor of his daughter-in-law. Why, right after his aortic dissection surgery, she changed the password on his bank account and started funneling money out in $5000 hunks. Fortunately we caught her before it went too far."

"Did she pay it back?"

"No."

Then we were both silent, listening to the ice cubes melt and tinkle against the glass. I sighed again and looked at Hart, who appeared genuinely confused and a little lost, having leaned forward to prop both elbows on the desk and rest his jowly chin in his chubby mitts.

"You said that the property had been sold, right?" I finally asked him.

"That's right. All 100 acres." He showed me the bill of sale. There, next to Sisi's chicken scratch was my signature, as genuine as if I had signed it right then and there, and next to mine where I expected to see Eddie's signature, or Boon Percy's, there was this: Laurel Hill Energy Ventures, LLC.

"What's Laurel Hill Energy Ventures, Steve?"

"Oh, it's just a group of guys, investors, who are buyin' up property, leasin' property and so forth to get the mineral rights. The Tuscaloosa Marine Shale has been very productive in St. Helena Parish just south of here, so these firms are out snatchin' up land like crazy, then, if there's shale underneath – and they say it's about 11,000 feet down – they lease the land to the big oil companies to extract the natural gas. "

"You mean the oil company comes in and builds a well on the land?"

"Oh no, that's pretty unlikely. They go in horizontally from a central well. The landowner generally sees no change to the property."

This all sounded very familiar, though it hadn't occurred to me until then; it was the only reason my father held onto the land in the first place, hoping to strike it rich. I was aghast.

"And my sister, in all her profound economic wisdom, decided to sell. Why the fuck – pardon my French – I mean, if she wanted to do something behind my back, why wouldn't she just lease the mineral rights? Were you advising her on this deal?"

I could see Hart's little gossamer threads prickle on the top of his head – I guess my tone was a little accusatory but I was by then so beside myself I could barely breathe. All my various surgeries – the rotator cuff, the spinal fusion, the broken ankle, the nerve pain – every cut of the knife was simultaneously dialed up to a raging ten while the familiar sweat started squirting out the pores on the back of my neck. Then my brain shut down except for one nugget of overarching awareness: it was time for my meds. So

I shook out my pills, adding an extra oxy for good measure, and poured 'em down, but the Coke was far too fizzy for pill taking. I started to choke and cough so violently Hart was forced to get his massive girth up and out of his swivel throne, squeeze around his desk and swat me on the back. But the pills made it down to their destination, which was at the moment the only thing that mattered.

"Jesus, Howard. I told you we would be able to work this thing out, and we will, so don't up and die on me." We chuckled, him louder than I perhaps in hopes that I would forgive him this egregious error. At the very least he should have called me to confirm that I was in agreement with the deal, which made me very suspicious about this little club of investors that were buying up land and leasing it back to the big oil companies. But, since the sale was a fraud I should've been able to return whatever cash Sisi had made off with and get the land back.

"So did Sisi get a good price?" I asked. Just then the grandfather clock in the reception area chimed twice and Hart heaved himself up, handing me one of the manila folders.

"She actually came to the table with a number, which the Laurel Hill Energy Group agreed to immediately, since it was only about a third of what the land was actually worth."

"Oh good God, Steve!" I snatched the folder from his chubby mitt, and he left his hand there, motionless in the air, before slowly lowering it down, indicating that he would have little patience with any further impolite behavior, or at least that's how I read it. He lowered his chin – now three chins – and stared at me with his baby blue eyes over the rims of his readers and under his thick silver brows, his jaw set and his lips pursed.

"Son, I hope you're able to calm down and proceed in a rational, professional manner, like your daddy would have done. Your sister is going to be in serious trouble with the law for forging those documents."

I thought about this for a moment. *Did I really want to get my only sister thrown in the klink?* So I asked Hart: "Do you think the police will put a warrant out there for her arrest?"

"If we file charges, yes. But I wouldn't recommend that. Not yet. I always think it's better to fly under the legal radar and try and work things out in a gentlemanly way, first. Most little snafus like this can be fixed over lunch round these parts."

The door opened and "darlin'" announced that the attorney's next appointment was waiting.

.

Shaking hands I said, "Okay counselor, I'll follow your lead," and walked out under the bruised sky into the sultry, sticky afternoon, feeling like that Union cannonball fired from the Mississippi had landed smack dab on my head.

22 Camille's Ghost

That afternoon I felt like I was coming down with the flu. My gut, which had always been where I stored my chronic anxiety and lately, my father, was in revolt against Southern cuisine. After the meeting with Stephen I had a fried oyster Po' Boy, sweet potato fries, sweet tea, cornbread and a couple of fried dill pickles to top it off. I was sure it was the pickles that did it. Or the Coke. After several hours in and out of the can I finally curled up around 8:30 p. m., empty and exhausted, and slept.

I woke up at 4:30 a.m., my blood boiling with fever and my troubles demanding attention. I couldn't fall back to sleep; the noise in my head was too loud, too cacophonous, too insistent to allow me to slip back into the unreality of dreams. Even a nightmare would've been preferable to the banter in my brain. Asking the eternal "how could Sisi do such a thing" was as pointless as it ever was. Her reasoning, or lack thereof, was so disconnected from rational thought, so inscrutable in its twisted logic, that there was no point in even attempting to understand it.

It pained me deeply to think that Sandy was, once again, right on all counts, and I wondered if I should tell her about this latest development. It would probably push her right out the door for good. Whether Sisi intended to hurt me, or simply never considered my existence, was beside the point. If Sandy would have me back, and my son, bless his heart, took his typical "everything happens for a reason" stance, maybe we could sell off what we had left and make enough to move to Ecuador, or Costa Rica. Someplace where I could divorce the very idea of having ever had family; move forward, the three of us – oh and Elke, too – and never look back.

I finally dozed off with that thought in mind – the thought of trading our house for an Airstream RV and hitting the great American road. And the Mexican road, the Central and South American roads all the way down to Tierra Del Fuego, where we would take an icebreaker to Antarctica and live in an igloo until they started selling real estate on Mars.

I awoke to the sound of Johnny's ATV. Like angels, or perhaps medics, Johnny and Bessie brought me a basket of fresh hushpuppies, scrambled eggs with Andouille sausage, and some kind of yogurt/granola parfait.

"What's this?" I asked.

"This here is a California breakfast, accordin' to the Internet," Bessie explained. She took my breakfast into the kitchen and served it up, smiling and jiving like it was the most fun she'd ever had, serving yet another member of the extended family of Browns, Sublettes, Percys, Bowmans and all their uncles, aunts, cousins once, twice, three times removed all the way back to William the Conqueror. Still, as good-natured as she was, it made me uncomfortable. Surly and resentful would have made more sense.

"Okay, Mister Howard," Johnny said. "Have a nice quiet breakfast and I'll be back in a little bit to take you on a tour of the property."

After breakfast I felt somewhat restored; still feverish but sort of revved up as a result. So I had a closer look through the restored plantation house. It was a simple home, just an old English farmhouse, really; nothing like the grand Greek Revival plantations with their columns and dormers and such. Later, I learned that the area south of the state Mississippi line and east of the Big Muddy, all the way down to New Orleans, was once considered West Florida, which was the property of the British Empire, along with Canada, as the result of the Treaty of Paris and the conclusion of the French and Indian wars in 1763. Many settlers from the British Isles arrived, including Alexander Stewart, our Scottish patriarch who arrived at Thompson's Creek near St. Francisville in the mid-1770s. After the American Revolution and the departure of the Brits from Florida and West Florida, the Spanish took it over again. So Alexander Stewart received his first land grant from the Spanish in 1787, which really doesn't mean much except that the Cajun Creole coonass business that everybody associates with Louisiana doesn't apply as much to West Feliciana and the other parishes south and east of the Mississippi.

Briarwood was a box, perfectly symmetrical from the two beds of violet petunias astride the white picket gate, to the giant century-old camellia bushes bursting with crimson flowers on either side of the wide stairway up to the covered front porch. The interior floor plan differed little from the larger plantation homes: a wide central hallway extended from the front door and out the back, allowing the sultry and dense air to breeze through. Unlike the other plantation homes, the stairway went up at the back of the hall rather than the front, where it led to a landing facing the rear of the house. Also unlike the larger plantation homes, there was no separate stairway for the servants. So the main stairway had been reversed so that it would be more proximate to the kitchen, which was originally in a separate building behind the main house.

On either side of the wide central hall were the main rooms: the parlor and the dining room on the left; the master bedroom and study on the right, each with dormant fireplaces except for the parlor. The back porch has been enclosed as a sun and reading room. Since the place had become a weekend retreat for the Sublette family, more or less, it was done up the way Eddie's mother, May, felt most proper, and aside from the kitchen and the bathroom, it followed the fashion of the time when it was built: 1832. Most of the furniture were reproductions, but they looked as if they were installed in 1832 and hadn't been moved since. Especially the mahogany wingbacks with the ancient needlepoint, the marble vanity that was identical to one from 156 Woodland, and the little stepstools required to climb into the beds which were, like the four-poster in my parent's master bedroom, at least four feet off the ground. I went outside and waited for Johnny in one of the teak rockers, pondering why folks felt the need to have their beds so high.

"Keep the snakes out," Johnny told me.

The air, most always ponderous, was cool and thick with mist, but not cool enough to keep the sweat from beading up round the back of my neck. "We may see a little sunshine this afternoon," Johnny said when he returned. "It's like that in the fall down here. Always cool and grey in the mornin' but by n' by a little sun might shine. We're supposed to get a thunderstorm, or maybe a hurricane, but you never know. Mother nature can be mighty fickle in the fall."

He had his beautiful brown cable-knit sweater on over denim overalls and a red and black-checkered hunter's cap with earflaps pushed out by his unusually large, fuzzy, pink-rimmed old man ears. His heavy black plastic framed glasses magnified his big brown eyes, so dark the pupils were indistinguishable and the lids so heavy it looked like he either just woke up or was about to fall asleep. The wrinkles on his chin were so deep as to be unshaveable; white stubble grew like willows in a desert seep. But when he smiled it was like the sun had burst through the clouds; he wore his oversized titanium white dentures like a medal of honor, showing them off every chance he got, even when he was relaying bad news, which I learned soon enough.

We bounced up the single lane dirt farm road up past the house overlooking the good-sized pond – big enough for a power boat – where Johnny said he had caught the biggest large-mouth bass in the parish just last spring, so big he stuffed and mounted it over his fireplace in the cabin he had shared with his 89 year-old wife Bessie for nearly 60 years.

"It was so big I put my whole fist in the mouth all the way to its belly," he said as we pulled up to the edge of a shallow ravine choked with vines, bushes, small hardwoods and many good sized, mature trees.

"This here is your property," said Johnny, waving his hand over the ravine. "Yours and your sister's. 100 acres, 50 each."

I decided not to tell Johnny that the property belonged to Laurel Hill Energy Ventures, just to keep the noise level down. Still, looking through the quiet forest, golden leaves periodically dropping from the upper branches of the giant hardwoods, swaying slowly on their long descent to the forest floor, I felt a powerful emptiness and suffocating sense of loss. This had been mine. My hideaway, my private refuge, a place where I could have slowed down and let my wounds heal. Instead I was running around in circles, heaping insult upon injury, and letting the world toss me around like one of Mr. Booper's tennis balls in the waves. This was my land to do with as I pleased, but now I didn't own a single tree, a single branch, a single falling leaf, much less a million-dollar oil lease. I wanted to break down and cry.

Slowly the mist melted away in the grey flannel daylight, which now spread its weak November shadows across the pond and the dense woods beyond. We slowly headed back the way we came, Johnny twisting his head around and jabbering at me. "I didn't tell you this last night 'cuz I thought you might turn around and get back on the plane home," he started, "but some folks think your sister is a ghost".

"Oh come on, Johnny," I said, "she may be white, but she's not that white." Johnny laughed briefly, then continued, dead serious.

"Not all ghosts are white around here. Some folks are saying Elizabeth Stewart has come back for revenge." Johnny pulled the ATV under a huge magnolia and we sat down in the shade with our backs up against the trunk. I felt a grumble across my gut and suggested we go make some lunch.

"Okay, but first you need to understand something." Johnny said. "You know that big old plantation house down near St. Francisville, the Myrtles?"

"I've heard of it," I said.

"That's all? You just heard of it? Your great great grandmother lived there, Howard!" Johnny cried, dumbfounded. I explained that I didn't know much about Louisiana, or my ancestors, but was hoping to find out a few things.

"Well, we'de best get us some lunch. This might take a while."

We headed back to Johnny's cabin: rough-hewn timber with the traditional chinking of clay and straw still visible in large portions of the outer walls, reinforced with cement in some parts. The front door opened directly into the main room, and from what I could tell all of the furniture was handmade. The front room had a dining area on one side and a living room on the other with a big woodstove in between, an open kitchen beyond the dining room and a bedroom walled off behind the living room. The floors were cedar like the main house but remained unfinished, and the walls were rough-hewn logs like the outside, though the chinking inside was all cement.

It was cool and dry in the cabin, with the odor of cedar mixed into the powerful scent of southern cuisine. Bessie had made up a simple lunch of cornbread, crawfish etouffee and spicy greens. The flavors exploded like a three-ring circus across my entire body, and though I was a little worried about how my sensitive digestive system might react to this incursion of foreign flavors, especially after the gastric distress of the previous evening, I wasn't about to take a pass.

After eating we cracked a couple of cold beers and sat in the big rockers on Johnny's front porch, since the sun was out and the day was warming.

"Now I personally ain't never seen a ghost, but I seen what they done and sometimes it ain't pretty. Now, you listen good 'cuz what I'm gonna tell you might explain some of the things that are goin' on around here."

I hunkered down in the rocker and looked across the meadow to the pond that had taken on a café au lait color with the sun low in the autumn sky. I watched a flock of Mergansers slide in for a landing, and thought that I could sit on that porch watching duck landings and takeoffs all day, possibly for the rest of my life. But it was a very short-lived thought; my phone buzzed in my pocket and I thought for sure there had been a sister sighting or perhaps the state police had located her, but it was an automated message from the pharmacy in San Anselmo informing me that my prescription was ready. I felt like throwing the phone in the pond right then, though it was over 200 yards away.

"How much do you know about Ms. Elizabeth Stewart, your great-great granny? Do you know that she and her children were supposedly poisoned by a servant girl named Camille?"

"What?" I gasped, duck landings blasted from my brain.

"Yessir. I can't believe you ain't never heard this story. It's on the Internet, they say."

I told Johnny that I had no idea that the woman my sister was portraying in her schizophrenic episodes was poisoned. I had never heard of anybody in our family being poisoned.

Johnny stood up and started clawing through the pockets of his overalls, finally extracting an old pipe and a sack of tobacco, then sat down.

"Well, your great-great granny had a servant named Camille, and as the story goes Camille was a busybody, an eavesdropper, a real nosy kinda girl. One night Camille got caught with her ear up to a keyhole to the parlor, and when the master asked her what she was doing she said her ear had a bad itch and she was trying to scratch it on the doorknob. Well whoever heard of such a thing? So he took her out to the wood yard where they chop the logs for the fire, puts her head on the choppin' block and…whack…chops her ear off!"

Oh for fuck's sake, I was thinking, I should be conferring with a lawyer instead of drinkin' beer and listening to this old man tell ghost stories. But Hart asked for a couple of days, and I've got the posse keeping an eye out for Sisi, or Elizabeth Stewart, so…what else can I do?

So I didn't move a muscle. My internal English teacher was sucked into Johnny's story as if he were Edgar Allen Poe himself. There was also something so poignant about listening to what I assumed to be the grandson of a slave talk about these people, what I assumed to be his people, and the brutality they suffered. It almost sounded like he thought Camille got what she deserved.

"But that's just the start," Johnny continued, taking a long draw off his pipe, which I suspected was highly illegal contraband to Toya, but obviously not Bessie. She might have been having a chaw while she cleaned up in the kitchen.

"Poor Camille couldn't be a house servant anymore, with one ear, so they turned her out to the kitchens where the work is much harder. But she decided to make the best of it, you see, 'cuz she wanted to get her revenge. Or at least that's what most folks think. Other folks think she was trying to make herself into a hero and get her house servant job back. Anyways, she went out to the woods and picked a mess of oleander leaves, very very poisonous to people, you see? She took that oleander, makes a paste out of it and baked it into a cake, and serves it up after supper. Mrs. Elizabeth had some cake and so did her two older children, but not the baby 'cuz she already asleep in bed. And the master said he didn't want any cake. Well it wasn't long before the Mrs. and the children were terribly sick and who should come runnin' but the one-eared servant Camille, shoutin' that she has the antidote to the poison and everybody is going to be saved! So she gives the Mrs. and her children the antidote and nothing happened, so she gave them a little more, and still nothing happened until sure enough they were dead."

Johnny paused to have a smoke while I rolled my eyes and scratched my head. "What year is this?" I asked, either because Johnny didn't say or I couldn't remember.

"1820's, around then."

A flock of ringed-necks came in for a landing while the Mergansers took off, but they were just a sideshow.

"So what happened to Camille?"

"Oh the master fixed her good. They took her to the river, tied her up with bricks, took her out on a flatboat and dropped her in. Bye bye little miss green turban."

"And now she haunts the Myrtles plantation?"

"Yessir. Folks say they've seen a little girl in them old dresses wearing a green turban. But that's not why I'm tellin' you this story, Howard. Mrs. Elizabeth Stewart and her two poisoned chillens are down there too, livin' in a mirror. See folks then believed that they should get rid o' all their mirrors when somebody died in the house, but Master Brown was too sorry to remember all that, so the spirits of Mrs. Stewart and the children moved into this one big old mirror that's been there all this time. Lately, people have been sayin' that they've seen Mrs. Elizabeth in the mirror more and more, but that ain't all. Seems she's all over the Myrtles, botherin' the tourists and the guests, then disappearin' just like that."

"Well, my sister may be a very talented actor, but so far as I know she has not learned how to make herself literally disappear."

We sat in silence on the porch for a bit, listening to the creak of the rockers on the planks and the cacophonous fauna that, even in the cool autumn afternoon, still managed to chitter, chirp, quack and tweet voluminously. Inside I was cursing myself for getting mixed up in this strange, messy state of affairs. I could only hope we would get something squared away soon. With any luck, we would be home by Thanksgiving.

"Well, Johnny, I must admit after all that excitement I'm a little bushed. I think I'll go back and take a little siesta. I didn't get much sleep last night. "

"Well sir I think that's a fine idea. I hope you don't have any nightmares about one-eared servant girls. Let me give you a lift."

I told Johnny I would rather walk, since it wasn't even a quarter mile down the gravel road. When I got back to the plantation house I stretched out on the parlor room sofa, lightheaded with fever, feeling completely and utterly bamboozled, and fell asleep in an instant.

.

23 Sisi's Warning

I awoke in the dark, my skin crawling with an army of red ants, each of them nibbling at my flesh while my heart pounded like a pile driver at five alarms: I had slept through my dose. Panicked, I stood up and patted my jeans pockets where I usually kept my pillbox, but my pockets were empty. Thinking that I probably emptied them someplace before my nap, I raced into the kitchen, swerving like a drunk. When my still-tender shoulder collided with the doorframe I howled like a New Delhi street monkey, which got my vocal cords working: *Okay, okay, where the fuck? Where the fucking fuck did I put them? Fuck. Jesus. Fucking son of a bitch. Come on now, stop, think: what did you do before the nap? Where were you? Oh shit God please!*

There was no sign of the little red and white capsule-shaped pillbox in the kitchen, or in the downstairs bath. *I didn't go upstairs, they can't be upstairs.* I staggered back into the parlor and ripped the cushions off the sofa…nothing. Again I patted my pockets in deadly earnest and…ahh, there they were, in that little change pocket!

I shook out the methadone and a couple of extra oxys and popped them, almost choking on their chalky bitterness, then went to the kitchen to wash them down. Instantly I was relieved. Instantly the sweats, the shakes, the armies of nibbling red ants: gone. I wondered if the doctor prescribed a banana every six hours the effect would be the same: completely psychosomatic.

I realized then in my instant calm and pensive state, standing in the parlor where my ancestors drank bitters and nursed their gout, that my brain has been rewired by drugs. Or perhaps a long dormant transistor has been awakened and activated. But the much louder realization was that I was addicted to those pink and white pills. My internal English teacher could almost hear John Cheever's description of Ezekial Farragut, the incarcerated murderer and protagonist of *Falconer*: "Farragut was a drug addict, and felt that the consciousness of the opium eater was much broader, more vast and representative of the human condition than the consciousness of those that had never experienced addiction." *Broader consciousness?* I wondered. All I knew is that I needed the drugs as surely as I needed air to breathe and water to drink, human condition be damned. The little pillbox, for so long a necessity for the relief of real pain, had become as heavy as Frodo's ring.

When I stepped outside for a smoke there was a FedEx package from Sandy leaning against the front door that contained two pieces: a thick business-sized envelope from my sister, which I suspected might have something to do with the estate – perhaps she'd finally decided to inform me that she'd sold the land – and a plain, unmarked, eight by 10 manila envelope.

Back inside I got a fire going in the parlor, then sat down on a plush velvet antique wing-back chair and tore open the envelope from Sisi, expecting to see the bill of sale that Hart showed me in his office the day before, only to discover several pages of lined note paper covered in her frantic curlicue scrawl. I checked the postmark: New York NY, November third, two days after our father's Halloween trick. *What the fuck?* I knew she hadn't been to New York. I thought back to the last time I had actually seen her, bawling in the emergency room the day after the storm, a week before our the old man checked out. Had she gone to New York? Hadn't Eddie said he first spotted her in St. Francisville November first? Or was it Binx that spotted her? Wasn't she down here selling off my property? I quickly read the first few lines, trying to get my bearings.

Dear Big Brother,

Wow I'm sorry this got so fucked up for you. You seemed pretty angry when I picked up my voicemails this morning but I honestly don't know why. Just because Dad said he couldn't die without me and all that other bullshit doesn't mean that I have to be his little slave, which is the only reason he wanted me there anyway – so he could boss me around. Besides Sandy was there and Sandy has everything under control and Dad likes Sandy, plus Sandy doesn't care if she's bossed around.

Oh boy, here we go, I thought. *A rant for the ages.* Lamb Chop's "Song That Never Ends," immediately started rattling around in my head:

This is the song that never ends
It just goes on and on my friends
Some people started singing it not knowing what it was
and now they'll keep on singing it forever just because
this is the song that never ends… (and so on and so forth)

I was tempted to toss the whole scrawly mess into the fire but instead just flipped it onto the nearby sofa. I knew I would have to read it soon, just in case it contained any clues to her whereabouts.

I undid the metal clasp of the other manila envelope and extracted about thirty pages of photocopied typewritten double-spaced text, all of it blurry and slightly askew on the page, hinting that the copy was made in the early days of Xerox machines. The first page began with this single paragraph:

Foreword

For the past thirty-three years I have been an employee of the Standard Oil Company, during which time I have served in various capacities ranging from laborer to Vice-President of the Parent Co. and President of two of its subsidiaries.

These experiences are here related for the purpose of preventing if possible, another victim from under-going the same tortuous proceedings that I did.

In order that you may better understand my reactions to certain situations herein related, I wish to state briefly my background and early environment.

Excited, I quickly scanned through the thirty pages, and it didn't take long to deduce that the words were my paternal grandfather's: Howard Easton Brown, the man Stephen Hart described as a "fearsome fuck up."

"Aha!" I shouted aloud. Then I noticed a small handwritten note on the floor that must have come out of the manila envelope from Sandy.

Hi Howard,

I found this when I was at your parents' house straightening things up the day after you left. It was in your dad's closet, stuffed under a couple of cigar boxes all the way to the back on the top shelf. At first I wasn't going to read it but I changed my mind. It's kind of a sad story but very revealing about your grandfather. Did you know that he was accused of being "dangerously insane?"

The letter from your sister came to our San Anselmo house. I didn't open it but it's curious that it was postmarked in New York. Maybe that's where she really is and you can come home, though I don't know why your cousin Eddie would make up such a story.

I emailed you some pictures of a few items that have gone missing since we took inventory after your Mom died. Many of the antique sterling silver spoons from the collection are gone, as is the soup tureen, the sterling butter dish with the cow on top and two complete sets of silver, all worth a lot of money. Keep an eye out for them.

It turns out Linda and Willy are on the outs in a big way. Maybe even divorce. I think Linda thought having me around might help calm the situation, but I think I made it worse. It was too uncomfortable there so I'm back at home. Besides, the commute to school was over an hour from their house!

Tripp called. Sounds like he's got a great adventure planned. He said you'd be going to the fishing camp after you get Sisi "squared away," whatever that means. Good luck!

Sandy's words washed over me like a wave of warm sweet cream, or like the feeling you get after struggling to wake up from a nightmare to discover you're actually in your own bed, safe and sound, and the fear was all in your imagination. I had been hoping that her spasm would pass, and the tone of her note indicated that perhaps it was passing, as it has many times since the beginning of our relationship. Even so, her potential reaction to Sisi's attempted sale of our land – her land, too – was likely to send her spinning again.

My grandfather's memoir was very tempting, but in true Calvinistic tradition I'd been taught to "save the best for last." So I continued reading my sister's letter instead.

It might be different if it were her own father. If she knew half of what dad did, or if you knew, you wouldn't have lifted a finger for him. I was his slave, Howard. His slave!!! Everything he ever gave me was so that I would be the little golfing junior leaguer, the champion at the club, leader of the ladies auxiliary, member of the DAR. It was like nothing else mattered and if I didn't fit in with the plan he would just dangle more and better shit in front of me: the BMW, trips to the Del Monte Lodge so I could play with the pros at Pebble and Spyglass, credit cards, and all I had to do was act the part. And Mom just went along with it, even though she knew it was making me miserable, because she was so afraid of him. And it goes as far back as I can remember – he had it all planned out with Grandmother Brown. Their little girl was going to be an LPGA champion, and if she wasn't quite good enough for that the country club championship would do. Grandmother was pulling the strings like she pulled on my hair when she was blind from the glaucoma, yanking Dad around like a puppet because she knew his little secret, she knew he was fucking every local chick he could get his hands on down in Laurel Hill when he was recuperating from the polio. Hell if they were still slaves like Grandmother Brown pretended they were we would have a whole house full of milk-chocolate brothers and sisters. Just wait 'til they find out the old man croaked, they will be coming out of the woodwork looking for their fair share. You'll see, Howard. Why do you think Dad never wanted to go visit his cousins in Laurel Hill when we were kids? It's cuz he didn't want to meet up with his girlfriends, probably big mamas by then. I swear, Howard some half brother or sister is bound to show up. Even aunts, cousins, uncles – the entire line of Howard Browns has been cross breeding for generations – St. Francisville might as well change its name to Brownsville. If you had ever been there you would know. I know because I've been there and I can feel it just walking down the street. It's amazing they haven't turned Laurel Hill into a golf resort, seeing how obsessed our ancestors were with the stupid game.

Golf. Did you ever really think about how fucking crazy Dad was? I remember when he got so frustrated at the driving range because I couldn't change my grip the way he wanted me to change it – my hands just didn't go that way – so he goes yelling at Mom right in front of everybody on the range that she had to go give me a "girl" lesson and get me straightened out or else. We were both so embarrassed that finally that goofy pro –LeRoy – he came down and gave me a ½ hour free lesson right on the spot, just to get Dad to stop making a scene on the range, and I was hitting the ball great. But as soon as LeRoy left Dad was back at me, tellin' me and Mom that LeRoy was a greasy wop and didn't know shit about golf and next thing you know I can't even get the ball off the ground. Mom and I got so upset that we started crying and Dad just stormed off the driving range, straight to the purple Mustang in the parking lot and drove off in his golf shoes. Mom and I went to the pool which was a very bad idea because when Dad came back to see us at the pool and not the driving range he had another fit, ordered us to get dressed and go back to the driving range, but by then it was getting dark and time for Mom and Dad to hit the bar. So while I was instructed to practice my putting on the barely lit putting green Mom and Dad were having a few drinks with their friends on the patio, and next thing you know Dad is cheerful again. On the way home Dad, with his usual jumbo Dixie cup of draft beer nestled in his crotch, gets pulled over by the Fairfax cops. Turns out Dad knows the cop who is also a golfer and they start shooting the bull while I am freezing my junior nipples off in the back because I forgot to bring a sweater. The cop doesn't even ask Dad to pour out his beer and lets us go with a jolly guffaw, after Dad had peeled a hundred out of the roll in his money clip and slipped it to the cop, all right under our noses as if Mom and I were invisible. So now Dad is really cheery and decides we're going to Pinky's Pizza at 9:15 on a Sunday night. The guy that ran the joint then – Tony? – is closing up so Dad instructs Mom to go bang on the door and since he knows us he comes out. The pizza cooks are gone but he has a couple of cold ones that can be reheated at home, but Dad has to have Canadian bacon with pineapple, so he slips another hundred to Tony who slaps on his apron and fires up an oven, and they sit there drinking wine waiting for the pizza to cook while Mom and I curl up in a booth and go to sleep. When we get home Mom and I immediately go to bed leaving Dad to deal with the pizza. Dad goes to the bar, pours a scotch, sits down in his big easy chair and passes out. The next morning he doesn't say a single word the whole time I'm getting ready for school and he's getting ready for work, though the transistor in his bathroom is blasting away as always. When we go out to the car we find that it's covered in bits of pineapple, tomato sauce and torn up white cardboard box, along with the tracks of the family of raccoons that live down by the creek. Who gets to clean up the mess? Whose fault is it that the pizza didn't make it from the car to the house the night before? I don't know where you were Howard – college maybe, or summer camp. But as usual you weren't there for me.

You probably never heard about the abortion either, or maybe you did. Mom and Dad told me that if I ever told anyone, that if it ever got out, they would disown me; kick me out and leave me completely on my own. I can't believe I never told you. Maybe I was afraid you would have the same reaction, especially since the baby was mulatto and you're such a racist.

Hearing this accusation, I had to pause. Racism, as I understood it, meant that a person believed they were superior because of their race. At that time in my life, I felt markedly inferior to just about every living thing on the planet, human and otherwise. But then I caught myself: *my sister had an abortion?* I think back upon that moment now as perhaps the first evidence of my shift in perspective; just a tiny glimmer of awakening. My sister was telling her story, and it wasn't about me. The shift in my point-of-view wouldn't last long, but at least it was a start. As for her accusation of racism, I didn't know. Perhaps her reasoning would be revealed, so I kept reading.

It was his baby and he really wanted to keep it. He wanted to get married and live in Berkeley, I was going to get my Masters and PhD and live the academic life while he played jazz. He was nuts about me. I'm sure you remember him. I think he even sat in with your band once or twice. Charles White. Chaz. That's what everybody called him. Jazzy Chaz. Obviously I tried to keep the whole relationship a secret. Obviously. I don't think I need to explain why. But there was no way I could keep the pregnancy a secret and I knew it would never work out. Not in a million years. So I went to Mom and told her that I was pregnant with Matt Benedict's kid, and that it was a one-night stand and Matt Benedict didn't even like me and she's all "you should force him to marry you!" But that's Mom, you know. Get pregnant by an upper class white guy and she's hearing wedding bells. Anyway I lied my way through the whole thing and poor Chaz was devastated. I haven't spoken to him since, and I would've had his baby and married him if it weren't for my bigoted parents. They would have disowned all of us and we would've been out there on Telegraph Ave., Chaz playing his trumpet for spare change. Luckily the truth never got out. You've never heard about it, have you? Now you're the only one who knows. If you tell Sandy trust me you will never hear from me again.

Did you ever hear about Dad's suicide attempts? Of course not. You remember the supposed gall bladder operation when you were in college, when Dad ended up recuperating at home for about six weeks and grew his little Abe Lincoln beard and had those stupid pictures taken of him with the shotgun and his pipe looking like some sort of backwoods hick? That was no gall bladder operation. One night I woke up as usual thinking about having a little snack – ice cream, cookies, donuts, cake – my nocturnal appetite was the opposite of my daytime diet, where I ate like a rabbit all those years. Well, this was right at the height of my bulimic period where I would wake up and pig out on sweets, then throw it all up and go back to bed. Before Mom figured out what was going on and started locking me into my bedroom. Had I been locked in that night Dad would have been dead 35 years ago. I got up and as I stopped in front of the kitchen slider I heard a car running. So I go looking out the back door at the carport and there's Dad sitting in his Buick, a garden hose taped onto the exhaust pipe and run through a crack in the wing window. I bust into the car, turn off the engine and start shaking Dad but he's not responding. I go wake up Mom, which was like waking up a retarded person or something she's completely helpless so I call the Sherriff – no 911 in those days – and in a little bit we had fire engines, cops, and ambulances all crammed into the driveway. They drag Dad out of the car, still unconscious and barely breathing and they give him mouth to mouth. When he comes to and saw me staring down at him he said, "Get out of here." That's what I got for saving his life, Howard. "Get out of here." He refuses to go to the hospital, but these cops aren't letting him off the hook – attempted suicide is a crime, right? So he goes and from the hospital they ship him to a rehab. Mom and I have already been sworn to secrecy so there's nothing we can say. I ask Mom why he did it and do you know what she said? His golf game had gone down the tubes and he said… he said, "I give up." That was it, Howard. That was it. "I give up. I can't make a putt." Fuck if that isn't totally fucked up I don't know what is, Howard. Can't make a fucking putt so you gas yourself in your fucking Buick. Jesus.

The more I think about you, Howard, the more I realize that you and I didn't really have the same parents at all. We were under the same roof but did not live in the same home. Maybe now you can understand why I had to get away from the whole scene. The whole death Dad's way schtick. He's always got to be the center of attention and I just couldn't take it anymore. Dad needs this, gotta get Dad that, etc. etc. and never once did he pause and contemplate his end-of-life issues, never did he want to talk about all the bullshit he created and bad sins he's committed and now he's going to carry it around with him in the spirit world and try and pawn it off on whoever is nearby. From the moment he died, 5:00 PM on Friday, right? I know because as soon as he did I felt this pressure like someone leaning on me or sitting on me, like a parasite trying to attach onto me. It was nothing of course, but I swear I felt it. I'm glad I wasn't there because if I was I would have been possessed like you probably are now. He's a bad person, Howard. A devil.

I know you think I'm going crazy but you don't know what's really going on anyway so you can't be the judge. A long time ago when I was having those eating problems I went to a shrink who said I had borderline personality order and was bipolar too. Mom and Dad didn't want to share anything with you, figuring you would go blab it around to all your friends and Sandy and all her friends. And I'm fine as long as I'm taking my meds but I don't like the meds. They make me feel dull and sleepy, like my brain is just a block of wood. I can't feel anything. Anyway that's why you think I'm crazy, and I'm sure you'll go rush over and tell Sandy and the next thing you know it will be all over town but I don't give a shit about Sandy. She's a control freak, a busybody, and a two-faced bitch. I've tried to be her friend but she just hates me. She hates me, that's all there is to it. I wanted to help with Dad, I really did, Howard, but SANDY WOULDN'T LET ME!! Now you've gotta get rid of his stuff and sell the house and I'm sure Sandy has it all under control. Good. Keep all his shit, I don't want any of it. I took what I needed when Mom died, another big deal for Sandy who didn't have a right to any of Mom's stuff anyway. If you want to have a relationship with your sister you should get rid of her. She's got you PUSSYWHIPPED!!! And you can't even see it. Too bad for poor Howard. And it's always been "poor Howard" in our family, hasn't it? Howard's sad, Howard's depressed, Howard doesn't have any friends, Howard had a bad golf game, be nice to Howard he's not feeling well. GOD! NEVER ONCE did anybody give a shit about me and how I might be feeling. It was more like Sisi's a pig so let's lock her in her room at night so she doesn't clean out the refrigerator, Sisi got straight As again big whoop! Sisi got into Stanford, Sisi's got a scholarship to grad school, Sisi can't handle it so let's send her to an institution! I get so mad I want to strangle something. Oh. I guess I already did. Ha! Don't you see, Howard? If I didn't do something bad Dad wouldn't have known I existed.

You don't see the good things either, Howard. All the things I've done for you in the past, lying about your drugs to Mom and Dad, standing up for you whenever you got drunk and in trouble, but you're so unbelievably selfish, just the way you were brought up, that it's all exactly what you expect. Not one thank you. Not one. Well, not anymore bucko. I'm outta here.

Okay, don't come looking for me. Please. I do love you, I really do. Maybe in a year or two we can be friends, when I get through this divorce and the kids are squared away and the estate is all settled and everything is calm, (and Sandy has had a lobotomy) we can be like brother and sister again. If you even want to.

Love,
Your crazy sister Elizabeth

Enraged, my head spinning, a gnawing pain deep in my gut, and my momentary awakening extinguished, I threw the pages of the letter into the air, scattering them around the parlor. I was tempted to tear it up into very small pieces and toss it into the fire, but stopped, thinking that it might prove that she had serious mental problems – evidence that might facilitate getting our property back – even if it was written prior to her adventures with luxury RVs and paranoid schizophrenia. So I picked up the pages, carefully folded them into threes and returned it to the envelope where she'd scrawled our

San Anselmo address, thinking that her scrawl alone might be enough to deem mental incompetence. Then I noticed that she'd drawn tiny hearts, each impaled by an arrow, along the edges of the envelope. I hung my head and prayed aloud: "God, help us. To do what, I don't know. But please, help us anyway."

24 Disturbance in Chakra Number Three

After breakfast with Eddie and a couple of my elderly agents at the Birdman Cafe I hung around downtown reading the papers on a park bench in front of the courthouse, hoping I might run into Stephen Hart so I could light a fire under his gargantuan posterior and get the proceedings moving. After a while I gave him a call, only to get "darlin's" voice mail informing me that he was fully booked that day – probably at The Bluffs golf club – and to leave a message. I told Hart that my sister was still at large and that I wanted to meet with him at the earliest opportunity to see what kind of case he planned to build to get my property back. Then a warm, sticky drizzle set in so I returned to Briarwood.

Grandfather Brown's 30-page memoir, which I read the previous evening over a grilled cheese, tomato soup, and a bottle of red had only created more questions, and the few answers it had provided were disturbing. It was the classic story of a neglected stepchild: young HB, as he was called, lost his own father, "Brownie" Brown, a sharpshooter with Stonewall Jackson's brigade, when he was only eight, to suspected suicide. His mother Harriet remarried army colonel Harry B. Cooper within two years, so they left the family compound in St. Francisville and young HB commenced to get bounced around from one relative or boarding school to the next until at the tender age of 14 he was enlisted in the Army. Eventually he became a bigwig with Standard Oil of Ohio, though not nearly as big a wig as he felt he deserved to be. It became clear that the "tortuous proceedings" he alluded to in his foreword were related to office politics, where he was ultimately accused of being "dangerously insane." His memoir ends with his arrival at Briarwood, to recuperate from what he claimed was the flu but sounded more like a nervous breakdown, perhaps related to a relapse of malaria, which he contracted while building an oil refinery in Tampico. The most disappointing aspects of the memoir are the brush-aside treatment of his marriage and his children and his involvement in The Great War. He died at age 57 in 1949. My father said he had a heart attack while trying to pull on his hunting boots.

Talk about bad chemicals. Mix the supposed suicide of my great-grandfather "Brownie" with his son Howard the fifth, together with my sister's various psychoses, my father's "red reds and blue blues," the alcoholic death of my maternal grandfather at 41, Mom's anorexia and Alzheimer's, my own roller-coaster emotions and…well, one might observe that my sister and I had been dealt a bad hand from a loaded deck.

After a shower I poured a glass of red, took my meds and parked my exhausted ass in a front porch rocker to breathe in the thick, damp autumn musk. Everything was so still, so quiet, so unperturbed that I wished I could pry open my soul hole and suck it all in until I was so full of peace and quiet I could barely zip myself up again. But my reverie was short-lived. Soon Johnny puttered up on his ATV with a cooler of victuals. "Hello, Mister Howard. Bessie thought you might want some of this shrimp gumbo, greens and cornbread for yo' supper. She just cooked it up all nice and fresh."

"Well I guess I don't have much choice but to eat it, do I?" I said jokingly and we had a good laugh. "Wanna join me for a drink? I would like to ask you a few questions."

Johnny and I went inside to mix up a couple of toddies, then returned to the front porch. He looked so shriveled in his overalls underneath that huge cardigan and oversized hunting cap, perched on the giant teak rocking chair – like a famous dancing California raisin – that I was tempted to take a bite out of him.

"Why do you think Eddie cooked up this ridiculous story about my sister posing as the ghost of Elizabeth Stewart just to get me down here. Seems a little…a little devious, don't you think?" Of course I wasn't sure that Eddie or his brother Binx "cooked up" a story to get me to come retrieve my sister, but I wanted to see if I could get Johnny to spill the beans, if there were any beans to spill.

"Well, I don't know what Mr. Eddie's thinkin' or what he has up his sleeve. He can be tricky. When he was younger he was more likely to tell a whopper than anybody I ever met in all my born days."

Eddie Sublette, for all his English West Floridian gentility, was starting to seem a bit like the Wizard of Oz. He even looked like a wiry version of the Wizard, though even more like the guy with the traveling magic show in Kansas: "Oscar Zoroaster Phadrig Isaac Norman Henkel Emmanuel Ambroise Diggs," aka O.Z.P.I.N.H.E.A.D. Eddie was no pinhead, but he might've been the "man behind the curtain." He certainly had been expertly avoiding attention, busy with this and that, always coming and going. If he swapped the duck pants for a green tuxedo and a turban, I might've asked him why it was taking so long for the great OZ to find my sister.

We sat in silence for a while, listening to the bullfrogs in the lake and the hypnotic drone of the Louisiana nightfall, as if the electricity from the coming storm was starting to buzz through the woods.

After Johnny left the darkness set in, followed by the first rumbles of distant thunder, ominous and creepy. In a spasm of fear I rushed through the house and turned on all the lights, even upstairs where I had yet to set foot. The upstairs bedrooms were just as warm and cozy as the rest of the house but I left the lights on anyway. I guzzled what was left of my toddy, poured another glass of red and called Sandy.

"Have you found her yet?" she asked immediately. It was so grounding just to hear her voice; we shared such a simple, down-home connection that in spite of my better judgment I found myself talking about the land and the possibility of the Tuscaloosa Marine Shale sleeping 11,000 feet below the rolling, snake-infested, swampy woods, leaving out the fact that at that moment it wasn't ours. But I would say anything to get her back.

"The chances of a discovery are probably a hundred to one, at least. The only reason the old man kept the property was because it cost him nothing, it was something he could pass on to us, and the land leaks oil in this part of the world, even if it hasn't started leaking at Briarwood."

Sandy laughed and, not surprisingly, read my mind: "We could park a big old doublewide down there, spiff it up with a white picket fence, a few yard ornaments and a windsock or two…"

"LSU flag, honey, plus the flag of the West Florida Republic, which lasted about 6 months…that's what everybody in St. Francisville is flying."

"No windsocks?" she said in mock disappointment.

"Oh, yeah. There are windsocks. Everybody has at least one of 'em."

"Good. So now you're thinking you would like to hold onto the land?" she asked, taking a bite of what I guessed was a rice cracker slathered with guacamole.

"Yeah, so long as you think we can live without the proceeds from a sale. If nothing happens in a year or two we can unload it, though I think you better have a look at it first. Really, you have to get a better look at this whole area. It's awfully nice, even if you can't go outside 60% of the time."

She hemmed and hawed a little, weighing whether she wanted to get into a future fantasy or stick with the immediate issues at hand. When I shared that the whole masquerade business looked very sketchy, and I really wasn't certain what to do except wait to hear from the police, or the posse, or the morgue, she suggested that I gather Tripp, come home and forget about it. There appeared to be no urgent need to sell the land (which of course she didn't know had already been sold), Tripp had been having a fine time according to the posts his companions had made on Facebook, so why not get the hell out and let Sisi's second cousins deal with whatever the hell she's doing to alarm the genteel Southerners.

Finally, after a little more hemming and hawing Sandy admitted that her reaction to my decision to come down here in the first place was embarrassingly childish. She admitted that the very next day she felt so bad she almost got on an airplane to follow me, but when she considered that being with me down here would involve a Sisi confrontation she decided to sit tight and hope it would be over soon.

"We have a new temporary roommate," Sandy said, switching gears. "Elke's little three-day adventure in Nevada City turned out to be a disaster – her friend's boyfriend is a heroin addict and tried to steal just about everything Elke brought with her – so she's keeping me company until y'all get back."

"Did you just say 'y'all'?" I asked, and we both started laughing so hard tears came to my eyes. When we finally stopped I noticed that the thunder was getting louder.

She asked about the contents of Sisi's letter, figuring that my sister probably lambasted her and blamed her for just about everything that could possibly be wrong with our relationship, which I neither confirmed nor denied. There was no point in sharing the ugly details of a Sisi letter with Sandy or anybody else for that matter, since I was convinced that very little of what she said was true.

"Oh Howard," she said, as if remembering something that she had intended to remember and just now realized that she forgot, "I told you the family silver was missing, right? And all those other items I wrote you about? I've been tearing through the house as you know, trying to get it cleared out for the painters and carpet guys, and am discovering all sorts of things missing. All the turquoise jewelry that your grandmother insisted be split equally between Sisi and me – gone."

Suddenly the lights flickered and the bearded live oaks outside were illuminated in a white flash – a veritable celestial firecracker –followed by that nervous silence that supposedly tells you how far away you are from getting electrocuted, so I counted: one, two, three, four, five BOOM! – just like a cannon shot from a Union flatboat on the Mississippi. It was so loud it rattled the pictures on the walls.

"Did you hear that?" I asked Sandy.

"Hear what?"

"The thunder! First crack of what's supposed to be a ripping thunderstorm."

Then, as if God had kicked over a watering can, the rain started. For some reason Sandy decided it was a perfect time to pour nasty reality on our fledgling recovery, just as the storm moved in.

"Howard, I've been trying to decide whether to send this to you or tell you about it, but…I guess I just did decide, didn't I? Your sister is trying to file a lawsuit, accusing me, personally, of stealing all of those things I just told you about, plus a bunch of other stuff too."

"Huh? When? Did this just come today?"

"From the lawyers, not from Sisi."

CRRRRRAAACK!! Another thunderclap shook the 300-year old chandelier and the house lights flickered off, along with the cell service. I tried the landline a few times, then the cell service a few more times and got nothing but noise. Sandy had teed up a cliffhanger and the next thing I knew the show was over. For the next five minutes the power flashed on, then off, then on again, and I could hear Sandy's voice among the Greek choir of voices wondering what had happened to their connection until finally the only sound was of the storm.

I really had the creeps. Outside the hoary oaks were putting on a textbook display of hoariness, moss waving around like the beards of a thousand ancient flying Chinamen. All I wanted to do was climb into bed. I start pawing around for the flashlights and found one on the bedside table, then followed the beam into the bathroom. After another deafening whack of heavenly rim shots and the accompanying lightshow, I headed back out into the front hall, then through the dining room where my half-full bottle of red awaited. After pouring a full glass I went back to the dining room and sat down, afraid to go to my impromptu battery-powered workstation since it was so close to the window. Outside it was blowing harder and harder and the cabinets were rattling like there was a wind tunnel in the walls, and with each blast I felt my knees grow weaker until I was down on the front parlor floor, just hoping that my evening dose would calm me enough to at least temporarily pass out.

I didn't know how long I'd been asleep, but when I awoke the storm was still raging. I was cold, I had a crick in my neck from lying on the floor and unusually strong pressure bearing down on my soul hole. Then, in the next flash I saw my father sitting on the sofa in the parlor in a white tuxedo, smoking a pipe. But when I directed the beam of the flashlight at the sofa it was deserted. Then I heard his unmistakably deep, sonorous voice, the famous voice of "de lawd" in *Green Pastures.*

"Your mother and I never liked my Southern relatives much, Howard. Yet here you are, chasing your poor mentally ill sister, who is trying to get you to believe that our family was a great uncouth, brutal posse of cruel slave owners. And that I was some sort of Don Juan of Highway 61 having my way with local negresses. Howard? Howard, are you listening to me?"

Another great flash of white light illuminated the old man, without all his accouterments of death, sitting with his long legs crossed in a red velvet wingback chair and bedecked in Mark Twain white from head to toe. I pointed the flashlight at the chair: nothing. Then as if Stephen King himself had scripted the scene, a roaring flame kicked up in the fireplace and the room was bathed in flickering firelight.

"It's so difficult to have a decent conversation in a thunderstorm," said the man in white, seated now in a dark corner of the room with the shivering shadow of his frame cast against the wall. I slowly crawled up and took a seat at the end of the long sofa.

"You see, Howard, there are two sides to every story. In my line of work there's no right or wrong, black or white – just shades of grey, some lighter, some darker. Take your sister's letter. She claims I was an evil man. Maybe I did a few things that seemed evil, from her perspective, but that does not make me an evil man, any more than your proclivity for drugs makes you an evil man."

A long peal of thunder that sounded like it was ripping the heavens asunder ended in a deafening boom that rattled the windows, followed by successive flashes of lightning that first revealed my father on the ancient wingback Victorian, then on the sofa, then standing by the fireplace, like three photos of different poses. My soul hole was buzzing like a bare wire.

"There's just one thing I would ask you to understand, Howard. Perhaps you can explain this to your sister in one of her rare moments of clarity. Like many of my contemporaries – kids that grew up in the Great Depression, especially in the South – I wasn't really raised by my parents. My sister – do you remember Aunt Margaret? Tall, skinny, voice somewhere between Lauren Bacall and LBJ, depending on how many toddies she had under her belt?"

It was easy to picture my father's sister, Margaret, six feet tall – or 5' 12" as they liked to say – an alkie Jimmy Durante shnozz just as purple as an eggplant, with wispy, fly-away charcoal hair under an array of head gear, always in a pants-suit to disguise her thick, manly calves. On the scale between 100% male and 100% female she seemed about fifty/fifty. She smoked like a chimney and drank like a fish, as did her husband, both just as old South as they could be.

"My sister was shipped off to one set of relatives and I was shipped off to another. As soon as we were old enough for boarding school off we went. For a long period of time we had no family home. My father would be bounced from one Standard Oil job to another, sometimes with my mother in tow. Other times she would stay with her family in Baton Rouge and Briarwood while we were in boarding school. I guess if there was one place where the four of us gathered from time to time it was here, until my father died and my mother moved out to Albuquerque to be closer to her sister..

The point is, when you kids came along I had no playbook, no model, no instructions, nothing besides my mother's Southern Baptist discipline to guide me as a father. And her belief in the cleansing powers of golf. That's where it came from, you know. Not my father. He didn't even play the game. You grandmother was a fanatic."

I don't know how to respond to this. There was thunder crashing and lightning flashing like Briarwood was under siege, but my father's voice was clear and calm.

"If there's any advice I can give you from down here in your third chakra – which is quite comfortable, by the way – I would say don't go digging too deep into our family history down here in West Feliciana…"

CRRRRACK…CRRR…CRRR…ACK! BOOM! Several successive flashes went pulsating though the parlor followed by an almost instantaneous explosion directly overhead, and out in the middle of a fallow green field a solitary, ancient live oak exploded into a ball of flame, beating back the rain with a fierce, single-minded intensity. Grabbing my flashlight I rushed out on the front porch, but all I could see in the flashing night were the bright flames and the outline of the giant, moss-laden tree alone in the field. The live oak must have been 150 years old, but within 20 minutes was reduced to a charred, hissing hulk of smoke.

Then without warning the entire front yard was awash in yellow light, sending the impenetrable shadows and their voices from the past back into the storm. After a while just sitting on the parlor floor, feeling as if I might have suffered some electric shock myself and rubbing the subsiding ache in my chest, I warily plodded through the house turning off lights, then turning them on again, then off, then on, in every room until I was certain that I was completely alone. The fire in the parlor was out as if it were never lit in the first place – there were no burning embers, no evidence to suggest that I'd been visited by my father's ghost except the throbbing of my soul hole.

Then I noticed something on the wingback chair that hadn't been there before. I asked myself *was that already there? Did my father drop it off? Did he somehow remove it from the shelf so I wouldn't miss it?*

It was a big blue hardback, about two inches thick, encyclopedia-sized. The cover read: *Alexander Stewart and Anna May Hereford in Spanish Feliciana. A genealogy!* Here I was wondering why my father was so circumspect about our family history, but then he seemed to want to make sure that I at least…at least do what? Memorize the family tree? But, as it turned out, it wasn't just a genealogy, or at least it wasn't like other genealogical books I'd seen. I opened it.

"When Alexander Stewart arrived at the settlement at Thompson's Creek from Angusshire, Scotland, in 1777, the territory was ruled by the Spanish…"

25 A Rogue's Gallery

I read as if in a dream, listening to the thunder rolling away south and watching the flashes recede, until the first of the local critters began to herald the arrival of another day. The book was a cross between a genealogy and straightforward history, and the author had taken great pains to focus on the Brown branch of the family, once Howard Henry Brown entered the picture as a child from Anterim, Ireland around 1810. Howard Henry built Briarwood in 1832. The Browns hooked up with the Stewarts when Howard Henry's grandson, Sydney Howard Brown, my grandfather, married Alexander Stewart's great granddaughter Mary Stewart in 1919 and produced my father, Hal, in 1924.

The Browns were farmers, then soldiers, then after the Civil War got involved in the fledgling oil business. But such pedestrian details were of no interest to me, so I scanned the book for stories, anecdotes, bills of lading and other snippets of information that might reveal more about the makeup, the essence, of my ancestry. My mouth dropped open when I came across the list of assets that were recorded for the 1793 census. There among the horses, cattle, hogs, and 3000 acres of crops, were 26 slaves – for Alexander Stewart, his wife and one son. I shuddered. Were Johnnie's ancestors in this bunch?

But then I came across the story of my great grandfather, Howard Lemuel Brown – "Brownie"– the supposed sharpshooter with Stonewall Jackson's brigade. To my surprise it was written in third person, with dialogue, as if someone had attempted to create something more than a simple battlefield anecdote.

As the story went, Captain Brown was riding in the first battle of Manassas when his horse was felled on the battlefield, breaking the Captain's leg. The horse had fallen on a downed Union soldier, who Captain Brown took for dead. No sooner than he began to root through what he thought were the dead man's pockets than the Federal pulled his revolver and pointed it at Brownie's head.

"I should shoot you dead right now, as you are the enemy, but if I did that I might never get out from under this horse," said the Federal. As the battle continued to rage all around them, Brownie and the Federal – neither of whom could move – got to talking about home, about their wives and children and the farms they planned to return to. Colonel Flaherty, the Union soldier from the north side of the Ohio River, across the water from Kentucky, told Captain Brown of Louisiana about all the slaves that he had helped liberate.

"I wouldn't be surprised none if some of dem folks don't belong to my family," said Captain Brown, and they commiserated for a little while about the crazy war. Eventually the bullets stopped and the victorious Confederates started to help the wounded off the field while taking Union prisoners. When they found Brownie and the Federal Flaherty, the Union captain surrendered his gun and was to be taken prisoner when Brownie started caterwauling from his stretcher: "Let him go! Let him go! He'll die of starvation in that prison camp and never see his sweetheart nor his young'uns no more! He's a good man, I tell you. He coulda shot me right between the eyes if he wanted to but he didn't!"

"Is that right, Cap'n Brown? Well then, I suppose we should return the favor," said the sergeant, whose name was Hickock.

So Hickock gave Flaherty a crutch and, dragging his bloody leg behind him, the Union soldier started to make his way back over the battlefield, stepping over and around thousands of dead soldiers and horses to the Union lines. Then, with Flaherty not 50 yards across the field, the Confederate sergeant shouldered his rifle and shot the Union soldier in the back.

After that first battle of Manassas Sergeant Hickock went on to ride with Stonewall Jackson alongside Captain Brown. But even though Brownie and Hickock fought side-by-side for two years, all the way to Gettysburg and back down to Appomattox, and saved each other's lives more than once, Brownie never forgot what Hickock did to Flaherty from Ohio.

After the war Brownie went back to the family homestead at Briarwood and got into the oil business with Standard of Louisiana. Hickock kept on soldiering, since his family's homestead in Georgia was burned in Sherman's march. It turned out that Hickock didn't care much who he fought, so he was one of the few rebels to join the US Army to go fight the Indian Wars in the West. One night around 1898 the two men met by accident at a horse race in Baton Rouge. By then Hickock was too old for soldiering and had become a professional gambler. Brownie recognized Hickock at the race and after collecting his winnings followed him to a noisy saloon. If Hickock recognized Howard Brown he did not let on. They got into a card game, and as the story goes, it was after midnight and Brownie was fleecing Hickock good when he said:

"Beggin' your pardon, Mr. Hickock, but you look a mite familiar."
Twirling his mustache, the gambler pushed back his bowler, gave him a long, hard stare, then said: "You don't. And I never forget a face."

"Is that right?" Brownie said, knocking back a shot of whiskey, "well I suppose you remember the face of the Union soldier you shot in the back at the first Manassas."

The table went quiet as the two men, now in their late fifties, stared each other down. Brownie didn't believe that Hickock couldn't recognize him since they had spent a couple of years at each other's side. He had also seen plenty more of Hickock's cold-blooded cruelty as the war raged on: rapes of union women, confederate women, slave girls not more than 14 that he shot and dumped into the nearest well or river when he was finished with them; murders of innocent civilians; hangings of runaway slaves and worse yet, runaway rebel soldiers. His appetite for killing was bottomless. He was the devil incarnate, Brownie knew it and had resolved to put a stop to it.

Just then there was a blast – a gunshot – and Brownie's chair exploded in splinters as he went flying backwards, a bullet crushing his knee. The dancing girls screamed and ran for the dressing rooms while the other guests hit the floor and the bartenders ducked. Brownie then jumped up, oblivious to the blinding pain, and before Hickock had time to even stand up Brownie shot him in the forehead, popping his bowler straight up off his crown as it whiplashed back on his neck and then forward, his gambler's arms flying outward as if preparing to embrace his killer as the chair tilted slowly back and finally fell. Then Howard Brown hobbled over to where the dead man lay and peppered his face with bullets until it was hardly a face anymore.

Finally a bartender fired a shot over Brownie's head and the carnage stopped. Then while all the people watched in horrified silence, Captain Brown supposedly drank what remained of the bottle until the last shot, poured it on what was left of Hickock's face, whisked the candle off the table and lit the dead man's face on fire.

Even though the Captain's kneecap was hanging out of his torn pant leg, he shouldered his bag and somehow walked out of the saloon where a man awaited in a carriage, and before the sheriff arrived he'd gone cantering off into the night. The next morning they found him at home in his kitchen at Briarwood, dead with a bullet hole through his skull.

It is here that the story gets vague. One theory suggests that when he burst through the side door into the kitchen at two a.m. and started crashing around down there somebody thought it was a burglar and shot him. Others think that he knew he would be convicted of murder and sentenced to hang, so he ended it right there. One story has Brownie inviting the driver of the carriage into the kitchen and requesting to be shot. Another story has it that Brownie's eight-year-old son – my grandfather – took his father out with a pistol. By request.

26 On the Road to Serendipity

By the time I was finished with *Alexander Stewart and Anna May Hereford in Spanish Feliciana*, I was too churned up to sleep. Not only had I been visited by my dead father – not just visited, but warned about looking too closely into our family history – I also found out why. So I dozed, imagining the horror of being eight years old and having your father say, "Son, I want you to blow my head off." This, I decided, could not possibly be true, because if it was…if it was true, well, then what? Should God order a universe-wide quarantine of Howard Brown genes and systematically destroy each and every one of them? Did I have a ticking genetic time bomb somewhere in my brain that would someday instruct me to light the next person I met on fire, then ask some grammar school kid on his way home from school to put a bullet through my skull? How about my son? My sister? Her kids? Were they face-burners waiting to happen?

As I lay there I resolved to show the book to Eddie and maybe Johnny, especially Brownie's story, to see if there was any truth to it. I also resolved to quit smoking. But when I finally fully awakened, startled by the sound of somebody rooting around in the kitchen and equally alarmed that it was already 10AM, I couldn't find the damn book anywhere. I stripped the bed, I checked all the drawers and closets in the bedroom, I looked under the carpets and behind the hanging paintings – places a book couldn't possibly hide – all to no avail. When I finally limped over to the kitchen, there was cousin Eddie clearing out the contents of the fridge into a big cooler: almond milk, eggs, rice bread, yogurt, coconut water – Northern California style food items that he probably thought were made out of bird seed and rabbit pellets.

"Hey, sleeping beauty! That storm keep you awake last night? Power go out?"

"Uh…yeah, I…Eddie. Have you ever seen a thick blue hardback book around here, a family genealogy?"

"Sure, Aunt Sarah put that together oh, maybe 20 years ago. But I haven't seen one around here in ages. I must have lost it." He paused his cooler-loading and looked me over.

"Whoa y'all look you could use some coffee, sport. Here, I made up a pot." Sleeping beauty? Sport? Did I detect a note of diss? I was just about to tell him that I'd found the book when he said: "Hey! Good news! We've found your sister!"

·

"WHAT?" I shouted, incredulous, my knees buckling to the point where I had to steady myself on the kitchen counter. I quickly took a stool.

"Yessir," Eddie said, grinning ear to ear and setting the coffee down before me. "It so happens that she has been shacking up – oh, excuse me – she's been spending some time with her psychiatrist down in New Orleans, Dr. Raymond Cobb, and Dr. Cobb has a fishing camp next to ours on the Little Tensas Bayou. When Lola and her son arrived yesterday afternoon to spruce the place up for our little visit..."

"Our little visit?" Nobody had mentioned a fishing trip to me, except Sandy who said Tripp intimated that at some point during this escapade, after we got Sisi squared away, we would do a little fishing. But things had gotten so mixed up in the last forty eight hours that whatever plans might have been made were just irrelevant scratches on a calendar.

"Yes, well, I had a conversation with Mr. Hart yesterday afternoon and he brought me up to date on the little misunderstanding y'all had regarding your property."

I felt the hair on the back of my neck bristle. "He called you?"

"We had a conversation, yes, and he told me about the forgeries and so on. I must say your sister is very clever when she has her wits about her." Eddie was so smooth, so slick that I felt like any objection I might make or pointed questions I might ask would slide off him like a politician at a town meeting.

"Why?" I asked, trying to keep my growing anger and this sense that I was being played by a posse of geriatric Southern thugs under control. I was thinking that Eddie must have something to do with Laurel Hill Energy Ventures, and that Stephen Hart was the attorney that put the deal together.

"Why? You mean why did I have a conversation with Mr. Hart? Actually we had a little golf game yesterday and he told me about it then." Eddie's composure was not about to be ruffled.

I was inclined to tell Eddie to keep his bulbous purple beak out of my business but, for a change, decided to let the truth reveal itself, which I was certain it would in time. Fomenting contention was likely to do me, and Sisi, more harm than good. So I redirected the conversation. "So how do you know my sister is at this fishing camp with her psychiatrist?"

"Ah...as I was saying Toya and her son were getting the camp ready when Dr. Cobb floated over to say hello and who do ya know is riding alongside the good doctor but Sissy Mae Brown. Toya said she recognized her at once and tried to call you last night here at the house but the storms had already knocked the power out up here."

"Eddie, do you know if my sister knows that I'm down here looking for her?"

"Well that depends on what Toya might have said, I guess," Eddie replied, starting to get a little impatient with my cross-examination. "Listen, we can talk about all this in the truck, Howard. No you go on and get yourself dressed. You don't need no gear. We got everything you need at the camp. Just a couple changes of clothes, a nice warm jacket in case the weather turns, and all your good luck. Not that you're gonna need it down at Serendipity – catchin' fish down there is like shootin' ducks in a barrel."

"Well, it there's a way we can talk to Toya, that'd be good, cuz if my sister knows that I'm coming she will disappear like a Vegas magician."

"Oh, I don't think y'all got to worry 'bout that, Howard. Unless she's got a boat." Eddie chuckled.

Once dressed, I helped Eddie schlep the cooler out to the car and it dawned on me, watching him heft the heavy box, that Eddie really was an old man. His typical male pattern baldness, evident in almost all the males in the dozens of family photos around the old house, was hemmed in by a monkish ring of silver curls, and his gaggle was like so much raw chicken breast hanging under his chin. He had steely blue eyes that bugged out under the thick lenses of his glasses, and his skin, pink and mottled, looked more likely to burn than tan; freckles, moles and other growths on his arms belied a little too much exposure to the southern sun.

Outside I met Robert J. Sublette, the infamous troublemaker that everybody called "Binx." Our meeting has formed one of those mental images that I can recall simply by closing my eyes, because instead of the usual buzz in my soul hole, I felt something more like an electric shock. I felt like I had already had an altercation with this man, though I knew I had never met him before. He was a good four inches taller and at least ten years younger than hunched-over Eddie, with a bad auburn-colored toupee, a classic middle class belly sagging over his belt and a voice that sounded like he was gargling gravel. His oversized mirrored highway patrolman sunglasses concealed a good part of his face, but I could sense the look in the eyes behind them. Binx Sublette may not have looked much like Mr. Road Rage, but I felt sure on that first meeting that they were cut from the same cloth.

"Obliged," he said, looking directly at the hole in my chest. He gave my outstretched hand one quick squeeze, then turned and spat on the ground.

"Let's go," he added, kicking some gravel over his spit. His demeanor was so textbook cold that I had to chuckle.

Binx's son Bolling and his twin brother Jack, both in their late teens, were sitting in the back of the monstrous Chevy Tahoe. Bolling, clean-shaven, with high cheekbones and jet black hair, wiry like his uncle Eddie and not much bigger than my sister, was glued to his cell phone. Jack, his short, pudgy, shaggy-haired, bearded twin was staring out the side window. Bolling acknowledged my introduction with a sullen grunt but Jack was overjoyed to see me, leaning over the back seat and extending both arms like he wanted to give me a hug. Immediately I could see that Jack suffered from a mental disability of some sort: the glazed, eager lips, the constantly working, thick-fingered hands, and the unkempt beard with bits of breakfast ripening in the whiskers were the first clues. His eyes –huge, glassy grey orbs behind thick magnifiers – were practically rolling around in their sockets.

The day was as crisp as a ripe Golden Delicious, the air oxidized and power washed by the storm. The enervating weight of the atmosphere had dissolved: I felt like I could stand up straighter, my shoulders back in testimony to the refreshing lightness of the late morning.

We were headed to the family camp way down on Little Tensas Bayou several hours away in the land of the Cajuns, Creoles, coonass bayou rats, Voodoo priests, Hoodoo witches and, of course, zombies. It was at Camp Serendipity that we were to meet up with Tripp, who has been touring the southern Bayous from Baratatia Bay up through the Little Tensas Bayou, Bayou LaFourche and anywhere the little posse of professional fly fisherman wished to go. One of his associates had been posting photos and videos to Facebook that I'd quickly browsed over on my phone. The redfish Tripp had been landing were spectacular, though I can't say I'm attracted to the monstrous catfish the other fisherman had been yanking out of the mud.

Out of deference and respect for my giganticness, I got to ride shotgun next to Eddie, who was as proud of his state as anybody could be, even though he didn't have a particularly high opinion of the residents of the southwestern parishes. The early November countryside was a muted palette of fall color: ochres and siennas with the occasional blood red burst of sumac, surrounded by wide open fields of green that made me think that a good portion of the state could be turned into one giant, thousand-hole golf course. The colors were subdued compared to New England but psychedelic compared to Northern California, which by contrast is considered a semi-arid environment versus the wet, hardwood jungles of the south and east. The

Louisiana woods were for professionals, with dozens upon dozens of varieties of hardwoods alone: the live oaks, beech, sumac, Laurel, dogwood, horse chestnut, hornbeam, laurel, sycamore, birch, the namesake magnolia and the omnipresent baldycypress, punctuated with groves of identically-sized loblolly pine, under which nothing grows. I felt a pang for my former naturalist son, who at age nine would have been having a field day with his tree books. All I could say was "look at all those fucking trees!"

I was eager to pick up where Eddie and I left off regarding the "conversation" he had with Hart on the golf course. Since Eddie was a retired real estate attorney, it occurred to me that he was probably one of the partners in Laurel Hill Energy Ventures, if not the principal. "So, Eddie," I said, turning down the nauseating "new country" music station that had been blaring since we left. "You spoke with Mr. Hart, you said. Would you happen to be involved with Laurel Hill Energy Ventures, the outfit that bought the property from my sister?"

There was a long pause: I didn't take my eyes off Eddie and Eddie didn't take his eyes off the road. For the first time since we'd met, my second cousin was at a loss for words. Then he smiled, as if a perfect response had just walked up to him and sat in his lap. "I would rather not discuss this matter in the current company," he said in a low half-whisper. I glanced back at his Binx in the back seat, who was drinking a beer and texting with someone, not listening to us up front. I assumed Eddie was concerned that his brother would hear something that he shouldn't. Then Eddie said, "Howard, listen. We'll get everything ironed out, I promise. Your sister has made a grievous mistake, but we're not going to leave you high and dry, so please try not to worry."

After cruising along with the music at low volume, which really wasn't bad at all because I couldn't make out the ridiculous words, I forced my thoughts toward my ulterior motive for coming down here, which was to see if I could get the straight scoop on our family history in this strange, sticky part of the world. Watching the woods roll by off the edge of the highway, it occurred to me that our family history was just as dense and impenetrable as those walls of growth, thick with shrubs and vines that would scratch and poison if you tried to enter and ominously dark once you got inside. I knew Eddie had family stories that he thought I should hear. So I asked him straight up.

"All right then," he began, " you and me had the same great grandparents, Mister and Missus Howard Brown. Mamie Brown had two daughters and one son, Samuel Howard Brown, your grandpa, May Bolling Brown, my granny, and Annabelle, or Nell Brown, Boon Percy's granny. Your grandpa married Mrs. Louise Evans, while my grandma married Captain Claude Sublette, and Boon's granny married Mr. Clyde Percy."

"Okay, Eddie. I get that," I said. "I won't remember it, but I get it. But what I'm really after down here is some sort of genetic explanation for the ongoing mental... uh...aberrations that, for example, are causing my sister to either believe she is somebody else, or, best case, decide to become a practical joker." What I didn't mention was my own worry that I had a time-release plaque bomb ticking in my own brain that would some day start shutting down the various substations that have allowed me to function in society without a great deal of trouble. Nor did I mention the evidence of alcohol and drug abuse running through the family tree like a great vein.

Eddie paused a long while before responding, perhaps taken aback by my apparent lack of interest in the machinations of our contorted family tree, which I'll admit is intellectually stimulating, even fascinating, but far from what I thought I was trying to accomplish. I immediately wished I hadn't said anything, because in truth I didn't know my second cousins any better than I knew the UPS guys. I might be setting myself up for all sorts of trouble, not to mention Sisi and the entire branch of Howard Browns that hung so precariously on the family trunk.

"Well for God's sake, Howard," Binx piped up in back, surprising both of us with his sudden appearance in the conversation, as Eddie was passing a pickup at about 80 on the two-lane blacktop and just barely squeaking back in before a big rig went roaring by. "Everybody knows that your great-granddaddy, the one that rode with Stonewall Jackson in his sharpshooter's brigade, blew his own head off when your granddaddy Howard was just eight years old, just down the road from Briarwood at the old Laurel Hill house."

I felt my heart go thumpa, thumpa, thump thump thumpa, as if it'd been thrown off the tracks. I wanted Eddie to pull the circus bus over so I could drag Binx out into the bushes and pound his ass, spouting such bullshit in front of his kids. Fortunately Bolling appeared to be asleep, and Jack was busy knotting and unknotting his fingers.

"Okay Eddie, Binx," I said as calmly as possible as he pulled off the New Roads exit and headed for the fancy new bridge over the Big Muddy just south of St. Francisville. I paused for a long moment, watching the cables of the new bridge sing by in the noon sun. "Listen, there's one person that's never heard that story and never will unless it's told by me, and that's my son, Tripp."

"Oh…" Eddie said hemming and hawing while the boys awakened from their short midmorning siesta, "Okay, I understand. I completely understand. We're sorry for being such a crawdad-headed motor mouths, but we are interested in this stuff down here, as you can see."

"Yes, I can see that, fellas. But let's just keep that last bit between us."

"What last bit?" Young Jack hollered in his cracked falsetto from the back, with a touch of strange hysteria in his voice. Again I wondered what was wrong with Jack, who had been softly muttering to himself in the wayback seat. When I turned to look back at him he was staring out the window, his shoulders hunched and almost imperceptibly rocking to and fro.

"Ain't none of your business, son," Eddie said, very stern.

"You mean the business about uncle Howard's Civil War ancestor that blowed his own brains out?" Jack squealed, spraying spittle across the side window.

"Jeez, Jack!" his brother Bolling shouted, frantically wiping at the back of his neck and head, "Say it, don't spray it!"

Then, in an instant the Tahoe was fishtailing through the muddy grass on the shoulder. Eddie leapt out of the car, yanking both boys into to the weeds and cuffing them so hard that they both went down into the tall, heavy grass. Then Binx jumped out, grabbed his 74 year-old brother and pitched him against the side of the truck.

"Jesus, Eddie. You tryin' to get us all killed?" Another big rig roared by rattling the SUV and blowing his air horn. Binx shoved Eddie into the backseat, while Bolling and Jack clambered back in. He looked back at the oncoming traffic and waited as a line of cars went ripping by, then, when there was break in the action, he rushed into the driver's seat and swerved out of the soft, muddy shoulder, tires kicking giant clumps of mud and grass into the roadway and the engine squealing like it might explode. "Jesus mother fucking Christ you stupid hot headed son of a bitch why the fuck did y'all go and do that for?" Binx shouted.

Eddie was silent, glaring out the window with his hands in fists, flexing closed and open, closed and open. Just as the scene began to quiet, Jack screamed so otherworldly loud that I almost opened the passenger door and jumped out.

"Aggghhh! Aggggghhh!" he wailed like a frightened child. "Pull over, pull over, there's a cottonmouth in the truck! Oh God help me!"

I turned as far as I could in my seatbelt to see Jack, red-faced and crying, trying to squeeze into the back storage area, his blubbery frame pinned between the ceiling and the seatback. Binx was looking for a place to pull over but the grassy shoulder dropped steeply into thick shrubbery and forest. Eddie had snapped off his seat belt and was searching the floor for the snake when Binx reached down between his legs and hurled the snake into the way back.

"Goddamnit y'all fuckin' chowderheads!" Binx shouted. "Y'all look at that snake. That ain't no cottonmouth, that's a fuckin' gopher snake!" Then Eddie reached into the seat behind him and snatched it up, laughing. "Jesus Christ, boys. Jesus fucking H. Christ."

Finally Binx spied a turnoff and within a minute or two we were in the parking lot of a little strip mall. He jumped out, pulled his buck knife out of it's holster and swiped the head off the snake with a deft move the likes I'd never seen. He then threw it back in at the twins, guts squirting all over everything. The two jumped out the side doors, white as ghosts.

"Boys, y'all go on and get that harmless little snake out the back of the truck right now, you understand me?" said Eddie. Bolling, obviously the bolder of the twins, rooted round the groceries in the back until he found it, then took it over to the woods astride the parking lot and hurled it like a limp spaghetti noodle.

Jack got the bulk of the guts in his hair, but he didn't notice and immediately curled into fetal position in the way back, quietly sobbing and snuffling.

"Sorry, Howard," Eddie said. "We have a history for having a bit of a temper on our side of the family."

"Boy you can say that again," Bolling shouted from the back. I looked over at Binx who was beginning to smile a little bit.

"Yeah. I'm not so sure it's just our side of the family, Eddie, if you know what I'm talkin' about," Binx growled, obviously referring to some secret he shared with his brother. Eddie shook his head. "How'd that snake get in here, anyway?" Binx added.

"Yeah, *Howard Brown*," Eddie said jokingly. "How *did* that snake get in here?"

It was all I could do to keep from crying, listening to this 74 year-old man behave like a 14-yr old, and I was thinking if there's one way to attest to some faulty wiring in the family's mental schematic, my second cousins were providing the best case study I'd ever seen. Given Jack's obvious mental disability, I wasn't at all certain he could keep great grandfather Brown's supposed suicide a secret from Tripp. But I doubted Tripp would take Jack seriously, even if he couldn't see Jack's obvious disability.

Overloaded, my conscious mind finally cried "uncle," my eyelids grew heavy looking at mile after mile of green, ochre, and soft auburn woods, their dark undergrowth and green carpet, all of it against a sky so clear and blue it was almost impossible to imagine any creature in the realm harboring a single hurtful thought. And thus to the steady drone of rolling wheels I dozed.

27 Aboard the Sissy Mae

When I opened my eyes the day had grown gray and steamy and the land had lost its bucolic country charm. Gone were the dense, uniform forests of loblolly pine and rolling hills of hardwoods, along with the whitewashed fences and grand expanses of green grass, the gnarly, knuckly oaks with their long beards and emerald cashmere coats, all of this has been replaced by a broad, flat savannah of low shrubbery dotted with the native bald cypress surrounding a maze of channels, bays, canals and waterways. The short view was mostly concrete: strip malls on either side of a two-lane highway divided by wide grassy swale that sat atop a giant French drain. The line of frontage businesses was interrupted by fenced-in vacant lots and warehouses, behind which began the doublewides and small, shoebox homes on stilts.

The banter in the SUV had finally quieted down. I guessed that Binx was on his sixth beer and his son Bolling on his fourth. Eddie, like me, was not a daytime beer drinker, though he did have a flask of something that he'd been taking a pull on from time-to-time. Finally we turned off the main highway and onto a non-descript street with a gas station/bait store/adult video shop on one corner and a topless bar on the other.

After we drove a few blocks past the peculiar little houses on stilts, we arrived at a large marina with watercraft of all ages, shapes and sizes. Just when I was thinking that many of the boats had been abandoned and left to sink into the mud, people appeared on the decks of these dilapidated craft; boat people in stained tank tops, beers and cigarettes in hand, watching in silence as Binx pulled the SUV into his designated spot. A few of the women looked like they might've worked down the street at the topless club, with giant ballooning breasts underneath their black heavy metal band tanks, hair cropped short as to better accommodate a wig. I smiled and waved from the passenger seat but they just stared at me like I was a monkey in the zoo. I had forgotten that I probably looked like a gorilla.

The Sublettes owned a 50 foot-long flatboat with a pilot's cabin in the stern and about six vinyl padded swivel chairs on four-foot posts – fisherman's thrones – with two benches between under which life jackets, lanyards, nets and such were stored. I had never seen such an unusual watercraft – it was more like a river barge than a fishing boat – but I had never been in such unusual water. But not everything about the craft was foreign, for there across the stern in elegant cursive was her name: The Sissy

Mae, of West Feliciana, LA.

As we chugged slowly out into the bayou under a low and heavy sky the color of Japanese eggplant, I was quickly distracted from my sisterly ruminations by the surroundings. The banks of the wide channel were humming with life: snowy egrets marched deliberately in the water off the shore like sentinels at their stations, freezing periodically over some potential prey, then stabbing their bills into the water, coming up with a morsel that they quickly swallowed, wiggling their long white spaghetti necks to help it down. A great blue heron perched on a low cypress branch scanned the water before spreading it's wings wide, flapped a few times then glided low to a new perch. Black cormorants bobbed on the oily-looking surface, disappearing below for long periods, then reappearing twenty yards away, sometimes with a fish in their beak but more oftentimes not.

As the channel snaked deeper into the southern jungle, my English teacher's brain flashed, once again, on Captain Marlowe and the telling of his fateful journey up the Congo River in search of Mister Kurtz. Long buried images from the story were suddenly before me in stark relief: the elegant queen of the cannibals in her brass leggings and gauntlets, her helmet-shaped hairdo, her barbarous baubles jingling like finger-cymbals as she followed us through the dense shore growth – I half expected Camp Serendipity to be fenced in by posts adorned with severed heads and surrounded by spear-toting natives in loincloths. *Mistah Kurtz* said the voice in my head, *he dead.* *Mistah Howard*, the voice corrected with a buzz of my soul hole, *he dead.*

Jack was perched in the bow with binoculars, scanning the banks for gators. Bolling was in a fishing chair near the pilot's cabin, a fresh beer in the coozy, getting in few texts before we lost service. Binx was at the helm of the vessel, high in the pilot's cabin looking across the water for potential snags and trouble spots, leading us on his mission to the heart of darkness.

As the channel narrowed I began to notice the odd roots of the bald cypress and the strange phallic "knees" that emerged from the chartreuse duck weed at their base. I was once told that these knees provided an extra dose of oxygen to the tree, but later read that, like tent stakes, they provided a buttress to the main trunk. Marveling at these trees as we chugged deeper into the bayou I got that otherworldly feeling again. Like Eugene Henderson in the dry and remote villages of the Arnowe and Wahiri, there was a quality to the surroundings that suggested the possibility of a search that might awaken the soul's spirit. Perhaps it was this quality that had awakened the spirits of the great Southern storytellers – Faulkner, O'Connor, Walker Percy

– though if you grew up here I imagined the bizarre landscape would be as common as palm trees and papayas to a Hawaiian. Still, were it not for the tangible problems that needed my attention I might have spent more time coming to an understanding with my past – those events conscious and unconscious that have shaped this awkward and self-absorbed bundle of nerve endings. Then I might catalogue it all and refer to it as needed. Why? I honestly didn't know.

All of a sudden there was a commotion in the bow; Jack was jumping up and down, howling and pointing starboard about 30 yards up. "Gator! I see a gator!" Of course alligator's are not at all unusual in Louisiana's bayous, and to see a full grown man of nineteen, shaggy and bearded in what must be a very uncomfortable fleece lined denim jacket, jumping up and down and bellowing like a four year-old over what must be a common sight was disturbing. Still, I'd never seen an alligator in the wild so I grabbed a pair of binoculars and scrambled up to the bow.

"Ugh," I grunted as I got near Jack. He had pissed himself with gator thrill and the stench just about knocked me over. *Shit*, I thought, *wait'll his daddy sees this. He's liable to beat the crap out of the poor dimwit.* I quickly scanned the bank, thinking how I might get Jack changed before Binx found out, but I didn't see any gators.

"Where is he, Jack?" I asked.

"Oh he went back in the water," he said matter of factly. "But boy was he big. Mighta been the biggest gator I've ever seen, and I've seen lots of gators, more than a thousand, I think."

"Oh really?" I asked. "Do you have any pictures of them?"

"Oh I sure do, on my computer. Wanna see?"

So Jack took my hand. "Come on," he said, his pant legs rubbing together with that scratchy rasp of wet denim. I glanced up at the pilothouse where Binx sat behind the wheel drinking a beer and flipping through *Hustler* magazine. Jack pulled me through a small hatch into the dark hold where our duffel bags and such were piled with other supplies – the stench of his pissed jeans was overwhelming.

"Jack, take those wet jeans off."

I instantly realized that my request was too direct by the horrified look of recognition on the 19 year-old boy's bearded face. Just when he was about to scream I clapped my hand over his mouth. "Jack," I whispered, "I am not a homosexual, I only want to get you cleaned up before your father finds out you've pissed your pants. I'll bet he gets pretty angry when you piss your pants, doesn't he?"

He nodded slowly, rubbing his hand on his inner thigh, smelling it, then repeating with his other hand. "Okay Jack," I continued in a whisper, "you're gonna be extra quiet now, right?" He nodded again. When I let him loose he jumped away from me, still scared. "Turn around," he said, "please." So I averted my view, suddenly wondering if he even had a spare pair of pants. "Okay, don't turn around. I've got my wet pants off. My underpants are wet too. Should take those off?"

"Yes, of course," I said, looking at the pile of duffels and trying to determine which might be his. "Don't the wet clothes make you uncomfortable?"

"Oh, not really. I'm used to it."

"What? You mean you piss your pants and then wear them until they dry out or get washed? Why? It must be very uncomfortable, and stinky too."

"My daddy says I can't have any more pants until I stop messin' the one's I got," Jack said, like such an arrangement made perfect sense. I didn't bother asking him if this meant that he didn't have a backup pair of pants, or underpants. I couldn't turn around to size him up, and it seemed awfully cruel to make him put the wet pants back on right after I'd instructed him to take them off.

"Okay, you just sit tight, I'll think of something," I said, pulling my red duffle from the pile.

"What if there's no place to sit?" he asked in his squeaky man's voice. *No place to sit, no place to sit,* I was thinking.

"Well, stand tight, then." So this fat, hairy kid was standing behind me, a pair of piss-soaked jeans and underpants at his feet, while I picked through my duffle, which was really pointless because Jack was probably eight inches bigger around the waist than I was.

I heard some shuffling behind me, so very, very slowly I turned my head to see what Jack was up to, catching a view just as he was sliding his wide, hairy ass into a pair of rubber coveralls – rain gear – and I immediately thought *good god, this kid's not as stupid as I thought. Not only did he find some substitute clothes, all we have to do next time he has an accident is hose him down.*

As soon as he had the coveralls all the way on, I whispered, "can I look yet?"

"Okay," Jack whispered back. So I turned full around and there he stood looking like a big fat lemon, the yellow straps hanging over his stained v-neck t-shirt. He pulled on his fleece-lined denim jacket and zipped it up to his chin so it looked like he had on a pair of rubber yellow trousers, ideally suited for a latent bed-wetter.

"Brilliant," I said, softly clapping my hands. "Where did you find those?" He pointed to the wall where there must have been a half-dozen identical yellow slickers hanging from a hook, and I got a distinct sense that this had happened before. "Will your father be upset about your pants?" He lowered his head and nodded, looking at the floor. It occurred to me that we could probably dip the piss soaked jeans and underpants in the bayou water to remove the stench, but I couldn't think of any way to do this without Binx noticing. Just then a shout went up topside and Jack went barging past me through the small door and out onto the deck in his yellow rubber pants.

"Land ho! Land ho!" he squawked in his loudest Barney Fife roar. "Bring 'er in, Captain! Bring 'er on in!" Tempted as I was to set eyes on the legendary Camp Serendipity, I had to do something with Jack's stinky clothes. To imagine his own father would make him wear those piss-soaked jeans and soaked-through undies, letting the urine dry of it's own accord in all it's smelly, nauseating glory was so far beyond the realm of acceptable behavior I felt like giving Binx a dirty whirly. Had he never heard of Depends?

Naturally the hold was full of lanyards and lines of all widths and lengths, so I grabbed a line and tied it through the belt loop of the jeans and the wiener door of the undies and looped it back over, knotting it tight. Then, with maximum stealth, I tip toed out of the door of the hold, threw the piss packet overboard into the chartreuse duck weed, waited for it to sink, then cleated the line, hoping that we would tie up to the dock on the other side of the boat. Later, I could fish out the clothes and get them into a proper washer/dryer. At that moment it seemed the best course of action. Even though Binx might question why Jack was decked out in rain coveralls, if it forestalled a beating and got poor Jack into some dry clothes, and maybe even got him thinking about pissing in the toilet, then I planned to say my mission in the matter would be accomplished. Had I known my mission in the matter was just beginning, I might have let poor Jack stew in his own piss forever.

28 The Junebug Two-Step

When my father used to talk about his Southern family, the plantation, the man-made lake, and all of it I figured there must be money – big money, old money, cotton money, oil money – behind the operation. Looking across the inky channel through the fluorescent duckweed that showed the way to the dock of Camp Serendipity that late afternoon, I saw my assumptions, like always, were wrong. This place – like a picture out of a swampland storybook full of voodoo princes, giant alligators, water moccasins, and screaming zombies flying through the cypress – was about to crumble into the mud, leaving no trace but the tin roof and a long dock attached to nothing.

A single pier of cedar planks, at least a hundred feet long – long enough to accommodate the Sissy Mae on one side and several shorter craft on the other – extended from a rickety dock into the deeper water of the channel. A short gangplank led from the pier up to the dock, which was several feet lower than the front deck of the house itself, which stood on wooden stilts above the muddy shore. Nature appeared to have reworked the main structure and the surrounding cabins into a Disneyesque cartoon of acute and obtuse angles. Nothing – from the elevation of the dock to the front porch, the railings, the doorframes, window frames, and rooflines – was square. Nothing was level. The whole jumble of sticks, posts, planks, glass and rusted tin was completely crooked and totally cattywumpus. Had skulls on posts surrounded the property it would have made perfect sense.

The sight of Toya and Reggie calmed my nerves. After Bolling threw Reggie a line and tied up The Sissy Mae, we disembarked and went trudging up the rickety pier single file. Suddenly I realized I had forgotten my duffel. "Hey, what about our stuff?" I asked Binx just ahead.

"The help will take care of that, Howard," he grumbled without turning, "you just relax."

The help? There was something in Binx's tone that confirmed my belief that he was of the same archetypal stock as Mr. Road Rage. Aside from Binx's toupee and lack of visible tattoos, they were appearing more like twins every passing moment. The heavy mustaches, the trucker's caps, the mirrored sunglasses, the drunken palaver – it was uncanny to say the least.

Before stepping up the gangplank to the sloping front porch I stole a glance back at the boat. At the same time I had a powerful urge to go get my things. The *help* indeed. Should I plan to tip them when they dropped off my duffel? Just when I started to return to the boat a familiar female cried, "Hey there, mister! Whaddya think you're doin'?"

I turned to see Toya and her son Reggie, each pushing a shopping cart, coming onto the porch from around the back of the house. Each had on a green golf shirt, short-sleeved and collared, with the Camp Serendipity emblem on the breast pocket. Uniforms?

Out on the pier it was almost dark, an almost imperceptible line of gray faded above the darkness of the trees into a solid wall of black while the lights from the camp spilled across the motionless green duckweed and water lilies. Instantly the air was filled with flying insects, even in the cool mid-November night, and I was reminded of my father and the fumigator he would spray across the back deck and his putting green. It killed the mosquitoes, but it made the grilled burgers taste a little weird.

Toya, Reggie and I climbed over the gunwale onto the deck of the Sissy Mae and headed for the hold. "You know they's gonna wonder where you is," Toya whispered, as if I were committing some sort of crime.

I paused in the dark and she stopped as Reggie, ahead of us, clambered into the hold and flicked on the light. Toya and I remained on the deck and I whispered, "Have you seen her yet?" We were out of the beam of the houselights and I could barely make her out on the deck.

"No," she whispered, "but I've seen her doctor, Raymond Cobb. He motored over last night expecting the Sublettes, and you, to be here. When all he found was the help he motored back without even gettin' out his skiff."

"Really? Jesus," was all I could think of to say. Toya took my arm in the dark.

"Howard, something is not right about that doctor. In fact I think all these fella's is up to somethin' no good. It's just a feelin', but why ain't they callin' out for you right now?"

Just then – right on cue – Binx stepped out onto the yellow-lighted porch in a halo of bugs and shouted "Howard? Howard Brown where'd you get your Cali ass off to?"

"Well, there you go," I whispered to Toya, who was still gripping my arm. "Seriously though, Toya. What makes you think so?" I said, not knowing whether Toya knew about the illegal sale of my property or not.

Then, with an audible click, a powerful flashlight illuminated the pier, the boat and all of it. "I'm comin, Binx! Just gettin' my stuff," I shouted back, the both of us ducking out of the sweeping beam. A moment passed, Toya pulled me down under the gunwale.

"Wait here just a second, Howard," Toya whispered as she crawled over to the hold. Ten seconds later she was crawling back with my red duffel. "Okay, now you get on back there, Howard, stay low, keep quiet, and don't come mingling with the help no mo', you unnerstan' me?" She chuckled and gave my thigh a slap.

After a long moment rocking on my haunches, all I could think of to say was, "Yes, maam." We both laughed and I scuttled over the gunwale down the pier to the house.

"Well look who's here!" Binx hollered from the kitchen, where a half-gallon of Jim Beam was proudly displayed on the counter. "It's the nigger lover!"

"Binx Sublette you stop with that foolishness this instant," Eddie hollered. "This is our second cousin you're are talking to, our kin, and he deserves the respect you would show for any of us, even if he is from California."

Johnny and Bessie were in the kitchen putting away the victuals and behaving as if they were as deaf as posts. My blood was boiling. "Aww, it's okay Howard," Binx said, coming at me with arms open as if he was about to give me a big hug. I would've liked to throw him a right hook, catch him square in the jaw, lift him clean off his feet, and send him toupee and all into the hearth of the fireplace. But instead I took Binx by his broad shoulders and coaxed him into one of the several overstuffed yellow club chairs in the front room, which he plopped into like an old rag doll. Dutifully, Bessie brought him a tray of crackers and fried green tomatoes topped with melting orange American cheese, maybe even Velveeta, and a tall bourbon on the rocks. Binx smiled and bowed slightly to Bessie, indicating his thanks, and proceeded to stuff his face without a word. Bessie had obviously seen this behavior before.

My Chown Hoon Dong was pulsating like a hazard signal as I pulled Eddie onto the front porch. "Eddie, under the circumstances I think it's best if I collect my sister and head home as soon as possible. Our lawyers can deal with the buyback of the land over the phone." (I had already decided that Mr. Hart probably had a conflict of interest and that I would hire my usual attorney, Chuck Hanger, to manage it.)

Eddie reached up, put his wrinkled hand on my whacked shoulder and gave it a painful squeeze. "Listen, son," he began, "I've spent a good deal of my life apologizin' for my brother's behavior, just as you've done for your sister. Binx is what we call around here a Jekyll and Hyde drinker – the more he drinks the crazier he gets, which I expect is very similar to your sister's behavior. Of course his language is offensive, especially to a Californian. But once you know what to expect, as with everything, you learn to deal with it." I pondered his 74 year-old wisdom, warmth replacing the fierce throbbing in my chest. He was right, of course, but I wasn't quite sure why I should stick around and learn to deal with it.

"Eddie, you are absolutely right. I am sorry. You have been nothing if not hospitable, but you've got to understand..."

"No, Howard. *You're* the one that's got to understand, if you don't mind my sayin'. You're our guest here at Camp Serendipity, it's true. But this here ain't California, you unnerstand? My brother Binx doesn't even like the idea that you're down here at our family fishin' camp, and the only reason you are here is 'cuz your sister is right next door. Now I don't see it that way. You're my cousin, and it doesn't matter to me if your daddy made a mess of things down here and decided to move away, you're still my cousin. From where I stand, that means you've a right to everything the family has to offer. Now if you'll just relax and enjoy our hospitality, we'll take care of the business that needs taking care of with no further fuss. My brother will come around, just as I hope your sister comes around. How's that sound?"

Oh, Eddie Sublette, the smooth old silver fox in his topsiders, the slacks with the little ducks on them and his Camp Serendipity logo polo shirt. But then Toya and Reggie came in with a load of supplies; Johnny deftly flipped on a local Cajun radio station and before you know it the bon temps was set to roll. Eddie extended his hand and we shook. I would try to keep the peace until I could figure out what to do with my sister.

The November darkness settled over the bayou as if someone had drawn the curtains. Suddenly the yellow lights on the other side of the front door screen to the dock were a mass of whirling, spinning bugs, especially Junebugs, crashing to the deck and twirling on their backs in a five-minute Saint Vitus death dance. Upon seeing the bugs, Jack burst through the screen door, still in the yellow rain gear and denim fleece-lined jacket. "Mr. Howard," he blurted, "Mr. Howard come on this is real fun!" He pushed past me out to the fishing dock outside the screened in porch and started dancing on the helpless upside-down June bugs in his bare feet, sliding around on their squishy guts, whooping and hollering in his own Saint Vitus interpretative ballet. Inside Binx was beginning to stir.

"Jack!" he barked, "Jack you halfwit sumbitch!"

"Don't you worry, sir. I'll take care of it," Reggie called out as he rushed onto the fishing dock from around back of the house. Then Johnny said, "Mr. Binx, Reggie gonna get your son, don't you worry, he'll be fine." His voice was soft, soothing, like a mental health professional trying to talk someone down from a fit.

Reggie ran out onto the dock under the light, his bare feet sliding out from under him as he fell on his ass with a crash, shaking the whole dilapidated structure. I stepped out onto the slick surface of the dock, holding the doorframe and extended an arm to Reggie who pulled himself up, grabbing my injured shoulder. I howled with pain, thinking *I should have brought the goddamn sling.* Meanwhile Jack was sliding along the sloping dock, then jumping, slipping his feet around in an uncanny display of natural balance, all the while avoiding falling on his prodigious butt. Toya and Eddie were on the screened porch, watching Jack's crazy boogaloo and Reggie's flailing attempts to grab him, sliding and falling until he finally got his arms around one of the crooked posts and righted himself.

Suddenly Jack stopped and stared out into the duckweed off the stern of the Sissy Mae, probably twenty yards away where the yellow lights from the dock faded into the darkness of the channel. "My pants!" he shouted, pointing at small floating pile atop the swamp vegetation. "And my underpants!"

Goddamnit, I cursed under my breath. *I thought I saw those pants sink!*

Then, just as Reggie leapt for the tackle, Jack ran down the dock and right into the water, unaware of the line attached to his pants and underpants. The duckweed barely came up to his middle, and he parted it with a wide sweeping motion, like parting jungle growth on an expedition, steadily sinking in the mud with each step. I ran down the pier to where I'd cleated the line and attempted to pull the bundle closer to where Jack was thrashing in the weeds.

"Grab the line, Jack," I shouted. Then, just as he got his hands on it a deafening shotgun blast split the soft and heavy night.

"Leave him be!" Binx fired the gun into the sky again. "Leave him be, I say! The Lord has called his damaged child to the swamp, and it is there he must perish!" Then he leveled the shotgun at Jack and was about to fire when Eddie came up from behind with an almost-full half-gallon jug of Jim Beam and cracked his brother upside the head with a weak but effective blow. Binx staggered forward and fired, sending up a splash of luminescent weeds and water only two feet from where his son stood with the bundle of muddy clothes in his arms.

Binx dropped, out cold. Eddie pulled the shotgun out from under his unconscious brother and headed back inside, cursing loudly at this pathetic display of Southern idiocy. But before Eddie made it through the door Jack let out an earsplitting feral howl, dropped the clothes, let go of the line and started writhing in the water. A seizure? Puce foam formed around his flailing limbs, a greenish, ochre mass of bubbles, a bayou milkshake. Then the writhing teen was under water, drowning perhaps, then up again, wild, wiggling and screaming in the mud. "Get that boy a life preserver!" Eddie shouted, "but do not set foot or anything else in that water!"

There was a preserver hanging next to the door of the hold, so I jumped off the pier onto the gunwale, tore it off the wall and pitched it to Reggie, who in turn pitched it right onto the mass of bubbles.

"Jack! Jack! Grab the life preserver! Jack!" Reggie yelled. The boy emerged with a hellish bark, glasses down around his neck, head strap loose, eyes rolled back as he pulled a monstrous snake out of the water and hurled it onto the bow of the Sissy Mae. Arm hooked in the donut, he collapsed into the water.

"Mister Howard, get down here and help me pull him out. I don't think he'll let go of the donut. Come on!" So Reggie and I began to try and haul Jack – two hundred and fifty pounds of gelatinous flab – out of the muddy, weed-choked water. Meanwhile Eddie had climbed up to the pilothouse where, shotgun at the ready, he swept the emergency lamp around and over Jack as the boy sank deeper in the mud.

"Jack, just relax your legs. We will pull you out, promise," Reggie yelled.

"Ten o' clock, snake at ten o' clock," shouted Eddie from above. I turned just as the report shattered and sent pieces of water moccasin flying every which way.

"Arghhhhhhh! Ooooh! God save me!" Jack screamed from the water, thrashing his arms to ward off more attacks. In another minute we got Jack to the pier, but then we had to get him up. His terrified screaming was as horrific as anything I've ever heard come out of a human – a Barney Fife possessed by demons – and there was no doubt in my mind that his hysteria was speeding the venom through his system at triple the normal rate.

After Reggie, Toya and I managed to get Jack's whole limp body onto the dock a light approached from further down the channel in the direction of Dr. Raymond Cobb's camp, where my sister was supposed to be staying. The boat was screaming down the narrow channel at full throttle, creating a massive wake that splashed violently against the shore, probably awakening every cottonmouth and alligator in the area. Just before arriving the driver cut the motor and coasted alongside the pier, to where we stood around Jack. The driver jumped out without a welcome or introduction and started asking questions. Have we found the bites, did we see the snake, how long since he was bit etc. Finally Eddie said, "thanks so much for comin' over, Ray. I 'spose you heard the gunshots?"

"Yessir, and the caterwaulin' from this young feller, and all y'all's shoutin'," the doctor replied, cutting through Jack's muddy slicker. "Y'all know how y'all can hear a pin drop out here."

Our group was silent as the doctor looked for the bites. "Looks like more than one cottonmouth got a piece of this boy. You said he threw one of the snakes on board?"

"Uh, yessir," Reggie said. "I suppose that snake is up there someplace." The doctor wiped away some mud from Jack's calf to reveal a heinous wound, like the snake took a bite out of him. The calf was already bigger than a football.

"Well, it looks like he ripped the snake right out of his leg," said the doctor. "See if you can find that fucker, will you please?"

Just as Reggie jumped over the gunwale with a flashlight I heard a siren in the distance coming our way; whirling lights of red and yellow flashed in the treetops, then around the corner into our smaller channel. It was an emergency airboat, the water equivalent of a police car and ambulance combined. Behind us a screen door slammed; Johnny with a small suitcase – a first aid kit. But before stepping onto the pier he quietly shuffled to where Binx lay in the Junebug muck on the dock, still unconscious. Johnny shone his flashlight over the supine body, then bent over to see if Eddie's drunken brother was still breathing. Slowly he scanned the brother's face, shaking his head.

"Mister Eddie," Johnny called over the sound of the approaching airboat. "You best come over here and see 'bout your brother. He ain't lookin' too good." Eddie gave the doctor a pat on the shoulder and stepped quickly up the gangplank to the dock.

The four paramedics pulled their airboat up to the dock and rushed to the two victims, a pair for Binx and the other two for Jack. Dr. Cobb had cut off the legs of Jack's yellow rain coveralls and after the medic took a quick look at the snakebites they called for an airlift. They quickly prepared several injections while simultaneously cleaning and dressing the surface wounds. Finally one of the medics asked me: "Does this boy have a parent or guardian on the premises?"

"Yessir. That's his father, Binx Sublette, over there with the nasty rap to the head. That's his uncle Eddie Sublette looking over him." When he asked where the mother was, I was tempted to say *none of your business, sonny.* It was a stupid, insensitive question, but based on the available evidence to date, this was an unusually stupid, insensitive part of the world. I said, "She's not here."

"And who are you?"

"Howard Brown, a second cousin. Visiting from California."

The paramedic nodded, smiling. "Oh, of course. Sissy Mae's brother from Cali. Does everybody grow so big in Cali? I reckon you ain't never been nowhere like this before, eh?"

"No sir, I have not," I said with a slight chuckle, wondering how this cracker knew my sister. The paramedic chuckled a little, then bent over Jack, unconscious from the injections. He pulled his eyelids up, then the lower part down. He opened Jack's mouth and stuck a gloved finger under his tongue, lifted it up. Nothing unusual. But when we looked over his body there were strange concentrations of shuddering muscle, and the wounds themselves were massive bruises covering his legs, feet and forearms.

"Jesus," I said, shocked by all the bites. "Is this kid gonna make it?"

"Hard to say. Usually a bite from a swamp viper won't kill a man if you get to him in time, but I've never seen anybody with so many bites in so many different places. It was like he stepped on a nest, but when you pointed out the location...well, snakes don't nest underwater."

In the distant west the sound of a chopper approached. Jack was loaded onto a gurney and rolled to the dock, an oxygen mask across his quiet face. To look at him one might think he was just a typical overweight Southern teenager with shitty eyesight, a bad hairdo, and in need of a shave, though there was something about the shape of his mouth that suggested something was awry in his brain.

On the dock the Junebug guts had become white and sticky as Elmer's glue. The paramedics had father and son, both unconscious, on gurneys under oxygen with IV drips plugged into the back of their hands. The medics were more worried about Binx; his pulse was slowed and his face has taken on a tinge of yellow ochre. The lump on the back of his head was bad, but not bad enough to cause any bleeding in the brain, according to the medics.

When Dr. Cobb – technically a psychiatrist that keeps his EMT certification up to date for swamp accidents like this one, I'm told – examined Binx he came to an entirely different conclusion.

"Alcohol poisoning," he stated with authority. "We see it fairly often out here in the bayou, and Binx Sublette is a prime candidate, with his history."

The amphibious chopper came into view, flying low over the channel, then pulling up and circling above the camp. After a couple of times around it settled over the water, the wind from the blades kicking up whitecaps that crashed against the pilings of the pier and the dock like a hurricane was upon us.

Once the chopper was at rest in the water with its blades still spinning slowly, a skiff was lowered and two EMTs exited from the door behind the cockpit, jumped in and piloted it over to where the two gurneys waited on the dock. The gurneys were collapsed; Jack was loaded into the skiff and taken to the chopper. Once Jack was loaded in the skiff they returned for Binx. His other son Bolling shouted over the din that he would be the family representative at the hospital and joined the crew in the copter. Slowly the whirring blades picked up speed, the waves kicked up and splashed over the Junebug guts on the dock, and the chopper, with Binx Sublette and his two boys aboard, took off down the channel.

Then, for a what felt like a long, discombobulated moment as the medics prepared to depart, I had a profound sense of complete displacement – an abstraction of real self from virtual self – as if I was not who I thought I was, but was exactly where I was supposed to be. The day's events, especially those of the last hour, had presented a glimpse of a familiar yet foreign existence and, though I had a vague memory of my original purpose at Camp Serendipity it was being crowded out by…by what? Ancestral memories? Had this strange and dangerous environment been sucked through my buzzing Chown Hoon Dong to create a disturbance in the chakras? Where was my psycho when I needed her?

I paused to study the suddenly familiar scene – the backwards boat, Sissy Mae, tied up to the rickety pier, the yellow light throwing its beams into the all-engulfing dark of the swamp; the low droning thrum of crickets and cicadas rising up like columns of circling smoke, punctuated by the hoot of a solemn owl and the belch of the lonely bullfrog; the quiet, still water, blanketed in its neon chartreuse, smoother than silk; all of it part of me from the day I was born and perhaps before.

And then I noticed one more thing. "Goddamnit!" I muttered under my breath. There were Jack's jeans and his nasty briefs, still floating at the same spot, tied up to the line that was still cleated to the Sissy Mae.

I shuffled down the pier, pulled out the clothes with a few globs of duckweed, schlepped the whole mess to the dock and laid it out. Tomorrow I would get them washed with strong hopes and maybe even a little prayer that Jack would think twice before he pissed in them again.

29 Pixie Dust

After all the airboats, skiffs, helicopters, and EMTs had finally cleared out and Jack's pants were spread out on the dock, we sat down to a quiet dinner of peppery boiled crawfish, corn and potatoes – food that I needed to be trained to eat, given the delicate technique required to extract the caterpillar-sized meat from the crawdad's tail. Sucking the head – a Feliciana parish tradition – wasn't nearly as difficult. After dinner I finally got a chance to talk to Dr. Raymond Cobb in private.

The night was alive with the symphony of the swamp: wailing cicadas and crickets, beating wings of bats and night birds, chirps of tree frogs and the rhythmic croaking of their amphibious cousins below, and the occasional splash of a jumping fish. I imagined I could hear the snakes slithering around the shore and the breathing of the prehistoric alligators, their snouts resting on the giant lily pads. I conjured voodoo lords, sorcerers and monsters, people disappearing and never heard from again – far more dangerous than my father's home-hospital room and my brick patio in San Anselmo, even more so without Mr. Booper. Were it not for the comfy, padded wicker rocker, the big tumbler of red, and the chemical salve of my opiates (which I had neglected almost all day with surprisingly few ill effects), I might have been freaking out.

"I'm told that the patient at my camp is your sister," Dr. Cobb began. I sensed a bit of caginess in the doctor's voice, along with that air of superiority that can make it so impossible to talk to some doctors about the truth. Like politicians, they can be difficult to pin down.

"Yes, or so I'm told. She disappeared about a week before my father died."

"Wait, did you say *before* your daddy died?" asked the doctor, his bushy Mark Twain brows raised over his bright hazel eyes. Beside the eyebrows and a thick mustache, Dr. Cobb's head was quite the cranial specimen. I imagine most men with a full head of hair like myself wonder what their skulls look like, though I don't ponder it much; the dent from my forceps delivery still feels like a moon crater. His skull looked like a mottled ostrich egg.

"Yes. About six days prior, I think. Does she know I'm here?"

"No. Eddie was very clear about that, though I think the work we've done this past week has helped her realize that you are not her enemy," Dr. Cobb said, leaning back in his rocker and pulling a large cigar from his breast pocket. "Cigar?" he drawled, as in "see-gar?" I declined.

"God, I hope so. It's my wife Sandy she can't stand, not me!"

"Mmmm, hmmm. Well that kind of depends what day it is, doesn't it?" Cobb said. He swirled the ice in his bourbon glass with a rhythmic "chink chink chink" and fiddled with his cigar. "It depends on what she's had to eat, what she's had to drink, how much exercise she's getting, how her brain is processing her medication or if she's even taking her medication. Humans are very complex organisms, Howard, and when something goes awry there are likely to be several factors behind it."

I'll admit I've seen a few psychiatrists and psychologists alike, and if Raymond Cobb didn't fit the mold I don't know who does. It scared me that he had his hand in the cupboard of any number of psychoactive drugs that could turn a garden-variety manic-depressive into a drooling vegetable in a matter of days.

"And how did my sister come to be your patient, Dr. Cobb?"

"Oh, please, call me Ray!" he insisted, chuckling that good old boy "everything's cool" chuckle and firing up his cigar with a big fanfare of flame. In the yellow light from the porch and the flicker of the cigar I noticed that Dr. Cobb was probably closer to Eddie's age than mine. They shared the ruddy pink complexion, though Dr. Cobb's nose was less bulbous and more aquiline with a bony ridge down the center to the tip, which curled up slightly. It fit his long face and long triangular jaw line, which also suited the droopy silver mustache over his unusually small mouth. In general form, Cobb was Stanley Laurel to Eddie's Oliver Hardy, or perhaps The Scarecrow to Eddie's Oz.

"Okay, Ray. How did you get involved with Sisi?"

"You mean Sissy Mae?" he said, again with the insider's chuckle. "Well, Howard, when your sister showed up in the French Quarter around Halloween she was a very confused woman. Lost, I would say. Delusional."

I sighed, long and heavy. Had I stayed with her that day after the storm, had I insisted that she get tested, had I insisted that she stay under observation, none of this would be happening.

"Was she...injured?" There was no way the gash on her head could have healed in the week between her leaving and Halloween, the day our father died.

"Yes. That's how she ended up with me. The next day after a night at the Royal Sonesta, the most expensive hotel on Bourbon Street, she started carrying on in her period dress, claiming she was Elizabeth Stewart and accosting locals as if they were runaway slaves. The cops picked her up, took her to the psych ward, and she ended up with me."

"So. Ray, how did you, as her doctor who just said she was delusional, let the infamous Sissy Mae, or Elizabeth Stewart, sell our inheritance, our one hundred acres of Briarwood, to Laurel Hill Energy Ventures?"

The doctor smiled and shook his head. "I'm sorry Howard, but nobody needed to convince Sissy Mae to do anything. One of the first things she told me after I started treating her psychosis and we started to learn a little bit more about each other was that she wanted to sell the property right away. This would have been about four days after she arrived. Fortunately she responded well to the medication and besides being a little jumpy from exhaustion, her brain would function normally for extended periods. Well, when I told her that I had a satellite practice in St. Francisville and happened to know the fellas at Laurel Hill Energy I turned her over to Stephen Hart."

"Well…that's very interesting," I replied, trying to remember if Hart had specifically mentioned that he had worked directly with my sister to put the deal together, or if he even had an interest in Laurel Hill Energy. I don't recall seeing his signature on any of the documents. "I met with Stephen Hart day before yesterday. He didn't mention that he put the deal together on behalf of my sister. Did you know that the death certificate and my signature on the bill of sale are forged?"

Now Dr. Cobb was looking seriously flummoxed. He gazed at the ash on his cigar, slowly tapping it onto the dock and twirling the glowing tip on the arm of the rocker. "I don't know how that's possible, Howard. The state of Louisiana requires two witnesses and a notary to execute a deal like this. You would have had to sign the document in front of a notary and another witness for it to be valid. Just the fact that the document isn't notarized…"

Just then the phone rang indoors, and Johnny hollered out for the doctor. "It's Sissy Mae doc. She says she's scared that something happened to you, Binx and the boys, and y'all got to get back home right now!"

"What? Where's Lawrence? Hold on, let me talk to her," Cobb shouted, getting up and shuffling toward the front door.

"I'll go with you." I set my wine glass on the dock.

"Howard, please. Now is not the time. Christ, it's almost 11," Cobb entreated, pausing, but I was nearing a state of panic. The Southern hospitality house of mirrors was starting to crack right there in the deepest darkest depths of the Little Tensas Bayou and I wanted nothing more than to get out of there.

.

But then I realized Tripp was due to arrive the next morning. I wondered if he was going to be embarking from the same marina. Maybe I could commandeer the doctor's speedboat, grab Sisi and wait out the night in some hidden cove. I could intercept him at the marina in the morning.

Then, without arriving at any conscious decision the periphery of my vision faded to blurred darkness and my body went racing down the dock. I jumped into the cockpit of Cobb's tiny speedboat, lowered the motor, started it up and pushed the throttle down hard. The boat whined and bucked, the bow popped up but we weren't going anywhere – we were still cleated to the dock. I wrenched myself up from the helm to un-cleat the line but by then it was too late. In my tunnel vision Dr. Cobb ran up and grabbed me by the shoulders, pulling me away from the boat.

"Jesus, Howard, what the hell do you think you're doing?" he cried. "Goddamnit, boy, if you're so fuckin' eager to see your sister, well all right then, let's go see her. You don't have to steal my goddamn boat!"

Eddie, standing on the pier about ten steps back began to waver in my vision while sweat burst from my pores. A tremendous pressure started pushing on my chest and I was having trouble breathing when I started seeing pixie dust: phosphorescent snowflakes begin swirling out of the edges of the tunnel, around Eddie and the camp behind. My legs began to quake. I closed my eyes and reached for the doctor, who asked, "Howard, are you all right? Are you having a stroke? Howard, can you hear me?" I clutched his shoulders to avoid falling on my face, clenched my jaw and, with my eyes still closed, concentrated on pushing back the dust, clearing it from my vision while consciously trying to quiet my quaking legs.

"Howard, please, open your eyes!" the doctor entreated. But I refused to open them until the last silver sparkle was gone. Suddenly there in the swirling snow stood a woman under a parasol, black hoop skirts fluttering in the breeze. It was Elizabeth Stewart calling, "Hurry, Howard. Hurry!" Then a confederate soldier –"Brownie," of Stonewall's Sharpshooters – swooped in on a jet black steed from the cypresses, and, without breaking stride, took his Southern belle around the waist and galloped out over the channel and across the water, disappearing into the cloud of luminescent flakes, while the cloud itself was sucked up in the draft of the horseman and his girl. All went dark.

"Howard, here, lie down, please." Dr. Cobb wrapped his arms around my barrel chest just as I felt my strength returning. I opened my eyes and the pixie dust was gone.

"Holy shit, what just happened?" I continued to steady myself with a hand on the doctor's shoulder.

"Jesus, Howard. I don't know. You tell me," said Dr. Cobb, in a state of genuine bewilderment. "It looks to me like you were trying to steal my boat and had a seizure of some sort. Are you prone to seizures? I wouldn't be surprised if you were, given your family history."

I hung my head, unable to speak, suddenly cold, shivering in the heavy night air. "There was Eliza...Elizabeth Stewart..." I stammered, "and my ancestor, a confederate cavalryman, Captain Howard Brown, and a black horse..."

"Come on, let's get you inside," Cobb said softly. Slowly we made our way down the pier, Cobb and Eddie doing their best to support my mammoth frame between them. I felt like my legs were floating and I was tumbling head over heels down Tripp's front steps again.

The men coaxed me down on a hard, single bed, a bed designed for fishermen for whom sleep is inconvenient necessity; fishermen who are on the water before the sky announces another day. They removed my sweat-soaked t-shirt and shorts, then heaped blankets across my shaking body while Toya used her soft, warm hands to rub the clammy skin on my shoulders, my legs, my chest, and my pelvis. After a cup of hot lemon sweet tea laced with bourbon, my trembling finally subsided. Then came the pain: every suture inside and out, every former bruise, every sprain, strain, cut and scratch began to burn and throb. My pillbox was on the nightstand but I couldn't move to get it, couldn't speak, groan or even whimper. But Toya knew, she could see my desperation, so she gently placed the pills on my tongue – all of them, a double dose, and I chewed, swallowed, chewed some more, delighting in the bitter taste of the chemicals.

Not long after, my body felt encased in a sarcophagus of warm paraffin, spreading lovely heat from the tips of the hairs on the top of my head down to the last cells of my gnarled toenails, and my eyes grew heavy. Then, just as the soothing wax began to close around my aching brain I had one final, clear thought, a realization that just when I thought I was taking charge, calling the shots, making my moves, writing my ticket, baking my cake and eating it too, I'd been called out, cut down, put back in my place. Life had, once again, pushed me crashing down the stairs; the father had flung the howling, helpless baby against the wall, only to have it break through and shoot like a rocket into the coldest, loneliest faraway place in the universe.

30 The Real Sissy Mae

That night after my pixie dust vision, my father buzzed me out of my doped-up sleep, or visited me in a dream – it's hard to tell the difference when you're communicating with the dead – to tell me that he was not surprised by my failure to grab the bull by the horns. It was what he had come to expect, he said. "Just like on the golf course, every time you had a short putt to win the whole shootin' match, you blew it."

"Of course I blew it! Good God can you imagine? I could see you in your charcoal grey business suit on the little knoll above the ninth green from the tee. I could see the smoke of your pipe. You watched my drive; you watched my second shot roll six feet from the pin. The coaches, all the other players and you, the only parent, watched as I lined up the putt. When I missed it you turned, walked up the knoll out to the parking lot, got in your car and drove home. Why did you leave me there without a ride home? Because I missed a birdie putt? Remember what you said at the dinner table that night? 'You know what I would be doing right now instead of stuffing my face? I would be out back putting until I could sink 20 six-footers in a row. Even if it took all night. But you? No way.' Right, Dad. No fuckin' way."

There was a long silence on the other end of the chakra line. He knew he had been a prick, even admitted it on his deathbed, yet here he was after death serving it up again. So I figured if I made him feel crappy enough about his bullshit he might decide to vacate my third chakra and go wherever it was he had decided was waiting for him – the black hole of infinite self-recrimination.

"Sisi claims that you tried to gas yourself in the Buick Regal. She says she found you unconscious with a garden hose taped to the exhaust. Was that after I failed to make the CU golf team? Or was it after you had to send Sisi to Baton Rouge for an abortion? Or was it after you found out that the baby was fathered by an African American?"

"Well," he said, "you've got your facts mixed up as always. I don't know why I ever imagined you could practice law. It is true that we sent your sister to Baton Rouge for a little procedure, then to Briarwood for a little while to allow her to reflect on her...uh... bi-racial transgressions. That was a mistake. Not the abortion, but putting your sister in the sights of Binx Sublette. Or vice versa. There was no way for your mother and I to know that she would have a twenty-year-long affair with him. Later, I mean. I doubt anything happened when she first went down there. Shit, she just had an abortion. But she admitted that Binx had been a perfect gentleman, even if he did seem to be a bit drunk all the time."

Binx Sublette? Shacking up with Sisi? I couldn't see it. "What's this about Binx Sublette?"

My chakra father chuckled. "You'll find out, trust me." A cruel response. What was I supposed to know? Did Binx have anything to do with the forgeries? Was he trying to bilk the "folks from Cali" – the folks that "he had little use for" – out of their Louisiana inheritance?

"Okay, if you want to play it that way, let me ask you this. You asked me, in those final days, if I thought Mom loved you. Did you wonder if she slept with other men on her European tours with her sister? The trips you refused to go on because golf was not on the agenda?"

Again, he had no comeback. Perhaps he was already packing and getting ready to go. Perhaps my eviction tactics were working. I went for the jugular.

"Do you ever wonder that if you had left Mom in bed when her tummy ached during those last days – if you had left her there instead of yanking her out of bed, pulling her jammies down and forcing her to sit on the geriatric can, thinking that her only problem was constipation – do you wonder if she would have lived longer if you hadn't taken matters into your own hands? When the caregiver showed up, shocked to see Mom cold and weeping on the senior potty, her jammies around her knees, she yelled at you, didn't she? What the hell do you think you're doing? Can't you see that she's in pain? She called me, she said get over here right away your father's out of control. What were you thinking? If Mom could just take her normal morning dump she would come in and make your breakfast like always? Were you thinking?"

Now I had pushed him over the edge, blaming him for expediting my mother's death. "Your mother…she…well, yes, she went on those trips with her sister so she could have affairs with foreign men, as if she was back in her twenties and traveling Europe for the first time. That's why she loved those river cruises. The Elbe. The Danube. She could pick one from the herd and shack up for a few days."

"That's not what I was asking about!" I cried. But he continued as if he hadn't heard a word I said.

"But she wasn't in her twenties. And when the young guys discovered she wasn't much more than a bag of bones under all the Talbots's, Anne Taylor and cashmere, under the push-up padded bras…she had no choice but to come back home. She probably caught the awful-awful from one of those shoe salesmen."

I would've hung up on him if I could. Besides, it was starting to get light outside – the birds were tuning up for their morning performance – and I needed several more hours of uninterrupted, dead-to-the-world sleep. Remarkably, the buzzing faded away. He must have felt so bad... if he was alive he would have rushed out and bought everybody in the family a diamond ring, a cashmere scarf, and a new set of golf clubs. That would fix it.

After our exhausting bout of finger pointing I managed to fall asleep for a few more hours. Later, after coffee, cornbread, bacon and sweet, buttery, creamy grits, I felt ready for a chat with Sisi. Or Sissy Mae. Or Elizabeth Stewart, though I wondered if Elizabeth Stewart would even acknowledge me as her brother. I was edgy, nervous, anxious and suffering from some related indigestion. A disturbance in the large colon, perhaps. But there were no silver sprinkles, no shakes, no pain, no wobbles. The nerves made me a little weak in the knees, but I didn't plan on chasing her around the Doctor's cabin.

It was a cool, clear autumn morning, just like it was the morning before in West Feliciana; the kind of morning that makes my teeth ache and my nostrils quiver; a shoulders-back, stiff upper lip, chin-tucked-under kind of morning that gives one hope for the future of the earth and its eternal power to cleanse the beings upon it.

Except for Dr. Raymond Cobb. He looked like the previous evening had been too much for his 70 year-old sensibilities; deep hound dog bags drooped under his eyes like his mustache drooped under his long, bony, purple-tipped nose. His egg-shaped dome was mottled, splotchy, and in need of a beanie.

"Sissy Mae didn't sleep well last night," he said as he pulled up to the pier without so much as a good morning. "Nor did I." I could understand why he was being a little wary of me after the previous evening. "I think the commotion down here – all the shooting and yelling and such – upset her. And when she heard about Binx and his son she fell apart. The nurse and I were up with her for a while before I finally gave her a little extra sleep medicine. So if she appears a little dopey, that's why."

The nurse?

We motored out into the channel where the water was the color of black tea, so dark that you might expect a bucketful to be black as well. The air was much lighter: the bald cypress and various types of brush, shrubbery, vines, and creepers looked as if a great weight had been lifted from them, making the sun's rays much easier to capture. The birds, too, were singing hallelujah to the clear cobalt sky; herons, ducks and egrets swooped down the channels in formation. The sinister swampiness of everything had retreated to the shadows.

"She still doesn't know you're coming," Dr. Cobb announced in his Garden District drawl as his neat, clean and beautifully built camp came into view, still a ways down the channel. "I want to do everything I can to keep her from withdrawing, which she'll do when frightened. So I've instructed the nurse to keep her in her room until you're comfortably settled on the porch. Then I'll inform her that we have a visitor and bring her out."

"Wow. She must have told you some real whoppers, if she's led you to believe that she's afraid of me," I said, slack-jawed at all the precautions he thinks are necessary. "Trust me, if anybody is scared, it's me. She can be a veritable Medusa when she's angry."

"Yes. Well, we've taken care of that."

"What? Her temper?"

"Yes. EST is very effective at controlling tantrums."

A sudden surge, a giant full-body hiccup, coursed through me. My heart jumped into my mouth, my jaw snapped shut and I had an overwhelming urge to crush the man's pinheaded skull with whatever blunt object I could get my hands on. Or gouge his eyeballs out. Yes, just like a commando. Wouldn't need any accessories for that.

"You...you..." I was having great trouble getting it out, "Wait, Ray...you prescribed shock therapy for my sister?"

There was a long pause as we chugged up to Dr. Cobb's pier. He cut and raised the outboard motor, slid the key out of the ignition and turned to me. "We're here," is all he said, heaving his tall frame out of the boat, then extending a hand to me. I took it, and stepped over the driver's seat but just before stepping out I gave his hand a strong jerk, as if to pitch him into the water.

"Listen, Dr. Cobb. We're not off to a very good start here." I paused to let the sounds of the swamp settle in: the chirps, croaks and rhythmic drone of the cicadas and Junebugs. I let the calming groove sink into my skin. "You fried my sister's brains without my permission? I mean, what the fuck...?"

Cobb smiled sympathetically, his tired eyes so forlorn on his long face. "In the state of Louisiana, shock therapy is prescribed when a patient is psychotic," he said in a low voice. "No permission necessary. And let me tell you, your sister is psychotic, without question. Or perhaps I should say that she has exhibited psychotic behavior, and probably will again. I can't guarantee that she won't need another round at some point."

I studied the doctor's gaunt visage, trying to get beyond my suspicion that he was hiding something. I didn't want to believe that any of it – Sisi's masquerades, her forgeries, Laurel Hill Energy Ventures – anything other than what it was on the surface. I wanted to believe the mute angel in my heart who was trying to say: *Look, these people are more like you than you think. Nobody is out to screw you, these are just people, and people make mistakes.* Bullshit my internal red devil hollered. *These crackers would like nothing more than to take a California hippy camping in the swamp.*

As I was thinking this, my heart now whump whump whumping in my throat and the beginnings of pixie dust forming at the periphery of my vision, Dr. Cobb stretched up and put his arm around my shoulder, coaxing me down the pier to his pretty little swamp house.

"You seem very nervous, Howard. How do you feel? Are you sure you're steady enough to have this meeting?" Dr. Cobb stopped; we faced each other as he gave me the once over, looking up to study my eyes. "Would you like something to help you relax? A little Xanax, perhaps?"

Never being one to turn down drugs, I nodded. I was very, very anxious on top of my normal heebie-jeebies. I checked my watch to see where I was with my dosing schedule, relieved that in an hour I would get 10 milligrams of methadone and 10 milligrams of oxycodone, which on top of the Xanax would calm me down to a level where I assumed most people function naturally.

A guy that looked like a retired NFL linebacker greeted us at the door to the screened porch, and just seeing this fellow was like a salve to my inflamed brain. My breathing began to relax as Dr. Cobb situated me in a comfortable rocker on the screened porch and retreated into the house to get the drugs. Meanwhile I marveled at this massive specimen of humanity. This miraculous man, at least my height at six-six and I'm guessing 260 pounds, didn't appear to have an ounce of fat on him, and he was at least 50 if not 55.

"Welcome to Little Tensas Mental Health Services, Mr. Brown. My name is Lawrence. I'm the doctor's nurse and assistant." His voice was so low and grumbly that to hear him say 'I'm his nurse' made me think of Bigfoot running a daycare center. I quickly shook his hand.

"I'm pleased to meet you, Lawrence. You remind me of a famous linebacker, also named Lawrence, who played for the New York Giants.

Lawrence Taylor."

"Thank you sir. I humbly admit that you're not the first person to make that association." Lawrence set down a tray of finger sandwiches, fried green tomatoes dripping with Velveeta and topped with shelled crayfish, a basket of popcorn shrimp, two ice-filled glasses and a pitcher of sweet tea. Since it hadn't been much more than an hour since my sweet n' buttery grits, I wasn't inclined to start stuffing my face again so soon.

"Ha! Really?" I said, still standing, "Well you do look a lot like him, or I guess you look a lot like what he must look like now."

"Thank you, sir." Lawrence replied with an enigmatic grin. As he poured the tea Dr. Cobb returned with a couple of pills.

"Here are two. Take one now and if you're still shaking in your boots in twenty minutes take the other one. If you don't mind I would like have a chat with you about these episodes...or at least about the episode you had last night. I suspect there's something that can be done for that." *Yeah, right. Hook my brain up to the jumper cables and turn 'er over.*

The doctor took a seat and put his spidery, long-fingered hand on my spastic knee, which was jumping up and down as it often does in stressful situations. "There's a cure for this too," he said, softly pressing on the knee until it stopped its relentless twitching.

"Sorry, I can't help it."

Lawrence laughed. "Yeah, the old restless leg. I had that too for a long time, but the doctor here helped me whip it, didn't you, Doc?"

"Yeah, LT, we whipped it," said Doc, using the famous linebacker's old nickname. I looked up at the imposing figure in his casual white T-shirt and shorts. His blinding smile made him look like he wouldn't hurt a flea.

After Lawrence retreated to the kitchen, Dr. Cobb gave my knee a squeeze and said: "Your sister seems pretty good today, somewhat tired as I expected from last's night's poor sleep. But mentally she's lucid and rational, if a little dreamy. I'm going to go get her and bring her in now, then I will leave you two alone. Just ring this bell if you need assistance or anything else."

"Doc?" I asked, suddenly with visions of a drooling, drop foot, claw-handed mongoloid. "Will she recognize me?"

"Of course! Unless she chooses not to, that is. I'm sure you can understand why she may decide on that approach."

"Oh yes," I said, thinking back on my sister's semi-pro acting abilities. I sat down, listening intently for the sound of her voice over the incessant squawking and buzzing of the swamp. Finally after what felt like an eternity the front door opened. I stood, turned and, upon seeing her felt a distinctive, painful hiccup in my heart. Her image became blurry, wavering about five feet before me, and the only thing I could think of to do was open my arms, which I did. I opened them as wide as I could, smiled, and said "Sisi! It's me, Howard! Your brother!" But she just stood there, a bemused little grin forming and fading, forming and fading on her lips.

Finally Dr. Cobb said: "Sissy Mae, are you going to say hello to your brother? He's come a long way to see you." Sisi looked up at the doctor, then over at me, then reached in the front pocket of the knee-length pale pink smock, under which she wore a very loose fitting semi-see-through white cotton blouse. She pulled out a silver cigarette case, one of our mother's heirlooms, but her little birdlike claws were shaking so bad she couldn't get a cigarette out. Then the case fell from her hand and cigarettes went spilling across the floor.

"Oh dear," said Dr. Cobb quietly. "Don't worry sweetheart, I'll take care of it." The old doctor bent down, snatched a single cigarette, stood up, put it in Sisi's mouth and lit it. She took a long drag, her already caved cheeks sucking in so hard that her entire body appeared to fill with smoke. Exhaling slowly the smoke surrounded her head, curling up over her pallid, alabaster face up into her black and silver gray hair, still cut short and pushed into unkempt chaos. It was hard to believe the freak storm and her injury were just a short while ago, with all that had happened since.

"Sisi," I said, leaning forward with my arms still open wide. "You do recognize me, don't you?"

Then, in a voice so thin and quiet I thought our dead mother had joined us, she said: "Howard? Howard Brown? Is it really you?"

When the sobs came I took her in my arms, holding her emaciated body as tightly as I dared without crushing her, her head on resting my big stomach. On and on she cried, blubbering and coughing, her skeleton body wracked with barking sobs, until Dr. Cobb touched her shoulder and said: "Perhaps this was not such a good idea. Maybe we should try again another time. Take it slow, okay, Sissy Mae?"

But Sisi wouldn't hear of it, crying out meekly through flowing tears: "No! Please! Don't go, Howard! Please, Dr. Ray, don't make him go."

"All right, all right," said Dr. Cobb. "Why don't you just sit here and try and relax. I'll get you some medicine and we'll see, okay? We'll just see."

"Thank you, Dr. Ray," she whispered. He helped her into the rocker while I sat down, wishing I had a bottle of red wine to go with the Xanax, which was probably the only thing preventing a massive pixie dust seizure.

"Oh, Howard," Sisi said, reaching for a loose cigarette. "Oh Howard," she repeated. "Do you remember when I called you Junior?"

"Yes, of course," I said, feeling like I was talking to an old demented granny. "I liked it."

She was a waif, pale and delicate as dandelion seeds. The pink around the rings of her crying eyes was the only color in her pale, drawn face. The mole that once distinguished her chin was gone, and her eyebrows, once dark and masculine, had been shaved, replaced with what looked like black magic marker. The enamel veneers that covered the gray, stubby choppers of her youth were stained brown and yellow; her thin lips pursed over them in embarrassment, I suppose. Those veneers weren't cheap.

"What are you doing here, Howard?" she asked, taking my hand in hers. I could've said that I'd come to visit my cousins, or to sell the land, or move onto the land, or to take Tripp fishing – any number of things – but I decided that if I was going to expect her to be honest, at least to the degree that she recognized the truth in her fantasy world, then I'd better be honest too.

"I've come to take you home."

"But this is my home," Sisi said without missing a beat. "This has always been my home."

A part of me had been expecting this, assuming that the Elizabeth Stewart stories were true.

"You didn't ever live in Northern California? In Kentfield, California?"

"No, Howard! We've always lived here: you, Mom and Dad, right down the road in Baton Rouge!"

All I could do was nod my head and smile. A little twinge of foot pain was starting to break through the Xanax buzz, sending electric signals up through my ankles and into my legs, while my Achilles tendons both started throbbing right on cue. I cracked open my pill bottle and washed down a hearty dose, along with the extra Xanax, and waited. When Sisi got up to use the facilities, I signaled Cobb.

"This amnesia, I guess you would call it – this idea that she's lived here, or Baton Rouge, her entire life – does that come and go?" I asked him.

"The short answer is 'no,' at least not since her last EST treatment. Temporary amnesia after EST is pretty common. For now, she thinks she grew up in Baton Rouge, but that won't last," Cobb replied.

Sisi returned, and before she could sit down I asked her, "Sisi, where do you live down here? I mean, where is your house?"

"Oh, Howard! You should know! I live out in Briarwood, down the road from the old plantation house on the property we own back in the woods there. Wow! And I thought my memory was bad!" I shot the doctor a stern glance, *as if to say this better be temporary, Doc.*

Then, just as I saw Reggie pulling up to the dock in Eddie's two-seater fishing skiff to retrieve me, the phone rang. It was Tripp.

"Hey, Dad! Yeah! Awesome…" and he went on to tell me in that relaxed Big Lebowski dude-speak that *Outside* magazine got some great video, photos etc. of him landing big monster redfish and even a sailfish in the gulf, all on a fly, (though he can't see the pictures, of course) and that they've left the marina, they're on the way, and that he has a couple of surprises for me.

"Oh no," I whispered, "you know I had a little meeting with my sister today—I'll fill ya in but suffice it to say that I don't know if I can handle any more surprises."

"Oh, don't worry, Dad. You'll love these."

He hung up, saying that we might have time to take the boat out for some redfish fishing in the evening. The temporary distraction of his ebullient energy had probably helped to avert a pixie dust attack, since my sister's irrefutable insanity, exacerbated by her claim that she lived on the land that she had sold to Laurel Hill Energy Ventures, was rattling around in my head like a racquetball. How she managed to go completely over the top in a week or so was a mystery that I would need to take up with Dr. Cobb. Did the blow to the head in the Sprinter jar loose some especially noxious brain chemicals?

"Who was that?" Sisi asked, as I got ready to go. We never got a chance to discuss the forgeries, or the masquerades, neither of which she seemed capable of carrying out, or at least not in her current condition.

"That was Tripp!"

"Tripp?"

"Yes, Tripp, my son, your nephew." I didn't want to ask how her kids were doing, or her ex, or Arno, for fear she wouldn't even remember who they were.

"Oh? Your son? Is he piloting the Sissy Mae?" I looked up at Lawrence, who probably didn't know anything about Tripp, same as Dr. Cobb, and decided to let her ignorant bliss carry her for as long as it would carry her. Maybe she would remember that her nephew was blind, maybe not. Maybe she wouldn't even recognize him. Hell, maybe I would have a couple of more pixie dust episodes, lose my mind, forget my past, forget my parents, forget my addiction, forget my son's accident, forget my chown hoon dong and the peanut gallery in my soul, forget that I've been married for thirty years and fall in love with old six-foot Sandy all over again.

31 One Stitch at a Time

When I arrived back at Camp Serendipity Tripp was there, surprises in tow: Elke and Sandy. After I practically got down on my knees and thanked the lord Jesus for saving my big fat lonely ass, the four of us put our squishy NorCal sentimentality on display on the dock while the cracker water taxi crew looked on, leering and spitting as if they were waiting for us all to get naked for a frisky four-way. Had Binx been there he might have thrown down some coin to make it happen.

Since arriving at Camp Serendipity I had felt like a Peace Corps worker dropped into the impenetrable backwoods of a mysterious, unknown third-world country with a collection of folks whose way of thinking was as foreign as the indigenous tribes of the Amazon rainforest. The arrival of my remaining family was like Dr. Livingstone being discovered in a giant cook pot being boiled by a tribe of restless, hungry natives. Now we could all boil in the pot together.

There hadn't been an opportunity to tell Tripp, Elke or Sandy about Jack, who was relegated to a wheelchair while his snakebites recovered. Nor had I told Jack that my son was blind. Jack's twin brother Bolling had seen pictures of Tripp, as had his father, in various fishing magazines, so when he showed up with his white cane, tapping on this and that to get the lay of the land, it was no surprise to them. But Jack had never seen anything like it, and Tripp had never been around anyone with an intellectual disability before.

"What's that stick for? And the whistle around your neck?" Jack had asked almost immediately after they were introduced. He had been sitting in his wheelchair on the front porch, watching the party disembark from the water-taxi. He saw how Elke held Tripp's elbow and guided him down the pier as he tapped the planks before him, not that her guidance was necessary – Tripp had been on more piers by the time he was 26 than most people are in a lifetime. Still, Jack wasn't quite sure what to make of the curly-headed blonde guy in the mirrored sunglasses with the white stick and the whistle around his neck.

Had Tripp been able to see Jack's shiny, wet lips, his scruffy beard, his magnified eyes behind his thick glasses, his rough hands and stubby fingers, and the way his fat gut hung out from under his soiled T-shirt, he would have guessed that Jack was disabled. But he couldn't. Still, there was something in Jack's voice – the high-pitched timbre, the declarative insistence of his questions, the childish tone, coupled with the knowledge that Jack was no child – that must have cued Tripp.

"These are my eyes," Tripp replied, taking the whistle in one hand, and tapping Jack's wheelchair with his stick. He put the whistle in his mouth and blew a short tweet.

"No they're not!" Jack immediately blurted like a cocksure four-year-old. "Your eyes are in your head!" He removed his glasses with one hand and pointed to his own eyes with the other, like a child identifying body parts.

"Oh, well, yes, that's true for most people," Tripp said, smiling, "but the eyes in my head can't see."

"Jesus Christ," Jack's brother Bolling interrupted, having so far been unable to take his eyes off of Elke, who in yoga pants and a hoodie must have looked like a gift from the Kit-Kat club to him. "He's blind, Jack!" Bolling continued. "Haven't you ever heard of Tripp Brown, the famous blind fly fisherman?"

Then Jack suddenly began to cry. "No!" he wailed, pulling at his stringy hair. "And I don't care! You can't make me!" He set his jaw and stared angrily at the planks of the deck. At this Elke shot me a curious glance, to which I only had to nod.

"Oh, that's okay, Jack," Elke cooed, reaching over and patting his shoulder. "We're so glad to meet you! Would you like to play cards with us?"

Jack looked up, frowning and sniffling. "How?" he asked, looking back at Tripp, who didn't need to hear the whole question to know that Jack wanted to know how he could play cards if he couldn't see. Or how Tripp could possibly play cards with a stick and a whistle.

"Stick around, Jack. I'll show you how," Tripp said, smiling and tapping the wheelchair with his stick.

"This I gotta see," said Bolling, laughing and turning his brother around in his chair and heading back into the house. "Come on, Jack. Let's see how a blind guy plays cards."

Yesterday's warmth and sparkle had degenerated into damp, swampy, refrigerated mist that sunk into my joints like dried ice. Sandy, all six feet of her, was bundled head to toe in jeans and a parka, but to me it didn't matter if she wore a hazmat suit. She was in the swamps and channels of Little Tensas, two thousand miles from home, supposedly to help save her own worst enemy from…from…what? More shock therapy? Or to get our land back? Or simply because she would rather be together in hell than alone in paradise?

"Jesus, hon, what a crew!" she remarked. We lay in a single bed together, her skin warm and silky against mine under a pile of blankets, both of us stuffed with seafood gumbo, fried trout, redfish, oysters and crayfish, mustard and turnip greens, corn and potatoes and finally a berry cobbler from berries Bessie had picked in the summer and had frozen. But they were so sugared up I wouldn't have been able to tell if they were berries or dog turds.

The house was dark and quiet, save for the whisperings of Tripp and Elke in the room next door, and the rhythmic, gentle snores of the Sublette twins on the sofa bed in the front parlor. It was a chore getting Jack out of his wheelchair and into bed. He mewed and caterwauled like a midnight tomcat every time we touched his legs, so we finally picked up the whole chair – Bolling, Tripp, Reggie and I – and dumped him into the sofa bed while he screeched like a barn owl.

"Oh, baby. It's been like a three-ring country carnival with this gang. And I'm not so sure the fun has even yet to begin," I whispered, spooning her from behind with my tumescent wiener tucked between her fine pillowy buttocks like caterpillar in a cocoon, my feet and ankles hanging over the end of the bed. "You don't know the half of it yet," I said, wondering if I should tell her about my sister selling the property.

"Oh really?" she whispered, squirming around to face me and almost pushing me out of the tiny bed. "Which half don't I know?"

"Well, about the property…" I began.

"Sisi sold it illegally, I know. Stephen Hart called me to confirm that your father had died, and when I asked him why he wanted to know, he told me the whole story. He sounded disappointed that those death certificates were actually forgeries. I guess he thought that the real death certificate, the one you showed him, was a fake."

My heart started thumping and I pushed myself up on one elbow. "Oh, honey. That is so not good."

"Why? Wouldn't you do the same thing if you were him?" After pondering this for a moment, I said:

"I might if I had a vested interest in the property, which Mr. Hart has been careful not to admit. But if he really sounded disappointed then he's tipped his hand. He's a part of this Laurel Hill Energy group that took advantage of my mentally-ill sister."

Sandy propped herself up on one elbow so we faced each other, the sticky cold air sending goose bumps up my back. "Wait a minute, Howard.

Hart said that Sisi initiated the sale – she came to him with the forged death certificates ready to talk turkey."

It looked like part of Sandy was starting to see that all this time she'd pegged Sisi for a purposefully malevolent bitch when it may have been bad brain chemicals to blame after all. "You probably didn't know this, but this Doctor she's been seeing that has a house about a mile from here – he gave her shock therapy."

Sandy gasped. "You mean electro-shock, with the big...I don't know what they are...shockers, I guess."

"Yes. The kind they gave Randle McMurphy until they finally gave him the lobotomy."

Sandy grew quiet and turned her head to the wall. I wrapped my arms around her and rested my head on her shoulder. "Don't feel bad, honey. I didn't think her condition was this serious either."

"It's a bad business, Howard," she said without turning her head. "We've got to get her out of here."

I felt like something had entered the room very slowly, a warm vapor, yet dry, hovering above us in the bed, a pale canopy enveloping us. There's her, there's me, and there's the presence of us together, a palpable force that surrounds us, levitates us, protects us like a sci-fi force field. I gave her a hard squeeze, and she turned to face me. "Oh Howard, forgive me," she said in a broken whisper, warm tears on her cheeks. "Please?"

"Your wish is my command, my sweet baby," I joked, substituting cliché for whatever a true, meaningful heartfelt response might be. Chronic cleverness. I made a note of it and vowed to try harder.

We chuckled, then kissed and kissed some more, and we made love, again, very slowly, very quietly, and for a brief moment the impenetrable darkness outside the double-hung window turned a deep, luminous blue. After, not long after, we drifted off in what I have been unable to admit all this time but have known to be as real and true as the moon, the sun, the stars and the sky. We were in it; this force field, this cocoon, this halo – I could feel it. Am I afraid to admit its existence because I'll be embarrassed, like I might be if I admitted to believing in Santa Claus or the Easter Bunny in front of other sober, responsible adults? Or does it even matter, so long as I admit it to myself? Probably not. But it – this presence – was as palpable as the nose on my face. God in His Almighty Loving Glory was in the house.

33 Bayou Theory

Binx Sublette had probably never been a member of the tragically clever, self-absorbed or chronic wiseass class. Instead, he skipped that altogether and went direct to the top of the asshole class. He was also the first to admit it. So when Sandy and I awoke to hear that Binx had returned from his brief dry out and gone over to Doc Cobb's to pay my sister a little visit, I had some special cause for concern. According to the commentator in my third chakra, Sisi and Binx had been having an affair for years. But there was much more to know about my suspected adversary, so I figured I might just have to ask around, as they say. Then I saw Johnny in his deck chair fishing the channel from the end of the pier. He spied me and shouted: "Howard, get yourself a chair and get down here. Look!" He slowly bent over and pulled up a stringer full of fish. "The cold weather done got them bitin' like crazy, storin' up for the winter." *Aha! My mole!* I thought.

The younger folks plus old Eddie had commandeered the Sissy Mae for the day: Toya and Reggie, Tripp and Elke, and the Sublette twins had headed out to explore – and fish – the Little Tensas Bayou with Captain Eddie at the helm. Figuring Bessie and Sandy might be busy for a while I grabbed one of the folded deck chairs and a rusted spinning rig leaning against the side of the house, but as I was walking down the pier my soul hole buzzed and I was hit with a sudden hesitancy: it was the voice of my father, and he was saying, "Shouldn't you be going to collect your sister right now? Shouldn't you be contacting an attorney about contesting the sale of your property? (I would suggest Chuck Hangar)." And then, the classic summation: "Don't you have work to do?" Standing there on the pier in the crisp autumn morning, Bessie and Sandy and a host of other birds chattering in the background, white feathers of smoke from Johnny's pipe curling up against the dark wall of cypress, coffee in one hand and a fishing rod in the other, I silently told the old man to go fuck himself. The craziness would continue soon enough. Besides, I was gathering intelligence.

The water was clear of weeds and black as India ink out in the channel, but Johnny was casting back toward the weeds where the bass, redfish and speckled trout were feeding. The bayou was alive with cormorants, ducks, egret and other waterfowl, also cashing in on the late fall feeding frenzy. Johnny had his shotgun lying on the pier and, tied to a stringer floating in the water, a couple of the pestilential nutria rats. He said it was unlikely for gators to be active in the cold weather, which was probably sixty degrees and just perfect in my estimation. The dense, invasive cold from the night before had given way to light, brisk atmosphere that seemed to sparkle on the treetops and the sunny ripples in the quiet channel.

"Howard, reach in that cooler and grab me a bag of that frozen shrimp. The pink stuff."

I handed him the bag. He opened his pocketknife, carved off a hunk of frozen shrimp and baited the hook of my rod. "All right then, I want you to cast it out the other way, where the boat usually is tied up, just short of that duckweed. The fish is all lined up right there, chowin' down on water bugs like they're at one of those big all-you-can-eat places on Highway 61."

I tried to think back to the last time I cast a spinning rod, my fingers reflexively recalling to hold the line under my index finger of my right hand, open the bail with my left, and let it fly. And fly it did, about two feet before the line snapped back and the little ball of shrimp nearly knocked my cap off.

"Jesus. I am such an idiot," I grumbled, now having tangled the line around the reel and losing the ball of shrimp.

"Howard, I don't wanna hear you talk like that no more, you hear me?" Johnny's unexpected admonition threw me off. *Talk like what? No taking the Lord's name in vain?* "There's enough people like to call a man an idiot without him callin' himself one too, you unnerstand?" *Ahh...okay.* I got the sense that even though Sandy had just arrived the night before she had told everybody that Howard's gotta cool it with the self-deprecation, and to slap my hand every time I said something mean to myself. Like calling myself an idiot.

"Gotcha. Guess I haven't cast a spinning rig for a while."

Johnny carefully took the rod from my hand, deftly untangled the line around the reel with his soft, steady, big-knuckled fingers, then slid the rod back so he could bait the hook. Still sitting in his chair, he showed me how to hold the line against the rod with my index finger, and how to open the bale so that it stayed open.

"The bale won't close until you turn the handle clockwise," he said, opening the bale and clicking it shut with the reel handle. "Okay, here goes." He laid the rod out flat behind him, then cast, the reel singing while the line sailed high over the water and landed with barely a splash where the duckweed stopped. Johnny let the bait sink, one-one thousand, two one-thousand, three one-thousand, then began to reel in slowly, his gnarled left hand moving in rhythmic, deliberate circles, now and then twitching the rod tip left and right, hoping to startle a fish into biting. Once we saw the bait under the water he quickly reeled it in and handed me the rod. "Go get 'em, Howard," he said.

After a few tries I had it down, but after about twenty casts I still got no takers. I laid the rod on the pier and Johnny quietly re-rigged it with a bobber so I could cast it out and simply wait for a fish to come along and grab the luscious bait. Then there were footsteps up the pier. Sandy had come with a basket full of cornbread, muffins, hushpuppies, bacon, and a thermos of coffee.

"I hope you fellas know that this is the last time y'all can expect to be served around here," Sandy said sternly, but her smile gave her away.

Johnny started laughing like it was the funniest thing he'd ever heard. "Ha! That ain't the first time I heard that this was the last time I was gonna get served! Ha Ha!"

Sandy cuffed me across the head, knocking my cap in the water, which I quickly fished out. "No luck, eh?" she said. Johnny pulled up his stringer and she oohed and ahhed. "Yeah, but what about you, big boy? Where's your fish?"

"Still in there," I said, pointing to the water. "I'm letting 'em fatten up."

"Well, here. Gimme that thing." She took the rod, laid back her arm, then cast in a big looping motion, line flying in a grand arc out into the middle of the channel. Slowly she let the bait sink, then got a hit that bent the rod tip halfway down to the surface of the water. Deftly she set the hook with a strait upward jerk and started reeling. "Oh boy. It's a biggie, boys. I can tell. A real whopper."

The line drew patterns across the top of the water like a figure skater, back and forth, up and down, around in a circle with a curly-cue and a loop until the fish began to tire. She reeled it up to the pier and Johnny handed her the net. Down on one knee she netted the sparkling golden speckled trout, the rod under one arm and the net in the other hand. Quickly she reached into the fish's mouth where she'd been hooked, cleanly through the lip. "This one is preggers," she observed, quickly working the hook free with just a tiny spot of fish blood. "Go on and have your babies" she said to the fish, lowering the net into the water. Shocked and exhausted, the fish was motionless for almost a minute, gills expanding and contracting, dorsal fins working back and forth until Sandy finally gave the net a jerk and the fish darted back into the inky depths.

"Ok, if you catch her again you gotta let her go. Then you'll end up with ten fish instead of one," she told Johnny, who had been watching the display without a word, until he finally asked:

"I ain't meanin' no disrespect Miss Sandy, where did a girl like you learn to do that?"

She put a hand on Johnny's shoulder. "My son is a professional fisherman."

Laughing, she began to make her way back up the dock when I shouted out to her, "Hon, get a chair and come down. We need your good luck. Besides, Johnny has something he wants to share with us." Johnny looked at me curiously. "He's gonna tell us just exactly what's been going on with Binx and my sister. And maybe why Binx is such a nasty prick."

I was surprised that Binx was not in detox after the episode two nights ago. He needed at least a standard twenty-eight day program, but that may have been a California thought. He hadn't broken any laws, so a court order was out of the question. It was likely a point of pride, a distinctly Southern macho independence, for Binx to take care of himself. For him, it had become a matter of drinking, and dying, or not. Simple. And I could tell Binx was the kinda guy that wouldn't let one little drink kill him. If he was going down it would take a fifth, at least.

"That Binx Sublette has always been trouble, ever since he was a little baby boy," Johnny began after Sandy got situated. "He was a biter from the get-go. I remember he bit me the first time I even pick him up, before he could even walk. He walked up to another child, or even an adult, and just haul off and bite 'em, sometime right through the clothes. Well I tell you it took years for him to be cured of the bitin' sickness. He had to wear a muzzle when he went to school so he wouldn't bite nobody! Can you imagine such a thing? His parents were both respectable folks, and they were beside themselves."

Sandy and I looked at each other, recalling some of the kids in Tripp's pre-school and kindergarten that had biting issues, but I couldn't recall any muzzles.

"After the bitin' it was the fightin'. Young Binx Sublette got kicked out of every school in Louisiana, Mississippi, Alabama, Georgia, East Texas – finally when he was eighteen his daddy stuck him in the marines so fast would make your head spin. That seemed to straighten him out some. Were you ever in the service, Howard?"

"No, I was lucky," I replied. "Though they had the draft lottery in 1973, and my birthday, February twenty-ninth mind you, was number one, they didn't take anybody that year. That was the last year of the draft. And it was the only lottery I ever won." Johnny chuckled but Sandy scowled – fifteen-yard penalty for negative thoughts. I forgot to add that I wrote a long CO letter, which was rejected, but after I went to the physical they declared me 4F for the fractured collar between L4 and L5 anyway.

"Okay. So when Binx got out of the Marines and Vietnam he went to LSU on the GI Bill, pre-med, and for the next eight years he did okay. He still loved to fight, but the Marines made a boxer out of him, so now he didn't have to go out wastin' boys on the street at night, instead he got in the ring with them and got his ass kicked. After a while it seemed to start rattlin' his brain so the school made him stop. He would have gone back out to the streets but the law in Baton Rouge was watchin' him now. Plus they made him take some kinda medicine – lithium, I think – that seriously slowed him down."

A voice, not so little, was in my head saying: *Great. This is just great. So far we got one suicide and two clear cases, three if you count Jack Sublette, of severe mental illness.* Throw in my dad's bipolar disorder, his sister's brain cancer and subsequent dementia, and we're building up quite the rogue's gallery of nut cases. Given my recent episodes of pixie dust attacks and heart hiccups, I might have considered switching places with Binx. At least he could make the end look like an accident and his family could still cash in on the life insurance policies. That doesn't work if you jump off the bridge, even in the middle of pixie dust narcosis.

Still I couldn't imagine Charles "Binx" Sublette practicing medicine, even if his online profile indicated that he was a professor at LSU Medical School for over twenty years.

"Yeah, but he was drinkin', and drinkin' got him in such a nasty mood, he couldn't keep any nurses or office staff, so he stayed in the LSU lab and the classroom. He had articles in the medical journals, and folks in the doctorin' business said he was a big thinker. I guess if you didn't know him he was a respectable man. Then along came the twins and the sick boy, Jack, and old Binx just about threw in the towel. He got so down and out, his wife one day said she had enough and walked out, so now he said he was gonna kill himself, and she could have sick little Jack."

"Wait a minute," Sandy interrupted, signaling, "stop" with her hand like a crossing guard. "What woman is going to walk out on her disabled child? Who was this woman?"

Johnny fingered his stubble, puffed at his pipe, and stared up into the cypress as if awaiting word from God. "Miss Sandy, there seem to be some things that the good Lord intends to keep secret. The mother of Binx's children seems to be one of those things. Nobody knows for sure if he was married to the woman, or if it was just some girlfriend he was shacking up with. Whoever, whatever she was, Binx ended up with the kids and she disappeared. Or not. Who knows? She coulda been a hooker in N'awlins or a bank teller in Baton Rouge. Maybe she's workin' down there at the Kit Kat Club." We all chuckled and I thought to myself *if there ever was a perfect place for disappearing, this is it.* Then Johnny continued with his story.

"The suicide threats did not set well with the police, so one day when he disappeared I got a call axin' if he had come up north to Briarwood. I hadn't seen him at all, I said, but they said keep an eye out 'cuz he is dangerous. Then one afternoon when I was mowin' all the grass around the property – and you know there is an awful lot of grass out there – when I got way out yonder back of the house I saw Mr. Binx's truck. So I drove over and sure enough the engine was runnin' there in broad daylight, he had a hose hooked up to the exhaust pipe and he was sittin' in the cab out cold, an empty bottle of Wild Turkey in his lap. And he locked himself in, so I got a rock and crashed through and pulled that mask off his face. As you now know, he lived."

Sounds familiar, I was thinking, though I was still having a hard time believing Sisi's story about our father's suicide attempt in the Buick Regal. I wondered if the temporary lack of oxygen to the brain makes the victim's condition even worse.

"That was when the twins were little, about fifteen years ago now, I guess." Johnny's eyes were starting to cloud over, and I got the feeling that Binx's biography was over. "The end," Johnny said. "Heh heh heh." Then he pulled the flaps of the checkered hunter's cap over his ears, pulled the brim down over his eyes, slowly lowered his chin to his chest and nodded off for his pre-lunch geriatric nap.

I was tempted to do the same, but the idea that Binx Sublette was chattin' up my sister at that very moment made me want to hop in the speedboat and speed over there.

"I think I should go with you," Sandy said as soon as I told her my plan. "She needs to know that I'm on her side, that I want to help her."

Sandy's transformation from suspicious, estranged in-law to caregiver had been so sudden, it was almost unbelievable. When she was on her own for those few days she must have had an epiphany and realized that Sisi was a victim of powers beyond her control, and had been for a very long time. I was curious about her moment of awakening, mainly because it had taken me so long to accept that my sister was mentally ill. But it wasn't really until I saw her the day before that it sunk in.

"That would be great if she thought she needed help," I tried to explain as we gathered up the gear from the dock. "Actually, the ideal scenario would be if she didn't remember you at all, like she did with Tripp. First she didn't recognize the name, didn't even know I had a son. Then she figured, "Great! He can help drive the boat.""

Sandy paused, put her hands on my forearms and studied my face under the brim of my cap, her sparkling gold-flecked eyes searching from side-to-side, reading me. What did she see? Confusion? Sadness? Regret? Anger? Suspicion? Love? Perhaps all of the above, for it was all there, slithering around under the surface like anacondas in the asphalt. She took my hand, pecked my cheek and said, "Okay. Come on, let's go take a shower."

34 A Sister Found and Lost

Sandy decided not to accompany me to Cobb's place, perhaps having noticed that I needed a little more time to figure out the right approach. She was right, of course. It was also too soon for Sandy to reappear – it might've triggered an unwanted reaction.

Just then Johnny squeaked in through the back door with a bucket full of freshly cleaned fish, a big wide smile on his leathery face and his eyes shining like marbles in his deep sockets. Once he saw me dressed to go visiting he said, "Hold on a second, Mister Howard. I don't want you losin' your way out in that swamp. The two-seater is out back, and gettin' through the swamp to the main channel ain't exactly easy."

"Johnny, I'm sure I can find my way out there. What are you gonna do while I'm trying to reason with my sister?"

"I'm gonna fish. What else am I gonna do? Read the Bible? Besides, the fishin's pretty good at Doc's place."

Johnny drove us through the swamp and out to the main channel without bumping a single cypress knee or squeezing under any fallen branches, smoking his pipe with his shotgun across his lap.

"Johnny?" I asked after we pushed off the back pier. "Would it be okay if you don't shoot anything for a little while?"

This cracked the old man up. "Of course, Mister Howard! What's the matter, are your ears gettin' tired of all this racket?"

"Yeah, I guess you could say that. Where I live, you can't just up and shoot at stuff, you know?"

"Sure, I know! I lived in the city once. Ain't no need for no shotgun on Bourbon Street! Nossir. So long as there's a trumpet and a saxophone, nobody need no shotgun. Heh heh heh."

"Oh, is that right? When did you live in the city?"

"Long, long time back, when I was just a little child. Before my pappy started messing with the white women, we were a happy Freejack family, living in a nice house with help of our own. My mammy was a voodoo queen, you know, as popular with the folks as Madame Leveaux. Once we had to move up north to St. Francisville, things were different. When word got up that way 'bout my pappy's indiscretions, a posse of country boys came up to our house, dragged my pappy out the front door and strung him up to an old oak right there in our own front yard."

We floated for a while in silence, my gut churning with the horror of the injustice and barbarity that these people have had to endure, even the Freejacks, and I couldn't help but double over in pain. Indignity! Ha. What dignity is left when you're watching your daddy twitch at the end of a rope?

"You miss your dose, Mister Howard? Miss Sandy gave me your dose right here case you need it."

Such nice words, but this pain was far beyond anything a drug could reach. All I could do was whimper, Mr. Clever Retort cut to the quick.

"Howard, it's okay," Johnny said, patting me gently on the back as we pulled into the main channel. I was still doubled over like I was about to throw up. But that wasn't it and Johnny knew it. I thought about my grandfather's memoir and his "torturous proceedings." Good God as if being humiliated by a bunch of corporate double-crossers was "torturous" then Johnny's experience had to be...well, torture isn't strong enough to describe what I could imagine young Johnny and his family felt when they saw their father lynched in their own front yard.

Johnny pulled up to the doctor's pier next to Cobb's identical two-seater, but it was some time before I could bring myself to stand up and go in. I was stuck wondering if any of the members of that lynch mob were relatives of mine. But, as Johnny explained: "We couldn't live in St. Francisville no more, so one day a white man in a Model T with a wagon hitched in tow came to our house and he said, "I got work for y'all if you need it. Good wage, respectable lodgings if you need 'em, family doctor, and a nice pond full of bass and catfish."

"My mammy looked at this young white fella up and down and said 'where y'all live?'

'Up north of Laurel Hill,' he said. 'Little plantation called Briarwood'."

"So Mammy and the family piled in the wagon with all our belongings, and we just left our house there in St. Francisville, which we couldn't own anyway owin' to the law, and set out to Briarwood. I couldn't been more than five years old, I reckon. And I've been there ever since. Eighty five years."

I sat there for some time just breathing, trying to calm the churning and trying to beat back the invading pixie dust on the periphery of my vision. It was no time for a pixie dust episode. I clenched my jaw, closed my eyes and took deep breaths, in and out and in and out until I could finally see Johnny clearly in the driver's seat and the bright blue sky behind his beautiful smiling face.

"Howard, I wouldn't trade my life in for nuthin' o' nobody, you unnerstand? It's been a good life, and when I see folks out there pushin' and shovin' and hollerin' 'I want mine! Gimme what I got due!' I turn the other cheek. Those folks ain't go no peace and never will. But me n' Bessie, we know. We's got our peace right here in the lord Jesus Christ and ain't nobody can take that away from us. Not even that old Binx Sublette. Heh, heh, heh."

The source of Johnny's peace rang a loud bell. Didn't one of those billboards say something about giving up your troubles to Jesus and relaxing, sort of? I'll admit I was becoming more intrigued by this possibility, but the social aspect – the reverends shouting and pontificating from their pulpits and all the worshippers carrying on – if I could get past that I might be saved, but it was tricky proposition for a Marin Country liberal, even a lapsed Catholic.

"Johnny," I said, straightening up and putting my hand on his hunched shoulder, "you have been more helpful than you could possibly imagine." I stood up and stepped onto Doc Cobb's pier. "Keep an eye out, okay?"

"Yessir. You know I will, Howard."

Lawrence greeted me on the dock. "It's a good thing you've come, Mister Howard. I think Dr. Cobb could use your help."

"Why's that, Lawrence?" Looking at this living testimony to physical grandeur, it really was hard to imagine that we were both humans, born by a sperm and an egg. I can only imagine that the sperm and egg that wrought Lawrence were supercharged with a superior strain, like highly prized and pampered Pinot Noir grapes.

"You'll see. I don't wanna steal the thunder, ya know?" When Lawrence smiled with those gleaming teeth I swear I saw a little twinkle and heard the little ping of a tiny bell.

"Howard, oh Howard! You'll never guess! Never in a million years!" Sisi cried when I arrived, her voice on the edge of hysteria, crackling with electricity. Her eyes were huge, wild, bulging like a lemur's, and her dry pink lips trembled on her shining, polished porcelain face. Though her cheeks were collapsed under angular cheekbones, she appeared to be at the height of an exploding mania. I looked over at the doctor for some kind of explanation, for there was no denying that my sister was overwrought, to say the least.

"I can't get her to take her meds. Lawrence can't even coerce her," the doctor said. "Maybe you can." I took this under consideration – I'd never seen her quite so worked up.

"Hi!" I finally said. "Wow, you sure are excited. Can you hold on a second until I sit down and Lawrence brings me a drink?"

"No!" she shouted. "You have to guess!"

"I have to guess what you're so excited about?"

"Yes! Guess!" she hollered, jumping up and down on an invisible trampoline. I look around briefly, assuming the empty chair next to Sisi's is where Binx Sublette had been sitting.

"Where's Binx?" I asked, forestalling the guessing game.

"He's getting ready, of course," she said. "Now, guess, come on! Come on!"

I don't know that I had ever seen her act this way, at least not since she was eight years old. She was dressed like an eight-year-old too, a creamy sleeveless dress over a pink camisole, her arms like pale twigs hanging off sharp-edged shoulders attached to a breastbone so prominent she almost looks like an Appalachian coal miner's consumptive wife. Her neck was so thin it looked like her round head might flop over like a tired peonies.

"Okay. My guess is…that you haven't been taking your medicine like you should and now you're worked into a frenzy. So, before we play any more guessing games I think you should take your pills."

Such an ultimatum was probably a big risk under the circumstances, because she was clearly enjoying herself, but there was no way I could talk to her about the land situation, the falsified documents, the impersonations, the lawsuit she'd filed against Sandy or anything else with her in that condition.

In the wink of an eye Lawrence was beside her with a cup of pills and a glass of water, which she instructed him to leave on an end table. "Binx! Howard's here!" she shouted, then turned back to me, fixed me in an almost sane gaze and said: "I don't like the pills, Howard. I hated them in college and I hate them now. They make me feel dull, and I don't like feeling dull. Believe me you wouldn't like it either. But after you guess, I'll take them, just to make you happy. But I'm not going to let you ruin my special moment!"

She jumped up when Binx walked in the room, looking his best yet. His mustache was trimmed, his toupee greased back and his mirrored sunglasses freshly polished. If I didn't know his history, I would have thought he was a movie star, what with his square jaw, sculpted cheekbones, ruddy complexion, heavy, bushy brow and fine white enamel dentures. He even had on a clean Camp Serendipity polo and khaki slacks as if he was headed for the first tee. Only the buck knife in its sheath hanging from his belt reminded me of who he really was.

"Howard!" he exclaimed in a clear, deep voice, "It's good to see you."

We shared a firm handshake, then he turned and put an arm around my sister, and she wrapped her arms around his waist.

"Okay, Howard. Can you guess now?"

God, it was cruel! She was cruel. Even in her mania with all the deceptively innocent energy and enthusiasm of an eight year-old, she was hell-bent to wreck me. And she was going to make me say it: the one thing that promised to cut me out of my half of the estate, my half of whatever she had a mind to share.

"You're getting married," I said in what must been an obvious tone of defeat. I forced a smile. "Congratulations." I shook Binx's hand again. He smiled, but it was the kind of smile that opponents in the boxing ring might share before trying to kill each other. I gave my sister a weak hug. She had tears in her eyes, overcome with manic happiness, and I felt tears welling up in my eyes too, knowing that this was likely to be her biggest, and quite possibly her last, mistake. I handed her the cup of pills and the water. She hesitated, then looked me in the eye with a conniving grin and drank them down, even opening her mouth for me so I could see that they were swallowed. Finally, Dr. Cobb broke the tense silence.

"Congratulations to both of you," he said. But then it dawned on me that...did my father say something about them meeting when Sisi was down here getting an abortion?

"Hold on, how long have you known each other?" I asked.

"Oh Howard, I've known Binx for years. He's always been sweet on me."

Outside, an airboat whizzed by at an illegally high speed, sending waves up onto the dock and over the pier. Lawrence burst through the door and ran down the pier to try to catch sight of the perpetrators, but all that remained was their wake. The beating of the wide wings of egrets and herons filled the air as they sought refuge from the screaming engines, but Sisi didn't seem to notice any of it. Slowly, she let go of Binx and sat, lighting a cigarette with shaky hands and dabbing at her tears with a tissue. I wanted to ask how they've known each other for so long but Sisi's eyes were already glazing over. Maybe Toya knew the facts, as it sounded like Sisi had been visiting down here on a pretty regular basis for a long time.

"There are a few legal matters, in addition to getting the marriage license, that you and I, and perhaps Howard, will need to attend to," Dr. Cobb said in his soft-spoken drawl. "The state of Louisiana requires that people in the direct, daily care of a psychiatrist, as you are Sissy Mae, prove that they are mentally competent enough to enter such a union of their own free will. I think it's evident why such a law needs to exist: there have been many cases where a perhaps insincere individual will marry a mentally ill patient and go on to take advantage of them in ways that are unacceptable in our society."

While Doctor Cobb was sharing this information I was watching Binx out of the corner of my eye. Sisi's eyes were at half-mast from the quetiapine – most likely a recent addition to her pharmacopeia – and as her chin fell to her chest, Lawrence scooped her up in his tree trunk arms and carried her to her bedroom. Binx watched with peeved curiosity.

"Wait a minute, doc. Does this happen every time she takes her meds? She hasn't been like that when we've been together in the past. What the fuck are you giving her?" Binx said, nodding to where she was sitting before Lawrence carried her away.

"Oh no," said the doctor. "Only when she's missed two or three doses and has worked herself into a frenzy. Had she stuck to her schedule her bipolar symptoms would not have been so readily apparent – she would have stayed on an even keel. It's only when she pretends to take her meds, hides them under her tongue, spits them out or fakes it in one way or another that she will slowly start to display symptoms of mania. She won't sleep, she won't eat – it's something that you, as her husband, will need to learn to manage very carefully. It may be that your experience with your son will be helpful."

Now Binx had a nasty sneer on his face. "My son is retarded, doc. Ain't no pills can help that sorry fat-ass boy. Just a good whippin'. That's all that works for him."

Both Doctor Cobb and Lawrence blanched, and it occurred to me that neither of them had seen how Binx abused Jack.

"Well, let me just say, Mr. Sublette, that any attempt to do any such thing with my patient will land you in jail," said Cobb, who pulled his hunched shoulders back, shoved out his old-man chest, and jutted out his chin like a cock o' the walk. Binx casually leaned forward, shook a cigarette out of Sisi's case, lit it, inhaled long and slow, then deliberately blew the smoke in the doctor's face. The Doug Dennikan/Mr. Road Rage/Mr. MacDickFuck resemblance was uncanny: his movements, his expressions – had he been wearing a wife-beater tank top, a backwards Raiders mesh cap, and no toupee, I might not have been able to tell the difference. When he took a step forward toward the door Lawrence clamped his bear paw onto Binx's bicep and whipped him around, pulling Binx's face close to his.

"Mr. Sublette, sir, I believe you owe Dr. Cobb here an apology," Lawrence said, quietly, almost in a whisper.

Binx looked up into Lawrence's eyes, while his right hand crept down to the sheath on his belt. "Get your nigger paws off of me, or you will experience the wrath of every coonass Cajun on this bayou tonight and end up swingin' in the big cypress over yonder by the firelight of a hundred torches."

But Lawrence did not let go. Then, just when Binx reached for the knife in it's sheath, Lawrence reached around with his other hand and took Binx by the wrist, turning it while Binx tried to turn his body the same direction until he could twist no more. Lawrence gave the wrist one more brutal wrench and Binx's wrist bones splintered like firewood. Then Lawrence dragged Binx, now howling in pain, out to his little fishing boat, past Johnny clambering up from his beach chair, and pitched him into the boat head first. As Lawrence turned away, Binx was trying to crawl, his good arm outstretched across the bench, for his shotgun in the bow.

I watched in horror as the scene unfolded in slow mo before my eyes. Lawrence, back turned to Binx, strode up the pier wiping his big pink palms together as if cleaning his hands of the matter, and Johnny, mouth agape, fishing rod in one hand, looked frantically toward the shotgun in the two-seater.

Then I saw myself as if in a dream, ducking through the front door, instinctively opening the hall closet and grabbing the shotgun that I somehow knew was standing in the corner. Without a thought I stepped back over the front threshold onto the porch, clicked off the safety, pumped the gun and fired into the air, the blast reverberating through the house and echoing down the channel in successive booms.

Binx froze, Lawrence froze, Johnny froze; they all looked across the dock to the front door, at me, Mr. Wimpy Giant Northern California Howard Brown himself, the perennial big-oaf onlooker now suddenly center stage. I had the shotgun in my hand, and I must have had the stupidest grin in the world on my face, because slowly the three men on the pier – Lawrence, Johnny, and even Binx – started to laugh. Soon I heard Dr. Cobb chuckling behind me. Standing there with my heart pounding like the bass drum in a second line parade, my ears ringing like Sunday bells in Vatican square, and a warm, wet sensation spreading through my boxer shorts, all I could do was shake my head in wonder. The bull, at long last, had been taken by the horns.

35 Eyes in the Backs of Our Heads

The following day was Eddie's 75th birthday. In typical old-fashioned backwoods Louisiana style, the birthday boy decreed that the men would spend the day fishing while the women would prepare for that evening's "throw down," as they called it on the bayou. Elke privately bristled over this arrangement. "Do you think I should tell these crackers that it's the 21st century?" she commented as we were boarding the Sissy Mae without her. "I can fish circles around these chumps."

The chumps weren't many. A couple of Eddie's silver and no-haired cronies from New Orleans, widowers like Eddie; a friend of Bolling's from Baton Rouge, Doctor Cobb, Johnny, Reggie, me, Tripp, Jack, whom we had finally extracted from his wheelchair, the old silver fox himself and his injured brother, who insisted on piloting the craft with his one remaining good arm. Doubtless the pain in Binx's bandaged wrist was being treated with the same kinds of drugs I had grown so fond of, along with his own personal liquid remedy, Jim Beam. The two together promised to turn our captain into a slobbering idiot before long, but when we shoved off from Camp Serendipity that morning Binx was as dangerous as a sulking slug, and just about as green.

From the moment we stepped on board the Sissy Mae, Jack latched himself onto Tripp like a cross between a guide dog and an adjutant. At first my son appeared a little put off and slightly humiliated by Jack's slobbering, spastic fawning. He hadn't expected it, nor had I. Brother Bolling was initially embarrassed and irritated by it, and, after reminding Jack that Tripp had been on more boats and done more fishing than all of us combined, he and his friend skulked off to the stern. The only person on board who seemed happy with the unwelcome partnership was Binx, who insisted that Tripp's legend as a blind fly-fishing virtuoso was nothing more than media hype for Sage, Patagonia, and other gear manufacturers. "He can't do anything by himself," Binx had proclaimed in slurred disgust from behind his mirrored sunglasses the previous evening, his toupee askew and his broken wrist wrapped in ice. "He's lost without that little hippie bimbo. Hell, he'll even take help from a retard."

First Jack led Tripp to the bathroom, which I hoped meant that he intended to use it himself when he felt the urge. Later, when we finally had a private moment, Tripp said, "You know why he goes in his pants when he's on the boat? He's too fat to get into the head, and too embarrassed to whip it out and piss over the side."

Then Jack led Tripp around the perimeter, showing him all the various obstacles a blind person might run into: the chairs bolted to the deck, the stairs to pilothouse – "The ladder is very, very dangerous" Jack warned Tripp, "don't go up there without me," – and the hatch to the hold. I was waiting for Tripp to say, "Okay, thanks Jack, but that's enough. I can manage," but he didn't.

Eddie had arranged to tow a couple of sturdy aluminum canoes and a four-man aluminum fishing boat, because there were many stretches of water in the Little Tensas that were inaccessible to boats the size of the Sissy Mae, either because it was too shallow or the channel was too narrow and overgrown. After sailing for about an hour we anchored in a shady cove of bald cypress, out of the way of whatever other light boat traffic there might be on the hundreds of channels, canals and waterways of the Little Tensas. I teamed up with Tripp and Jack in the fishing boat with the 2-stroke outboard – it was the only boat that could manage our weight – and motored down a narrow channel until we were out of sight of the Sissy Mae and the canoes.

Though the sun was out when the day began, the temperature had been dropping steadily all morning as a thin cloud cover developed. Soon it was cold enough to warrant parkas and wool beanies. Tripp had his own fingerless wool gloves, since he was used to fishing in all types of weather, and after fly-casting for a while I switched over to a spinning rig, just because I could warm my hands up in my pockets between casts. Jack seemed impervious to the conditions, though his broad nose turned crimson while it leaked a steady stream of snot into his mustache and beard. The local fauna grew noisier with preparations as it became increasingly evident that winter had arrived.

As he had on the Sissy Mae, Jack was riveted to Tripp's every move, and even though Tripp had demonstrated how he could use his echolocation skills to cast under branches, over stumps, between trees and ultimately find fish, Jack insisted on being his eyes. The only trouble was that Jack's ability to describe distance and location were primitive at best.

"Okay," Jack whispered, "you have to throw your fly over there." He sat behind Tripp on the center bench facing the starboard gunwale, his legs wrapped around him like he was riding on the back of a motorcycle. Then he would situate Tripp's arms.

"Okay, how far should I throw it, Jack?" Tripp would whisper back, smiling.

"You should throw it medium far, but not too far," Jack said. Clearly the concept of standard weights and measurements had not been included in his education to date.

"Sounds good, Jack. Are we ready?"

"Roger that. On your mark, get set, cast!" bellowed Jack, forgetting to whisper.

It was too cold for the fish to be feeding off the surface, so the boys were fishing with nymphs that Jack selected from Tripp's collection, some of which he had used just a few days prior with the *Outside* crew. Jack's choices were completely based on his personal color, size and texture preferences, having nothing to do with the entomological realities of the local bayous, the time of year or the type of fish. Their effectiveness was remarkable.

An hour and a half-dozen released fish later – Jack wanted to let them go just as much as Tripp, mainly because he didn't like the taste of fish – Tripp suggested they switch positions, but Jack wouldn't hear of it. "I can't," he said. "I don't know how."

"I can show you how, Jack. My dad can be the eyes."

"No, I'm the eyes. I'm the eyes," he insisted. Tripp did not object, and even though I was freezing my gargantuan ass off, I could see that the two of them, both conscious of their individual disabilities, were enjoying the simple act of helping each other. I can't say that I had any sort of epiphany at that moment – I was too wrapped up in the complications surrounding my sister and the apparent theft of our land – but later I would be able to look back on that day, and the unlikely friendship that was born in that little aluminum fishing boat, floating peacefully on ebony water under darkening skies, and see that the first of many clues to the source of my salvation had just been dropped smack-dab on top of my thick skull.

36 Big Fun on the Bayou

When we returned, the camp was already ablaze with yellow light and birthday party buzz. There were even tiki torches illuminating the pier and the dock, and between them were strung tiny colored lights, the work of Toya with the help of Elke. The night smelled of burning citronella, Cajun spices and the dense, heavy odors of vegetation dying back for winter, dampened by the growing cold. Johnny said to expect cold rain later that night and the following day, though the day's earlier cloud cover had dissipated and the clear, moonless sky was blanketed with a million stars. I was reminded of the night Tripp and I arrived in Downieville, the very first night of the infamous sister search while the old man was still yuckin' it up with his caregivers. What a long time ago it seemed, standing in that parking lot while my baby boy snoozed in the passenger seat of the old Saab, imagining that ancient light, created millions of years ago and just now making the connection with human eyes. Such incomprehensible truths never fail to stir up the questions that I, like most people, try to avoid asking, if only because the mind will not be able to comprehend the language of the answer.

Despite the cold, Eddie and Sandy were on the screened-in porch, talking intently about something, which I rudely interrupted.

"Sandy, my sister is going to be arriving any minute."

Eddie excused himself and Sandy put her hands on my shoulders, looking up with a slight smile. "Are you nervous?" she asked.

"Am I nervous? I'm always sort of nervous around her. But I was wondering if you were nervous."

Sandy sighed and shook her head. "Well Howard, you've been telling me for some time that you've thought she was losing it, and based on how you've described her since you've been out here on the bayou, it sounds like her psychological problems – borderline personality disorder and so forth – have become full blown psychiatric problems: bi-polar episodes, psychotic episodes. I wouldn't say it exonerates her from everything she's done, but there doesn't seem to be much point in beating her up over it now. It sounds like she probably doesn't remember half of it."

"Ahoy!" came a shout from down the channel. Dr. Cobb, Lawrence, Binx and Sisi were arriving, with my sister in the prow dressed in the royal outfit of a Mardi Gras Queen. Not the skimpy little bikini that hookers

.

parade around in on Bourbon Street, but a white gown with a long tail, and a white feathered head-dress that stood at least two feet above her crowned head. Her lipstick was bright red, but other than that she was all white, from the elbow-high white gloves to the white 3-inch heels. I wondered where she got the getup. Binx leaned against her in black top hat, black topcoat and tails over a purple and gold New Orleans Saints Jersey, jeans, cowboy boots, the irremovable mirrored-sunglasses and his injured wrist in a sling. I figured he had to be pretty shitfaced to wear such an ostentatious outfit, considering the real Mardi Gras was a couple of months away.

Sisi stood up in the boat with her scepter raised high and blessed the crowd on the dock. Then with a crack in her voice she declared, "Laissez les bons temps rouler!" Everybody cheered and she started showering the party with purple, gold and silver beads, as if Eddie's birthday and Mardi Gras were interchangeable celebrations. On cue, Toya rushed into the house and cranked the stereo and despite what was growing into a bitter cold night – as cold as it gets in these parts, I imagined – everybody started dancing to Clifton Chenier singing "C'mon baby let the good times roll."

Boats from up the channel and down – two or three, then another few – pulled up to the pier. Partygoers unloaded, laden with food and drink, bottles of tequila, bottles of wine, bottles of bourbon, cases of beer. Soon the smell of pot filled the air and the stereo was almost drowned out by an otherworldly roar, people dancing up and down the pier, on the dock, up on the deck of the Sissy Mae.

Time felt like it had come to a screeching halt. We danced and drank and sang until my recently repaired body parts started to scream for relief, so we retired to the fishing chairs on the deck of the Sissy Mae and watched like fans at a football game as the party raged on. Then I noticed that the Mardi Gras queen was not in her throne, nor was her king, and instead a couple of scantily clad young women had found her scepter and were leading the crowd in song. We clambered down to investigate.

"Hey, has anybody seen the Queen lately?" I shouted over the roar of the crowd. Eddie and Dr. Cobb scanned the mass of writhing bodies, shaking their heads.

"I wouldn't worry, Howard," said Dr. Cobb, "Lawrence is keeping an eye on her."

But I was worried, because if there was one guy Binx would like to cut, it was Lawrence, though he would've have a hard time battling anybody with his left arm in a sling.

"You never talked to her, did you, Sandy?" I already knew the answer, since Sandy had been by my side the entire time.

"She did not even acknowledge my presence, though I don't blame her, being the queen and all."

I was compelled to look for her, figuring Lawrence would make her easy to find. Sandy didn't feel it necessary to track down my sister and wanted to dance instead.

"Come on you old goat. You've had your rest," she insisted.

"Just let's locate her real quick," I replied, logging the "old goat" reference for later. "She's gonna be the one dressed like a queen next to the six-foot-six two-hundred and sixty-pound linebacker."

Sandy laughed and said okay. More people were in the parlor, and in the screened porch, dancing and singing, passing pipes, bottles, vials and every manner of contraband. Out on the dock a fight broke out; I heard drunken shouts and a splash, laughter and another splash. Inside the air had grown close, smoky and dense. Women were shedding their blouses, men their shirts, some women their bras, and the party took on the air of a Roman orgy or spring break in Daytona Beach as guys poured beer on bare breasted women to wild hoots and cheers. I suspected that the birthday boy, feeling ignored and out of place, had snuck off somewhere to play cards with his cronies.

As we were winding through the hot and sweaty bodies, the opening strains of the famous song by the Neville Brothers, "Fire on the Bayou," (pronounced "fi-yo on the bai-yo") with Leo Nocentelli's trademark wah-wah intro, slowly built. The dancers were soon wailing like wild natives, bumping and grinding to the funky groove and bellowing the words to the chorus as if it was the last thing they would ever do.

Every time the chorus hit, the house buckled, like the floor was going to give and everybody would end up in the mud below. The girls in the wingback chairs were joined by more bare-breasted ladies, some jumping up and hanging from the rafters, spilling bourbon right out of a quart bottle as the chairs tottered forward, then back. I got a sudden and distinct flash of impending destruction.

"Come on, let's get outside," I said, feeling like the little cattywumpus structure was on the verge of falling off its stilts. We made our way through the dancers on the dock and out to the pier, looking for Lawrence. He wasn't in front, so we picked our way through various couples making out on the boardwalk to the back of the compound. The kids – Reggie, Tripp, Elke and

Jack – were in Toya's cabin playing cards. Nobody had seen Sisi, though Tripp said he heard a boat depart from the back dock. We went back outside where it had become very cold. The bass and drums echoing through the cypress and the light from the tiki torches in the Spanish moss felt like a scene from a voodoo mystery, and when Sandy and I rounded the corner of the boardwalk there was Lawrence, prone in a canoe, out cold.

"Lawrence!" I shouted, gently slapping his big flaccid cheeks. Sandy grabbed the bailing bucket, filled it with swamp water and splashed it across his face.

"What the…" he cried, bug-eyed with dismay. "Ooooh," he moaned, holding his head, "Where am I? What the hell you folks doin' here? Where's Sissy Mac? Where's that son of a bitch, Binx Sublette?" He looked around, dazed, angry.

"Lawrence, what the last thing you remember?" Sandy asked, gently touching his head, checking for injuries.

"Me n' Sisi were sitting back here catchin' our breath and havin' a smoke, and Binx was in the bathroom. Then Sisi dropped her crown in the water, so I gave her my drink to hold while I got down on my knees, right over there," he pointed to a spot close to where the canoe was tied up, "to fish it out. After poking around the mud with my hands I found it and gave it back to her. She handed me my drink and I took a big gulp and after that…after that I don't know what happened."

While Lawrence was trying to recall how he ended up napping in the canoe I scanned the pier. The two-seater, which Johnny and I drove back to the house the previous evening, was gone.

"Ugh. Sounds like Sisi slipped you a mickey. It's about 10:15 now. What time do you think it was when you were having a smoke?"

Lawrence rubbed his head and looked at his watch. "Pockey Way was playin', that's what I remember." Almost two hours had passed.

Then, as if the interloper in my third chakra had commandeered my consciousness, I was suddenly overwhelmed with suspicion. I was convinced, at that moment, that we had been duped all along.

"Binx and Sisi are making a run for it," I concluded.

"Making a run for what?" Sandy asked.

"Making a run for the Justice of the Peace, honey! Binx is going to marry my sister and take her for everything she's worth!" While I'd had this thought before, it suddenly became very clear that Binx Sublette, as drunk as he seemed, had been masterminding the entire charade. I may have been a little lit, maybe even drunk, but I was as certain as Sherlock Holmes that the jig was up.

"Get married? Did you tell me they were getting married?" Sandy asked, genuinely wondering if I mentioned it, which would have stirred her up. But she was as lit as I was and I couldn't honestly remember if I told her or not. When would I have told her?

"By a Justice of the Peace? Howard, I don't think so," said Sandy. "If Sisi, or Sissy Mae, is going to get married she's going to do it in style."

"You're thinking of the Sisi from six months ago. Sissy Mae won't be able to tell a JP from a Catholic priest."

With "Fire on the Bayou" still filling the swamp with pulsing rhythm we pushed off in the aluminum fishing boat and, with Lawrence's direction – he was far too discombobulated to drive – we bumped our way into the back channel. As we picked our way through the cypress knees for the next half hour, the music slowly fading with the lights of the camp behind us, a strong sense of unreality – that feeling of floating with no place to land – coupled with a sudden fear for my son, whom I'd left back at a wild party that could have easily blown up into a dangerous, violent scene, got my teeth on edge, my hackles up and my brow suddenly dripping sweat.

Then, as if she could sense that fear and paranoia were clouding my senses, Sandy put her arm around me and chuckled: "Who would have ever imagined that settling Hal's estate would lead to this?" Laughing, I thought to myself: is that what all this is really about? Correcting a few little mistakes that my poor psychotic sister has made? But what if my worst fears, my paranoid suspicions, are true? What if there's more to it than the land grab? What if Dr. Cobb, Stephen Hart, Eddie Sublette and his brother Binx, the principal guys behind Laurel Hill Energy Ventures, are conspiring with my sister to cut me out of the land deal? What if they already know that the Tuscaloosa Marine Shale is loaded with oil and natural gas eleven thousand feet under our private patch of forest? And, Bugs Bunny's famous sixty-four thousand-dollar question: what did I do to deserve this?

"We've got to turn back and get Tripp and Elke," I announced, backing off the throttle.

"Why?" Sandy asked. "I thought we had to catch up to your sister before she eloped."

"Fuck that. I have a very bad feeling about this whole thing. We've got to get Tripp and Elke, gather up our things and get the hell out of here."

"Howard, are you crazy? Ever since Hal died you've been convinced that your sister is in danger and needs to be saved because she's too nuts to take care of herself."

"Honey...don't you see? This is all a sham, a charade! My sister is no crazier now than she was when she started funneling money out of the old man's bank account, three weeks before he even died. After the blowup at the emergency room she decided to fix me good, once and for all, and came running down here where she knew her bayou boyfriend would help execute her plan."

"Howard! This is ridiculous! What plan?"

"The plan to bilk me out of my half of the property, which is already known to have a very fat and healthy vein of Tuscaloosa Marine Shale running right underneath it!"

Sandy was silent, and in another minute I had the boat turned around and we were gurgling back the way we came. The cold night had silenced the various chirpers and chitterers, and aside from the occasional hoot of an owl and the water lapping against the cypress trunks, it was very quiet. Then I heard distant sirens, and I wondered if they were real or if it was my chronic tinnitus. Sometimes the tinnitus can sound like chopper wings going *woof woof woof* in my head, but then we all heard the real thing. Sandy pointed up at the searchlights and said, "Uh oh, sounds like Eddie's birthday bayou rumble got a little out of control. Just like a high school party, it's not a success until the cops come." We shared a nervous chuckle. "I guess it's a good thing we're going back for the kids, considering..."

I was too wrapped up in my conspiracy theory to pay much attention to police boats, fire boats and medi-vac helicopters to worry, since we were already going as fast as we could through the bumper car back channel. "Listen, Sandy," I began, continuing to explain my suspicions, "my sister may be bi-polar, but she's not psychotic. This business with Elizabeth Stewart and her antebellum charades was just a ploy to get me down here. Now they expect me to fall for the idea that Sisi – or Sissy Mae, I should say...oh my God...she was in touch with Eddie before the night of the storm. She smacked her head on purpose, then used that as an excuse to start her Sissy Mae charade. Amazing!" I clapped my hands in wonderment. Now that the pieces were falling together in my discombobulated brain I could only marvel at my sister's ingenuity. After all, she was a straight A student.

"Howard, you're sounding as crazy as your sister. Why would they want you down here? Wouldn't it be easier for Sisi and her posse to simply execute their deal and leave you in the dark out in California? Sure you might have wanted to come down yourself once you discovered that your half of the land had been sold without your knowledge. And what about all that family research you've wanted to do? Disprove the rumors about your father's philandering, find the crazy gene that has infected your sister…and now maybe you! I find it hard to believe that Eddie or your sister would want to lure you down here. There's no reason, and besides, we would have come down here on our own steam, eventually."

I heard Sandy talking but my mind was so full of the intricate plan that my supposedly psychotic, shock-treated sister had wrought; I didn't hear a word. Then, to our surprise, Lawrence was awake.

"Howard Brown you sho got some wild-ass imagination. Whoo wee!" he said in his deep, soft, velvety tone. "You sound like some kinda mystery writer…you know, Agatha Christie or something. Too bad what you sayin' ain't true, 'cuz if it was we would be havin' ourselves a time!"

I peered through the dark at the giant nurse who was pretending to be a former hall-of-fame linebacker for the NY Giants, wondering what he knew that I didn't. "Mister Howard," he continued, "I hate to be the one to tell you this, but your sister is mentally ill. For sure. When the police in Nawlins picked her up off Bourbon Street she was in a bad, bad way. They cleaned her up at the clinic before we started workin' with her, but I've seen pictures. She had a dirty rag wrapped around her head, all soaked through on one side with dry blood, her hair stickin' strait up like French fries in a Mickey D box, dirty jeans under a ratty skirt, and a man's checkered sport coat. She didn't know who she was, where she was, what she was doin' – she was so scared she couldn't nearly talk. They took her to the hospital and that gash on her skull was infected, and the infection gave her fever and delirium, and on top of that somebody drugged her on the street and took advantage of her. But after her head was sewed up proper and when she got assigned to Dr. Cobb to be her psychiatrist, she kept asking 'where's Howard? Where's my brother? I gotta talk to Howard Brown.'"

Drugged her and took advantage of her! Sisi Brown? Impossible! Naturally I suspected Lawrence Taylor was in on the scam as well and maybe even a partner in Laurel Hill Energy Ventures. I was sure his little speech has been scripted and planned for just the right time.

Sandy put her hand on my thigh and gave it a squeeze. "See, Howard. You're making up a sinister plot out of nothing. When was the last time you had your pills?"

It surprised me that Sandy, who had borne the brunt of my sister's toxic vitriol for thirty years, was now defending her. I was also astonished that she was suggesting that I take a little chemical time out. I looked at her sideways for a long time, when finally the lights of the camp came into view. "Ok, whatever," I finally said. "I'm going to get Tripp and Elke and we're going home. Binx Sublette can have Sisi. I wash my hands of her. The lawyers can hash this out over the phone."

"Don't forget the silver and the other stuff she's nicked. It will be interesting to see how far gone she was when she supposedly pulled that little maneuver."

"Sandy, Sisi is not operating on her own. I swear. You'll see. That stuff will go up for auction in the next few days and Binx Sublette will be waiting to take his newlywed's money and head for the hills."

Sandy sighed as the lights of the camp in the treetops came into view. The music had stopped. As the back channel opened up and we approached the camp it became apparent that the party was over. The tiki torches looked tired and forlorn, their flames dwindled to nothing, and there was the powerful odor of charred wood. Lingering smoke curled around the torches.

"Looks like there's been a fire," Lawrence said, jumping out of the bow onto the back pier. After cleating the boat Sandy and I rushed to Toya's cabin but it was empty save for the card table and a game that had been abandoned in mid-hand. Meanwhile Lawrence ran down the boardwalk to the house and we followed. Soon we discovered what I feared was going to happen: one of the big yellow wingback chairs fell into the fire and went up like a Molotov cocktail, having been soaked in bourbon. The parlor area around the fireplace and the whole corner of the house was nothing but black, smoking cinders. The curtains were gone and the windows blown out, the walls burned black. The burning chair had been thrown through the window and onto the deck, then pushed into the water where I imagined it sizzled like onions in hot oil until it became nothing more than a charred and mucky mess.

As I examined the damage a fireman clomped through the front door in his chartreuse jacket and fireman's helmet. He didn't look much older than fourteen: his smooth chin was void of whiskers and he stood quite a bit shorter than Sandy. Lawrence and I were about twice his size.

"What are you doing here? It's unsafe. This residence has been evacuated," he said, irritated by our civilian presence. We asked him a few questions about the fire and he confirmed my suspicion that one of the yellow wingbacks had fallen into the fireplace and ignited into a ball of flames. The fire jumped onto the curtains, burned up some the walls and the rafters before Eddie and Johnny got it under control with fire extinguishers. Then the fireboat came and drenched the east side of the parlor, ruining everything from ancestral oil paintings to antique furniture to the vintage stereo. The fireman told us that some folks had boarded the Sissy Mae and taken the channel west, which he assumed was Dr. Cobb's place. We went back to the boat and took the back channel again, arriving at Dr. Cobb's around midnight, surprised to see the camp ablaze with the same yellow light, minus the tiki torches, that illuminated Serendipity. The night had clouded over, as Johnny had predicted, and now a freezing drizzle sparkled in the light like ice crystals. After spending over an hour and a half in the little aluminum fishing boat our teeth were chattering. Still, the dizzying odor of charred club chair hung in my nostrils, and there seemed no way to blow it out.

When Lawrence realized that Dr. Cobb had been playing host to all these shell-shocked guests he jumped out of the boat and ran up the pier like he was chasing a wide receiver, then dodged around the back so he could make a subtle entry. Then I noticed the little two-seater was in its slip, as were all of Cobb's other boats. My sister was still there!

A somber mood, heavier than the dense freezing mist outside, pervaded the parlor. Bolling was staring into space and Jack was weeping, while Eddie nursed a large tumbler of what looked to be bourbon on the rocks.

"What happened?" Sandy asked.

"My brother is dying, Miss Sandy," said Eddie softly.

"Right now?"

I felt like I had something caught in my throat. Like a hand grenade.

"Yes, ma'am. Dr. Cobb is in with him now, and the paramedics are on their way, but we've basically run out of time."

"I don't understand, Eddie. I just saw him in top hat and tails three hours ago. Or maybe it was four. He looked great. The king of the mardi gras."

I hadn't been able to get a close look at him behind his sunglasses. Obviously dying had not been part of his master plan, and I expected that it had thrown my sister – the conniving faker that had convinced everyone from the NOLA police to the folks at the public clinic to Lawrence, Dr. Cobb, Eddie and whoever else was involved in Laurel Hill Energy Ventures that she was mentally incapable of tying her shoes – for a real loop. I expected Binx had provided Sissy Mae with detailed instructions to follow during the auction process, assuming that Binx was going to be the shill.

"Howard, you better see about your sister. She's very shaken up, as you can imagine."

Before I could set up a roadside checkpoint that might limit the craziness I was apt to spew at times like this, I said: "Oh God, I'm sure she is. How is she going to unload the rest of the loot, now that her con partner is out of the picture?"

"Howard!" Sandy blurted, shocked that I would voice my crazy suspicions at such a time.

Eddie raised a hand in a pope-like calming gesture, almost affecting the dual finger Catholic salute. "Howard, I understand why y'all might be suspicious of everything she's done. I've neglected to tell you that two days after that freak storm sent her dream vehicle – a car that she truly believed was going to heal your shared wounds – into the neighbor's pool, she called me. It's a story I'll never forget, Howard, and now that you've confirmed that it's true, I too have wondered about Sissy Mae's motives down here. But let me tell you something, cousin: before that horrible storm and the accident – the gash on the head and the subsequent serious infection – she reached out to me like a foster child, like somebody that had never felt that her parents loved her or even knew her, despite the gifts that they bequeathed her. She said she would have reached out to you, but she was so afraid that your wife Sandy wanted to get rid of her that she never said a word."

Again, I was shaking my head. Eddie looked like he'd had enough bourbon to kill the normal Christian, or northern Christian, especially a seventy-five year-old Christian. Instead, it was younger brother Binx that was supposedly dying from alcohol poisoning.

"Is she in with Binx right now?" I asked Eddie, realizing that whatever he said was ghostwritten by Jim Beam, and there was nothing that could be done about it. I stared at the big tumbler of bourbon, wondering when my family was going to figure out that booze was poison in our family.

"You want a glass of sweet iced tea, Howard? I think this is going to take a bit."

37 A Brief Flash of Sanity

Okay. Assumption wrong. Had my olfactory senses not been steeped in dirty gym socks, soiled jock straps, teen hormones, and golf course fertilizer for thirty years I might have been able to discriminate between the odor of bourbon and the odor of sweet tea. I might have had the generosity to figure that Eddie was innocent until proven guilty. I might have had the sensitivity to give the grieving brother a break, whether he was drinking bourbon or fucking motor oil, but I was too confused by my own rampaging paranoia and suppositions.

The paramedics finally arrived, but not until Binx, in an eerie reminder of great grandfather Brownie's arsonist tendencies, deliriously poured a glass of bourbon on his head, sunglasses and all, and tried to light himself on fire. Still, Sisi was oddly disconnected from the seriousness of Binx's condition, repeatedly asking Dr. Cobb what was wrong with her fiancé. Not exactly psychotic, but strangely removed. After the medics got things quieted down Lawrence put Sisi in her room with her pills and expected her to pass out, but I suspected otherwise.

"Okay, I'm gonna to check on her." I told Sandy. I snuck into my sister's dark, cold room, where an occasional drop of moisture pinged the roof from wet overhanging branches. Her bed looked like a fleecy white cloudbank, down comforters piled three and four high. Then her little spectral cranium popped out like a Halloween toy and she whispered: "Howard. What's wrong with Binx? Is he better?"

She didn't sound in the least bit drugged, and had been obviously lying there listening to the action next door like she did when her room was just a bathroom away from mom and dad.

"Sisi, Doc Cobb told me he gave you enough quetiapine to knock you out for days."

"I don't want to go to sleep. I want Binx to get well so we can get married and take care of the boys."

"Yeah, okay, but how…"

Sisi revealed a pill container, shaped like a bi-colored capsule exactly like mine, only larger. It was full of pills she had successfully avoided taking, which given the distraction of the dying man next door wasn't surprising. Doctor and nurse had other concerns.

"Sisi, I don't think Binx is going to get well. Doctor Cobb is trying to

.

help him and the paramedics are trying to make him comfortable." Sisi stared out into the dark almost as if she was catatonic, so I continued. "Do you think you feel well enough to explain a few things to me?"

"Sure, I guess. Why not? I'm not tired. But I don't understand what's wrong with Binx? He gets drunk and throws up all the time. He has since the day I met him. What's so different now?" Suddenly, for the first time since I'd seen her since she ditched the emergency room at Marin General, I felt like this was my real sister. Her voice sounded almost normal, not like the space-case seven-year-old. How did she turn it on and off? Or did she even know that she was turning it on and off? If this was the sensible, albeit bipolar self that had been appearing less and less frequently, why couldn't she figure out that Binx had been drinking himself to death, and his time had finally come?

"I think Doctor Cobb believes that Binx's body has taken in so much booze that his internal organs are going to start to fail. Like his liver."

"Ahhhhhh" she said. "Well, can't he just go get a liver transplant?"

I was so floored by her sudden comprehension my jaw must have been on the floor. "I suppose if the Doctor and the paramedics thought that was a possibility they would medi-vac him out of here."

There was a long pause. The only sound was coming from the parlor: Jack was weeping while Tripp and Elke tried to console him. "Poor Jack," Sisi sniffled. "Poor, poor Jack. Bolling will be okay, but Jack…" An owl hooted through the sound of water lapping against the pilings. Slowly, real rain began to fall on the tin roof, usually a comfort. It must have been getting close to one in the morning.

"Damn. Well, Binx is sort of a prick, though pretty nice to me. I just want to be an official part of this big crazy family, that's all. They're all just as nuts as I am. I mean, look at Jack! Look at his father. Crazy as bedbugs. These folks understand my problems and can deal – it's all S.O.P. down here – though I wish Dr. Cobb would lay off the shock therapy. Jesus, Howard, if they give me a few more of those I'll end up a total vegetable."

Sisi's moment of lucidity was like a gift from the gods of mental health; like delicate antique porcelain, I didn't want to touch it.

"Ahhh, Howard. My head hurts. Sometimes it hurts so bad I can't think," she ruminated; staring at the sound of the light, gentle rain.

"Have you told Dr. Cobb? Or Lawrence?"

"No. Definitely not. They'll just dope me up, Howard. They've been doping me up from the day the cops picked me up in New Orleans. The stuff they give me for super high anxiety, you know, my kinda crazy spells? Doesn't do shit for the headaches. In fact I think it makes them worse."

"Well, maybe they can give you something that's just for headaches. Have you tried ibuprofen?" I was starting to feel a little anxious myself, knowing that this conversation could go south at any moment, like it did in the car outside Marin General hospital, and this was a rare opportunity to get some nuggets of truth out of her. Also, her lucidity, while welcome, only amplified my suspicion that this whole thing had been a clever act, and Binx's dying was one of the few unscripted parts.

"Huh? Shit, I can't even get my hands on baby aspirin, these assholes got me so wrapped up."

"Why? Did they get you doped up when you sold our land?"

There was a long, long pause.

"Howard. I know you think what I did was crazy. But I didn't forge anything. I told those guys: Hart, Eddie, Binx, Cobb…I told 'em that we didn't want the stinkin' land, based on how I thought you felt about dad. I figured given all the shit he did down here you would have just as soon severed all connections with Briarwood. But I was also completely out of my mind. After the shock treatment they could have dressed me up like a monkey and had me jump through flaming hoops, and I wouldn't have remembered any of it. So, they're the ones that did the forging, not me."

I took a deep breath, wondering how she knew that the documents had been forged if she was so completely out of it. But to press the matter – in that little bedroom, soft rain on the tin roof and my little waif sister hiding under the billowing white clouds of comforters – seemed unreasonably cruel, even if I still had my suspicions.

"Ok, Sisi. I believe you. How are you feeling now? Okay? Can I get you anything?" She didn't register my offer, and instead reached for her cigarette case, shook one out and lit it. Smoking around all those down comforters made me nervous, especially considering the latest conflagration at Camp Serendipity. Outside in the parlor Sandy, Tripp and Elke were having an intense, low-volume conversation over the whimpering of Jack Sublette.

"What about the impersonations of Elizabeth Stewart? When Eddie first called me in San Anselmo, he claimed that you were causing all sorts of problems in St. Francisville posing as our great, great, great grandmother, looking to exact revenge on…"

"Ugh! Howard, stop! I don't know what you're talking about! After I got picked up by the New Orleans cops and dumped into the mental health system, Dr. Cobb came into the ward and snatched me up like I was a long lost daughter." Sisi puffed hard on her cigarette, blasting smoke out with a pop of her lips. My mind was racing. Eddie said that Sisi had called him before her head injury.

"Eddie says you called him a couple of days before the storm. Said you felt like an orphan, and..."

"Howard, please. Please stop. I don't remember calling Eddie. Don't even know when or why I would have done such a thing. I felt like I was getting cut out of my own father's death. The hospice people wouldn't listen to me, you wouldn't listen to me, Sandy was completely taking over and it was pissing me off. My husband left me, my kids blamed me for driving him out when he was already fucking and had been fucking every administrative assistant that came through his front office. I may have called Eddie. I probably did, but I can't remember. These people actually like me down here, if you can believe it. I fit right in. But why does it matter, Howard? You're my brother, right? This is what's left of our family, now that my Binx is throwing in the towel. Right?"

She hit her cigarette hard a few more times, shook another out of the case and lit it off the butt. I didn't know...really didn't have any idea...how to respond to this. It was the most sense she had made in weeks, maybe months. Maybe years. But things were starting to get tattered around the edges of our cool, calm, collected, rational conversation. It was hard to believe that she really couldn't remember dressing up like an antebellum planter's wife, parading around plantation tours and accosting the locals. But I really didn't know anything about psychosis, or paranoid schizophrenia, or even bi-polar disorder though I've certainly had been around it long enough. In some ways I felt like I barely knew this skinny little waif hiding in a mountain of comforters, her nervous eyes fixing me in an electric gaze, a tractor beam, then the frantic blinking, the hazel orbs deep with bottomless black pupils darting left, then right, then again fixing on me, waiting. Was this really my sister, the last remnant of the Browns from 156 Woodland Road, Kentfield, California?

"Well, I know what you mean, Sisi, about family. I got your letter. But what about your family? What about your kids? Do you know where they are? Do they know where you are?"

"What kids, Howard? You mean Kenny's kids? The ones I am prohibited by law from ever visiting again? Besides, they're grown, gone, out in the world. You keep hangin' round your kid –poor guy can't get away.

Don't you think it's time you turned him loose?"

I rolled onto my back and covered my face in my hands. I'm reminded of a speech my father once gave me about being "too available" to my wife and children. He said I needed to spend more time doing things – like playing golf – without worrying about spending time with my kids and wife. If I made myself less available, they would appreciate me more. But he never said anything about kicking them out into the world. He never kicked us out, but he didn't have to. We left of our own accord.

"Tripp can go wherever he wants to go and do whatever he likes to do. Turns out he likes hangin' with his mom and dad. And frankly he needs our help. He's blind, you know." I was tempted to mention Ward, just so she might understand why Tripp was so important to us. But I couldn't be sure she would remember him, and I didn't feel like telling her about the little boy that died of cancer.

"Yeah, but what happens when you die? Here you got this kid hooked on you like a drug and then you cut him off. That's fuckin' cruel, if you ask me. If I had become stepmom to Binx's twins, the first thing I woulda done was kick Bolling out. Then I would have put Jack in the state loony bin."

I studied my sister, her cigarette dangling from the corner of her mouth where the red lipstick from her Mardi-Gras Queen outfit had smeared and faded, wondering where this hard edge, this cold vein that sometimes drove her life came from. I guessed if I was the wiseass, she was the hardass.

She pushed her lower lip out and blew smoke up in a long stream, tickling her nose, then scrunched her eyes and laid her head back on the headboard, staring at the ceiling. Oh, what I would have given to be able to see what was going on inside her brain, the thoughts scrolling through her consciousness like stock tickers.

She scratched her cheek and rubbed her eyes, took another drag and exhaled with an annoying pop of her lips. "Howard. Nobody knows you like I do. Nobody. Not Sandy, not Tripp. Maybe you think dad knew you pretty well, and that may be true. But all you know is that he didn't much like what he knew; you weren't the son he had in mind, just like I wasn't the daughter he had in mind. But I know you, Howard. I know what's going on with you."

It was strange, her talking to the ceiling like I was up there looking down, when I could have probably licked her ear from where I lay next to her on top of the comforters. Then suddenly she rolled over on her side, I turned, and we were face to face.

"I wonder if mom and dad ever really knew what a serious doper you've

always been. Did they ever bust you? Did you ever get in trouble for
snorting coke and drinking beer all night? I knew your routine. When you hit
the top of the driveway you turned out the lights, cut the engine, and coasted
into the carport. I would lay awake and listen to you climb up on the deck
and sneak in your bedroom window. I could tell when you were tripping,
when you were speeding, when you were smoking, when you were stealing
dad's reds, his Dexamyl, his yellow jackets, his bennies. Did he ever bust you
for stealing all his drugs? How about the Viagra? Did you steal some of that,
too?"

At this I had to laugh. Some time in his mid-seventies the old man
decided that getting old was fucking up his golf game. So he got a
testosterone patch and Viagra prescription, mainly because he was convinced
that if he lost his golf game and his sex drive, he might as well cash in his
chips.

"He must have noticed, don't you think? I wonder why he never said
anything. God, when Mom found my stash you woulda thought that I'd
murdered Julia."

Julia was the slow-moving, low-talking, tobacco-chewing, cigar-smoking
cleaning lady from Richmond that wore a white maid's outfit and watched
soap operas while ironing our clothes. Whenever Mom found contraband we
would always blame Julia because, obviously, she was the one with the drug
problem.

"See, Howard? Sandy doesn't know this stuff. She doesn't know how
you shuffled drunken chicks down to the guest room, or about the landfill of
broken hearts — all those one-night stands that you would dump like rancid
meat into Corte Madera Creek. I tell you, Howard, if you knew half of what
the girls said about you, well...maybe would have a little more self-confidence.
Of course they all came to me, wanting to know what you were really like.
They wanted to know if super tall guys like you had big dicks. I didn't get it."

Another long pause, visions of all the girlfriends I dumped into the
Corte Madera Creek like rancid meat failing to appear in my mind, along with
all the girls lined up to ask my sister if I had a big dick.

"When was the last time you had a day without pain pills, Howard? Five,
six years ago? Now you're onto the hard stuff too, but your pain is still the
same. Or is it?"

Pain. Sisi knows pain. And pain pills, voluntarily checking into rehab
when her Vicodin habit got out of control. But she didn't know my pain.
Nobody knew my pain but me, and now that she'd mentioned it, I realized

that my feet were killing me, throbbing, tingling, burning. I reached for my pills and the water by the bed and slugged 'em down. "Thanks for the reminder, Sissy Mae," I said half jokingly. She didn't laugh, but nodded her head and grinned.

"I'll bet you haven't had a single sober day since grammar school."

We smiled, as if she knew my secret and I knew hers, and we were still covering up for each other so our parents wouldn't catch us. "Are your feet better now?" she asked, knowing that they were probably fine because I'd taken my pills. Amazingly enough, the pain was gone.

"Yes, Howard. I know you. Your amazing talent, all of it shoved right back down your throat. By dad. By mom. By Sandy. I was the only one who saw it, Howard. I knew that the middle of the road, the family man, the schoolteacher, I knew it would kill you Howard. And that's what it's doing. Don't you see? Can't you see? And now you're too old to teach. Too old to coach basketball. Or too fucked up. Now what, Howard?"

We lay there side-by-side, face-to-face, and my sister the nut was telling me what a mess I had made of my life. Now what, indeed.

"Well, I thought I might get an RV and hit the road, go find myself, ya know?" I knew the minute I let this out of my wiseass mouth that I had made a grave mistake, making fun of something that I knew she took very seriously.

"Dammit, Sisi, I'm sorry. I know I shouldn't have said that." I grabbed her hand as big tears welled up in her shaking eyes. "I'm trying to stop being such an asshole. Really, I am."

"Oh Howard, you're not an asshole. That guy dying next door, he's an asshole."

There we were, chuckling in the face of death, in the face of illness, lying on our sides in that single fisherman's bed, Sisi under that mountain of down, just her impish little head and her short black and white hair sticking up, and I on top of the covers, one leg hanging off the side. I felt like we'd made a pact that, no matter what happened, we were going to stick together. Her claims of ignorance in the land deal were completely believable, and I was ashamed by my raging presentiments. But it was this feeling – more of confirmation, really – that the bond we shared was the oldest and perhaps strongest was, I thought, exactly what I had been hoping to feel when I followed her down to Louisiana. I knew it would be temporary, but I also knew that it would never, ever disappear completely, and that when the feeling passed there would be other times for it in the future.

.

Outside the rain had grown heavier, far from a downpour but steady, creating a single-note hum across the tin roof. It must have been at least 2AM and I was thinking everybody must be asleep except the medics and Eddie, looking after Binx. Then there was a knock on the door. I assumed Eddie had come to announce Binx's passing but it wasn't him. Sandy wanted to know if I needed anything. "Hi, how's everything going here? Can I get you anything? Sisi, are you okay?"

Tripp was standing behind his mother, and when Sisi saw him she popped up from under the comforter. "Tripp! My God. You look fantastic. Where's your cute girlfriend? I want to see her." She squirmed over me and out of bed in her skimpy nightie, looking like a waif in need of a year's worth of an all-you-can-eat smorgy, her drawn, sharp angled face positively glowing. Elke peeked around the doorjamb and when my sister saw her she bounded across the room and wrapped her in a hug, then grabbed Tripp around the neck and pulled the both of them down into the comforters.

"Oh, I've missed you guys so much!" Sisi cried, a hint of dangerous mania creeping into her voice. Within seconds Doctor Cobb was at the door.

"Please! Sissy Mae!" he whispered. "We have a patient in serious condition here."

"Ha ha!" Sisi shouted in manic joy. "You have a drunk in drunken condition here! My next husband!" And off she spun into a chilling cackle, causing Tripp and Elke to try and squirm out from under her grip. "Hey, no fair!" Sisi yelled. "This is my family, Doctor Cobb! Aren't they beautiful?" Elke shot a panicked look my way, and I signaled her to start working Sisi's shoulders like she did for Jack. Then I noticed a glass of water on the nightstand, Sisi's pillbox right next to it. Now I could see why Dr. Cobb and Lawrence needed to resort to drastic chemical measures to maintain the peace, as Sisi's mania was clearly a source of dangerous chaos. I poured the pills into the water and handed it to Sisi, who drank with abandon, then grabbed me around the neck and pushed her lips into mine, spitting her intended drugs into my mouth. Patiently, I spat the white and pink paste into her water glass, took her firmly by the wrist, and handed her the mixture.

What the hell just happened in her brain? Holding Sisi by the wrists, I tried to zero in on her eyes, which were now darting around. Eventually her breathing slowed and her frenetic shaking began to settle.

"Sisi?" I asked, staring into her like the person I was just talking to got up and left, leaving this poor, nervous maniac behind. She looked down at the glass of medication in her hand while everybody else, except Lawrence, quietly left the room. Sisi threw a glance toward Lawrence and smiled.

"Go on Miss Sissy Mae," said Lawrence. "You'll feel better."

I gave Sisi a hard stare, again looking, searching for my funny, wiseass, silly sister, but she was gone. Where? Then she started to cry. "Sisi," I asked, pleading. "What's happening? Just five minutes ago you were the sister I remember. Then you go off. If you hate the drugs, then why do you behave like you really need them?"

"Because I do." Then she grinned this weird "fuck you" grin that looked like it had come from somebody else's face, drained the glass until every drop was gone, crawled into her cloudbank and disappeared.

38 Incident on the Corner

It didn't take long for that feeling of blood-level connection to dissipate once the mania took over, but I still felt good about it. Almost elated. I felt a wave of relief wash away my apprehension and open my heart to her like an anemone in a tide pool. A flow of sanity had rushed in, and just as quickly began to ebb back out again. But, unlike the wise anemone, I didn't close up when the tide receded. After all the years of up and down, back and forth, wet and dry, I should have known better.

The barometric pressure continued to drop, though the rain had subsided by morning, giving way to an unusually cold, grey and damp November day, especially for Louisiana. Later in the afternoon, after Dr. Cobb, Lawrence, and Sisi had packed up camp and motored off in his launch, returning to New Orleans; after Eddie had departed with his brother and nephews for the Baton Rouge hospital, and the Stubbs family had gone back to Briarwood, Sandy, Tripp, Elke and I pulled our rented Ford Focus up to the Carriage House Hotel on Magazine Street in New Orleans, tired, hungry, stinky, unshaven, uncouth and in desperate need of a shower bigger than a sardine can.

Just as I was about to jump into the spacious teal-toned tiled shower, Eddie called to inform me that his brother Binx was dead.

"It was too late for a liver transplant. His heart had been weakened to the point where he couldn't have tolerated a transplant. So I sat with him – he was unconscious most of the time – but he did say one thing, Howard. He said, 'Please ask Howard to forgive me.' That was one of the few things he said. But I don't want to hold you up, son. Y'all go get your sister and bring her back up to Briarwood. We've got some business to take care of." Then he hung up. Just like that. Left me hanging.

My English teacher's brain thought there was something disturbingly Dickensian about the rapid demise and death of Binx Sublette. Had he really been as pickled as Dr. Cobb claimed he was, I thought it would have been more obvious, and since I didn't see him stumbling around, throwing up or passing out, I had figured he had more time. I guessed that after his failed suicide attempt he had decided to take the long way home; a sad end to an angry and bitter life that, if the stories were true, was brightened from time to time by none other than my crazy sister.

On the ride to New Orleans we had a discussion about what would become of Jack and Bolling, now that it was apparent that their only known parent would soon be dead.

"Doesn't the mother have to step up and take them in?" Tripp asked. He was stretched out across the backseat with his head in Elke's lap – I had to put the driver's seat so far back, there wasn't any legroom behind it – as she curled and uncurled his blond ringlets around her fingers.

"If they were minors, they might try and track her down and get her to take responsibility, that is if anybody knows who she is," Sandy said. "But they're not. Bolling is going to be on his own. If he doesn't take Jack under his wing, and no other family member will take him, he'll probably end up in a state mental institution."

Tripp's response was immediate, emphatic and unequivocal: "No way," he said, popping upright from Elke's lap. There it was, my father's favorite expression, coming out of my son's mouth. "We're going to have to adopt him."

"Really, Tripp?" Sandy said, turning around. "Where are you going to put him? How are you going to take care of him, out in Bolinas? He's going to need access to special services, services that I don't think he's been getting all this time. Besides, you can't just adopt an adult, even if he's got the intellect of a four-year-old." I couldn't imagine a judge allowing a blind man to take in a mentally disabled adult, but I kept it to myself.

"Doesn't matter. We've got to figure out a way to take him in. We promised we would take care of him. Didn't we Elk?" I looked in the rear view mirror to see Elke nodding the affirmative. Sandy and I looked at each other and exchanged one of the many invisible signals married couples unconsciously develop over the years. In that one glance, that one raised eyebrow, we agreed not to berate our son for making promises he couldn't possibly keep. We knew that all the practical reasons for keeping our big noses out of the Sublette's family business would just make Tripp, and Elke, more determined, more adamant, more contrary and irrational.

"Okay," Sandy finally said. "You're responsible adults. You do what you think is right."

"Don't worry, Mom," Tripp said, laying his head back on Elke's lap. "We will."

After lunch we drove our rented Ford Focus to Dr. Cobb's rambling wreck of a Victorian in the Garden District where Sisi had spent a few days after her release from the hospital psych ward under the care of the doctor, his sister Lucy, and their live-in assistant, Clara Bowman. Though Tripp and

Elke had wanted to take the car up to Baton Rouge to be with Jack, we convinced them that we could wait one more day. So, bundled up against the cold, they headed to Bourbon Street.

Dr. Cobb's sister Lucy was, as my mother used to say, a real pistol. From the hibiscus on the tip of her carrot-topped head to her daisy-painted toenails, she looked like a walking advertisement for the local florist. Everything was flowers: her scarf, her dress, her shoes – all of it wild floral prints from soft pastels to raging reds.

When Sandy complimented her on her joyful look, Lucy said: "Oh don't y'all just hate this cold and damp? I can't stand it. It seeps into my bones and makes me feel like the tin man. Remember him, from Wizard of Oz? 'Oil can, oil can.' Remember? Well that's how this awful weather makes me feel: all rusted up. So like any good Southern belle I fight back! There ain't gonna be any of that cold and gray in my bones. Nossir!"

Seeing that Lucy, like Eddie, could probably talk for days without taking a breath, I said: "Is my sister inside with Lawrence?"

"Uh, no, not exactly," Lucy stammered, casting her eyes downward. "I'm afraid we don't know where she is."

My heart burped. "What? Where's Lawrence? Where's Dr. Cobb? Why didn't they call me when they learned that she'd run away?"

"Wait a minute, Howard," she said, "First, the police have been notified and an APB is out. So let's just relax and I will bring y'all up to speed. Y'all just sit down and I'll get us some Cokes. Whaddya like, dearie? Diet?"

"Lucy, please," I said sitting on the edge of a very creaky antique, then re-locating to the couch. Lucy must have sensed that I was about to explode.

"When we got home there was a voice message from Eddie on the machine that said his brother had passed," Lucy explained. "Sisi heard the message and threw a fit, so Lawrence and Raymond gave her some pills and put her to bed. After a half hour or so Raymond went to his office and Lawrence went home, figuring Sisi would be drugged for at least three hours. When I went to check on her after an hour or so she was gone, and so was my car!"

"She took your car?" Sandy cried. Lucy had no explanation.

"Great. So she skipped the meds, grabbed the silver and is going someplace to unload it," I said. "Though I don't know what she needs the money for. Maybe she wants to buy our land back." Like being shot with a poison arrow, the feeling of sibling love and understanding melted in the face of another inexplicable money grab.

"Silver?" Lucy cried, jumping up. "That's not possible. I've got that silver stowed away where she could never find it. I'll show you."

Lucy led us up the wide, curved mahogany staircase to the upstairs parlor, then down a long hall where the walls were completely covered with family portraits and photographs, then to a small door at the end of the hall. When she saw that the door was unlocked, she picked up her pace.

"I know why she took the silver," Sandy said. "Now that Binx is gone, she thinks she'll end up broke, on the streets, indigent. It was the same after Kenny divorced her, wasn't it? Suddenly she felt like she wouldn't have enough money to buy a roll of toilet paper."

I would have responded but I was out of breath. Lucy led us up a very narrow and steep staircase – the servants' stairs. At the bottom of the stairs a flight below it used to open to the kitchen, but it had been walled in for almost seventy-five years. Going up, it led to a single, stuffy whitewashed dormer room with two tall, narrow windows on the far wall, stuffed with dusty boxes of family loot.

"Your mother delivered all of this," Lucy announced, waving her hand across the room, "soon after she learned that she had Alzheimer's. She wanted to stash it away so that a certain someone couldn't get her hands on it."

"So the things we thought she had stolen and the things she had accused me of stealing have been here all along?" Sandy asked in amazement.

"Wait, Lucy," I interjected. "Where's the box of silver?"

"Well, it should be right here…" she said, pulling away a sheet. No box.

Within minutes I was in the Ford Focus on St. Charles Avenue, rolling between streetlights sparkling with pre-Thanksgiving Christmas decorations in the frigid late afternoon mist, wondering if Sandy was right about the toilet paper.

When I got to the spot where there's a Wendy's on one side of the street and an Emeril's on the other I got a call from Tripp, who wondered if I could pick him and Elke up at the corner of Canal and Royal, which was exactly where I'd end up if I kept going straight down St. Charles.

As I was waiting at the light on the corner of St. Charles and Canal, I saw the familiar surfer kid, his buttery curls blooming from under his backwards trucker's cap, his wrap-around Vuarnet's creating a black band below his bushy blonde eyebrows and his white-tipped fish-stick tapping the pavement. He was arm-in-arm with his au naturale girlfriend, so lithe and lean in her pink skirt over calf-high black spandex, billowing print blouse and leather bomber jacket under the faux gas streetlamps up Royal.

My reverie was distracted by a shout and squealing tires: a sedan with headlights off came careening around a right turn from Chartres, jumping the sidewalk and shooting clear across Canal into the streetcar lane, cars screeching, honking, bicyclists pitching sideways, pedestrians scattering. Then the sedan swerved back across Canal toward the sidewalk on a bead for the corner where Tripp and Elke stood with several others under the tall French-style streetlamp waiting to cross. Some fuckin' douchebag with his head up his ass honked behind me and even though the light was green I couldn't move, transfixed by the unfolding carnage. Cries echoed across Canal, more tires screeched, and sirens blared as two police cars came racing up around the corner at Chartres. Then the out-of-control sedan crashed head-on dead center into the faux-gas French streetlight on the corner, ripping the hood of the car in half, glass exploding like a breaking wave as the bystanders dove for cover.

Except one: Tripp. He stood like a statue under the pole just a few feet from clouds of steam blasting out of the sedan's cloven radiator, his arms straight down his sides and staring up at the ornate iron streetlamp as the rectangular top slowly tilted and began to fall. "Tripp!" I shouted, jumping out of the Ford, but he couldn't hear me from across four-lanes of Canal Street above the screams, sirens and the squealing steam. He just stood and stared, mesmerized by the brightness of the falling lamp. I couldn't watch, covering my eyes in dread just as the iron lamp was about to crash onto his stupefied, gaping face.

Swirling luminescent sparkles washed across my vision, parting to images of little league games, CYO basketball, guitar lessons, swim meets, Disney videos, school carnivals, spelling bees, church plays, soccer and more soccer: the domains of a bright-eyed bushy-tailed boy awash in a world of colors; a world of bugs and squirrels and naughty puppy dogs; a world of Spiderman, Frodo Baggins, Prince Caspian and Power Rangers; a world of sparkling, gurgling, bubbling rivers, harlequin fly patterns, singing reels and iridescent, glowing trout. Then came his ninth 4th of July: hot dogs, lemonade, pinwheels, Roman candles and Piccolo Petes, a gaggle of shirtless boys on the sidewalk, a bright flash, a deafening blast, a scream, a cry, an oh my God! Pixie dust swirled across my vision, settled and parted to the gloaming, a world of murky shadows, indiscernible shapes, browns, umbers, and the dark greys of night under a fingernail moon until sounds, scents, sensations were all that remain.

The crash of the streetlamp on the pavement jolted me out of my instantaneous dream state. I sprinted across Canal through the gawkers in their cars, and pushed my way through the gathering crowd. Tripp lay on his belly, his white-tipped fish-stick still in his hand and his face on the pavement near a splash of blood, and Elke was by his side, her arms around him, the street lamp in shards on the pavement only a foot behind her head. I knelt and touched her shoulder; she stirred, slowly looking up, her face scratched and bleeding. Her eyes darted beyond mine left, right, then finally rested on the crumpled, bent iron, the yellow glass shattered and strewn across the sidewalk, the huge filament of the electric bulb jagged, twisted; then quickly she crawled to where she could see Tripp's unconscious face against the pavement, sirens now screaming, reflections of red and blue flashing and spinning against shop windows. Gently she slid her hand under his cheek and lifted his head, so slightly until she could see, with tearful, thankful relief that she had tackled him, wresting his stare from the enveloping light of falling lamp, just in time. Elke threw her arms around my neck, her voice softly breaking, buried in the shouts, sirens and the endless screeching hiss of the sedan's radiator; "Thank God, thank God" she cried into my shoulder, over and over. Beyond her head I could see the front grill of the sedan cloven by the streetlight, the front windshield smashed, airbag pushing through and no sign of the driver.

My heart stopped when I saw the vehicle's hood ornament on the sidewalk. Then I noticed the same emblem on the airbag: Mercedes. Elke let me go when the paramedics arrived, but as I moved toward the Mercedes - a 230CS - a gloved hand took me by the shoulder and firmly pulled me away from the wreck.

"Wait, I think that's my sister in there!" I hollered. I don't know why I suspected it was her because I forgot to ask Lucy what model Mercedes she was driving, but I knew with uncanny certainty that Sisi was under the airbag.

"I sho' hope not," said the fireman. "You just stand back a ways here, just right here..." he gently shoved me nearer the building on the corner. "Just tell the officers you'se family."

"That's my son," I added, nodding toward the stretcher.

The fireman looked me over, then Tripp, and said: "Okay. Now I *really* hope the driver is not your sister," shaking his head.

Elke remained huddled over Tripp's body as the paramedics rolled him onto a stretcher, removing his broken shades. One of them quietly asked Elke if she knew the injured man and if he was blind. She nodded, hugging herself with her legs pressed together, swaying forward and back on the balls of her feet. A female paramedic pulled her aside and covered her in a blanket while Tripp was carefully strapped to the stretcher.

Again, there was a gloved hand on my shoulder. "Mister, is this here your sister?" He helped me up and I saw her face and the gash, the same gash from before just behind and above her left ear, the matted grey and black hair, the blood bright red dripping forth. My knees buckled and the pixie dust swirled across my vision like a blizzard, just as I noticed the silver: knives, forks, spoons, soup tureens all strewn about the car, like a bomb had been dropped in the middle of a table set for a feast. The last thing I felt were the big-gloved hands under my armpits. Then it was lights out.

39 Miracle on St. Charles

After the paramedics jump-started me with some smelling salts and got me situated in the ambulance we screamed down St. Charles in the dark grey light and chill mists of evening to the Kindred Hospital emergency room. Sisi and Tripp were hustled into the ER on gurneys while I tried to handle the admitting duties, but it was no use. The lights were too bright and the pastel hospital colors too familiar. I was crippled by a sudden flood of memories of the past two years – shufflin' in mom, shufflin' out dad, shufflin' out mom, shufflin' out dad – over and over with increasing frequency until they each decided to face the end at home.

Sandy showed up with Dr. Cobb, admitting duties were handled, and after about an hour in the dimly lit faux-wood paneled ICU waiting room Elke, Sandy and I were allowed to sit with our unconscious son. Meanwhile Dr. Cobb attended to his psychiatric patient, Sisi Brown and almost Sublette, in another area of the ICU.

Dr. Singh, the attending physician, neurosurgeon and ophthalmologist, explained that besides a bad lump on his head and some as-yet-undetermined trauma to his eyes, Tripp was fine. "What's left of his vision might be worse or better, it's impossible to say. We only know that he experienced what would normally be considered "blinding" light, like staring into the light of the sun. But who knows what happens when eyes that are already damaged absorb such light? Once Tripp is conscious we can get a better understanding of his optical reaction."

Tripp's hospital room was, again, so familiar it threw me for an unexpected petit-mal pixie swoon. There were two beds separated by curtains printed in the similar barf motif of the old battle-axe nurse's smock, and it occurred to me that disgusting hospital décor is probably a conscious design strategy, requested by the insurance companies, to discourage patients from wanting to spend any more time there than is absolutely necessary. Tripp was in the bed nearer the window, the TV inexplicably playing softly up in the corner where the wall met the ceiling. A bandage was wrapped around his head and under his chin and it was obvious that a large patch of scalp had been shaved. A hydration IV was needled into the back of his hand and he wore a blackout sleep mask just like my parents used to wear.

The room was dimly lit aside from the TV and the lights of the various hospital gadgets at the head of the bed. It was so quiet in the adjacent bed by the door that I wondered if the patient had croaked, but I resisted the urge to look. Outside, night had closed in, encasing the parking lot lamps in halos of swirling, shimmering mist. After watching some TV shopping channel, Elke started shuffling through the channels until it fell on an obscure, low-budget sportsman's show featuring guys in Alabama and Arkansas floating around in tricked-out bass boats making major bank in fishing competitions. Then the show, "Live to Fish," cut to a segment on the famous blind fly fisherman Tripp Brown, about a recent expedition along the gulf coast and in the bayous of Southern Louisiana. The scene started with a montage of Tripp standing on a raised bench inside the a bass boat in the pink and yellow sunrise and casting into tricky spots – behind submerged logs, under low hanging willows, into small openings in dense patches of duckweed and other aquatic growth – and nailing fish after fish after fish. A low, sleepy voice thick with drawl was trying to be clever.

"For the past five years, young California fly fisherman Tripp Brown has been dominating competitions and simply amazing fishermen from around the world with his smooth command of virtually every cast in the book, his unorthodox yet remarkably effective home-tied flies, his winning smile, magnetic personality, and uncanny ability to find fish where nobody else can. But if there's one thing that really differentiates Tripp Brown from every other fly fisherman out there, it's his eyesight. Tripp is, for all intents and purposes, blind as a bat."

I was thinking that the one thing that would get my boy to snap back into consciousness would be hearing his name on TV. When I stole a look at him I noticed a little more color in his cheeks beside the sleeper mask, like his engine was beginning to warm up and would soon turn over. He was beginning to stir, just slightly, as the announcer was sharing Tripp's secret to blind fishing success.

"We asked Tripp Brown how he uses echolocation to determine where fish are, and how he controls his casts by feeling the weight and pressure of the line in his fingers." The camera cut from the coiffed, bearded announcer in his Sage cap and "Live to Fish" logo sports shirt to Tripp in a "Live to Fish" cap with his golden curls exploding out the side and the mirrored sunglasses covering half his face.

"Well, first, just so y'all know I'm not completely blind – it's not like looking into a black hole. It's more like a brownish grey hole of different shades and shapes. Depending on the light, I can make out the water line against the sky, or a bank depending on the contrast. The higher the contrast the more I can see. So I combine my ability to see some shapes in and around the water with echolocation, which is what bats use to navigate when they're hunting at night. I use this whistle to send the audio signals out, and..."

"Hey!" Tripp shouted from behind us on the bed. We turned.

"Hey, is that me?" He had pulled his sleep mask up on his forehead and was staring at the TV, his formerly milky eyes bright, blue and focused. Slowly his gaze wandered to Sandy, then Elke, and at last to me, and he started shaking his head. "This is fucking impossible," he gasped. "I must be dreaming." Sandy hit the nurse call button on the side of his bed, and ten seconds later she blustered in.

"Yes, yes, what can I..." She stopped abruptly when she saw Tripp staring at her. She stared back. "Oh my God," she whispered. Slowly she raised her right hand in a peace sign, index and middle finger extended. "Tripp? How many fingers?"

He looked at her hand, then slowly rose his, popping up the index, then the middle, his mouth breaking into a wide smile. "Well. I'll – be – a – mother – fucker," he said.

The old nurse, standing there shaking her head at the foot of his bed with her fingers still up, whispered "Me too." Tripp inspected the scene while the rest of us stood in suspended animation. I watched his eyes study us as if we were aliens just arrived from outer space, or amoebas under a microscope, while his blank expression blossomed petal-by-petal, unfolding and glowing as if illuminated from within, until his gaze came to rest on Elke. Then, like the eastern sun emerging from the long night to spread its nourishing light across the land, he opened his arms to his lover.

40 Brown Family Cosmology

We wept tears of joy, cried hallelujah, jumped on the hospital bed in a four-way hug (I hugged from the side, not wanting to destroy the furniture) and made such a raucous commotion that security was eventually called in, to which we started chanting "dispatch, dispatch, dispatch," promising no peace until our boy was released from the hospital.

But Dr. Singh, as flabbergasted as the rest of us but not quite willing to jump on the bed in the five-way hug, wanted Tripp to stay for the night. It was late already, and he wanted more films, X-rays, stress tests, cat scans, and it soon became clear that Tripp wasn't going far from the hospital until Thanksgiving. He warned of a possible relapse into blindness if Tripp was too active, or if the eyes were not cared for properly.

Dr. Cobb was equally stunned and amazed, but not ecstatic like the rest of us, which I assumed meant Sisi was in trouble. After ten minutes of his own family-style check-up on Tripp he pulled me into the corridor.

"Sisi will be undergoing emergency brain surgery. She's getting prepped as we speak."

"Is she conscious?" I asked.

"More or less. That's one reason why I came for you. Perhaps the news about your son will lift her spirits a bit. But you'll have to come with me now."

I didn't want to leave our celebration, but I felt compelled to see if there was some comfort I could provide to my sister. Part of me thought it was worth a try, the other part thought that I was probably the last person she wanted to see, considering we had, once again, caught her stealing from the family. But my instinct said go, so I gave everybody a kiss, even the old battle-axe nurse, and followed Dr. Cobb. He led me down corridors, up elevators, down more corridors, down elevators, and up an escalator until it seemed we were several blocks from where we had been, though it was all the same hospital. As we walked, or practically ran, he explained that the injury Sisi had received in late October in California developed into a tumor and started bleeding internally. Minutes before the collision with the light pole at the intersection of Royal and Canal she had a seizure, brought on by the swelling tumor, that knocked her unconscious and caused the accident. If there was any silver lining it was that she would not be charged with reckless driving, though she did ultimately get charged for driving without a license.

"The trouble is this, Howard," Dr. Cobb said, stopping in the corridor outside her room and taking me by the shoulders, looking up at me with his big hangdog, droopy-eyed expression, the hairs of his untrimmed silver mustache curling over his upper lip, "There are varying levels of success with this surgery, I guess you could say. Now, if we didn't do anything the swelling would continue and she'd turn into a vegetable, then die. She might be able to function for a little while at the level she's been at – maybe two weeks, a month at the outside. We could plug her in and keep her alive, albeit brain dead, for eternity. I don't believe that's a viable or even a humane option, since the swelling will cause a great deal of pain and the drugs she'll need to relieve that pain will make her relatively comatose most of the time. However, I'm not a brain surgeon, so you'll want to have a chat with Dr. Nakagawa as well."

"Okay, so the only other option is surgery?"

"Yes, well, there are drugs we can try that are supposed to reduce the swelling, but we've already tried the primary drug, which is designed to stop the swelling right away, and it was not effective. So, in answer to your question, yes, surgery is the only viable option."

I pondered, feeling my helpless anger simmering, and made a mean crack about electro-shock therapy, after which Cobb told me to "grow up," in so many words. Then he told me that my sister might lose her ability to speak.

"All the cognition is intact, but the part of the brain that forms words may be damaged in the procedure."

He explained that the tumor was in "Broca's Area," a spot just above and behind the left ear that was responsible for speech.

"But she could still text, right?" I asked. Cobb pulled on his mustache, looked up at the ceiling, then put his hand on my shoulder.

"I'm not the neurology expert, Howard, though I have helped many patients with speech difficulties stemming from psychiatric disturbances. The problem isn't just talking, per se; it's forming words in the brain. While it's possible she could try and text what she's thinking, she's likely to get the words mixed up. Sometimes she'll be close enough to make sense. For example she might confuse 'house' with 'hut,' or she might substitute 'cave' or 'teepee.'"

"But not 'boat,' right?"

"Yes, possibly boat, if it has a cabin on it."

"Provided she survives the surgery," I added.

.

"Right. It's a small sacrifice that may fix itself over time. Also, Howard, while I wish this brain surgery didn't have such negative repercussions, you also need to understand that this will have no effect on her brain chemistry. All of the manic depression, the occasional paranoid schizophrenia, the psychosis – Sissy Mae will continue to need her medications."

I felt flushed, losing control, withdrawal symptoms setting in. I reached in my pocket for my pills…when was the last time I had a dose? I couldn't remember, so I swallowed what was left in my pillbox. It was nearly 10PM.

Seeing my sister in this condition, so soon after seeing my son regain his sight, gave me an acute attack of vertigo, and I was fortunate Dr. Cobb was there to steady me or else I would've fallen flat on my face at the foot of her bed. With her eyes closed, her head shaved and the strange hot air bags inflating and deflating about her torso and limbs, it was hard to imagine the vivacious, beautiful, larger-than-life shit disturber that my sister could be when she wasn't imitating Cruella de Ville. It was even more difficult to imagine the majestic, willowy, glamourpuss with the sparkles on her high cheekbones and her long, lithesome neck. I couldn't imagine the cowgirl, the Buddhist or any of her various personas. It was even hard to see the lost, frightened little Morticia-haired waif, so delicate a steady breeze might blow her away. None of those women appeared to be there. Instead there was this shell, this empty cocoon with a beanie warming her bald head, her eyes closed and her mouth open. Dreaming, perhaps. I hoped so.

I approached her bedside and took her hand. Her eyes opened gradually, she saw me and tried to smile. "Hi," she attempted to say.

"Hi," I said, pumping myself up. "Something amazing has happened. Tripp has regained his eyesight. Your nephew can see again!"

She knitted her brow in hard concentration. "Son? Alive?" she said with great effort. I told her to stop trying.

"Uh…yes, Sisi. He's alive and he can see!" I said, but there didn't seem to be any use. My sister was someplace else entirely.

"You're going to be okay, Sisi. Hang in there."

I turned to go, but she pulled me back with all her strength and brushed her lips across my cheek. "I'm sor…sor…"

"I know," I said. "It's going to be okay." She dropped my hand and closed her eyes, and it was all I could do to hope, to pray even, that those words would not be her last.

41 Back to Briarwood

"The Lord giveth, the Lord taketh away," some wiseass said back in the dark ages. But on the same day? In the same family? The vertigo that I had felt standing at the foot of my sister's hospital bed only worsened, and I literally stumbled back to Tripp's room, all the while discombobulated by this notion of divine providence, and the idea that the universe is constantly trying to maintain a semblance of balance with this cockamamie system of reward and punishment, victory and defeat, life and death. If we're to go by some moral scorecard, there's no doubt that there would be a long string of black marks next to my sister's name, and a long string of gold stars next to my son's. If the big HP decided that the black marks were well over the prescribed limit and Sisi deserved to not only die but also go to hell for her sins, I thought I might have to abandon what little faith I had. But I knew that she wouldn't die, just like I knew that Tripp's vision wasn't going to reverse itself. I also knew that Sisi would have a very difficult time communicating, which, given her often vitriolic and forked tongue, even when she wasn't in the throes of a mental spasm, seemed an oddly appropriate punishment.

Tripp would also need to make some adjustments: his days as the famous blind fisherman were surely over. Still, from my perspective the accident, or miracle as some claimed, on the corner of Royal and Canal, had mended a wound that had grown so familiar that I would have trouble letting it go. My sister, once a cause of such worry and heartache – a time bomb on the loose, poised to further wreak havoc on me and everyone that had ever known her except perhaps Binx Sublette – was now safe. Not only was I convinced that she would live, I was also convinced that she would ultimately live with us, and that her footloose and fancy-free days as Cruella de Ville were over. And, after seventeen years of hazy, gauzy darkness, my son could see again. It was like I just had a painful goiter removed from the center of my forehead. Or my heart. Or both.

When we walked out of the Carriage House Hotel on Magazine Street Thanksgiving morning it was thirty-eight degrees, a record low for New Orleans in November. As the weatherman described it, a column of cold Canadian air was sliding under the oppressive blanket of gulf moisture, making the sky was one solid sheet of slate gray from horizon to horizon. A "wintry mix" of rain and sleet was predicted to begin around noon and the state patrol was urging people to have their Thanksgiving dinner at home to avoid what might turn into treacherous driving conditions later, but I doubted that it would keep our family from converging at Briarwood.

The roads were busy with turkey day travelers and the going was slow on the interstate, but Tripp didn't mind. What points of reference Tripp had as a nine-year old in Northern California didn't much matter in southeastern Louisiana – it would have been dramatically new whether he had been blind or not. Now he was not and it was wondrous, even under a freezing Thanksgiving sky that threatened to drop all manner of wintry nastiness.

"I've never seen anyplace so..." He paused and ran his palm horizontally through the air. "Flat," said Elke.

"It looks like nothing but water and trees," Tripp observed. Water, sky, trees, bushes, flowers, roads, buildings, bridges, birds, cows, horses: these are the things my boy could identify from memory. His memory of color had grown rusty, as had his ability to recognize shapes. He knew the difference between a car, a bus and a truck, but aside from very few vintage vehicles he couldn't place the manufacturers or models. Tankers on the river, barges, even tugboats took a few tries.

Despite the traffic jam and the sometimes alarming revelation that my son was, in some ways, 17 years behind the rest of the seeing world with his visual vocabulary, it felt so wonderful to be in the little Ford with my family that I could've stripped down, jumped on the roof and sang hallelujah. Then, just as if the forces of nature that regulate unbridled joy had registered my ecstasy, Dr. Cobb called. Since the phone was hooked up to the car's hands-free internal system, everybody got to hear the doctor's report, which was typically inconclusive. The tumor had been successfully removed without any obvious negative effects, but it was too early to tell if she would be able to speak. All in all it was a good report, given the alternatives.

We expected that by the time we arrived at the plantation everybody would have heard about Tripp's miracle, though we weren't quite sure how to characterize it. Was it a recovery? Do people "recover" from blindness? A restoration, perhaps, since Tripp had perfect vision until his accident at age nine? Tripp would need to be patient with his cousins, for each of them would want to hear how he felt, what it was like before, what it was like now, and, perhaps the hardest question of all, what was he going to do now that he wasn't the famous blind fly fisherman anymore.

"I'm just gonna say 'I don't know,' because I don't. I'm happy I can see, ecstatic, overjoyed, so don't get me wrong when I say this, but my career is fucked."

"Tripp, for chrissake you're only twenty six! You've made a ton of money. Just imagine how you'll nail the competitions with the combination of echolocation and sight!" Sandy exclaimed, turning on her power of positive thinking, which in this case was not nearly as annoying as it can be.

"You could be a professional surfer," Elke said, almost tentatively.

Elke had been pretty quiet when the four of us have been together since the miracle, but I could imagine how she must be feeling. Suddenly, Tripp would be able to compare his only partner, the true girl-next-door from Kentfield, to all the women that have been sniffing around Tripp's back door for the past seventeen years. But she's had a lock on him, even from before the accident when they played Ninja Turtles and Power Rangers together, hunkered down in front of *Bambi* when they were just babies, then *Mary Poppins, The Sword in the Stone, Cinderella, Snow White, Robin Hood, Dumbo,* 101 *Dalmatians*…all the Disney classics. Elke was one of the first girls to play little league with the boys until Tripp's accident, when she quit. Tripp has had his moments of resentment, especially at the beginning when it was uncool to be seen in each other's company, and Elke has had her moments of doubt about her man's ability to protect her. Now Tripp would get a chance to see how lucky he'd been to have Elke's companionship, among other things.

"Hey that's actually a pretty cool idea, Elk. We could travel to all the contests, surf, hang on the beach, maybe play some golf."

"Golf?" Sandy and I exclaimed in unified bafflement.

"Oh, sure. I love golf!" Elke said.

I decided to leave that one alone, though I knew Tripp loved playing with his Grandpa before the accident so long as the old man didn't lose his temper or over-instruct. But he always did, and I thought Tripp's affair with golf was poisoned as mine had been. Clearly, I was wrong.

The rolling countryside north of Baton Rouge was colder and greyer than New Orleans, dramatically different from just a week before when the autumn air was in transition from the last vestiges of sultry, damp humidity to a couple of real autumn sparklers to the refrigerated mist that has now turned the South into a freezing meat locker. Most of the psychedelic autumn was gone, and those few leaves that remained were mere spots of muted color in a tinker-toy jumble of grey branches. The live oaks, knobby and gnarled with their hanging moss, held onto most of their prickly, waxy little leaves. Then there were the loblolly pines, which in their dark uniform clusters looked like overgrown Christmas tree lots randomly dropped into the hardwood forests.

Having lived in a one-dimensional world of brown and grey shapes for the past 17 years, Tripp soon learned Louisiana was not all trees and water. He was enthralled by the bucolic fields and dense stands of timber, the cows and sheep in their white-fenced pastures, the palatial plantation homes with their grand oak avenues, and the squalid doublewides with their laundry lines, car parts and cyclone fences. His memories of similar scenes from childhood, especially in the rural hills surrounding Petaluma and Santa Rosa, made the landscape around the Blues Highway feel vaguely familiar. Still I wondered if it wasn't all too much visual stimulation: the dark horizon in the distance fading into yet more gray, the middle ground with its woods, fields, roads, houses, grocery stores, mini-malls, gas stations, the giant brick West Feliciana High School with the crumpled, crunched auto body on the vast lawn in front and its dark warning about drinking and driving, the industrial churches with their Jumbotron displays of fiery pastors and bake sales, the lone bar with the full parking lot.

Then there was the interior of the Ford to study: the dashboard with the colorful, backlit controls in flashing blue and yellow, the click-click of the turn signal with its dashboard lights, the computer display for the stereo system set to Pandora, the windshield wipers occasionally brushing away some light precipitation. And if all that wasn't enough to flood my son's brain with a cacophony of visual chaos, there were the two folks in the front seat that he hadn't seen in 17 years. The last time Tripp saw his mother she would have been 46 looking 26, her forehead without a crease, her eyes without the perennial puff bags that now dog her into buying miracle creams and tonics; her hair without a fleck of gray, thick, vibrant, with a shiny brown luster like Mr. Booper's sleek coat; and the skin tight about her long, elegant neck where it now sags, the ultimate, final giveaway of her true age. Was her voice different? Had he noticed the extra love handles, the padding, and the loose jiggling skin of the upper arms when he's hugged her over the past 17 years?

He must certainly have noticed his dad's inexorable march through middle age and beyond, inches heaped upon years, from a 34 waist to a 36 to 38 and finally to an impasse, unwilling to go up but disgusted by his overhanging gut and sagging man-boobs. Surely Tripp had felt how his parents' bodies had changed, along with their voices and their concerns. But nothing could have prepared my son for my head full of limp, shining white hair, the professorial salt and pepper eyebrows over the perennial scowl, the bulbous purplish nose and the thick light-sensitive glasses. Did he still have the mental image of a tall, straight, slender, tan, blonde, square-chinned, broad-shouldered basketball coach, golfer, swimmer, mountain-biker, skier, hiker, and runner throwing his boy high in the air at the swimming pool? Was he wondering where that guy went, and where the slightly hunched retired English teacher that'd taken his place came from? I could just hear the two 60-year-olds asking their 26-year-old formerly blind son, "Do you really think we look all that different than we looked when you were nine? We don't *feel* that different!" Which would, of course, have been the biggest lie of all.

Elke had seen all of this happen, including the changes to her lifelong buddy over the course of seventeen years of blindness. He'd never seen his pubic hair, the whiskers on his chin and the soft blond mustache across his upper lip; he had no idea how his hair turned to ringlets the color of baked winter rye grass in late summer, or that the muscles of his torso seemed sculpted from burnished bronze. From childhood through puberty, adolescence, teenager, young adult to now, a full grown man, Tripp has had to trust the reports of his family and friends to imagine how he might have changed since he last saw himself at nine. He was back among the seeing, for better or worse.

Besides being back, he was being a good patient, following Dr. Singh's orders: half hour with eyes open, half hour with eyes closed (or behind a mask), half hour open, half hour closed. It took him a full five minutes to completely remove the sleeping mask and open his eyes, by which time we had pulled onto the long oak-bordered avenue to Briarwood. Everything was frozen solid: the giant camellia bushes that frame the wide front stairs were limp and wilted, leaves turned under against the cold. All the flowerbeds that Johnny and Bessie tended with such fastidious care were fallow, and the circles of tulips and daffodils around the bases of the oaks were but a warm weather memory. Even the surrounding fields of grass were brown with frozen thatch, creating a scene more reminiscent of Thanksgiving up north in Indiana or Illinois than of this watery lowland. And the critters that normally make such a god-awful racket around here had gone silent too, probably hiding in tree trunks or underground trying to survive.

The Stubbs family rushed out to greet us.

"It's good to see y'all," Johnny said, "Especially you, Mister Tripp. You're a miracle in our presence, I reckon, a gift from God Almighty upon this family that has seen so much heartache these days. You's such a fine young man. From the first moment I saw you I've been prayin' to God to let you see again. And it sure looks like the Lord heard me, he did. Surely this is some Thanksgivin' we're gonna have! Now, let's get y'all off this old frozen

porch and inside where it's good and warm. Y'all can help us with the victuals, though I'm suspectin' old Mr. Howard here could use a nap."
Everybody laughed. Ha ha ha. Old Mr. Howard indeed.

The house was warm. Very warm. There was a fire in the parlor and the dining room, the old wavy windowpanes were all perspiring with condensation and the whole house basked in the aroma of roast turkey.

"Where's Eddie?" I asked.

"Oh he's hidin' in the upstairs parlor watchin' the football game. LSU is on, so he can't bear to miss a play," Toya said. Even though it had only been a couple of days since I'd seen her, I missed her easy company and playful flirtations. A part of me hoped that I wasn't "Old Mr. Howard" to her.

Suddenly Eddie was at the top of the stairs. "Howard!" he shouted as if he hadn't seen me in years, "get up here and watch the rest of this game with me. We're getting clobbered and could use a little of your good luck." *My good luck?* "And tell Toya we need some service up here!"

Oh, Eddie. You nasty old prick, I thought. *Is the master/servant business woven into your 75-year-old brain like shit thread in a needlepoint?* That's what I felt like saying, but didn't.

Though it was only early afternoon, the sky was getting darker and the desire for a Thanksgiving cocktail, followed by a quick nap and some heavy petting before the guests arrived was growing palpable. Toya handed me a tray with a bowl of popcorn, two mint juleps, and deep fried dill pickles direct from Bessie's deep fryer.

"Good to see you, Howard," Eddie said after a firm handshake. "This game is a goner, but I have some things we need to talk about." He paused, then picked up his glass in toast. "To the return of Howard Brown! And to the miracle that has restored young junior's vision. Cheers!" I took a tentative swig of the mint julep, marveling at the sweet, minty bite of the high quality bourbon. I followed with a healthy gulp.

Eddie turned the sound down on the TV and arranged things so we sat across each other with a wicker coffee table between us. Clearly Jack and Bolling used this room on their frequent visits to the country, even though the décor was hardly boyish. The furniture was all white wicker, from the desk to the chairs and even the bedframes. The bedspread was baby blue, the wallpaper flowery. There was even a little sign above the door: "The Wicker Room." Thankfully the only light came from the muted TV and the dim afternoon gray, otherwise the room would have been so insufferably bright I might've jumped out a window.

Eddie looked tired and grief-stricken, despite his ebullient spirits. Heavy bags drooped under his eyes like an old bird dog, his silver monk's curls didn't have their usual luster, and his cheeks sagged heavily in true sad-sack fashion. The house was overheated in reaction to the record cold outdoors, which may have explained Eddie's somnambulant look as well as the sweat across the back of my neck.

"Well, Howard, it takes Northerners a little getting used to down here. You'll be fine." He said this as if I was sticking around awhile, which I had no intention of doing. "So, ya'll are probably wonderin' 'bout a lot of things, so let's deal with the most pressing first: the land."

I wasn't really ready for this discussion: my sister had just had her brain cut open and my son was going through the biggest upheaval of his life – joyous, of course – but what a shock! Then again, I wanted to get it resolved. "Okay, Eddie."

"Good. Now. The main thing we all want to avoid is a lawsuit, criminal forgery charges, that sort of thing. My late brother, bless his soul, masterminded this whole business: the forgeries, all of it. We – the other partners in our little investment group – were just as duped as you were. He was not as romantically interested in Sissy Mae as he once was, given her obvious decline, but he gave her the idea that the only one cut out of the deal would be you. She was especially happy to see Sandy lose whatever interest she might have had in the land through you."

"Figures," I said. I would never tell Sandy of course, even if my wife now understood how sick Sisi really was and had been for some time.

"But like I said before, Sissy Mae's motivation wasn't to screw you, which is why all she wanted from the land sale was the cash, which she fully intended to split with you. Unfortunately, Binx talked her into investing the money in something…I don't know what. Perhaps it will turn up when we liquidate his estate. "

I desperately wanted to feel something; a deep current of sibling love and devotion; an epiphany of understanding. Had she not gone along with Binx's undetermined investment plan, and I had gotten my share, I might have felt differently about the whole escapade.

"So I've talked with my partners at Laurel Hill Energy Ventures, and they're willing to do one of two things. First option: you buy your half of the land back. We paid for it, so you'll have to buy it back. Y'all are free to do whatever you want with it. Now if y'all decided to turn it into a dog track you might get some objection from the community, including me. But if y'all just want to let it be, or build a house on it, or park a doublewide back off the road where it wasn't too obvious that Howard Brown is living in a trailer, that's fine with our group. Understand?"

I could hardly believe my ears. "Why?" was all I could think of to say.

"We were duped, pure and simple, Howard. After we saw how messed up your sister was, we were eager to squeeze her out, but then she turns around and sells the property, with your apparent blessing, and signature I might add. Or at least as far as we could tell. "

"Okay, but..."

"Howard, we're not crooks. None of the fellas in the group – Steve Hart, Ray, Lawrence, Boon and myself – felt everything was on the up and up with this deal, even though we agreed that getting you and your sister out of the picture was the right thing to do. Of course now that Binx isn't here to tell his side of it it's easy to just wipe it off the books and start over, which is what everybody has agreed to do. We could look into Sissy Mae's insurance coverage to see if there's any money there, but of course you'll have to make good on Lucy's totaled Mercedes too. It is unlikely that Sisi's coverage, if it exists, will cover driving without a license. But there is another option."

Another option? I guess at this point I was wondering how Eddie's option #1 was remotely viable unless I had fifty grand to buy my own land back, assuming they would sell it back for what they paid. "Okay. Since I don't have an extra fifty grand to buy my piece back, let's hear it."

"Join our group." Eddie could probably see the hackles on my neck, which were already partially stimulated, shoot straight up. "Howard, wait. Think about this for a minute. Your land remains in your hands – in effect, we give it back. We give your sister's land back. The previous deal is completely null and void. You can build your retirement chateau back in the woods or just leave it all to the snakes, the deer and the turkeys. If gas is discovered on any of our group's land we share in the profits. Why? Because the oil and gas companies want to lease large tracts of land to explore and possibly drill. Steve Hart can explain how it works better than I can. Also, because of the dreadful circumstances surrounding this whole affair, the fellas in the group are willing to transfer the deed to the property back to you and your sister, so long as you join our group."

Again, my head was spinning. What reason did Eddie, Boon Percy, Dr. Cobb, Stephen Hart, and Lawrence fucking Taylor have to be so generous? I couldn't imagine that there wasn't a *gotcha* lurking somewhere inside this deal, but given the choice between trying to drum up $50,000 just to get this swampy patch of forest back under my name and leaving Sisi to her own devices, or signing on as a partner in Laurel Hill Energy Ventures...well, I could see no reason not to simply join the federation.

"I'll have to think this over, Eddie, talk it over with Sandy and Tripp, and of course my sister if she's able." The LSU game was now over and the next game was ramping up between Auburn and Georgia Tech.

"Of course, Howard. It will be a distinct pleasure to have you as part of our group." Eddie made a move to get up.

"Wait a second, Eddie. I have a couple of other questions for you."

He stopped, one liver-spotted hand on the back of the cushioned wicker chair. "Yes?"

"Was that you that called and told me about my sister's hijinks in St. Francisville, and gave me the speech about family taking care of family and saying Sisi was going to get knifed and all that?"

Eddie sat again, scratching his monk curls and ruminating. "Now what's this? I called you and told you your sister was making a scene in St. Francisville?"

"Whoever it was claimed to be you," I said as the pieces of what might have really happened started to fall together in my mind.

"No, it wasn't me. I didn't even know you were comin' until Binx asked me to meet you at the airport."

"Yes. But why did Binx feel he had to impersonate you?" I continued. "Why couldn't he have just been himself? It wouldn't have made any difference to me which one of you called."

The blood was rising to my face, my scalp was crawling, I was breaking out in sweats and the evil sparkling dust had started to crowd the periphery. Fortunately my pillbox was full. I popped a couple and washed them down with a mint julep chug-a-lug for double instant relief. "So why the fuck did you fuckers drag me to Briarwood, when I could've flown to New Orleans and gone directly to Dr. Cobb's? I could've gathered up my sister and taken her to a doctor in my home town."

"Why? Because your sister, if you haven't noticed, does not want to go back to California! And as far as Binx could tell, your sister is an expert at giving you the slip, even when she believes she's an antebellum ghost!"

Now Eddie, Mr. Cool, Calm and Collected, was starting to lose it. And I couldn't blame him, really. Old Hal had left his sister down here while he went north, and their family had grown up without interference until Sisi, renamed Sissy Mae by her lover, Binx, started to appear. But only for a short while, I assumed, since Binx got married upon his return from Vietnam. Then after the twins came, one of them mentally disabled, Binx and his wife divorced and he started drinking in earnest. I wondered how much time Sisi spent down here with him then, since she too was married with children.

"Sorry, Eddie. You're right. The masquerade was dumb, but it's not the first time my sister has masterminded dumb schemes. Nobody ever realized that this is where she came when she pulled her disappearing acts. Or at least I didn't know. Maybe our father did. Maybe that's one of the reasons he thought she was a slut, abandoning her husband and kids to come down here and party with Binx. Well, she's always been a shrewd operator when she has her wits about her. And it worked, didn't it? Here I am with my whole goddamned family – having Thanksgiving at Briarwood for the first time, as far as I know. Ironic that the perpetrator of the entire charade couldn't be here."

Eddie nodded, took a final gulp of his mint julep, saw mine was gone, then reached over and flipped a switch next to the light switches. A red light illuminated with a loud "bong" downstairs, and my jaw dropped. I was still simply amazed that Toya allowed this servant bullshit to continue, but she was there in less than five minutes with fresh everything. I rolled my eyes when our gazes meet. She just smiled, shook her head, and waggled back down the stairs.

"So I assume the whole story of her ending up on Bourbon Street like a gypsy with her hair sprouting out of her doo-rag and an open wound on her head is also bunk?"

"Not exactly. After Binx collected her from the airport he took her to his apartment on Decatur and they went on a 48-hour drunk together in The Quarter. He never bothered to have her head checked out, never bothered to get her cleaned up, change clothes…nothing, as far as I can gather. Then he showed up at my place in Baton Rouge, without Sissy Mae, and he was utterly destroyed. After two days of blackout drinking and drugging he couldn't remember where he left Sissy Mae or even why, he just knew he had to get out of there. Later he wouldn't even remember coming to my house. So I called Dr. Cobb, but the police got to her first. So Cobb was able to go in, post bail for public drunkenness and disturbing the peace, and take her back to his place. Two days later – it was the Friday your daddy died, I believe, he took her up to his camp on Little Tensas Bayou and, with Lawrence's help, dried her out. Apparently there was quite a bit of cocaine involved too, so it's really rather remarkable that she lived through it. Then you showed up."

This was a side of my sister I barely knew. In high school and even in junior high she had been very careful to try get out in front of her manic binging before it got out of hand, but she wasn't always successful. She caught serious hell from the old man every time he had to pick her up at the police station or at somebody else's house where the parents were concerned for her safety. More obvious were the cookie, ice cream, cupcake binges that eventually got her locked into her own room at night. Typically, Mom was more concerned for her daughter's figure than she was for her mental health.

I imagined her at Kindred Hospital in New Orleans in one of those rooms with the décor that compliments vomit, unconscious with a giant bandage around her skull and probably in some sort of cranial stabilizer that prevents sudden movement. "You ever know anybody that had brain surgery, Eddie?" I realized just as I asked the question that he was watching twenty two men on the field that might at some point require brain surgery simply to shake all the brain bits back into their designated locations after being knocked around inside those helmets for ten years.

"No, but I suspect my brother would have been a candidate had he lived. There's got to be something that can be rewired in there that turns off a person's self-destruct sequence."

"Yeah. Wouldn't that be great?" I said, wondering if certain things were rewired in the brain they would get rewired in the heart and soul as well, as a sort of side effect. But I didn't want to go there with Eddie. Maybe it was question for the Doctor.

"Did Dr. Cobb tell you when we might hear how the surgery went, and when we might know if Sisi can speak or not?" Eddie asked. I had forgotten to pass along Dr. Cobb's update, so I did. As always, more was to be revealed.

"I'll tell you one more thing, Howard. You probably didn't know this, but after your daddy moved west and his mother settled in Albuquerque, within the space of a few years, I lost both my parents and my wife. I was a wreck, suddenly living alone in a big house in Baton Rouge completely rudderless. I couldn't practice law, I couldn't play golf, I couldn't do anything. I felt like I had spent the last five years of my life watching people die."

Eddie was looking at me like he could read my mind, as if there was some connection between us that didn't need to be consciously acknowledged but was a foregone conclusion nonetheless. "Your daddy came down here. Nobody asked him to, he just showed up at my house, a complete surprise. He had bought an old camper – a 1934 Airstream Clipper

– and together we took off down the gulf coast, down to Key West, back up the Atlantic all the way to Nantucket, then across to Chicago and on to Highway 61, which we drove all the way from Minnesota to Baton Rouge. It took us the whole month of April – must have been around 1950 or thereabouts. That trip saved my life, Howard." He paused to take long pull on his drink. I was speechless. "When I heard what you had been through – retiring after 30 years of teaching and coaching, only to help shuffle your folks into the great beyond – well, I figured you could use a little help, though I'm afraid it turned out to be more hassle than help."

We laughed. I suspected that Eddie's brother had taken advantage of his knowledge of my father's rescue mission and used it to get Eddie to buy into his scheme, both of them knowing that I never would have thought of coming down to Briarwood to try and get my post-retirement life on track again.

"Wow, Eddie. You're right. I had no idea. Wow. That's all I can say. I'm…I'm…"

"Aw, forget it, son. Though I got some good stories about that trip that I'll never forget."

We both stood up and shook hands, though mine must have felt like a slippery piece of warm liver. It was all I could do to keep from bawling like a baby. "Thanks for all your help, Eddie, you're a good man."

"I try, Howard." Eddie said. "I really do. It's good to hear that I get it right sometimes."

42 A White Thanksgiving

Thanksgiving generally makes me nervous. First, I'm afraid we'll have to go around the table and declare our gratitude for one thing or another; a tricky proposition when you're seated around a table with relatives that you had no hand in choosing and are likely to be that last people on earth you would be grateful for. Second, it's impossible to sit down to the traditional cornucopia of orange, sienna, umber, ochre and rust in the center of a carefully embroidered pale orange tablecloth without being reminded of the many disastrous Brown Thanksgivings of years past.

Mom loved to throw a party, but she couldn't cook Spaghetti-O's out of a can much less a sixteen-pound turkey. But it didn't usually matter much: by the time the bird got to the table the adults were too smashed to care about eating dry overcooked gravy-less turkey or candied yams with marshmallows. The kids found that if you slathered enough of the yams on a bite of turkey and chewed for several minutes it was possible to choke it down. We didn't have the benefit of J&B or Early Times to lubricate the evening, which almost always turned into a storm of insults between my mother and her sister Dottie. The cousins did not get along much better, and by the end of the evening the families had sworn never to have Thanksgiving dinner together again. But when the next year came around, there we were.

This turned out to be a far more civilized event, at least for a while. At the north head of the table sat Eddie, and at the south head sat Johnny and Bessie, the oldest residents of Briarwood. There was Boon Percy, the career Navy man who served in the Gulf of Tonkin, and his second wife, Lorraine, a stout but well-proportioned woman with fine, rosy cheeks, carefully coiffed, colored, piled and styled amber hair, and a silver diamond brooch at the top of her long, cloven cleavage. She was a good bit younger than Boon – probably mid-forties to his sixty-something. Like many high-spirited women, she was graced with tiny, light freckles that made her bare, meaty upper arms look good enough to eat. Next to Elke sat Catie Percy, a taciturn poetry student and Boon's daughter by his first wife, Margaret, a recent breast cancer victim. Then there were the familiar faces: Toya, Reggie, Jack and Bolling, Doctor Cobb's sister Lucy, (the doctor has stayed in New Orleans to monitor developments with my sister), Stephen Hart and matching humongous wife.

The Southern Thanksgiving cuisine was truly decadent: roast turkey, pear salad with raspberry cream, sweet potato cups, browned butter mashed potatoes, cornbread stuffing, green beans with mushrooms and bacon, grandma Bessie's cranberry sauce, Southern style butter rolls and pumpkin-walnut layered pie. We were about finished with our first go-round when Jack Sublette pointed out the window and cried "OOOH! OOOH! OOOH!" Outside in the illuminated ancient oaks a wintry mix had begun to fall. In the light it mostly look like rain and sleet, but periodically a big white blob – most likely an ice ball – raced to the ground like it had been shot from a gun. To Jack, anything white that came out of the sky had to be snow. Up he leapt in his red snowsuit, his chair flying backwards and cracking against the wall while his knees knocked the table, sending Thanksgiving dinner sliding into the laps of those on the other side, china and crystal cracking on the hardwood floors.

"Jack!" Eddie shouted, "you sit back down this instant," but there was no stopping him as he tore past us shouting:

"Snow! Snow! Snow!"

"Tripp!" Eddie shouted down the table where Jack had to pass to get into the yard. "Tackle that boy!" But Tripp could see in an instant that the damage had been done, and there was no sense in trying to stop Jack. He crashed through the double doors, stumbled down the steps and went sprawling on the lawn face first, grabbing fistfuls of slush.

Bessie shut the door behind him as he began caterwauling: "Tripp, Tripp come on let's build a snowman!"

The group around the table was silent. Those with the remains of turkey dinner in their laps, Toya, Reggie, Lucy Cobb, and Catie Percy were standing, brushing themselves off while Bessie retrieved dish towels. After a few minutes Bolling and Tripp went outside to where Jack was scraping slush up from the grass, trying to pile it. But the sleet was coming down hard, so I got a couple of umbrellas from the front hall for brother and cousin and, opening the door, I could hear that Jack was crying. His snowman, or slushman, wasn't cooperating like the snowmen he'd seen on TV.

"Goddamnit!" Jack shouted, hurling the slush back into the storm. "Goddamnit Goddamnit Goddamnit!" He was a formidable character in his red snowsuit, almost like a young Santa Claus with a youthful beard, but much wider, stronger, more dangerous, with his stringy hair matted to his forehead and those wild animal bloodshot eyes. The anti-Claus, perhaps. And here my son and his girlfriend were thinking of bringing this wild beast home to Bolinas.

Tripp and Bolling stomped their feet on the step and came in, wet but not soaked through. "Somebody oughta take that poor bastard out and shoot him," Bolling said of his twin brother, muttering under his breath as he passed the table and headed for the bathroom. Tripp grabbed a dishtowel and dried off, shaking his head. Still, nobody had seen fit to publicly comment on this disturbing display.

Finally Johnny stood and said, "Listen, let's take a little cleanup break and get ready for some of Toya's punkin' pie. Howard, Sandy, Eddie – let's have us a little chat. Boon, Lorraine y'all welcome to join us. Tripp, Elke – could you keep an eye on big Jackie out there?" Jack was still making slushballs out of the sleet and throwing them with all his might at the big oak, but no matter how hard he tamped them down they broke before they left his hand.

We retired to the front parlor, where Johnny wanted to discuss Jack's future. "Those boys are going to be legal adults in February," Eddie said.

"Yes, that's part of the problem, as I see it," said Boon, stirring the fire. "You heard what Bolling thought should be done with his twin brother. As soon as he gets a chance, he's gonna get as far away from the situation as he can."

There was a pause in the conversation. Turning Jack Sublette over to the state mental health system may have been conceivable to these guys that had been around him his whole life, but it obviously wasn't to Tripp. Still, I wasn't ready to share my son's sentiments, or the fact that he had apparently promised something to Jack at the fishing camp.

Sandy came through with a bottle of red and refreshed glasses all around, and suddenly, as if the giant puppeteer in the sky had just taken control of my strings, I said: "Honey, what do you think of us taking in young Jack Sublette, now that his daddy's gone and his brother doesn't want anything to do with him. We could get him squared away with some of the local mental health services in Marin, and…"

Eddie stood up. "Howard, that's awfully kind of you, but really, I don't think the boy will want to leave home."

"I don't know, Eddie," Sandy said. "According to Tripp, Jack is expecting to move in with he and Elke."

"Well, what that boy expects or doesn't expect doesn't really matter, does it," Lucy exclaimed in a tone not dissimilar from Jack's shrill Barney Fife. "It's not as if he can make his own decisions. Still, I Ray and I can help get him situated in a private institution, provided we're all willing to foot the bill."

This sounded like something my mom, Take Charge Marge, would say. I looked over at Lucy Cobb in her floral print dress, with her carrot-colored hair coiffed and sculpted, and recalled the litany of vitriol that often spewed forth from mom's brain. Sisi could be equally insensitive, of course, and I wasn't exactly Mr. Appropriate myself. But, right though she was – Jack Sublette was in no position to call his own shots – her tone still angered me. Was a "mental home" really the only answer? How could any of us have known what was best for Jack?

When we returned for dessert Jack had returned to his chair – a backup, since he broke the original – but refused to remove his dripping wet snowsuit. Toya gave his soaked square SpongeBob head a quick towel dry and his stringy brown hair a comb, but Jack didn't much care: he was eager to eat his pie and ice cream and get back out into the weather. Unfortunately the precipitation had stopped and the wind had come up, but Jack was unfazed: his attention was glued to the windowpanes and the meteorological events unfolding beyond. So, rather than having another tectonic event at the table, once the big boy had finished his pie we situated him in a chair right in front of the glass double doors so he could charge out should white stuff start falling. And after a while it did. The French doors at the other end of the enclosed porch swung back and we all turned to see our slow cousin in his red snowsuit, arms and mouth open to the sky, twirling under the oaks as first one, then another, and another snowflake drifted out of the ebony heavens. We watched as the big red figure twirled out into the dark fields, then back into the light, then faded into the shadows again, then reappeared, spinning under the oaks with his big tongue out as the air filled with the soft, light silence of falling snow.

43 Placentas, Placebos and Step Number One

After visiting my sister briefly the day after the historic Thanksgiving snowstorm, Sandy and I were invited for dinner at the decaying, rickety Victorian owned by Raymond and Lucy Cobb.

The visit with Sisi wasn't much more than a hug and a few tears – five minutes before she drifted off – the nurses hustled me out of there, accusing me of having upset her. They didn't know that Sisi was perfectly capable of upsetting herself – on command, it seemed – but I didn't feel obliged to share that with them. There's something about my tremendous size that nurses don't like. Perhaps they're afraid I'll bump into an important hospital gadget and cause a catastrophe, which I've been perfectly capable of doing both intentionally and unintentionally since I was 14.

Seeing my sister that way, with a giant white burka of bandages around her head and under her chin, both eyes ringed with purple bruises to her high chiseled cheek bones, the oxygen tubes up her nose and a ponytail of wires coming out the back where electrodes had been fastened to her skull to monitor her brain activity... it hit me like an elbow to the gut under the hoop, so hard I doubled over. Once I could look her in the eye a breathless emptiness seized my heart and the shimmering pixie dust began to crowd my vision. I tried to speak but could only squeak. Sisi smiled, took my hand in hers and gestured for me to pull up a chair, breaking what I thought was a heart attack in progress.

After I calmed down I tried to tell her about all the Thanksgiving excitement: the snow and Jack's crazy antics while staying away from the serious business about the land. I was still having a hard time believing that our land was ours again, but it didn't matter because after a minute or two she closed her eyes, slowly let go of my hand and drifted off.

Sandy could tell that I was shaken up when I rejoined her in the car, but she was kind enough to skip the usual cross examination that always happened after a private meeting with Sisi. She was dog tired and it showed: her eyes were uncommonly dull, her expression exhausted and sallow as if the wild events of the past week had drained her of every last smidgen of spunk. But as soon as Clara swung open the front door and released the delightful, tantalizing, mouth-watering scents of our San Francisco Bay Area home – Chinese takeout – our spirits buzzed.

"The closest y'all will get to Chinese food in Briarwood is Baton

Rouge," Lucy claimed, "and it ain't exactly a gung ha fat choy experience." I was surprised that we weren't having nasturtium salad, given Lucy's penchant for flowers. That night she had on an Asian version of her floral obsession: black silk pajamas (I don't know what else to call them) exploding with bright orange and yellow birds of paradise with an electric purple passion flower tucked between her flowing red tresses. With the orange/red lipstick and red-rimmed eyeglasses she looked like geriatric flower child. It was as hard to stay irritated with her as it was to stay irritated with a circus clown.

"Well, howdy y'all! Happy Thanksgiving!" cried Doctor Cobb, slowly making his way, leaning on a cane, down the front stairs into the foyer. All it took was one look at him to see why he was moving slow: the sagging basset-hound bags and wrinkles around his eyes behind the round wire-rimmed glasses were heavy and bruised. His skin, normally olive, recalled the texture and color of uncooked black cod in the freezer case at the meat market and he hunched in that old man way, like there was a football tucked at the base of his neck between the shoulders. Even the white mustache on his long face looked a little droopier than usual. When I made the connection that his appearance was the direct result of saving my sister's life I wanted to break down and weep all over the antique Persian rug. But still I could not.

"As y'all can see," he said, straightening with a rap of his cane, which I never noticed until then, on the carpet, "I need a drink!"

I felt a buzz in my soul hole and thought, *Yes, he sounds just like you, the Old Geezer, old G-Hal. You and your official announcement that the pre-dinner ritual of dominoes and scotch had begun.* Lucy got up, then immediately sat down again as Clara entered the room with a tray full of Chinese beer, and, to our utter delight, four steaming mugs – not the little Japanese ceramic cups, but mugs – of hot sake.

"Do y'all have small sake cups? I think this calls for a sake boilermaker," Sandy asked.

"A boilermaker?" Lucy asked. "You mean a shot in a beer?"

"You're gonna love it," Sandy insisted. And Lucy did. So did the Doctor. But after all the excitement of the last few days we thought we might end up napping on the Persian if we drank too much too fast, so before we were all completely snookered we sat down in the dining room for our Chinese feast. After green tea and fortune cookies, Doctor Cobb invited me into his office.

It was cold and musty in his den, with bookshelves of medical journals and other anachronisms of the analog age, every page having been scanned into digital systems long ago and now available at the click of a mouse. The big volumes were comforting, bespeaking knowledge painstakingly researched, hypothesized, lab-tested, and otherwise subjected to the rigors of the scientific method. Now, in this era of instant availability of everything, it is impossible to distinguish between truth and opinion, scientific fact and crackpot theory. Doctor Cobb's office had that air of permanence, of foundation, that reminded me of my father's office and his maritime law volumes of statutes and codes, surrounded by golf tournament trophies and first tee photographs. Cobb had seen fit not to mix hobby and profession in his home office, assuming that there was any hobby at all. My father would always say that golf was his true vocation and that law was his avocation. And though Dr. Cobb is a psychiatrist, it's obvious that his vocation is the health of the human body and the human mind.

What really reminded me of my father's home office was the high-backed brown leather swivel chair, creaky and worn in all the same places, cracked in the cushion with dry, frayed piping, crying for a little saddle soap and WD-40. Dr. Cobb settled into it and leaned back with a loud sigh, which was intended to cover up a flappy old-man fart but did not succeed. The Chinese take-out was already beginning to work its magic.

"I've neglected to tell you, Ray, that my father asked to be remembered to you in his final weeks. Evidently he thought very highly of you."

The doctor, still leaning back in the squeaky chair, rubbed his eyes behind his glasses in slow circles. "Ahhh, yes. Hal and I were very close when we were younger, before he moved to California."

"Really? That's good to hear, Doctor. My sister makes it sound like he was run out of here on a greased rail." I decided not to share Sisi's reason for our father's supposed unpopularity, thinking that Ray would bring up his general concupiscent behavior only if he felt it would aid my understanding.

"Ooooh no," said the Doctor, leaning forward in his chair. "Though I have heard the rumors your sister was trying to plant on her various sojourns with Binx down here."

There was a light tap on the door, then Clara came in with a pot of fresh coffee.

"Rumors of salacious behavior, am I right?" I asked as Clara poured. I could understand why my sister would have wanted to besmirch her father's reputation if the stories of her treatment at home are true, especially when I was away at school. But Dr. Cobb probably knew more about what prompted Sisi to paint such a gruesome picture than I did. Growing up with

Hal Brown could be rough, it's true; he even admitted it in those last few weeks. I supposed it was possible that I had buried the unpleasantness so deep that a few sessions with the Doctor might do me some good.

"Normally I wouldn't talk about my client's case with anybody; doctor/patient privilege and so forth. But this is an unusual circumstance, and since you plan on returning to California with her, you'll need a certain amount of background information so you can understand her triggers, topics to avoid and so forth."

The Doctor took a long, slurping swig of black coffee, holding the big blue ceramic mug with both of his long-fingered, liver-spotted hands. Tufts of white hairs sprouted between the knuckles, just as they did out of his ears and nostrils. Altogether with the mustache, he was one of the fuzziest people I had ever met.

"I also think it will be helpful if you get some psychotherapy yourself. Based on what I've seen, I don't think you need medication so a psychiatrist isn't necessary. But the therapist can make that call. If you find yourself going back on the opiates for anything but serious pain, or if you..."

"What?" The hairs stood up on the back of my neck as my forehead broke out with sweat. "Wait a minute. Did you say going back on the opiates? I'm sorry to interrupt Doctor, but as far as I know I've never been off the opiates. Far as I know I've been on fifty milligrams of methadone and sixty milligrams of oxycodone a day for the past 4 years. I may have missed a dose or two..."

Doctor Cobb held his hand up, a smile as wide as Mississippi spreading across his sagging jowls, causing his skin to gather in his cheeks like a squirrel with a mouthful of nuts. "Oh...I guess Sandy hasn't told you. Damn. I hope I haven't ruined it for her. You've been on a placenta for the past week or so..."

"A placenta?"

"Oh, sorry, I meant placebo. Jesus. I need some sleep."

"A placebo? You mean..." I jumped out of my chair in disbelief, almost looking for withdrawal symptoms to kick in.

"You're clean, Howard. As they say in the profession," Doctor Cobb said, his voice cracking. Then, as so often happens in my English teacher's brain, I flashed on Ezekial Farragut, Cheever's drug addict convict, and his similar placebo-based recovery. I couldn't recall if Sandy had read *Falconer* with me or not.

"Are you saying I went cold turkey and didn't notice? Doc...I mean, really?" I had both hands on his desk, staring him down, thinking, *how preposterous! Taking away my drugs without my permission?*

"Ha ha! No way! You would have been sick as a dog. No, Howard. Now, calm down, please, or else I'll have to hit you up with something serious." He was kidding. He couldn't hide it. But I sat anyway, letting it sink in. I couldn't remember a single day in the last ten years without some class-C prescription drug in my medicine cabinet. It sounded like Sandy was supposed to break the news, but the tired old Doctor had let it slip. I got up, opened the door and shouted for Sandy.

"Honey, I need some pills! My feet are killing me!"

"You should have some in your pillbox, honey." She shot a glance at Dr. Cobb, who was still smiling like a drunken chimp.

"I took 'em. They didn't work," I told Sandy. "The pain is just getting worse and worse. Are you sure they're the right pills?"

Sandy looked from me to Cobb, befuddled. "Howard," said the Doctor.

"Wait, Doc. Honey, I'm dying, really. I need some breakthrough oxy, bad." I don't know why I was being such a prick about their little switcheroo. Dr. Cobb and Sandy had, over the past weeks, weaned me off a drug that, if I kept going irrespective of any real or imagined pain would probably kill me in ten years. The honest truth was that, up until this Southern sojourn, I hoped they would kill me sooner. But I somehow had survived the past month – one of the craziest, wildest, purely chaotic experiences I could remember, starting with my father's final dying breath – while weaning off of the drugs that I truly believed were the only things that had kept me going.

"Sandy, Howard knows." Cobb spit it out so fast I had no chance to continue the masquerade, effectively putting a plug in my ridiculous, childish display. Sandy shook her head and gave me a "bad dog" look that was likely to get me scrambling under Cobb's desk with my tail between my legs. These two had played me.

"Okay, you guys," I said. "Okay. My feet are fine, honey. But it is amazing how those fake pills have managed to quell some pretty serious episodes the past few weeks."

Dr. Cobb pointed his finger at his noggin and drew circles at his temple – the universal "crazy" symbol. "It's all in your head now, Howard. I imagine it has been since you recovered from back surgery. There is no physiological reason for you to be in pain of any sort. So, I decided to see if there was a neurological reason. The only way to do that is to start at square one, which is where you are now and have been for about four days. The first two weeks we slowly weaned you down until all the pills were placebos. Now," Cobb paused for another slug of Joe, then turned, moved a few texts aside on the shelf and pulled out a full bottle of Maker's Mark. He poured a thumb-full into his coffee, then grabbed a couple of glasses off the credenza and poured two full glasses. "I want you to think about your pain episodes the last few weeks, Howard. Was it really pain in your feet like you experienced the first few years after the surgery, or was it a combination of panic, anxiety, and other emotional states you associate with pain?"

Sandy pulled up a chair next to mine so that now we were sitting at the Doctor's desk like a couple of patients. "Doc. I don't know." I was off the drugs. That's what I knew. I wasn't addicted to anything anymore. It was unbelievable. I felt like skipping to my Lou my darlin' all over town. "I don't really care," I said, feeling an upwelling, a big bubble of thanks, thanks that these two, and probably Tripp, Elke, Eddie, maybe Lawrence Taylor too, weaned me off the shit – a tricky operation even at the miniscule dose I had been on. It was a profound realization to discover that so many people believed me to be worth saving, because I certainly hadn't been feeling that way myself. For quite some time. Probably ever since I stood idly by while my son was fucking around with M-80s.

Sitting there next to my wife and best friend, soul mate and protector, and across from an old man that I never heard of until my father mentioned his name on his deathbed, and imagining that these two somehow joined forces when they didn't even know each other to help me kick the opiate pain medications...I simply couldn't believe that God or someone like Him or Her hadn't had a hand in this.

"Well, this is truly amazing. I swear those fake pills work just as good as the real thing." For once I had said the right thing. Sandy and the Doctor were in stiches, so happy that their scheme had worked.

"I gotta call Tripp. He is going to be so fucking happy that our plan worked!" Sandy announced, knowing that I knew when she dropped the F-bomb it was really, really serious. "You guys get back to what you were talkin' about. We don't want another night like last night. It's already nine o'clock, and I think we wanna check out of the hotel by tomorrow morning early, book our flights and head home.

I gave her a hug that was only a hint of how badly I wanted to hug and hug and hug, eliminating all possible space, time and matter between us while we melded into that impossibly imagined state of oneness. This I thought I might be able to get closer to, now that I didn't have an artificial sheath of chemicals shielding me from the direct experience of grace. As far as I was concerned at that moment, Sandy absorbed into my arms was grace enough.

44 What a Difference a Month Makes

After Jack Sublette's performance at Thanksgiving dinner, it became clear to Tripp and Elke that they would have to give his future more careful consideration. The idea that they could just pack him up and take him back to Bolinas on the plane was scuttled, and they decided that it would be best to go home and regroup. We also figured that a big family sendoff at the Baton Rouge airport was probably not a good idea, considering that Jack might be expecting to go with us, so we flew out of New Orleans the next day without so much as a handshake with anyone besides Dr. Cobb and his sister.

It quickly became apparent that traveling with miracle boy was going to be a hassle. From the time we walked into the terminal we were dodging inquiries from travelers who swore Tripp was the young man that had his sight restored by God on the corner of Canal and Royal in New Orleans. Even with the *Outside* magazine cap pulled low over his brow and jumbo cat-eye Vuarnet's shielding a third of his face, even hunched over in the window seat and buried in the in-flight magazine, people recognized him. Even with all 6'6" and 240 pounds of me next to him in the exit row aisle seat wearing the ugliest, grumpiest expression I could muster, and Elke dozing in the middle seat with a "do not disturb" card around her neck… we were unable to shield him from the Bible thumpers. Since we were flying out of New Orleans, which if not part of the Bible Belt was close enough, it seemed like everybody on the plane wanted to touch him and get his blessing. Finally the flight attendants had enough and asked the captain to turn on the seatbelt light and leave it on.

"Dad," Tripp asked after we both worked on our drinks in silence for a moment, "what is this miracle stuff all about?" I was caught a little off guard. Didn't Tripp go to catechism? No, of course he didn't. Neither did Sandy, and though I was raised Catholic I wasn't about to foist stories about Jesus and his posse of radical Jews on my young son. Except the Christmas story, of course. It was pretty difficult ignoring that one, what with nativity scenes just about everywhere you looked in the holiday season.

"Well, if you believe the Bible, Jesus performed a bunch of miracles while he was on tour for those three years before he got crucified."

Tripp looked out the window, sipped his drink, then turned back to me. "You mean besides virgins having babies?" I wanted to laugh but it was clear that it was no laughing matter to my son.

"Yeah. That's one of God's own miracles. The miracles that matter, I guess, to these people, are the ones that Jesus pulled off."

Tripp nodded. "Such as...?"

So I told him the story of Bartimaeus, the beggar that Jesus healed. He listened intently, sucking and chomping on ice cubes, patiently holding onto his questions while I tried to tell a few of the other miracle stories, stories I loved as a kid. The idea of this long-haired dude in robes roaming around the desert on a donkey, making bread out of rocks, turning water into wine and trying to make life more tolerable for the lower classes...they were downright inspirational. "That's why these folks are all over you, Buddy. They believe that God or Jesus has restored your eyesight. They want a piece of the action."

"Ahhh. Well, I guess it's as good an explanation as any other." He paused, looked out into the darkness over the Great Basin, then looked over at me, shrugged and smiled. "What the fuck," he said, more cheerful than I had seen him the entire evening. "I can roll with it."

And so we departed our paternal homeland, the English Coast of the Mississippi, the green of the countryside and the blues of Highway 61, as two profoundly altered Howard Browns. Tripp was of course the more visibly altered, having escaped a vague, gauzy filter of fog and entered, as he put it, "the wide, wonderful world of tits and ass." That's my boy.

As for the old guy peeking out from under a thick five-year layer of aggressive chemical and paternal interference between self and world, I sensed that getting doped up on the patio and playing chuck-it with Mr. Booper all day wasn't going to cut it anymore (though I had secretly sung to him every single day that I had been gone). Just when I figured that my branch had broken off of the family tree for good, with both my father and my sister headed for points unknown, the tables turned. We had picked up one stray and possibly another that we would have to figure out how to accommodate, along with one spirit that was now officially overdue – the Buddhists give chakra interlopers thirty days to clear out – for his tee time in heaven. But I was pretty certain he was still camped out in there, and that it was only a matter of time before he would have some acerbic comment about Sisi's brain trauma or Tripp's "no way" recovery. I knew it because I still couldn't believe that our month in West Feliciana, Little Tensas Bayou and the Crescent City wasn't a dream, and that I would wake up at the old man's rent-a-bedside, guitar in hand, Mr. Booper's soft tummy atop my aching feet, the girls twittering in the kitchen and the finches still scratching at the feeder, marveling at the old man's remarkable toes.

BOOK III
COON HOLLOW

I saw the light I saw the light
No more darkness no more night
Now I'm so happy no sorrow in sight
Praise the Lord I saw the light.
–Hank Williams, *I Saw The Light*

45 Later, That Same Evening

We returned to a copious El Niño deluge, the first of the official rainy season and a harbinger of what was to become a record-breaker in Northern California. The waters of the Pacific and the San Francisco Bay had warmed so dramatically that moonfish from the tropics were swimming alongside the sea lions, porpoises, bottle-nosed dolphins and humpback whales. Later there would be mudslides, floods, blizzards and avalanches in the mountains and beaches washed away on the coast. But then, in early December, the state was still so parched from two years of drought, even after the freak October storm, that folks were running naked through the streets yelling, "Keep it comin', Lord, please keep it comin'!"

Tripp and I were headed to Bolinas a good forty-five minutes behind Sandy and Elke, since they were in the short-term lot and my Saab was out in lower Slobovia. Sandy and I would stay over with the kids, pick up Mr. Booper, who with Odo had been looked after by a house sitter at Tripp's place, and go home in the morning. By the time Tripp and I took the long-term parking shuttle out to where my old custom-fit Saab had been chilling for a month, it was 1:30 a.m.

The rains had obviously been intense. Big puddles on the roadway had motorists feinting and parrying on 101, 380 and 280 all the way to 19th Avenue. Then the traffic thinned out, the rain held off, and we sailed smoothly over the Golden Gate, down the Waldo, through Tam Junction and up the Panoramic Highway until we hit Bootjack Camp, where we were suddenly drowning in pea soup.

"Shit!" Tripp shouted, slamming his fist on the dashboard. "If it's like this all the way to Bo we won't make it back 'til dawn." He was right: it was so thick the fog lamps could only cast a couple of weak, diffused beams about five feet ahead. And the Panoramic Highway is treacherous in broad daylight.

"God, I hope Mom and Elke made it through this okay. Shit, we should have gone to my place."

"Maybe they did," Tripp volunteered. "Maybe they were smart and checked the road report."

We continued crawling down the Panoramic, no sign of Sandy and Elke, completely alone in the pea soup. Big juicy drops of moisture fell from the redwood, pine and bay boughs in random rhythms. Around every corner there were piles of branches, some so big we had to stop and clear them. Obviously the womenfolk had gone to San Anselmo. Where the hell was the State Park patrol? After all, the road was open. Shouldn't they be checking for wayward motorists?

It was just as that thought entered my exhausted mind that we saw an odd, filtered light from the bottom of the Steep Ravine. "Dad, hold on," Tripp said quietly, calmly cracking open the glove compartment for the flashlight.

I buried my face in my hands. Maybe Sandy and Elke had tried going this way, swerved to avoid a pile of debris and went over the cliff. Jesus. I pulled forward into one of the dozens of turnouts on the well-travelled road, slowly crunching to a halt. About fifty yards down the road, the headlights of a vehicle illuminated the fog swirling about the giant trunks of second cut redwoods and Douglas firs.

We tried 911, but I knew before even trying that there was no service on this stretch. So we got out and started making our way down the road, the flashlight illuminating our next step but not much further. There was the strong odor of gasoline and oil. Further up, little chunks of glass sparkled in the flashlight beam. I checked my watch: 2:30 a.m. Highly unlikely any vehicles would be along. Then we noticed some skid marks on the wet pavement, fishtailing then ripping out the roadside shrubbery and disappearing over the embankment to where the vehicle rested, high beams fading into the thick, foggy darkness only 25 feet or so skyward.

We made our way down the road until we got to the point where the car or truck lost control and went over the side. Shining the flashlight over the side into the ravine, both Tripp and I realized that trying to access the truck – and it did appear to be a truck and not Elke's van – would be far too risky. The slope was almost sheer.

"Do you have climber's rope in your car?" Tripp asked, somehow confusing me with one of his *Outside* magazine sponsors. I checked my phone. Still no service. Obviously the rangers that patrol the state park had a radio system, but without a cell signal neither Tripp nor I could voice or text an alert.

It seemed like the best thing to do was split up, leaving one of us here just in case the driver got thrown, became conscious, and called for help. The other could drive back up to the Pan Toll ranger station and call from there. It was impossible to tell how long that truck had been sitting down there except for the strength of the headlights, which seemed at full power though it was hard to tell in the fog. I figured the wreck had happened in the last hour, probably when it was still pissing down rain on the mountain.

We were just starting to discuss our options when we heard a groan from down the road. I turned my light in the direction of the voice into a wall of fog. The groaning stopped. Tripp and I pushed forward, scanning the base of cliff. Nothing. All was silent save for our breathing and the sound of the drip, drip, drip in the wet forest.

"Maybe it was the wind," Tripp conjectured, knowing full well it was a human or a beast that sounded like a human. But where was it? We inched down the road. Then in the drainage ditch where the cliff ended and a culvert opened up to a seasonal feeder creek, 20 yards below the spot where the vehicle went over the cliff, we came across a scattering of Budweiser cans, a few oily rags and other trash. Then, deeper in the ditch, water from the feeder creek crashing over his midsection with his upper body sprawled against the far bank lay our mutual nemesis, Mr. MacDickFuck himself, Doug Dennikan.

"Oh for fuck's sake," I said, flashlight beam illuminating Dennikan's scratched and bloodied face.

"What? What do you mean?" Tripp asked. "Is it someone you know?"

Realizing that Tripp had never seen Mr. MacDickfuck before, except in shadowy, fuzzy outlines, I told him: "It's your neighbor, the one that's been harassing you guys. Mr. MacDickFuck."

"Oh. Is he dead?"

I slid down the small embankment, easily stepped across the rushing watercourse, then crouched over Dennikan's upper body and checked the jugular in his neck with two fingers. "His heart is still pumping," I announced, oddly relieved.

"How the hell did he end up over here when his truck is in the gully on the other side of the road?" Tripp asked, having never witnessed a car accident, particularly one where the driver gets thrown from a rolling vehicle.

"He was thrown. Listen, pal. Run back up to the Saab and drive up to the Pan Toll ranger station. You'll get service there. Tell 'em we're on the Stinson side of Panoramic about a mile down from Pan Toll. Here, take the flashlight." I tossed it over Dennikan's body to the other embankment where he caught it as if it was clear as day. I had almost forgotten that he was used to doing everything in the foggy dark.

"I don't really need this," he said, and tossed it back before I could object, landing the big Maglite directly on Dennikan's shaved skull. MacD groaned but didn't open his eyes.

When I heard the Saab's engine turn over up the road, I suddenly realized that Tripp had never driven a car, or anything else, in his entire life. On top of that, the unique configuration of the driver's seat made it almost impossible for anyone that wasn't six foot six to operate the car, even the most experienced drivers. I shouted into the fog and started running back up the road, but somehow he managed to turn the vehicle around. I heard Dennikan groan behind me. *Why worry?* I thought. *My son has spent the last 17 years performing miracles in the dark.*

I pointed the flashlight back at Dennikan. His ass had landed dead center in the creek pointing upstream so the water sprayed up and over his midsection, but his upper body was twisted so that he lay on his back, as if he were performing some contorted yoga pose. I was tempted to hook my hands under his shoulders and pull him out of the water, but I also knew that I shouldn't try and move him, even if he was getting a high colonic from the rushing stream.

So, with two fingers on his jugular I waited and silently prayed, after a fashion: "God, we both know this guy has been behaving like a supreme asshole and would probably be better off dead, but if you give him another chance, he might…" Then, overcome by a powerful déjà vu, I saw the face of Binx Sublette cradled in my arms, without the sunglasses. He had the ruddy, weather-worn complexion of a hard drinker, the purplish nose mapped with tiny capillaries and the dark grey pallor under the eyes and in the cheeks. He had the pockmarks from serious, unchecked teenage acne. But he also had the eroded, crumbling teeth of a meth addict, and I knew then that this was not the specter of Binx, who had moved on to some poor unsuspecting soul's third chakra, but of a guy that still had a chance. Unlike mom, unlike dad, unlike Binx, and unlike our little son Ward, this card-carrying son-of-a-bitch not only had a chance to live, but a chance to redeem himself and rejoin the human race, if he so chose. And if I so chose.

Looking down on his quiet, peaceful visage, as if he were a child asleep in my arms, or a buddy taken down on the battlefield, or a complete stranger whom I'd never seen before, I realized that I was on autopilot, wired by forces far more powerful than my own meager will.

Just then a spasm rocked Dennikan's upper body and, suddenly conscious, he jerked his head sideways and coughed up of dark glob of sticky blood. "Ooooh," he groaned, laying his head back in my arms, eyes open and staring into the beam of the flashlight. "Who…" he mumbled, his voice garbled with fluid. I illuminated my face. "Oh God, it's you," he managed to whisper. "I've died and gone to hell." I had to smile.

He closed his eyes and let his head fall sideways, the glob of blood running down his chin. When I returned my fingers to his jugular his heart had stopped. Fuck. I strained my ears for the sound of sirens, then, cupping his head in the palm of my hand, turned it upward. It had been seven years since my last mandatory EMT classes, classes that, as a basketball coach, I had to renew every few years. Still, in my thirty-year career on the sidelines I only used it once. The player, an extremely talented if somewhat flashy forward, had a bad heart that had been overlooked for 16 years. I put every ounce of bellows and every erg of muscle into reviving him, but he died anyway.

Nobody was going to care if I let Doug Dennikan die on purpose, except maybe the bartender at Smiley's in Bolinas. Still, I was going to try and save him. It was as if my entire being had been inhabited by a cosmic force, what some folks might refer to as "God's will." The body of Howard Brown had been appropriated by supernatural eminent domain, seized by the hand of God.

I wiped his bloody mouth with the back of my sleeve and bent over him, suddenly overwhelmed by the smell of stale beer, puke and blood. I pulled up, looked away and took a deep breath, filling my big barrel chest up with clean mountain fog, then fixed my mouth on his and started to blow. Three times. Four. Then with the heels of my giant hands together I pumped his heart, putting my own broad shoulders and back into every violent thrust. Nothing. Back to his mouth, then back to his chest, again, then again, until it looked like I was going to be zero for two in EMT saves. I hung my head, listening to sirens growing closer, when Dennikan suddenly jerked up like a rag doll, his head flopping forward, and let fly a glob of bloody sputum the size of a golf ball. "YES!" I shouted, smacking him on the back as hard as I could. Another glob, smaller, shot forth into the water. He looked around, wild-eyed and panicked as I slowly lowered him, my big hand still cupping the back of his head. His breath was coming in short, ragged bursts when a Ranger's truck pulled up, followed by the real EMTs in an ambulance. I made way as the professionals took their positions and assessed the scene, red and blue lights swirling above us in the fog, just barely reaching the shining boughs of redwood, fir and bay.

"Dad!" Tripp came bounding out of the fog like a gazelle, leapt the narrow creek and wrapped his arms around me as far as he could. "Well?" he asked, searching my eyes. I took off my glasses and wiped my forehead – I had broken out in the familiar full body sweat and had the beginnings of sparkling pixies in my periphery. He looked over to where two EMTs and a fireman were delicately trying to transfer Dennikan from the creek to a stretcher.

"I think I saved him, though I'm not sure he's going to be very happy that I did."

"CPR? He stopped breathing? Heart stopped beating?"

"All of the above," I answered. "Though I don't think he shit his pants." Tripp rolled his eyes. "I expect that, if he survives whatever internal injuries he has, he'll end up at least partially paralyzed," I added.

"Uh, I wouldn't be so sure about the bowel evacuation," an EMT said, not looking up from where he was cutting away Dennikan's jeans. Tripp and I took a sniff.

"Ugh!" Tripp exclaimed. I silently thanked the supernatural force that had subsumed my olfactory senses in the interest of saving a life. We backed away from the scene as they got Dennikan strapped onto the palette and loaded into the truck. Within minutes he was gone back into the fog. Meanwhile a shout came up from the ravine where Dennikan's blue Ford Ranger still sent its high beams up into the trees.

"There's a puppy in the cab! A little pit bull!" The spotlights of a fire truck, where two firemen examined the wreckage of the blue Ford Ranger, illuminated the scene below; it's windowless cab sticking up out of Steep Ravine creek. Tripp and I stood at the edge of the steep drop off where the truck had carved a path of smashed ferns and busted young trees leading to the rushing waterway below.

"A puppy?" Tripp shouted. A firemen's upper half emerged from the cab, a small ball of white in his arms. After a few seconds of examination, the fireman held the puppy in one hand over his head. "Amazing!" he shouted with delight. "There's not a scratch on him!"

46 Gesture of Balance

We weren't sure that we would ever hear from Doug Dennikan again, though we were all curious about his recovery. DeeDee, my bartender friend who frequently tended to Druggy (yet another nickname for MacDickFuck), told me about a week after the accident that he ended up paralyzed from the waist down, and that she was taking care of the dog while he was in rehab. If MacDickFuck had expressed any gratitude for being allowed to continue what had become the textbook definition of an unmanageable life, he hadn't shared it with DeeDee.

Tripp and I showed up at Smiley's, the only bar in Bolinas, on that cold, clear December afternoon for a bowl of chili and a beer. DeeDee rushed out from behind the bar to greet us, still a shapely if somewhat expanded 60-year-old. Her dimpled, freckled face, her long carrot-orange hair, toothy grin and general largesse pleased me then more than it had in the 3rd grade, though she was always a good choice for kickball. She took Tripp in a big woman bear hug, then grabbed me by the shoulder and pulled me in close to make a Tripp sandwich, and I thought for the first time in a while that I had ignored my old friends for too long.

"What the fuck? What the fuck?" DeeDee repeated several times, then turned us loose. Hot tears ran down her freckled cheeks, as she looked Tripp over like a long-lost son back from the war. "My God, you really are a miracle, aren't you? Look at those baby blues. Good Lord! Elke better watch out, that's all I got to say."

We sat down at the antique bar and she drew a couple of pints of Lagunitas Pale Ale, a local brew. Aside from a couple of bikers at the other end of the bar, we had the place to ourselves. After a little more chitchat I turned the conversation back to Dennikan.

"Rehab?" I remember asking while she polished glasses.

"Yeah. Physical, mental, spiritual – the works," said DeeDee, who could drink with the best of them but was not a drunk. Lucky her. "He'll be up at a minimum security clinic in Redding for a couple of months, learning how to operate his new wheels without the assistance of Budweiser and crystal meth."

"What about the dog?" Tripp asked. "What's his name?"

"Her name. It's Lila." DeeDee, like everybody else in Bolinas, knew that Tripp and Elke had absconded Dennikan's dog.

"What? MacDickFuck bought a female dog? What's wrong with this picture?" Odo, formerly Buddy, was a male. I figured he would want one as much like the one that he had inadvertently given up for adoption. "He didn't buy it. I did," she said, holding a glass up to the light. "I figured a little female vibe might help him mellow out a little, since he hasn't had a female companion since he lost Valerie. You probably never heard about Valerie," she said.

"No. Who's Valerie?"

"His wife. Drove her car off the Shoreline Highway about ten years ago. On purpose. And she was pregnant."

"What the fuck?" Tripp exclaimed. "She was pregnant? That is so fucked up!"

"She blamed Druggy," DeeDee continued. "Said he had ruined her life, didn't want to bring a kid into a world with him in it. It was heartbreaking. He wanted that kid in the worst way; it was all he could talk about. He was actually a pretty nice guy back then. He did all right as a commercial fisherman, operating out of Bolinas. He would cash in during salmon, crab and squid season, and in the meantime he caught plenty of halibut and cod to keep things going. But she commuted to Mill Valley where she was a hygienist or something like that, and after a while she got tired of commuting and wanted to move over the hill or to Fairfax. Druggy wouldn't hear of it, being a native Bolinian."

"So she drove off the cliff into the ocean? Sounds to me like she had a couple of screws loose."

When we told Elke and Sandy about Doug Dennikan's tragic marriage later that same early December day on Tripp's infamous front steps, there was some hemming and hawing at first, like it was inconceivable for such a professional asshole to have been married at all. But after a couple of minutes nobody had anything more to say about Doug Dennikan's tragic life, or say anything about what now seemed to be a very insensitive dog theft. A tragedy all around, almost too big to comprehend. Would Odo, formerly Buddy, have survived if he went back with his master, who had trained him to be a vicious killer? Now Odo and Mr. Booper were tearing around the yard, tackling each other and yanking on each other's ears, growling and howling with pure dog joy. But as soon as Tripp opened the front door, they were up the stairs and in the house, no doubt claiming their real estate on the sofa.

Then, Elke and Tripp got up and went into the house. "Don't move," Elke said, chucking me in the good shoulder. The winter sun had dropped into the ocean, leaving a plum-red stain across the horizon and a chill on Tripp's front porch.

"We're coming in," Sandy said, "it's getting chilly out here."

"Okay, fine," Tripp said from the doorway, "come in and sit on the couch. I'll light a fire. Or is it another 'no burn' day?"

"Yep, but it's okay with me. Breeze is offshore anyway," Sandy said.

The two of us sat on the old Kulim sofa that our friend Sally, who had died from ovarian cancer five years prior, had given them. The sofa was a perfect fit for the kids, and aside from the combination of dog hair, dog stains, and the two dogs that we had to shove aside to sit down, it was in fine shape.

"Well, Elke said as she returned from the kitchen, a bottle of champagne in hand and four small fruit jars on a tray. She set the tray on the coffee table in front of the sofa, then slapped her belly and said with a big-screen smile: "Guess who got knocked up at Camp Serendipity?"

47 Pink Confetti Bubblegum High

There are probably some who think that those that are enthusiastic about being grandparents have one foot in the grave, having surrendered their remaining days to baby talk, toy trains, Gerber's and old Disney films. My mother was one of them. She refused to hold Tripp and Ward, claiming a fear that her anorexic toothpick arms were too weak for a squirming baby and she would surely drop one on his head. She also insisted on being called by her first name: Marge. No Grandma or Nana for her. She had about as much enthusiasm for being a grandmother as she had for being a mother.

G-Hal was the opposite, or at least he was when the baby got past the blob stage. He loved to get down on the floor with the blocks, the tinker toys, the Lincoln logs and Playmobil. But he had his limits. When toddler chaos became too much he would try to get Tripp and Ward to sit still – completely still without moving a muscle – in a corner for five minutes. It beat hurling them across the room like a football, as he had done with me when I was in the blob stage. Still, I always felt like trying to make a three-year-old sit still for five minutes was cruel and unusual punishment.

As for the new grandparents-to-be, the news that Elke "got knocked up at Camp Serendipity" triggered a goofy, pink confetti bubblegum high in both of us that could have, and perhaps should have, resulted in a visit by the little men in the white lab coats. We were shivering with joy, and to think that my son and Elke had made this decision to get into a family way before the miracle on Royal and Canal made us shiver even harder. "Now that's big fat love," Sandy said.

Piloting Sandy's old jet-black Audi A6 wagon along the winding road along Lagunitas Creek to San Anselmo from Bolinas that night, a melody crept into my tired champagne brain that had been buried there since the late sixties. Sandy was snoring lightly in the passenger seat from champagne overdose and Mr. Booper was crashed out in the back.

> *My troubles are many*
> *they're as deep as a well*
> *I can swear there ain't no heaven*
> *but I pray there ain't no hell*
> *swear there ain't no heaven*

.

but I pray there ain't no hell
But I'll never know by livin'
Only my dyin' will tell
and when I die
and when I'm gone
there'll be one child born
in this world
to carry on

The "Blood, Sweat and Tears" version of the old Laura Nyro tune rung in my ears as if it were playing on the car radio. But there was something in the lyrics that wasn't sitting right with me. I thought, "I swear there *is* a heaven/and I *know there ain't no* hell." This was, of course, in keeping with my "pick your own afterlife" philosophy.

Then, inspired by the seeming reckless abandon of bringing more children onto a planet preparing to explode, we sold 156 Woodland and our Sleepy Hollow beach-less beach house and moved to a ramshackle property on the coast known to the locals as Coon Hollow. Tripp and Elke discovered the place on one of their now frequent bike rides out to the Palomarin trailhead north of Bolinas.

"It's a compound," Tripp said when he called from the place. "There's three separate buildings: a main house, a guest house and a studio that could be converted into a guest house, or at least a detached bedroom. And it's only five minutes from our place." Perfect for full-time babysitters, though he didn't say that. He also didn't mention that we would be able to accommodate both my sister *and* Jack Sublette in the compound, but I knew that was what he was thinking. The idea of taking in a mute 58-year-old paranoid schizophrenic and an intellectually disabled 18-year-old so soon, after all we had been through the last five years, was completely overwhelming. Babies I could handle. And we had expected to accommodate my sister, at least for a while. Jack Sublette was another matter, and a big part of me had hoped that once Tripp and Elke were home they would leave Jack to his own family in the south. Since our return, we had yet to discuss Jack's fate.

The property was graced with a spring-fed creek that ran year around down the north side of the hollow. In January we could see the clear water cascading over rocks and boulders, imagining that most of the year it would be covered by sword ferns and the round, thin pancake-sized leaves of the nasturtiums with their electric orange flowers. Further down the creek amidst several round, Volkswagen-sized boulders were some giant black conical seed pods, each around four feet tall and surrounded by the blackened, dead stalks and giant leaves of some prehistoric-looking plant.

"Chilean gunnera," Tripp told us. "In the summer the leaves get up to six feet wide, perfect for dinosaurs." I could practically see the 60-foot-long neck of a brontosaurus stretching up the hollow to munch on such a plant.

To the north a steep ridge covered in blackberry, pyracantha and potato vine rose about 200 feet to the top of a rock outcropping and a dense stand of Monterey cypress, pine, and bay, blocking the view of the Pt. Reyes peninsula but also, I suspected, blocking the stiff northerlies that can buffet the coast year round.

The south side of the property rose up from a large, mildly sloping grassy space that fell to the creek. A rotten, dilapidated plank fence, held together by 30-year-old ivy vine, bordered the south slope. On the gentle hillside sat a modest frame structure of gray, moss-covered shingles that looked as if it might crumble into the creek at any moment. Ivy and thorn-less blackberry vines were creeping up the walls and under the shingles, but otherwise the place looked serviceable. The other building, a bona fide one-room guesthouse with kitchenette and bath, overlooked the ocean from the hill on the east side of the main house.

It didn't take long for us to decide that Coon Hollow would be our legacy, our gift to generations of Browns far into the future. I liked the idea, so did Sandy, as well as Tripp and Elke. So, we sold our San Anselmo house and bought Coon Hollow. Then came six weeks of madcap moving. For the first time since I retired from teaching, coaching, death-march management and manboob maintenance, I woke up every day with more chores than I could possibly hope to complete. I almost totally forgot about the looming arrival of my sister and Jack Sublette, I forgot about my father and his almost nightly appearances in my dreams, I forgot about pain and pain meds and I forgot about what I was going to do with the rest of my life because there I was, doing it: packing boxes, taping and labeling boxes, unpacking boxes, moving boxes, both of us in a mad, frenetic, feverish state. We went through the leftovers of my parents' lives like a tornado, sucking up clothing, furniture, cookware, blankets, books, records, pictures, paintings, board games etc. etc. and spitting it all out several miles away at the San Rafael Goodwill.

As Einstein once said, "Not everything that counts can be counted, and not everything that can be counted, counts." In the process of distilling that which counts, I had discovered, or re-discovered, the simple joy of busywork. Like chopping wood and carrying water, the task of boxing up both my parents' and our lives and physically moving them from point A to point B was mysteriously rewarding, so much so that I was looking forward to all the work that awaited us in Coon Hollow. So I stopped keeping a scorecard of things that didn't count – all the heartaches of the past – and focused on carving out a new existence for our growing family, for grow it would. And there was work to do.

48 Boxed In

We moved into Coon Hollow in early spring, a historically short season on the Pacific Coast when the northerlies kick up whitecaps every afternoon while the rain stubbornly subsides. Some time in May a heat wave would usually cook what remained of the poppies, lupine, purple aster and green winter rye, so by June the hills would be signature golden brown and the fog would blanket the coast like a fisherman's rag wool sweater.

The place needed some serious fixing-up, and we were so occupied with painting walls, refinishing floors, replacing broken toilets and the like that I had almost forgotten about the impending arrival of my sister and possibly Jack Sublette. Then, one sparkling spring afternoon while we were unpacking boxes, Dr. Cobb called.

"The latest tests showed the beginning of some plaque development in her brain, Howard," Dr. Cobb hesitantly informed me. I had suspected that Sisi would eventually begin to develop Alzheimer's, just like my Mom, her sister and her mother had. Throwing memory loss on top of the existing pile of mental problems felt like a classic case of adding insult to injury, but Dr. Cobb said Alzheimer's might actually relieve some of Sisi's other symptoms. "I once had a patient, now deceased, that was an alcoholic and a chain smoker. When she developed Alzheimer's, she forgot her 11AM toddy. She forgot to smoke. Eventually she didn't know what cigarettes were for. She ended up healthier than she had been in decades, and actually lived a lot longer than she might have otherwise. The Lord works in mysterious ways, Howard. Keep that in mind."

I sighed and sat down on a stack of unopened boxes in our new great room, feeling like my enhanced and expanded brotherly responsibilities had come home, literally, to roost on my shoulders. Obviously, Dr. Cobb and his sister were eager to get rid of Sisi. Her insurance stopped covering her in-patient rehab in February, and she had been living with them in the Garden District ever since.

"It's a good thing she can't talk," he said in his characteristic deadpan, "though she has written several very...uh...colorful notes. Fortunately they're not exactly coherent." I could imagine. Her penchant for blue language was legendary, a product of seventies feminism and growing up with me. If anything, the loss of speech had made her written tongue even more foul and disgusting. If her emails to me, at least those that made sense, were anything

.

like the notes she shared with Lucy Cobb, their housekeeper Clara and the Doctor, I could understand why they wanted to get rid of her. Written comments like "that goddamn mothercock fucksucker has his bottom so far up his face he's turd choking" were bad enough, but when she directed her invective at Eddie Sublette and Stephen Hart, our so-called business partners, it was particularly embarrassing. "Oh, and that's not the half of it. She's got a surprise for you and Sandy. I can't tell you what it is but I can tell you that after a couple of days you'll probably want to throw it in the ocean."

I couldn't imagine what little gadget she had that made her more...more expressive...than she already was on paper. I'll admit I felt at least partially responsible, sparing her none of my own blue language and obscene imaginings when she was still wearing a plaid jumper and pigtails.

"Lucy can't take it anymore, Howard. The worst of it is, when Lucy objects to certain foul notes and text messages, Sisi claims no responsibility whatsoever. Whether this is selective memory or the real thing, the 'awful awful' as your daddy called it...well, it's too early to tell. It could be either." I couldn't argue with the old Doctor. She couldn't exactly stay up at Briarwood with Eddie, particularly after accusing her cousin of buggering his mentally challenged nephew in his room at the private mental institution. The time had come to get her out of Louisiana. But back here? With Sandy? I was starting to second-guess the whole plan now that we had discovered the peace and tranquility of Coon Hollow.

"I plan to fly up with her and Jack next Thursday," Ray said.

"Whoa!" I shouted, "Did you say you're flying up with Jack, too?"

Suddenly the box I was sitting on collapsed, and all two hundred and forty pounds of me crashed to the hardwood floor with the loud thumping blast of breaking pottery – I had been sitting on the box that held the kids' clay sculptures. Ward's pig, one of several pieces he made in the children's cancer center, didn't look recoverable. Nor did Tripp's castle. While Cobb kept on blathering over the speaker phone – I don't know how he couldn't have heard the crash – I slowly heaved myself up, went to the fridge, opened a Stella, went out on the upper deck and downed it in a single gulp.

"Yes, I've been in contact with Tripp and Elke," the doctor continued, "and they said they're ready..."

"Wait a minute, Doc," I interrupted, phosphorescent sparkles twinkling on my periphery. "Tripp hasn't said anything about any of us being ready for Jack Sublette." I had entered that familiar state of unreality, as if I were watching myself in a Hitchcock film. Cobb's words fell to the floor with the shards of broken pottery, waiting for me to pick them up and arrange them into intelligible form.

"I gathered that," said Dr. Cobb.

"Gathered what?" I was thinking that I should probably gather up the pieces of broken pottery on the floor.

"I gathered that Tripp has not discussed his plans for Jack with you or Sandy." Cobb paused. I might have been crying, or sobbing, or making some other worrisome sound, because then he said: "Howard, are you all right?"

Just then Sandy walked into the great room, saw me sitting on the floor with the broken ceramics and screamed: "Oh my God! What happened?"

"Howard!" Dr. Cobb yelled over the speaker. "What's going on?"

"Oh, Dr. Cobb, is that you? There's been an accident here. Howard's not looking too good."

"An accident," I muttered, feeling a little warm blood on my ass spreading through my shorts. I'd been impaled by Ward's pig. "Just one big fucking accident."

"Oh dear," Cobb said. "What sort of accident?"

"Nothing serious," Sandy replied, rolling her eyes at me. *Nothing serious?* I thought. *Our son has made arrangements to adopt a drooling 250-pound mongoloid who will most likely end up living with us, and it's nothing serious?"*

"Well, y'all take care of whatever needs taking care of there," Dr. Cobb said in his most soothing shrink tone. "Call me when you're ready."

We swept up the shards of Ward's ceramic pig, laying them out carefully on the dining room table like puzzle pieces, leaving the rest of the broken clay sculptures on the floor. Before I could mention our son's plans, Tripp and Elke walked in the door.

"Oh no!" Elke cried, both hands on her burgeoning tummy. "What happened?"

I almost said, *Dr. Cobb just told me that Jack Sublette is moving in with us, so I destroyed all the pottery before he could get to it.* But before I could drop my snark bomb, Sandy quietly explained that I had been talking to Dr. Cobb on the phone and accidentally sat down on the wrong box. "Did he say something that upset you, Howard? The box had 'kids ceramics' written all over it," she added.

"I know why dad sat on the wrong box," Tripp said. "Dr. Cobb must have told him that he was flying up here with Sisi and Jack next week." Tripp took a seat at the dining room table. "We came over here to let you know, in person."

"But…" Sandy began, "when…how will you…who's going to…" She pulled up a chair close to Tripp. He smiled one of his toothy bright white smiles. At the same time I had a palpable, physical craving for narcotics, though the physical pain in my giant ass was minimal. I suddenly felt cold and naked without them, but I knew that there were none at all in the house. I clenched my jaw, wiped the beading sweat off of my forehead and went to the fridge for another beer.

"Ahh, so…" Tripp continued, his blue eyes flashing, "Dr. Cobb must have forgotten to tell you, for some reason."

"Oh, he told me all right," I said, trying to control my dismay but not doing a very good job, "he said he was flying up here with Sisi and Jack…"

"…and Lawrence," Elke quickly butted in.

"And Lawrence? My sister's nurse, big LT?" I gasped in amazement, frozen with the bottle opener in my hand.

"Oh my God! Where in the world are we going to put all these people?" Sandy cried, jumping up. Tripp just continued to sit there grinning like a Cheshire cat, tilting his head and looking at the shards of Ward's pig from different angles.

"Here," Elke said.

"Where?" I shouted, "in that falling-down shed outside?" The pixie dust had returned to my periphery, my heart was pounding double-time and I felt faint. We had planned to put my sister in the existing guest cabin, which had a fresh coat of paint, freshly refinished hardwood floor and several new appliances. But the other structure – it had probably been used as a storage shed – was completely rotten from floor to ceiling.

Just then Tripp got up, went to the front hall, retrieved his backpack, returned to the table, pulled a manila folder from his pack and laid it on the table.

"Tomorrow morning at precisely 8AM, a crew will arrive to tear down the shed and begin building this." With a flourish he pulled out a color photograph of a 21st century two-story cottage, or cabin, or, as people refer to them now, a tiny home. "It's completely pre-fab, and totally green. It comes with it's own solar panel heating system, composting toilet, double-paned windows. Pretty sweet, huh?"

Sandy and I studied the picture of the little cottage that Tripp and Elke had chosen to accommodate two oversized individuals, Jack Sublette and Lawrence Taylor. Would it have oversized doors, extra-wide for Jack and extra-tall for Lawrence?

"Yes," Elke said. "We've asked for a few custom features."

"And it will be ready by the time they arrive next Thursday?" Sandy asked.

"Yep. And furnished," Tripp said. My heartbeat began to return to normal. Then, knowing that Tripp knew that Sandy and I could not afford to build the guest cottage, much less furnish it, I asked who was picking up the tab.

"Jack's daddy!" Tripp shouted, as if of all the amazing news he had just shared with us was dwarfed by this unbelievable fact. "This was all his idea!"

49 Mystery Money

I could no more believe that Binx Sublette had set aside money for Jack's care than I could believe in the physical manifestation of Santa Claus. I had witnessed enough demonstrations of physical and mental abuse, from attempted murder to repeatedly referring to his son as a "goddamned retard," that I figured Binx must have been forced, somehow, to provide for Jack in his will. Tripp could shed no additional light on the subject. "Dr. Cobb said the whole family was surprised, and Eddie most of all," he said as the evening sun gave itself up to the depths of the blue Pacific.

I immediately texted my sister, knowing that if I waited much longer she would be down for the night in the Central time zone —she was averaging 16 hours of sleep a day — and I would have to lay awake all night hypothesizing. But I was too late. Either that or she didn't want to respond for some other reason.

The next morning I felt like the thick coastal fog had been sucked into my head through my ears overnight, following a half dozen Stellas, the remains of a bottle of Hornitos, and several glasses of California red blend. When I awoke at daybreak to feed Mr. Booper, every cell in my body cried out for chemical relief, though my pain was nothing more than a garden-variety hangover. So I shed my nightclothes and soaked for a while in the hot tub, watching the fog swirl around the flat, geometric branches of the Monterey cypresses like smoke in an opium den. My C-channels, as Burroughs so lovingly referred to them, were open and humming for love.

When I returned to the sack my cell phone on the nightstand was humming as well. Sisi had texted me a short note:

Jack protection rescue loot was my hunch. I recite Binx no more my pussy if Binx not extricate dinero for wet times. Hart assembled ledger for Jack solely for father termination function but moola largely Kenny's. And Dad's, congenitally. I am not so disadvantageous, am I?

As I laid in bed trying to decipher her text – the neurologist's description of the disruption to Broca's area and the resulting speech disorder was surprisingly accurate – I tried to divine what had attracted my sister to Binx Sublette in the first place. I would have understood a brief fling – a novelty fuck – as a form of rebellion against the private girl's school and country club life. She had, after all, began her relationship with her second cousin when she had been quarantined at Briarwood after aborting a black man's baby. With Binx, she had pulled a complete 180-degree about face, from a pot-smoking hepcat jazzer to a redneck, alcoholic country doctor. If there was any similarity, it was in the extremity of her choices. *Hart assembled ledger for Jack solely for father termination function but moola largely Kenny's. And Dad's, congenitally.* It sounded like my sister had old Mr. Congeniality, Stephen Hart, set up a trust for Jack Sublette, but how did it get funded? By her ex-husband? And our father? *Congenitally?*

"Yes, Sisi came to me shortly after we learned of Binx's attempted suicide up at Briarwood," Hart told me in his syrupy drawl when I called him in the midmorning. The summer fog was beginning to burn off the ridge north of Coon Hollow, but the air remained damp and chill on our deck overlooking the Pacific. I sat in my bathrobe sipping coffee with Mr. Booper in his customary position atop my aching feet. "Jack wasn't even 3 months old yet, and Binx had already decided he wanted nothing to do with him. Your sister managed to change his mind about that, at least partially." I could picture him all pink and puffy in his little antique office across from the St. Francisville courthouse, a fresh, fizzing Coke on the rocks before him.

I wondered how my sister got the leverage over Binx. He hadn't seemed the type to be cowed by women, and Sisi couldn't have visited him very often, especially once she was married with children. "Oh, Howard, I suspect the woman your sister was when she was with Binx was a woman you've never met," said Hart. "Of course, my knowledge is all second hand, you unnerstand, mostly from Eddie. But I tell you…Sissy Mae and Binx could light up the Quarter like a goddamned bushfire. When she wasn't around, which was most of the time, Binx would sulk. Oh how he could sulk! He would hire a hooker now and then, but most of the time he would come home from work and park his ass in front of the TV with mess o' Mickey D's. When Sissy Mae came down here he was all of a sudden a mister hail-fellow-well-met, buyin' rounds for the house, dancing 'til dawn. That sort of thing. Yes, she had some power over that boy. I ain't never seen anything like it."

Now he's dead and she's brain damaged, I thought. I was familiar with Sisi's wild streak, just as I was familiar with her shy, retiring, academic streak. She was, at heart, an actor. But a philanthropist? Then I was hit with a thought so unexpected, so novel, so abrupt that I interrupted my call with Hart, and instead went looking for Sandy. I found her in the guest cottage, soon to be Sisi's abode, measuring for curtains.

"Honey, I feel like we've been dropped into the heart of a Dickens

novel," I exclaimed, gooseflesh rippling over my body in electric waves.
"Really? That's good to hear. I was getting really tired of *Heart of Darkness*," she said, standing on a stepstool with a pencil behind her ear and the tape measure stretched horizontally across the top of the window frame.

"No seriously, you won't believe this," I cried.

"Okay, just a sec, let me write this measurement down before I forget it." She pulled a notepad from the back pocket of her cutoffs, snatched the pencil from behind her ear and quickly scrawled down the number while I paced, not noticing the amazing transformation she had been making to the cottage. For my sister, no less.

"Okay," I said, breathless. "You know how everybody has been telling us that Binx was married after he came back from Nam, and how his wife walked out on him when she learned that Jack was retarded."

"Howard, we don't use the "r" word anymore, remember?" Sandy scolded.

"All right. Whatever." I was too excited to be politically correct. "So, you know how Tripp said that Binx had set aside money in his will for Jack's care, and that my sister says she had Hart set up a trust account for the money, right?"

"Is that right?" Sandy said, now curious as she plopped down in one of the overstuffed club chairs from the Sleepy Hollow house. Of course she didn't know that, because I had just learned it myself from counselor Hart.

"Oh sorry, I've been on the phone with Hart. He says Sisi basically blackmailed Binx so that he would be forced to fund the trust."

"Blackmailed? With what?"

"I don't know. Fun. Sex. Dancing. Good times. Apparently they were quite a pair."

"Well, I guess we kinda already knew that," she said, smiling. "They certainly put on quite a show at Eddie's birthday party."

Quite a show. The grand finale, at least for Binx. "Yeah...so," I said, my voice dropping to a whisper for no good reason. "What if there was no wife."

"You mean what if Binx didn't actually get married when he returned from Vietnam?" Sandy said, her eyes growing as white and wide as cue balls. "Then whose kids...?"

I stopped my pacing and caught Sandy's stupefied gaze. Then she stood up, shaking her head so violently that the yellow kerchief on her head let loose and flew to the floor. "No! No, it can't be," she cried. "There's no way. No way Sisi could keep something like that secret. It would have shown when we were all at the fishing camp. I mean, really, Howard. Your sister, God bless her, had absolutely no control over what came out of her mouth down there. She would have spilled the beans in that condition, with her two sons right there with her, don't you think?"

I paused, then sat down in the club chair. Now she was pacing, gently shaking her head from side-to-side, hands in her pockets. "What if she forgot?" I said, very deliberately, very slowly. "It wouldn't have been the first time she'd forgotten something really big or important."

While my wife kept pacing the floor of the cottage living area, walking back and forth from wall to wall, I thought that, if the twins belonged to her and Binx, she wouldn't have needed to bend his arm for funds. But she had also mentioned that Kenny, her ex, was involved, as was our father.

"Howard," Sandy announced as she tied her kerchief back into her hair, "it's an interesting theory, and you're right – very *Great Expectations* – but given all the other circumstances, I don't think it's possible. First, how did Sisi conceal her pregnancy? Second, who would know the truth now? Eddie? Dr. Cobb? Lucy? Jack & Bolling?"

I smiled, stood up, clapped my hands on my wife's shoulders, leaned forward and gave her a kiss. "Johnny," I whispered. "He'll know. He knows everything."

50 Kissin' Cousins

By the time the dense, dripping summer coastal fog had returned for the evening, after an afternoon of unpacking and theorizing, hypothesizing, conjecturing and guessing, Sandy and I decided that, in the final analysis, it made no difference whether Jack was a product of Binx and my sister or a product of someone else entirely. That didn't mean we didn't want to find out, but if it meant causing a rumble in the family, we would have been content to leave it alone. Jack and Sisi were coming to live with us, and if they wanted to act like mother and son, or not, it was fine with us. Besides, I doubted that my sister would even remember Jack by the time they got here.

We also came to the realization that, whether or not Sisi was Jack's mother, her role in his life threw all judgment of her behavior out the window, leaving the two of us feeling like guilt-ridden shit. At the same time, she had expertly concealed her own charity for almost twenty years, so she couldn't exactly expect a commendation.

Still, we took time out from unpacking to compare the photos we had taken of Jack and Bolling in Louisiana to various shots of my sister over the years, looking for similarities. Considering that the truth had no bearing on our lives moving forward, some might accuse us wasting our time. But the whole Dickensian drama had us in chokehold by then, and I was starting to feel like Pip to Sandy's Estella.

The resemblance of Jack to my sister wasn't obvious, but once discovered, it was striking. But when we stood Sisi and Bolling side-by-side the likeness was remarkable, and we both felt dimwitted for not noticing it before.

There were several group photographs from Camp Serendipity and Briarwood, but none with both Sisi and the twins. There was one of the twins with Tripp and Bolling's fishing companion taken the grey, cold day of Eddie's birthday fishing expedition, all except Tripp with a stringer of fish. Neither Bolling or Jack wore sunglasses. Then we found a photo of Sisi from her freshman year at Cal Berkeley with her then boyfriend, Chazz, taken at some party. They held a fat joint between them with shit-eating grins pasted across their stoned faces. We zoomed in on Bolling in the fishing picture, then held the photo next to it.

"Oh my God!" Sandy cried. "They look like brother and sister! Look at the shape of the eyes, Howard. And the hair color, and the heavy brows."

"And the high cheekbones," I said, amazed. "That's what really does it for me. They look like their faces were chiseled from the same mold."

Then we zoomed in on Jack's face. "I'll bet if he lost 75 pounds and shaved the beard, we would find more similarity underneath all that fat," Sandy said. "Who can tell if he has high cheekbones or not? His face is just big pink blob."

"Yeah," I said in agreement, "but look at the shape of the eyes, and the brows."

We looked, and looked some more. Eventually we were both convinced that the boys belonged to Sissy Mae and Binx, and that there was no marriage to a mystery run-away wife after Binx's tour in the Marines. Still, there was the perplexing pregnancy. I couldn't recall my sister disappearing for more than a long weekend while she was married to Kenny. Then, just as we were turning in for the night, in that quiet moment when the brain begins to shift gears and the dreams of the previous evening briefly replay across the mind's eye, it came to me.

Sisi had been married to Kenny for five years already, and they had produced two beautiful children, the second right around the time Tripp had been born. Then, before their second child was two years old, Sisi claimed to be addicted to a variety of anti-anxiety and pain medications and, after a very public breakdown, checked herself into a rehab clinic. Nobody knew where the clinic was located, and her doctor had given very strict orders that she was not to have face-to-face communication with family members for six months.

"But Kenny had to know!" Sandy exclaimed in the kitchen the next morning. As always, she had risen before me and was already doing chores by the time I made my breakfast. "What husband is going to agree to being ex-communicated from his wife for six months?"

"Well, she claimed that he was a big part of her problem. The babies too," I said, scooping freshly ground coffee into a French press.

"I can't believe it, Howard. If Kenny agreed to this arrangement, I'm certain Hal didn't."

I wasn't so certain. Perhaps the old man was aware of the whole charade. Maybe Kenny was, too. It was entirely possible that Kenny and my father had agreed to provide matching contributions to Jack's trust, on the condition that Sisi kept her mouth shut. Considering their professional reputations – and Binx's – I could imagine how my sister might have managed to extort money from all three of them, in return for keeping the secret of her Southern family to herself.

"I think it's probably best to keep it that way, don't you?" I asked Sandy. "At this point, nobody has anything to gain by knowing the truth."

Sandy was standing by the French door to the upper deck, watching the fog slowly receding from the ocean's surface as the first rays of sun flashed across the water. Then, without turning, she said, very quietly, "Except Jack."

51 Mayo on the Side

We did not discuss when, where, who, or how Jack would be told that the mute, chain-smoking woman that looked like Cruella de Ville was his mother. First, unless Sisi came forth, we had no way of knowing if our suppositions were true. Even if Johnny, or Eddie, or some other family member confirmed our suspicions, my sister could easily deny it. That would be even tougher on the twins, especially poor Jack. She would have to decide that she wanted Jack, and Bolling, to know who their true mother was, and in so doing might further complicate her already tenuous hold on reality. Still, Sandy and I felt like we were walking around with time bombs in our heads. Tick. Tick. Tick.

The sensation that something was about to explode was acute on that bright, clear summer morning we were to pick up Dr. Cobb, Sisi, Jack and Lawrence at the San Francisco airport. The weather was rare for the Norcal coast in summer. The fog had retreated to someplace so far out on the Pacific we couldn't even see the usual horizontal gray stripe that divided ocean from sky. Such a departure from normalcy surely portended catastrophic events, I was thinking. Best to tackle such events in a state of satisfied satiation.

"Honey, would you mind whipping up some turkey sammies? We should have some lunch before we hit the road, don't you think?" Sandy sat at our new fifties ultra modern dining room table among the pieces of Ward's ceramic pig, surfing the web for wall sconces to cover the bare bulbs we'd been living with since we moved in back in the spring. As always, she wanted to get it just right. All killer, no filler: that's her motto. It doesn't matter if it's the most expensive sconce, rug, chair, lamp or other home accouterment on the planet. If it's a fit, it's in.

"I know what I want for lunch," I said, cocking an eyebrow.

"Oh, Howard, please! We have to pick up Tripp in 45 minutes!"

"Oh. Gee, yeah I guess that's really not enough time, considering my incredible...uh...fortitude."

"Howard, we've been married what...34 years? And you still think that sex is like...I dunno...like making a turkey sandwich. You just slap a little meat between the buns and..."

"Listen to you! Wow! I like that idea!"

"Really, Howard! What about romance? What about kissing, and

297

cuddling, and back rubs...you know, foreplay! Love! You make it sound like the five-minute drill, or a quick game of around-the-world."

"Oh come on, sweetheart. I was just kidding."

Long, pregnant pause. I opened the refrigerator, got out the gluten-free bread, the supposedly heart-healthy goat cheese, the ultra-lean organic free range humanely-raised turkey, the fake mayo, the organic Dijon, my pickles...

"Just kidding?" she asked. She'd snuck behind me and wrapped her long arms about halfway around my ever-expanding gunnysack gut.

"Yeah, sorta. I mean, once my sister and wacky Jack are here I think we're gonna get pretty busy..."

"You mean we won't be able to do it in the kitchen anymore?"

"Well, probably not, unless we want to give Jack some lessons."

She held onto me as I popped two slices of the gluten-free rice bread in the toaster. It's inedible unless it's toasted. Then she undid my belt. "Just kidding, eh?" she said, going to work on Howard Jr. Oh. I guess I can't call him that anymore. What did Lady Chatterley's lover call his wiener? Arthur?

"Keep making those sammies, Mister. We'll eat them in the car. I'm just going to make some mayo, here."

God, what a woman! The next thing I knew she had her shorts around her knees and we had meat between the buns every which way. I was thinking *how lucky can a guy get* and *what did I do to deserve this* and *thanks be to God* and *hallefuckinlujah!*

Until, of course, the phone rang.

"Let it go to voice mail!" Sandy shouted, her head down on the cutting board and her long hair in the mustard. The voice? Dr. Cobb. "Howard, there's been a change in plan. I hope you're not on your way to the airport. If you are, turn around. Then please give me a call back. Thanks."

"Turn around?" Sandy wailed, laughing. "Okay!"

We hit the showers, soaped up and went another round. I didn't even need the vitamin V, now that I'd been off the pain pills for a while, and not when my perfect forward was making her move to the basket. Heaven! God bless Sandy Brown! God bless America!

Later, noshing on turkey sammies with fresh toast and hairless Dijon, Dr. Cobb called back.

"A change in plan? How so?" Sandy jumped out of her chair and put the phone on speaker.

"I'm not at liberty to say, exactly. But it looks like our arrival will be delayed by about a week."

"A week? Why?"

"You'll see. Meanwhile, enjoy the peace and quiet while you can, okay? That's really all I can tell you."

"Hold on, Doctor," Sandy said, affecting irritation but smiling like a Cheshire cat. "We were just about to leave for the airport. You know picking someone up at SFO is a long drive. Three hours round trip. And Howard drives like a little old lady."

"Eh?" I grumbled, "Little old what?"

"I'll give you plenty of advance notice as soon as plans firm up, don't worry."

"It's still just the three of you, right?" I asked.

"Yes, I think so. I'll let you know," he said. I could tell the old Doctor was uncomfortable in his role as secret-keeper. My Southern relatives were a cagey bunch. Were they coming by train? By boat, through the Panama Canal? Would they drop in like paratroopers? Greyhound bus, perhaps?

Regardless of how they would arrive and who was on board, we had prepared the compound for three new citizens of Coon Hollow. Three. No more. One incontinent developmentally disabled teenager, one brain-damaged, foul-mouthed, late-fifties mute, and one former linebacker for the New York Giants. We were ready for them, or at least as ready as we could be. Under the circumstances, we both decided that the best thing we could do at that juncture was to take a nap. So we crawled under the covers in our big, soft, warm, bareness to cuddle and spoon, listening to the waves crash and hiss on the beach below like thoughts, surfacing and receding, surfacing, then receding until all was quiet. We slept.

52 The South Will Rise Again

They arrived on a June Thursday afternoon in great clouds of dust from behind the ridge. At first I thought the fog was trying to trick us by coming in from the land instead of the ocean. Then I was reminded of the years after the Civil War, when the United States government decided to get rid of the tribes on the Great Plains: the Arapahoe and Cheyenne, the Kiowa and Sioux, and down south the Comanche and Apache. In the movies the clouds of dust darkening the horizon moved with the advance of the braves on their horses, riding to certain death in the face of Union soldiers with their Gatling guns, cannons, and other Civil War weapons of mass destruction. Here they came again, an entire tribe, a convoy, an invasion. Had we a Gatling gun we might have been wise to use it.

We sat on the deck that overlooked the ocean to the west and the bramble ridge of Monterey pine, blackberry, poison oak and ancient bay trees to the south, where the long gravel road snaked and switch-backed down to our gated entrance, which went on for another 500 yards until it reached our garage and deck outside our front door. About a tenth of a mile past our driveway the road met with a turnaround surrounded by dense thickets of willow and creek alder where adventurers might park and take the rugged trail down to the cliffs where the spring-fed creek spilled into the ocean. At low tide some folks might slide on their butts down to the rocky beach, then scramble back up when the water came back up to the base of the cliff. Still, visitors were infrequent. Until that Thursday afternoon in June.

Mr. Booper and Odo, both of whom felt something rumbling along the ridge before anybody else could hear or see anything, heralded their arrival. They went charging up the drive to the gate where they ran back and forth barking, growling, and jumping around like dogs possessed. The dust began to rise, kicking up a cloud that must have alarmed the pot farmers and recluses of the Third Mesa in Bolinas. Then the convoy dropped over the ridge from the first switch back and...and...there they were. Two Mercedes Sprinters, one dark and one light – I had come to recognize the distinct boxy shape of these vehicles – followed by a mid-sized Winnebago RV, inching their way down the narrow dirt track.

Tripp jumped up first and went running, up the stairs and out the side exit to the driveway, then up the gravel where he swung open the big wooden gates. Looking on from the patio, I wasn't certain the big Winnebago could make it through.

I lumbered up the drive, Sandy and Elke at my side, to where Tripp stood ready to escort the convoy through. "Jesus fucking Christ," I said. "I thought I told these clowns we could only accommodate three: my sister, Jack and LT."

"Oh Howard," Sandy said, taking my hand. "Don't you see? It's a celebration! How much you wanna bet that they struck gas in Briarwood? Come on," she said, grabbing me around my big waist so we were tummy to tummy. "How much? A million? Five million? Come on, let's bet."

"No way," I said, intoning my father's favorite expression of defeat. "There isn't any gas under Briarwood. Even if there was, it wouldn't be worth much these days."

"Bet me. Come on. $500,000."

"No way."

"A thousand."

"No..."

"You sound just like your fucking dad!" Sandy shouted, punching me in the man-boobs. "Think positive, Howard. Come on! We've struck it rich!"

I so wanted to think positive. If I could imagine the land of milk and honey with 40 naked virgins scampering around like bunnies in a wild strawberry patch, why couldn't I imagine suddenly becoming filthy rich through no power of my own? Why the fuck not? But I couldn't. This was reality, over which I seemed to have no influence. Dreams were entirely another story.

Through the gate came the Sprinters, the first piloted by Lawrence Taylor with a wide white grin. My sister was riding shotgun in the same long white sleeveless dress with a pale yellow long-sleeved T-shirt underneath and waving a white kerchief out the window like she was in a Mardi Gras parade. Her hair was done up in the same mustard bandana, sticking out the top in silver and black dreadlocks. At least she wasn't throwing Fat Tuesday beads into the ivy and shrubbery of the border fences.

Another identical navy blue Sprinter followed with Reggie Stubbs behind the wheel and Jack Sublette riding shotgun. Well, not exactly shotgun. Jack had the entire upper half of his five-foot-eight 250-pound frame hanging out the passenger side window, yelling and waving a pair of jeans. *Oh for the love of God*, I thought.

The June dust was now so thick that my eyes were watering and my lungs burned. Sandy and Tripp had covered their mouths and noses with cowboy bandanas and I decided to do the same. Meanwhile Lawrence Taylor and Sisi, the leaders of the convoy, had jumped out and run over to where we stood on the entrance-level welcome deck by the front door.

"Howard Brown!" Lawrence shouted, his tree-trunk arm around my sister's impossibly thin waist, dragging her along like a rag-doll. He shook my hand and left me with my sister, her looking up at me with a bemused expression as if to say, "Well, here I am." Slowly a wry smile stretched across her wrinkled face. She reached into a front pocket, extracted a smartphone, and with two thumbs quickly typed in a few words, then pressed a button and out of the device came, stilted and strange, her own voice.

"Hey bro," said the phone, "how the heavens are thou?"

"I've been fine," I replied not sure if I should be addressing the phone or my sister. "Just fine. I'm so happy to see you. I think you'll like it here." With two thumbs flying across the miniature keypad, she created another message in five seconds.

"Love me your hollow!" she announced, her speech defect sounding like a combination of dyslexia combined with word substitution, but it was a little early to tell.

"TRIPP!! ELKE!! HOWARD!! SANDY!!" bellowed Jack Sublette, spittle arcing across the front porch in the early afternoon sun. "I LOVE YOU!" He galumphed up to me in his uneven gait in a pair of urine-stained jumbo diapers that bounced in rhythm. Throwing his arms around my midsection, he straddled my thigh in his warm, wet Depends and shouted "I'M HOME!"

"Jack! Jack!" I said, intently whispering into his ear, the sharp, eye-watering odor of fresh urine making me woozy. "Go put on a fresh diaper, okay?"

"OH YESSIR MISTER HOWARD I WILL DO AS YOU SAY RIGHT NOW!!" Then he let me go and wobbled barefoot back up to his Sprinter, the back of his Depends heavily skid-marked as well and a wet, acrid, stink stain across my thigh. It was clear that the last five months in a private mental institution hadn't done much for his incontinence
. Reggie called out: "It just happened as we were pulling up to the gate. He wouldn't leave his seat and go to the can because he didn't want to miss a moment of our big arrival, so he just let loose. Otherwise he's been pretty good. The Depends help, that's for sure."

As Reggie helped Jack back into the camper, I noticed that my sister had taken a few steps in their direction, then stopped. Sandy was watching her, too. Sisi was craning her neck to get a better look up the driveway, then her hand went to her mouth as if she were silently giggling. Sandy cocked an eyebrow at me, and I couldn't help but smile. My sister, la misteriosa mujer, the queen of conundrum, the master obfuscator, was doing it again.

Slowly the rest of the Sublette family and the Stubbs family joined us on the entry deck. After quickly sneaking into our nearby bedroom for a fresh pair of shorts, I stood by the door greeting everybody as they came in, like it was a White House reception. After my sister and LT came Johnny, Bessie and Toya, each of them with a bit of wide-eyed fear and amazement at the view just beyond my welcoming girth. "My Lord," said Bessie. "Is that the Pacific Ocean out there, or am I dreamin'?"

"No ma'am, you ain't dreamin'," I said, instantly infected with the drawl.

"Well I'll be hogtied, Howard Brown," Johnnie Stubbs said, looking me over, "I din't thinks folks could keep growin' at your age, but look at you! You as big as a house!" I smiled and nodded, patting the old man on the shoulder and thinking that it wouldn't take much – a little constipation, maybe – for my heart to burst like a water balloon.

Toya grabbed me around the waist and made a point of trying to hook her hands together in the small of my back, her short hair smelling of vanilla and warm, fresh-baked peanut butter cookies. But our mutual tummies collided. Harder and harder she squeezed, squashing my corpulent midsection with hers. "Here, let me help you with that," I said, reaching behind as if to unhook my manboob bra, grabbing both her wrists and pulling them together with ease. "See, nothin' to it," I said.

"Oh Howard Brown," she laughed. Then Reggie and Jack came in, Jack in a fresh pair of overalls, greasy hair slicked to one side, freshly shaved and baring his bad teeth in a two-mile smile. Once he got a look at the ocean he had to go, right that minute. Tripp was ready and willing to oblige, itching as I could see to flee this sudden and unexpected reunion, as was Elke, who at six months was almost as round as I was.

"Hey there, cousin! What do y'all think of this?" Eddie said, clapping me on the back, attempting to pull me aside into a private conversation that I wasn't at all ready for. He didn't look much different than he had six months prior. He had on the same Kelly green slacks and Camp Serendipity jacket that he had worn the entire time out on the bayou, obviously laundered but worse for wear. What was left of his silvery curls may have started to get a mild tinge of standard geriatric Naples yellow, and his stoop may have been a little stoopier. But his eyes still had that boyish, mischievous glint that made

him seem a bit of the back room wheeler-dealer. Or maybe I was just
noticing it now because of our own wheeling dealings over the land. "You
had a look at your email lately? I suspect that you have not, given your lack of
response to the big strike."

"Big strike? At Briarwood?" I asked.

"Naw, not there. Way out in St. Martin's parish," Eddie said.

"Oh. That's great, but…" I was wondering what a big strike in St.
Martin's parish had to do with me.

"Son, you oughta pay a little more attention to your investments. You're
a partner in Laurel Hill Energy Ventures. We got claims all over the state."

"Investments?" My soul hole gave a sudden tingle, and I thought I heard
my father's voice. "I told you Briarwood was dry as a bone, didn't I?" Then
Eddie piped up again.

"Since I own the lion's share of the interest, I thought I would buy the
partners with smaller parcels a little present. Which is now in your driveway."

"A present?" I asked, not believing my ears once again.

"Sure. The RV – that is the Mercedes – is on me. You deserve it,
Howard, after all the heartache we've put you through. But we can talk details
later. Meanwhile, all your cousins and relatives have driven all the way from
Laurel Hill to see you and your family. Come on now, let's have a party!"

"Wait a minute," I said, scanning the crowd of Louisianans all now
transfixed by the ocean. "Where's Dr. Cobb?"

"Eh? He's not here?"

"I don't see him," I said, suddenly worried that something bad had
happened to my mothballed pain doc and active psychiatrist. I excused
myself and went into the bedroom to call him. I got his voicemail. "Doc,
where the hell are you? We're all waiting for you to come and mix us up some
down home toddies." Given the ridiculous drama of the West Feliciana
convoy showing up on a June afternoon out of nowhere, I half-expected
Cobb to drop out of the sky in a parachute.

I went over to the bedroom picture window overlooking the ocean,
whitecaps kicking up in advance of the summer fog, trying to collect myself
in the face of this surprise incursion, wondering how we were going to feed
and water this group when we could barely feed and water ourselves. At least
we wouldn't have to find sleeping quarters for all of them, though I imagined
that some of them – Reggie, Lawrence Taylor, maybe Toya – were dying to
escape from the cramped quarters of RV living.

Suddenly all the hubbub made me weak in the knees. I staggered over to the sofa and collapsed with a crash, just as the phosphorescent sparkles began to cloud my vision. In a panic, I reached for my pillbox, forgetting that I hadn't carried it in my right front pocket for almost seven months. Eddie looked at me with alarm.

"Here," he said, brandishing his flask of Beam like a St. Bernard in the Alps. I took a gulp and gasped. Seeing that I was in a precarious state, Sandy and Elke decided to clear the main house and take the crew on a tour of the property. Then the portable land line in my pocket buzzed. Cobb, Dr. Raymond. I hobbled to the bedroom and closed the door. "Hello, Howard. I assume the family has arrived?" he said, all Southern deadpan polite.

"What the fuck, Doc? Yeah, they arrived all right, and immediately set to destroying my house," I said. "Knowing you, Doc, you've decided to hang back in the Garden District, free and clear of the Stubbs, the Sublettes, and their resident NFL nurse."

"I'm almost there. I had a little delay, but I've rented a car and am on my way out."

"You're alone?"

"Yes," he answered. "Lucy was so happy to get rid of your sister, I don't think she'll be joining us for family events any time soon." We hung up.

I sat shaking on the edge of our bed, phone on my lap, waiting for the pixie dust to subside and for the fog to settle in over Coon Hollow. Instead, like the pixie dust, it receded, perhaps in deference to our visitors. I watched the cousins explore the yard, with its unique aloe plants, yucca trees, butterfly bushes, the phallic 20-foot-high stalks of echium (known locally as "Awesome Willy"), ripening blackberries and the prehistoric gunnera, as well as Jack and Lawrence's fancy new digs. It would be several hours to the mid-June sunset, and should the fog decide to stay out at sea the daylight-time darkness would settle in very slowly.

Sisi was exploring the creek, just a trickle in June but a torrent in January. Her dress was hiked up around her knees as she bent over the pools, pulling stones and other items out of the water, examining them, then carefully putting them back. Then the lower south side gate flew open and the boys came in, Tripp holding Jack's hand and pulling him through. It looked as though Jack was soaked from head to foot, shivering uncontrollably with a blue pallor to his skin and laughing like a hyena while my son screamed, "Dad! Elke! LT! Anybody! Get down here, I need your help!"

53 The Heart With a Mind Of Its Own

Sandy, Johnny and Bessie were studying the six-inch conical pods of miniscule white flowers of the butterfly bush, dodging the angry hummingbirds that had claimed the bush as their own. They all jerked around at the sound of Tripp's voice and Jack's strange bleating. Sandy leapt up the stairs to Jack's future quarters and emerged with an armful of towels as Tripp led Jack through the front door. Sandy shut the door and the creepy baying became muffled. I wondered if Jack had been hit by a sneaker wave, or had fallen in the rip tide, or had simply run headlong into the shark-infested waters of the Pacific.

And then my sister caught my eye. She stood frozen under the massive leaves of the giant gunnera plant, looking like a decorative yard ornament – a dwarf, perhaps, or a gnome – watching the scene unfold on the deck of the new guest house in rapt consternation. Again, her hand went to her open mouth, but she didn't look like she was giggling this time.

A giant bubble of anonymous emotion blew me open, knocked me sideways onto my bed, and I blubbered, dry-eyed as always, into my pillow. What the fuck were we – Sandy, Tripp, Elke – doing by bringing these damaged, disfigured, almost mutilated souls to Coon Hollow? I asked myself *what is this, what is this? Shit fuck goddamnit motherfucking cocksucking son of a bitch! Was this not the right thing to do? Was it not in our power to help this kid? Was it not in my power to help my sister? Wasn't this the real thing, the right thing, the honest thing to do?* No. I knew at that moment that I never should have allowed this scenario to happen, despite my son's insistence that we could somehow nurture Jack Sublette into some sort of manageable state. It was an idiotic, naïve and completely impractical notion, conjured in an overly optimistic, almost narcissistic, moment of mental and moral weakness, that would no doubt result in a lose-lose situation all around. Jack wouldn't get the care he required, and we would go crazy trying to provide it, Sisi most of all. Tripp's idea of getting him a job at Safeway bagging groceries wasn't going to happen, and it was only a matter of time before we would have to ship him out or hire a half dozen LT's to control his wild fits.

"Howard Brown."

My bedroom was silent save for the conversations of the cousins in the yard below and the muffled caterwauling of our resident idiot, the summer twilight glowing salmon pink on the whitewashed walls.

"Howard, sit up now. Come on, son."

Johnny Stubbs sat on the edge of the bed, his spine bowed, looking out over Coon Hollow, the line of willows, alder, the quiet Pacific and the wall of gray fog on the horizon. I must have been blubbering so hard I didn't hear him come in.

"Johnny? What the fuck? Get outta here! Can't you let a man cry in peace, for chrissakes?" I sat up and gave his bony ass a half-hearted shove. He just laughed.

"Come on now, sit up here and have a little toddy. I know you Browns like your toddies."

I sat up and swung my tired and tingling legs over the edge of the bed.

"Shit, Johnny, I was just tryin' to take a little nap."

"The hell you was," he said, and handed me a large glass of sweet bourbon on the rocks with a spring of wild mint from the hollow. I didn't have the heart to tell him that I thought Southern cocktails tasted like cough syrup. I took a little sip. It went down smooth as buttermilk, like nothing I had ever tasted before. Johnny had added something. Sweet light crude, or some other Louisiana contraband. I took a long draught. "You ain't never had one of Johnny's toddies, Howard. Now you gonna see why I've lived so long."

He smiled, big dentures luminescent in the twilight. The dusky, leathery skin on his grizzled chin and deeply grooved forehead seemed to glow from underneath like a charcoal briquette, turning the umber shades of his cheeks into the warm sienna of sun brewed tea. Or fine Kentucky bourbon.

"Son," he said, laying his long bony fingers across my shoulder. "You gotta stop beating yourself up."

"Eh? But I'm not…"

"Just listen, Howard. All right?" He took a drink, so I did too, clinking the cubes around in my glass and watching how they picked up the colors of summer twilight, wondering what down home chicken shack country wisdom the old Freejack had for me. A wild war whoop echoed through the hollow: Jack, naked, stood on the deck of the little studio below, pounding his chest and bellowing like Tarzan while Sandy, Tripp and LT tried to coax him back inside. I shook my head. "Jesus, Johnny, what the hell was I thinkin'?"

Johnny sat silently nodding, watching Tripp trying to pull Jack, who had the raw strength of a Downs victim, minus the other physical features, back into the cabin.

"You weren't thinkin'," Johnny said, "at least not with your noggin'."

He paused. "My guess is you were listenin'. Listenin' to some other voice, maybe just a feeling coming from inside you, maybe coming from somewhere else. Because nobody in his right mind is gonna get involved with that boy."

Johnny chuckled his signature "heh heh heh" while I wondered what the hell he was talking about. Acting on impulse? Taking orders from a higher power? "Wherever it comes from, you gotta stop beating yourself up about it, and about a whole lot other mess in your life. Listen, son, you think I asked for my daddy to get hisself mixed up with a white woman, or two white women, or a whole goddamn neighborhood of white women? Nossir. You think I asked for him to get himself strung up? Nossir."

"Jesus, of course not Johnny. It had nothin' to do with you," I cried, standing up and going to the window. Tripp, Sandy and LT had wrestled Jack in and were probably trying to dress him. *Maybe he's just overexcited to be here*, I thought. Meanwhile my sister stood stock still under the gunnera leaves, eyes glued to the drama on the deck of the new guest house.

"That's right. No more than Mister Jack asked to be born with a...with a..."

"A disability?"

"Yeah, sure. He didn't ask for that, and he didn't ask for a mystery mother, or for his daddy to get drunk and beat on him." He slid his bony ass off the corner of the mattress with a grunt, clearly uncomfortable, and looked around the room, finding a rocker in the corner. I moved down to the end of the bed. "Here," he said, holding up his copper-colored silver flask. He poured us both a freshener. "We gonna need us some fresh ice pretty soon," he added, as if we could possibly be forgotten in the bedroom. I was certain our conversation would be interrupted at any moment. Then he pulled two packets of sugar and several sprigs of mint from the breast pocket of his chocolate-brown cardigan.

"Okay, so my daddy didn't ask to be strung up, but who you think has been going around most his life all broken up about what happened to his daddy? You said I had nothing to do with it, and you right, so how come I blame myself for losing my only daddy?"

"Well..." I started, swirling the toddy around the glass, "That's just..."

"Human nature, right? Okay. You tried your damndest to keep your daddy alive, didn't you? When you saw that the good Lord had made up his mind to take him, you tried your damndest to find Miss Sisi and bring her home, but it was no good. His heart broke and he died not knowing if his little girl was alive or chopped up in the dumpster like you said. And there wasn't a damn thing you could do about it. So who goes around beating himself up for not making everything all right? Eh? Howard Brown, that's who."

I looked across the ocean, now the deep Prussian blue of the very top of oncoming night. Johnny was right about most of it, but I certainly didn't feel like I was beating myself up. No, for many years I tried very hard to make certain I didn't feel anything at all.

"You didn't ask for no heartache, and you didn't ask for no pain. You didn't ask for no bad back just like I didn't ask to be born black."

Bad back? Born black? I was getting confused and maybe a little drunk, but I kept my mouth shut. "Listen Howard, what I'm tryin' to say is your pain and the medicine you had to take...and you had to take it, I know. I never told you why I limp so bad – damn horse crush my pelvis way long time back. I'm lucky to walk again, but you think I don't know about pain? Least you didn't get strung out on no morphine let me tell you."

"Holy Christ, Johnny!" I cried. "That's serious shit!" I thought I sounded like an idiot. Bemoaning our ailments was not what Johnny was getting at, I felt sure.

"But our bodies healed, didn't they, son? We ain't the same as we was but we okay for now. For today, anyway. Ain't that right?" I nodded. After all the surgeries, the titanium cage in the lower back, the industrial strength Velcro casts and slings, the pain pills – all that shit – my body seemed to be as good as it was going to get, though I knew I would do well to be rid of a good portion of it. But if I was still getting around on my two legs at 90 like Johnny and Bessie, well, that would be right up there with the miracle at Royal and Canal.

"But you know, it's too easy to get down and out. You get old, your neck gets weak and the next thing you know you're always looking at the ground. Dammit, Howard. You got to look up!" He took a drink, so I took one too. "I've been thinkin' on this a lot, son. Thinkin' about what might have happened to your boy if he was lookin' down at the sidewalk when that light pole come down. But he wasn't. He was lookin' up! He looked up and he saw the light!"

"Boy, did he ever," I couldn't help but observe. I hadn't spoken to Johnny about what he clearly perceived to be a miracle, or what it meant, why Tripp was chosen, and if our family could count on a few follow-up miracles in the future.

Johnny chuckled his signature "heh heh heh," then paused to ruminate, looking up at the darkening sky out the window as if for guidance. Then he made a fist with his right hand and gently tapped his heart. "What about this, Howard?"

There was another long pause. Johnny took a drink and I looked out the window to see if the fog had decided to come in, not wanting to address this heart business in the least. But Johnny knew that I was wondering what he meant by it, even though I had a pretty good idea. "I know this gonna sound silly, maybe even a little crazy, but I've come to thinkin' that the heart has a mind of its own. Not like a brain, addin' up figures, remembering vocabulary words and such. The mind of the heart don't speak to us directly. It makes its own decisions. Hell, sometimes the heart's mind will decide to do something that the brain's mind thinks is some kinda cockamamie nonsense. Like takin' on Mister Jack there." Johnny gestured with his head down to the cabin below where yellow light now glowed in the windows; a warm, cozy, clean and well-lighted place. What would the 18-year-old do now that he knew he was safe with his adopted family? Would he calm down once this initial excitement wore off? "My personal feelin' is that the heartmind, as I call it, is my direct line to my Lord Jesus. If I'm upset about somethin', any little thing, all I got to do is tell my brain mind to quiet down so I can ask my Lord for help. It's the heartmind that does the askin'. And he always brings me help and comfort, because he loves me, just like he loves you. Y'all's decision to try and help Mister Jack? That ain't no brain mind talkin', you know what I'm sayin'? That's the Lord talkin' to your heart mind, and he's sayin' you help that boy and I will help you."

I was staring out the window at the stars coming out over the deep purple wall of fog on the horizon, listening the ice cubes in Johnny's toddy glass shift as he poured the last of it down his talked-out throat. *The heart has a mind of its own. The heart has a mind of its own.* I thought back almost a year, when my father really was ready to die. Was it the heartmind that said go get the golf balls, the putter? Was it the heartmind that instructed me to go find and help my sister, despite all the nastiness she had heaped on my family and me? Was it the heartmind that instructed me to help an idiot change his pissy jeans to avoid the wrath of his drunken daddy? Or save the life of a drunk who threatened to kill my son and his girlfriend? Was it the heartmind that lead me to try and show hundreds of simpering, zit-faced and greasy teenagers that reading great stories would make their lives better? Or that a well-executed fast break was all that was needed to win basketball games? And all this because a fellow purported to be Jewish and his posse wandering around Palestine 2000 years ago told us to "love thy neighbor?"

"The heart has a mind of its own," I said aloud.

"Yes, it does. Heh heh heh."

I cocked an eye at old Johnny. The room was nearly dark, the last of the summer sun long gone. But the great room was quiet. Where was everybody? Then, on cue, a knock at the door. "Hey sweetheart, is Johnny in there with you? Bessie and Toya are wondering where he ran off to," Sandy asked.

"Yeah baby, we're havin' a little chat."

Sandy came in, turned on the light. "Jesus, Johnny, everybody thought you walked down to the ocean and fell in." We chuckled; she nodded, leaned over Johnny and gave him a peck on his grizzled cheek. "I suggest you check in with your wife, Grandpa," she said to Johnny. She surveyed the both of us. "Well," she said, "have y'all got it figured out yet?"

"Almost," Johnny said, "just a few little things to wrap up."

"All righty then. Let me know if you need a hand. Everybody has gone back to their quarters to rest up before the feast that Howard and I haven't prepared, but I hear you, Toya and Bessie have a little something in mind."

"Yes ma'am. But don't go just yet, mon cher. Me n' Howard got to ask you something."

We do? I suddenly get the idea that Johnny's secret to longevity is this sweet Southern concoction, though it has knocked me completely on my ass. Sandy comes and sits beside me on the bed, leaving the door to the great room open.

"Okay. Shoot," Sandy says.

"Why you wanna take care of young Mister Jack, Sandy? You got your son, your daughter in law, your grandbaby comin', Howard's sister. What you need Mister Jack for?"

"Johnny," she said without hesitation. "We don't need Mister Jack. Mister Jack needs us."

54 An Unexpected Stray

I didn't have much time to think about Johnny's theory, except that there was something about it that made me feel better. Or maybe it was the toddies. Either way it was good to know that my occasional suspicion of divine intervention was not a unique hallucination. Nor did I have time to tell my wife that I had been instructed by the heartmind to do what I could to help Jack Sublette. Had I mentioned it she probably would have me committed to the state mental institution in Napa right along with Jack.

Slowly our extended family gathered in the high-ceilinged great room, a combination of kitchen, dining room and living room. When Jack came in, freshly scrubbed and combed in crisp denim overalls, Tripp holding one of his pudgy mitts and Elke the other, I could see that he was still agitated. His magnified eyes darted around behind his thick glasses as if he had walked into a room full of crocodiles. Tripp and Elke appeared a little apprehensive as well, until Jack's eyes landed on the shards of Ward's ceramic pig, which we had so far neglected to move off of the dining room table.

"What's that?" he said, pointing with Elke's hand still in his and dragging the two of them across the room. He stood looking down at the wreckage, transfixed by the shining multicolored fragments of pottery.

"It used to be a pig. My brother made it," Tripp explained.

"A pig," Jack declared, as if it was obvious that the broken pieces had once formed a whole, and the whole was a pig. He dropped Jack and Elke's hands and sat down. "The pig goes like this," he said, without taking his eyes from the jumbled arrangement of shards. Then he started picking up the pieces, matching edges to other edges like he was solving a jigsaw puzzle. Tripp caught my eye across the room and beckoned me over.

"Should we get some glue, Jack?" Elke asked. It seemed obvious that Jack wanted to repair Ward's pig.

"The pig goes like this," Jack said, not taking his eyes from the shards as he continued matching the pieces together. Meanwhile it was time to prepare the dining room table for our big family feast.

"Well…" I began, looking up to see Sandy watching from the kitchen. She shrugged. "Jack, we need…" I continued, thinking it best to relocate the repair operation to some other table.

"Dad," Tripp interrupted. "Could you go get some glue? He's almost got this figured out." I looked at my son, who was still watching Jack deftly match the larger shards with the smaller chips of Ward's pig as if he could see the finished sculpture in his mind. "Get some newspaper, too," Tripp added. "We don't want to slop glue all over the table." Then, just as Sandy appeared at the table with a bottle of Elmer's and a sheath of newspaper in her hands, there was a knock on the door. I shook my head, smiled at Sandy, said (with a nod toward Jack), "I don't know what could be better than this," and went to the front door.

As expected, it was Dr. Cobb, but he was not alone. Instead, there on the landing next to the old doctor was a man in a wheelchair, face partially in shadow, dressed in a light gray three-piece suit with a pink tie. It was Doug Dennikan, scoured and polished like a TV minister.

Slack-jawed, I said nothing. "This man says you saved his life," said Dr. Cobb, moving around behind the wheelchair as if ready to roll him in. I wondered if I should make way, invite him in, or tell Cobb to take him back to where he found him.

"He was down at your local watering hole drinking ginger ale. I stopped in for a bracer about an hour ago and he overheard me telling the bartender, the freckly redhead, that I was here to visit you. He asked, or I should say the bartender asked on his behalf after he handed her a note, if I would bring him out to, as she put it, make amends. We stopped at his place so he could get prettied up." Cobb chuckled. Dennikan did not.

I studied the man in the wheelchair. Gone was the Fu Manchu, the shaved dome, the backwards trucker's cap, the Maui Jims. His thin auburn hair, neatly trimmed, was swept across his balding pate, held in place by some high-powered, sweet-smelling fixative. The skin across his face remained rough and red, though more mildly pockmarked than before. There had been some work done to smooth his cheeks and forehead but his neck was still deeply cratered. But the most telling change of all was in his eyes. For the first time since I had met him at the onramp to 101 South, his hazel eyes were clear and bright, almost sparkling. Still, he looked at least ten years older in his TV minister three-piece suit.

"Hello, Mis...mist...Brow...Brown," said Dennikan, arm outstretched. I took his hot, sweaty, shaking hand in my giant paw and gave it a hearty squeeze. We both smiled. The old meth-eaten stubs had been replaced with beautiful dentures that seemed a good fit for his rather small, pursed mouth. He craned his neck to see around my girth, still blocking the doorway. Now he was shaking all over like a dope-sick junky.

"Hey Doc!" Eddie yelled from behind. "Get in here! Johnny's making toddies that will knock your old dick in the dirt!"

"Eddie!" cried Toya and Bessie. I looked around. Right behind me stood Sandy, and Sisi, staring like zoo-goers studying a strange beast in a cage. Tripp and Elke remained with Jack at the dining room table, but I could see that their interest was piqued. I stepped aside and Dr. Cobb pushed Dennikan into the foyer.

"Hello," he said. "I...I...just sto...stop...stop, stop, stopped... by...by..." He bowed his head and folded his chafed hands in his lap. "I...I'm...I'm sor...sor...sor" he said with a stutter too painful to hear. He hadn't stuttered when he accosted me at the mini-mart, or when he was stringing epithets together like popcorn in Tripp's front yard, or even when he announced upon seeing my face in the fog that he had "died and gone to hell." Like a rusty machine, he'd obviously needed lubrication to get the words out.

"Hey, let's get out of the foyer. You can play with that up there. LT!" I hollered, "We're gonna need your help." Dennikan jerked his head up as LT fixed his hands underneath the crippled man's armpits and lifted him into a standing position. Then Tripp and I clasped hand-on-wrist underneath his thighs and we carried him up the stairs. Sandy and Elke quickly followed with the heavy wheelchair and we gently set him back down. Still sweating and shaking, eyes bugged out; he looked up at LT in awe.

"Who...who are...are...you?"

"Lawrence Taylor from the NY Giants? Yes. After football he went into nursing," I answered. "Perhaps you would like a drink, Doug."

He reached into the breast pocket of his suit, pulled out the neatly folded shiny pink handkerchief that matched his tie, and extracted a worn card that had scrawled upon it: "Thank you. I don't drink. Do you have any ginger ale?" Fortunately Bessie had brought ginger ale, preferring weak Brandy Presbyterians to Johnnie's dick-in-the-dirt toddies. She made him a ginger ale on the rocks and brought it to him. He bowed his head and smiled.

When his hands began to quiet down, he took a drink then set it in his wheelchair cup holder. All of us except Eddie and Dr. Cobb, who had gone out on the deck for a cigar, and Jack the sculpture surgeon, were watching the man in the wheelchair. Then Toya, Bessie and Reggie got up, busying themselves in the kitchen with shrimp and crayfish they had carted on ice all the way from Baton Rouge. A Toya playlist of New Orleans jazz and funk played quietly off my iPad.

Sisi, who had been watching Jack repair Ward's pig from a chair in the corner, still as bug-eyed as she had been under the gunnera leaves, now pulled up next to Dennikan and handed him her smartphone, typing something first. He shook his head. Then he started typing, hunting and pecking with a single thick, scarred index finger, periodically wiping his forehead with the pink handkerchief. The suit appeared to be making him extremely hot and uncomfortable. "Do you want to take your coat off, Doug?" I asked. Sisi jumped up to assist as he leaned forward, sliding his coat and vest over his outstretched arms. Underneath his long-sleeved white button-down dress shirt we could see the shapes of tattoos across his chest and shoulders, clear down to his wrists. A flame crept up the side of his neck. His sweat had added another acrid odor to the sweet pomade on his sparse comb-across hairdo. I got up to open a window.

We conversed for a little while Dennikan typed, for it was slow going. The middle finger on his right hand was almost completely gone – just a stub, really – as was the pinky on his left. Finally he was ready. He held the smartphone near his mouth and attempted to mimic the robotic mail voice coming from the tiny speaker.

"Hello. My name is Doug Dennikan and I have come to make amends, as prescribed by steps eight and nine in the twelve steps of Alcoholics Anonymous. I am an alcoholic and have been a stutterer for as long as I can remember. The only time I didn't stutter was when I was drunk, which was, eventually, all the time. Then not much good came out of my mouth." The synthesized robot voice, sounding like a cross between Commander Data, Hal, and the answering machine at CVS pharmacy, would have made the whole scene laugh-out-loud hilarious if it wasn't for the content and urgency of Dennikan's confession. "In steps eight and nine, we make a list of all the persons we have harmed, and become willing to make amends to them all," the phone voice said. "This took a long time because there were many people on my list that I still believed deserved the pain I had caused them. You folks were not among those people. To Elke, Tripp, Sandy and most of all to Howard I say I am truly sorry for my behavior. Some have said that I have good reason to be angry at the world. My father beat me for stuttering which only made it worse. My mother left when I was very young. Later, I met a woman and we were going to have a family. But we were both alcoholics and drug addicts, and she killed herself and our baby. After that, well. You know how I was. Then Howard and Tripp found me dying in a ditch after rolling my truck off a cliff. They saved my life when, considering how I had treated them, they would have been perfectly justified to let me die. If it weren't for them I wouldn't have had this second chance. For that I am truly grateful. I hope you will accept my apologies."

He handed the phone back to my weeping sister, but she let it fall to the sofa, got up and, bending over, threw her arms around Doug Dennikan. The rest of the group sniffled and sobbed and for several minutes it seemed nobody said anything. Then Jack Sublette, who had been distracted by the robot voice and was thinking that somebody from outside had called to make their confession, left his post, got up and hugged Sisi and Dennikan, then, standing back, asked, "Why did that sad person call us?"

Dennikan was now eager to go, reaching for his vest and jacket on the sofa. Apparently Cobb had agreed to drive him back to his house, five minutes away, when his mission was completed, but Sisi wouldn't hear of it. For all I knew Sisi thought Doug Dennikan was her own Binx Sublette returned to her in slightly worse-for-wear condition. She invited Dennikan to stay for dinner, and nobody seemed to have the heart to say no. Not even Elke, who Mr. MacDickFuck had crudely (putting it mildly) propositioned a dozen times, or Tripp, whom he threatened to "waste his blind gay ass" every time he saw him. The rest of the family had never even heard of Dennikan or any of his exploits. But, as I suppose my heartmind, be it God or Jesus or the Higher Power, informed me, now was not the time to share MacDickFuck stories with our cousins.

Jack had almost completed repairing Ward's pig – there were just a few holes left in the sculpture and it was obvious where the remaining pieces fit – so we moved his rescue operation downstairs and prepared for dinner. Once all twelve of us were seated at our eight-person oval table and the steaming crawfish shrimp etouffee was dished out Johnny decided to say grace, as he had on Thanksgiving, our only other gathering of family, or what was left of it. When he thanked his Lord Jesus for sparing the life of his wayward lamb, Douglas Dennikan, I felt a little pang of awareness, a mini-epiphany, wordless, a soft glow, and with it almost an aura over the entire table, like old Johnny had summoned his old friend Jesus to bless us. Profound for me, business as usual for Johnny, or so it seemed.

Then I noticed Dennikan curiously staring at Tripp, registering something amiss. "Tripp," he blurted. My son jerked his head around like he had been lassoed. "You can see," Dennikan said, without slightest hint of a stutter. But then it set back in, as if permission had been granted and then revoked: "Ho...how...c-c-c-an...you...d-d-d-d do it?"

Tripp smiled. Now that he was almost finished helping Jack with his reconstruction project, he might have been waiting for Dennikan to notice. "Well Mister MacD," Tripp said, slipping in the truncated nickname so that it actually connoted a certain respect and gravity that "Druggy," Doug" or "Dennikan" didn't carry. "I suspect you've become a pretty avid computer user. So I am going to send you a few links. What's your email address?" Sisi quickly typed a reply and texted it to Tripp's phone. "Good, okay," said Tripp, picking up his vibrating device. "I'm told that what happened was a sort of miracle, like Christ healing Bartimaeus." I looked over at Dennikan, who had tilted his head a quarter off center like Commander Data when confronted with something illogical. "Are you familiar with the Bible, Doug?" I asked, then quickly added. "Neither am I. But let me tell you, when Tripp regained his eyesight every Bible-thumper below the Mason/Dixon line was cryin' hallelujah." For the first time the whole evening Dennikan laughed out loud, throwing his head back and slapping his knee, as if the idea of a miracle in this day and age was the most absurd thing he'd ever heard of. We all laughed along with him.

Then he paused, little-used smile lines forming deep creases in his ruddy skin, and signaled Sisi for the phone. He slowly punched in a text-to-speech message. "Well I guess we've both been pretty lucky," said the robot voice.

When I crawled into bed several hours later my soul hole started to buzz like a hive of angry hornets, stinging almost as bad as the irritated nerves in my feet. I rubbed some of the special painkilling cream over it, but it was impervious to the drugs in the compound. I was wondering what would happen if I made a little smoothie out of the stuff with some banana and yogurt when my father's voice came through loud and clear:

"So, it appears you've discovered our little family secret," he said, a droll syrup coating his chakra voice. "If you want to maintain peace in the valley with your sister, I suggest you keep your discovery to yourself. It's not exactly a point of pride with her."

I was about to pepper him with a thousand questions: Did Kenny know about his wife's second family? Did you know she was stealing from you to fund Jack's trust, or did you fund it yourself? Did the money from the land sale go into the trust? Why didn't she abort Binx's twins as soon as she knew she was pregnant? Was the rehab treatment just a cover up?

"But that's not why I'm calling," he quickly added before I could get a word in. "I want you to do one more thing for me before I go."

I tried to say *before you go? Where are you going? Is the chakra landlord finally evicting you, officially, since all my efforts failed?* But again, I couldn't get a word in.

"I want you to tell your sister that I forgive her. And I want you to ask her to forgive me, too."

And then he was gone. Just like that. My soul hole went as still and silent as a stone. I ran my fingers over the indentation in my chest, then got out of bed and studied it in the bathroom mirror. There it was, unchanged. A birthmark, nothing more. I half expected it to close up like an anemone, or like a portal to another world. But it didn't. *Dad, wait* I said in my mind, but I knew it was too late. I wanted to say *What about me? Am I forgiven, too?*

I got back in bed, laid on my back and stared at the ceiling, waiting for some sort of final sign-off, a "that's all, folks!" Then I began to wonder how I would explain it to my sister: my soul hole, my extraterrestrial communications with the dead, my visions, my pixie dust seizures. I thought perhaps I should start with Dr. Cobb, and at least get his recommendation on how to proceed. Then I thought, *naw, I'll just tell her that she is forgiven, and that Dad asks for her forgiveness in return, and let her figure the rest out. All I can do is deliver the message.* She may already assume she is forgiven, and that if anybody needed forgiving it was Hal Brown. Then, silently, I blew a kiss into the ether to the both of them – father and daughter – just as I had blown kisses to Mr. Road Rage and everyone else that appeared to need kissing. When I was finished I rolled over, spooned my warm, soft, sleeping wife and closed my eyes.

54 The Resurrection

When we emerged from the safety and comfort of our bedroom to face the family circus, the first thing we saw was Ward's resurrected pig standing proudly in the center of the dining room table. Clustered around the pig were several other clay sculptures from the same era, sculptures that had been in the same box and pulverized when I had heard that Tripp had arranged for Jack to come live with us.

"Amazing, isn't it?" whispered Tripp, who we were surprised to find stretched out in a sleeping bag on the living room sofa. On the floor between the coffee table and the sofa, sprawled across the furniture cushions, lay big Jack Sublette, and despite the obvious evidence that these two young men had been up all night repairing our collection of little boy's pottery, I found myself hoping Jack hadn't peed on the dining room rug. Sandy was evidently thinking the same thing; before getting a closer look at the pottery she bent over our sleeping cousin – perhaps nephew – and examined the area around him, which appeared to be dry. We would have to wait until he awakened for a complete inspection.

"He's wearing his Depends," Tripp whispered with a chuckle. "I checked."

I went over to the table and examined the repair work. "Jack did most of it himself," Tripp continued in a low voice. "I just helped with the glue."

As Tripp had remarked, it was amazing. I had heard about "idiot savants" that had particular, specific gifts that were far beyond the capabilities of "normal" people, but I had never suspected Jack had such a skill. Even on the fishing boat, when Jack was acting as Tripp's eyes and doing the delicate work of tying on the flies, I had simply figured it was something he had been trained to do. But looking at a pile of broken pottery pieces and conjuring a pig – not only conjuring it but rebuilding it just like the original – that was another matter altogether. And to think that the very person who had caused the reaction that broke the pig in the first place would be the same person to resurrect it – it all seemed too much at the time. Later, when I considered the eventful wake created by my father's physical departure, and all of the unusual, portentous events that followed, I might have expected miracles from Jack to be as natural as the sunrise.

After a week of sightseeing and toddy drinking the Briarwood gang departed, some by Winnebago, some by Sprinter, and some by air. A week later Jack and LT settled into a routine that included several days a week at a school for the intellectually disabled in Ross. A few more weeks after that, LT had taken a part time day job at the school, and Sisi was left with Sandy and me. It seemed a perfect time to tell her that our father had forgiven her, and in turn asked for her forgiveness. I also wondered if I should ask her about the money from the land sale, and if it had, as I suspected, gone into the trust that had eventually paid for her son's luxury cabin in Coon Hollow. But at the same time Sisi began to get involved with Doug Dennikan, and before long she had moved him into the upper cabin. By then I was not at all sure that bringing up her past, and especially her strained relationship with our father, was the right thing to do. Besides, the developing romance with Mr. MacD, who was more like a recovered version of Binx Sublette – a kinder, gentler version, perhaps – than I could have ever imagined, provided plenty of drama.

At first I was circumspect to say the least. But Sisi attached herself to MacD in the same manner she had attached herself to males since she was 14: like a wet blanket. Her prey, immobilized in his wheelchair with no place to run, didn't appear to have much choice in the matter. She steered him and his wheelchair up the asphalt path to the upper cabin and locked the front door. If he had any objections he kept them to himself, which is to say he didn't text me, or Sandy, DeeDee or anybody else, pleading to be set free. All of that remaining summer and into the fall the two of them sat on the porch of her casita in Coon Hollow reading and texting, reading and texting, Sisi sometimes sketching or doodling in her notebook, with Doug's young pit bull pup, Lila, at their feet. Midday they would disappear inside for several hours for lunch, naps, and doing whatever a couple can do when the male is paralyzed from the waist down. Then they would return to their perch for the late afternoon and evening.

Meanwhile, Jack decided he wanted to be a farmer. "Look," he said one afternoon when he had been digging up clumps of native grasses and grouping them together to form a tiny lawn in the same fashion that he had pieced together the shards of Ward's pig, "I've already got the uniform." Sandy had equipped his wardrobe with overalls of varying types and colors, mainly because Jack knew how to get in and out of them without assistance, and could quickly drop the suspenders when he had to go. Somehow Jack realized that overalls were standard-issue farmer garb, and, with Tripp's help, he started a garden on the weekends. It was too late in the season to start summer vegetables and too early for winter vegetables, but there was plenty of work just building the terraced bins. Doug Dennikan, a fisherman by trade but a carpenter as well before his professional drinking and drugging career, mapped it out, ordered the lumber and irrigation supplies and directed the construction. But once Jack got his hands on the hammer and nails, the project quickly devolved into a sort of free form hammering exercise. Next thing we knew much of the lumber had been filled with hundreds of bent nails. Eventually Tripp persuaded Jack to trade in his hammer for the shovel and, with Mr. MacD's help, completed the veggie bins.

By then, it was time for my son's real work to begin.

55 Two Pups Born to Carry On

I don't know why I never figured out what Sandy, Sisi, Tripp and LT appeared to have known for months. Perhaps it was because every time I noticed that Elke's tummy looked to be on the verge of exploding, even back when the Briarwood gang invaded, there was some other distraction. Had I not been absorbed by the various logistical challenges of housing three disabled adults and a former NFL linebacker I most certainly would have asked Tripp about his girlfriend's unusually prodigious girth. Had she had been mistakenly impregnated by a Sasquatch, or perhaps a gorilla? Was she toting two, maybe three ape babies in her supersized womb?

As it turned out I had been purposefully kept in the dark, and it wouldn't be until Sandy and I awoke in our Sprinter outside Tripp and Elke's Bolinas bungalow – there was never any question that it would be a home birth – in the cold, socked-in pre-dawn of August – that they finally turned on the lights. It started with Tripp banging on the door of the RV. Sandy and I had slept in our get-up-and-go warm-ups and T-shirts, ready to provide assistance to the mid-wife if needed, or to run interference on Elke's mom, Helga, whom as we had learned could insert herself into situations in any number of awkward ways.

"They're here!" he shouted when I opened the door.

"They?" I asked, starting the coffee maker.

"Ha ha!" Tripp laughed, reaching over and switching off the coffee maker. "Helga's already made coffee."

"Alright. How many babies are we talkin' here?" I asked, ducking through the door and cocking a rueful eye at Sandy as Tripp assisted her down the step. The old "let's play a trick on the old man" game might have pissed me off under other circumstances, but not this morning, even as cold, wet and foggy as it was.

"Two. Howard and..." Tripp paused and glanced at his mother, who nodded almost imperceptibly. "...Elizabeth."

"WHAT?" I gasped. For the first time in months my birthmark buzzed. I stopped at the first step to the infamous front porch, feeling the damp sink into my bones and taking hold of the rail in a sudden swoon, looking skyward at the fog swirling overhead. "'Howard makes sense. I mean, there's lineage there, you know? But there's no lineage on Elizabeth Brown. I mean, if you wanted to name her..."

"Howard," Sandy said softly, taking my hand and escorting me up the steps, Tripp on the other side, "Calm down. You look like you're about to have a stroke. Let's go in and have some coffee."

"Geez, Dad," said Tripp. "We thought our choice would make you happy." The disappointment in my son's voice cut me to the quick. I took him in my arms and squeezed as hard as I could.

"Any choice you've made makes me happy, Buddy," I said, forcing my knee-jerk reaction to the idea of another Elizabeth Brown in the world into a dark, airless corner where I hoped it would suffocate and die.

After a couple of quick jolts of Helga's Norwegian coffee Sandy and I were about to navigate through the flotsam and jetsam of a living room that had clearly been a staging area for baby making, or baby-having, when I stopped. "Okay, no more surprises, right? All the babies' fingers and toes are in place? No ghastly, hairy growths sprouting out the middle of the forehead?"

"Howard, really!" Sandy cried while Tripp chuckled.

"No more surprises, Dad."

We stepped into the quiet, dark birthing parlor where Elke lay propped up on a mountain of pillows, a baby on each breast, one in a blue beanie, the other in pink. The remnants of birth – the placenta, cords, bloody towels and other accessories – had been ditched already, though the heavy, pungent aroma of blood and guts lingered. The red light from the display of a digital clock radio, a gift from *Rod & Reel* magazine, lent the room the rich, velvety texture of an opium den. Or what I imagined to be an opium den.

"Nice work," I said, bending over to give Elke a peck on the forehead. Her tired eyes, bags drooping underneath like a basset hound, told the story of a long, painful, massively exhausting labor that culminated in two back-to-back push-a-thons but had paid off. The babies, though small, were in good working order according to the midwife.

"Ward came first," she said. "He was slow going, all tangled up in his umbilical, but once I eased him out and cut the cord, Sissy shot out like a cannon ball. Literally less than five minutes later."

Sissy, I thought. *You're going to actually call her Sissy? Really? Why not Sissy Mae? Why not Elizabeth Stewart? We could sign her up for the local chapter of the D.A.R. Or the KKK.*

"How are you feeling?" Sandy asked the new mother.

"Lovely," Elke said, a goofy, doped-up smile on her face. Then her eyes rolled back and her head lilted to the side, obviously ready for a few hours of sleep.

Sandy and I sat on the edge of the bed hand-in-hand for what felt like hours but must have been less than five minutes. We watched these little creatures, who seemed more like kittens, or puppies, or piglets, than humans. But they were not piglets; they were our grandchildren, the great grandchildren of G-Hal and Take Charge Marge, and of Sandy's long-deceased parents, and the children of many generations of Howard Browns going back to some unpronounceable place in Ireland. We watched them until I felt myself getting sucked into a swirling vortex of emotion that I could find no words to describe, my Chown Hoon Dong ringing like a church bell full of ancestral welcomes. Yet through all this confused cacophony, one thread glowed and buzzed far louder and stronger than the rest, an unmistakable spine of universal electricity that a voice from within – the heartmind, perhaps – told me was all that mattered: the divine Love of God. Eternally ours for the asking.

56 First Words, Last Words

Months later I found myself on the beach in the morning with Mister Booper, walking and chucking, walking and chucking, and, just like the old days, singing a silly little tune – something about hopping like a bunny, stinging like a bee, flying like a birdie and swimming like a brown dog in the sea. I had trained Mister Booper to drop the ball about five feet ahead of me so I could scoop the ball into the mouth of the chucker without breaking stride, and within a few minutes of walking got into a rhythm that, coupled with the crash and hiss of the ocean on the sand and the little ditty in my head, hypnotized my overactive brain into a meditative state. After a while I realized that for the first time in as long as I could remember, I was not worried about anything. I also realized that, try as I might to find something to worry about – my sister's encroaching dementia, the possibility that my surfing son and his betrothed would be eaten by great white sharks and our dogs eaten by coyotes, the likelihood that Doug Dennikan would take up the bottle again or that Jack Sublette would drop a rock on one of the baby's heads, the condition of our democracy, the price of oil, global warming, Islamic extremists, the relentless destruction of our gardens by rapacious gophers, and the general proximity of the end of my life – there wasn't a damn thing I could do about any of it. Except perhaps the gophers.

I returned to Coon Hollow around noon, hoping Sandy had concocted something to accompany my daily lunchtime dose of Jackson's Honest salt and vinegar potato chips. The rest of the family appeared to have similar hopes, so we all gathered on our sunny patio.

I sat across from Tripp and Ward, little Ward, Ward II, the return of the Ward, the Wardmeister – the baby in my son's arms, his big blue eyes glued to the glistening, flashing diamonds on the waters of the Pacific. I couldn't help but marvel at the resemblance Tripp's baby had to his own little brother, Ward the first, and the images his resemblance had kindled in my own mothballed memory over the past four months since his birth.

I recalled a Halloween parade at The Art & Garden Center in Ross, where my mother and babysitter had taken us as children several days a week to play with other small white people in a locked playground surrounded by carefully manicured gardens. That Halloween, three-year-old Ward was dressed as a little lamb, the same little lamb costume that Sandy had made for Tripp a few years earlier that he had outgrown to become a Power Ranger.

Tiny Ward was so light I almost forgot that he sat on my shoulders, hands gripping my forehead high above the parading children in their cowboy, princess, kitty cat and teddy bear costumes. After we had marched the garden paths the children were turned loose to play under drooping branches of an ancient magnolia on the central lawn. The kids would disappear into the canopy of the tree then out the other side, running and diving headlong onto the grass. But after ten minutes of in, under and out our little lamb disappeared, so I crawled under the branches over the crunchy, waxy leaves and damp clumps of rotting white flowers, calling "little lamb, little lamb, the big bad wolf is coming to get you." Just days before, such a warning would trigger peals of laughter, but not today, for our little lamb lay breathless at the base of the giant magnolia trunk. I pulled back his lamb hood and touched my cheek to his blazing forehead, knowing then as if given a summons that our little boy was not long for this world.

The new Ward is a towhead, with Elke's liquid sapphire eyes and a strong Norwegian brow, but aside from that he's just like the original. Or so I imagine. Sandy can see no resemblance whatsoever.

Sisi sat beside me on the patio with her Southern namesake, Sissy (minus the "Mae") bundled in a blanket and sleeping in her lap. My sister wore her usual white sleeveless dress and yellow fleece vest over a peach long-sleeved tee, her long silver and black hair – now more silver than black and finally freed of the dreadlocks – tied back into a ponytail. While most of us had our chairs angled toward the electric ocean, with the midday sun throwing jewels across the water to the horizon, she had her chair angled toward the yard. Below, LT sat on the deck of the tiny guest home he shared with Jack, reading with one eye and watching Jack with the other. At intervals, Sisi would direct her attention to the scene below, where Jack was building his version of a dry stone wall, fitting the rocks together with uncanny precision. Her expression would soften, and it appeared as if she might want to call down to him, "Jack! Jack! Go get a lemonade for your mother!" But of course, she couldn't. It had been over a year since her brain surgery and she had yet to utter an intelligible sound. "She will," Dr. Cobb reassured us, "and I hope you won't rue the day."

Meanwhile Mister MacD was pulled up on the other side of her in his souped-up wheelchair with built-in umbrella, text-to-speech unit with a full-sized keyboard on a retractable arm, watching the migrating grey whales through a pair of binoculars he had rigged on a boom over his head. Next to him sat Elke, on the edge of the splintered Adirondack chair, bending forward, index finger outstretched for the baby boy in her husband's arms. (There was a hasty marriage in the fall when Elke's dad decided to visit from Norway, where he had returned after Helga walked out on him.) She was trying to communicate with her little son, pointing at Tripp and saying "daddy," then pointing at herself. "Mommy," she said. Ward's huge liquid blue eyes followed her finger as she pointed. When she pointed at me, she said, "Grandpa." I smiled at the little bugger.

"Happy grandpa," I said, pointing at myself.

"Dad, come on," Tripp insisted. "You'll only confuse him." Elke then pointed at Sisi, who gazed at the child like she had established telepathic communications and knew all that he knew, head empty save for bliss. "Auntie," said Elke.

This went on: Daddy, mommy, grandpa, auntie. Daddy, mommy, grandpa, auntie. Daddy, mommy, grandpa, auntie, all while baby Sissy slept in my sister's arms. Then Sandy called down to us from the upper deck. "I made some tuna if you want some."

I rose to go and took a step toward the house when I heard a familiar sound, a sound I hadn't heard for a very long time.

"Da."

I looked back, and there was Ward with his little arm raised, index finger barely outstretched, pointing at me. "Da" he chirped, waving his arm in my direction.

"No, no, no," I said. "This is your daddy." I took his tiny paw in my thumb and forefinger and put it on Tripp's hand.

"Daddy," I said, pointing at Tripp. But he insisted, and pointed back at me.

"Da!"

"Hmmm. Maybe he's trying to say 'dumbshit'," I said.

Then little Ward looked up at his own daddy and swung his arm around. "Da" he cried.

"There ya go," I said.

"Sandy! Come down! Ward's talking!" Elke called up to the house. Sandy came bounding down the stairs, apron around her waist, like she was on a fast break. Pretty spry for an old gal with bad knees.

"Da!" Ward sang, now pointing at me again. Then repeating, pointing back at his real daddy.

"No, no," Sandy said softly. "This is grandpa."

"Da!" Ward insisted.

"Sounds like he's thinking of guys – you and me – men in general. We're all Da to him. Maybe he thinks he's Da, too," I said. But my thoughts had already jumped down the rat hole. *Oh Jesus, here we go. Poor little bastard has discovered his own little self, a male species in the primordial soup, destined for a life of quiet desperation...* but I stopped myself. I listened. Whose voice was it, really? My own voice, or my own Da's? Had the old man willfully vacated my third chakra to make room for the little bugger in my son's lap? I paused, listening for the sound of his voice, the unmistakable sense of his presence in my essential bodily fluids, in my consciousness where it had been since his blue steel-eyed shot from his stun gun a moment after his own heart had stopped over a year ago. I felt my soul hole, closed my eyes and waited for a buzz, a ping from my third chakra. I listened, my breathing quickened, and all was quiet. He had done as he said he would: he had moved out and let me go. Or I let him go.

I looked over at my sister, who was watching little Ward intently, as if trying to divine the secret that had allowed the baby boy to match a word to an object. But I had a distinct impression that her curiosity went deeper. Not only had the baby boy matched word with object, the object just so happened to be a father. First me, then his own father.

She looked at me and smiled, then got up, handed Sissy to Elke, kissed Ward on the forehead and walked over to the railing at the edge of the patio overlooking the ocean. Was she thinking about our father? Was she thinking about the prayer, "Our Father?"

And forgive us our trespasses
As we forgive those
Who trespass against us

She reached into her haversack, extracted her device, and looked as though she was going to type something. A shout went up from the yard below. Jack had managed to build a wall of rocks, about four courses high and 3 feet long. Unattached to anything on either side, there aside the conical black seed pods of the dormant gunnera plant, it looked like a primeval Druid shrine from 5000 B.C. Tripp took his baby to the railing and pointed at Jack, "Ward, look! Jack made a sculpture!"

"Da!" shouted Ward.

Then there was another sound, but not from baby Ward.

"Da."

Where is that coming from? Who's saying that? We looked at each other. Tripp cocked an eyebrow, Elke looked up and cupped an ear, Sandy looked behind her. Who is here? "Da!" Louder now, a female voice. Mr. MacD wheeled around and rolled over to Sisi. From the end of the patio she was opening her arms to the ocean, the infinite water. The outline of her frail body underneath her full-length white cotton dress – more of a nightgown, really – as all sharp angles, from the skeletal curve of her neck and bumps of her collarbone down to jutting hipbones and toothpick legs.

She turned and walked up to me, reaching straight up and placing her little bird-like claws onto my shoulders, her eyes filled with tears. Tears of rage? Tears of wonder? Tears of love? I couldn't tell which. She searched my eyes curiously at first. Looking for what? Forgiveness? I've tried to tell her that forgiveness is not mine to give, but if it was I have forgiven her for every transgression, every crime of passion, every purposeful effort to hurt me, every sin real and imagined under sun and moon. Sandy had done the same with every ounce of resolve, every ounce of honesty, every ounce of forthright sincerity she could summon. Before the plaque started shutting down Sisi's memory circuits, she wrote long and heartfelt amends to everybody she had ever known. For what? Being crazy? Bi-polar? Schizophrenic? Psychotic? Alcoholic? Anorexic? For some unknown reason she continued to think that she had it in her power to do better, to stop the bad chemicals and misfiring neurons, the voices, the nightmares, the imagined abuses, the masquerades, charades, and bold-faced lies. Even Dr. Cobb's best efforts to convince her that she simply got dealt a bad hand had failed to assuage her guilt.

There on the patio, the Pacific shimmering with electricity, everyone sat transfixed by her bizarre, sudden intensity and the way she gripped my shoulders. Even her nephew, who had just spoken his first word. She looked them over and smiled. Then, turning back to me, she leaned in very closely, just inches from my face like she was going to whisper something in my ear or even kiss me on the lips.

"You're beautiful," I said softly.

Her smile grew wider and the tears started coursing down her cheeks. Then she opened her mouth, and, after a brief moment of hesitation, said "Da!"

"Holy Mary...!" I shouted, jumping up and squeezing her bony frame. Mr. MacD suddenly wheeled over.

"You...you...you talked!" he shouted.

"Da!" she cried, grabbing her man by the shoulders.

"Da!" cried baby Ward

"Da!" I shouted, throwing my arms up in the air, hopping around on the patio and high-fiving everybody: my blonde, wide-eyed laughing son with his squealing, squawking baby; his lovely forever soul mate, dimples deep in her smiling cheeks, baby Ward chanting *Da! Da! Da!* And my wife, my love, my foil and protector, straight man to my heartmind, eyeing me with never-ending "oh now what" curiosity; Doug Dennikan with both arms up, a big toothy smile under his auburn whiskers; LT watching in wonderment from the cabin deck below and Jack running up and down the yard shouting "IT'S GOOD, IT'S GOOD," like a referee at a football game. Then Mr. Booper, Odo and little Lila started yipping and yelping and leaping. And I swear, though Sandy insists it was my imagination, that I saw a pod of migrating grey whales blow their spouts simultaneously beyond the breakers.

Finally Sisi Brown, queen for a day, woman of the hour, my sister, threw her arms up and signaled the winning basket, a three-pointer in overtime, against all the odds.

"It's good!" I shouted.

"Da!" she shouted in triumph.

She looked me up and down, smiling with a jubilance long forgotten, and, eyes flashing like the sparkling sea, fell into my arms.

THE END

ABOUT THE AUTHOR

Jeb Stewart Harrison is a freelance writer, songwriter, musician and painter in Stinson Beach, California. After many years as an ad agency copywriter, writer/producer, creative director, and director of marketing communications, Jeb now writes fiction and creative non-fiction, along with commercial works for hire. Jeb's debut novel, *Hack*, was published by Harper Davis Publishers in August 2012. In 2015 he received his MFA from Pacific Lutheran University at the tender age of 60. He also records and plays electric bass guitar with the popular instrumental combo The Treble Makers, as well as Bay Area favorites Call Me Bwana. Jeb was born and raised in Kentfield, California, and has lived in Boulder, CO; Missoula, MT, Hollywood, CA; Scottsdale, AZ; Indianapolis, IN and Ridgefield, CT.

Made in the USA
Coppell, TX
01 November 2019

10813111R00186